TO BE CLAIMED

WILLOW WINTERS

WOUNDED
KISS

From *USA Today* best-selling author, Willow Winters, comes a tempting tale of fated love, lust-filled secrets and the beginnings of an epic war.

His chiseled jaw and silver gaze haunts both my nightmares and my dreams, though I've only ever gotten a glimpse of either.

There's a treaty between us and them; mere mortals and the ones who terrify but keep us safe. The contract demands that every year there's an offering and this year I'll walk across that stage presenting myself. We have no idea what to expect if they choose someone, since they haven't done so in generations.
The only thing we know is that the ones they take belong to them forevermore. If chosen, you don't come back, or so the story of the treaty goes.

Gather and present yourself.
This is the offering …
… and I … belong to him.

PART I

The Offering

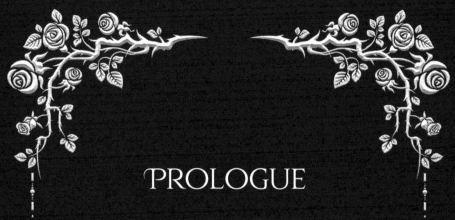

PROLOGUE

Their authoritative presence is felt before anything else. My heart skips a beat and my blood runs cold. *They're here.*

The voluminous cloaks cover their bodies entirely and their faces are mostly concealed by their hoods. Standing with their broad shoulders squared and hands tucked behind their backs, they emanate sheer masculinity and dominance.

His baritone voice whispers, and his breath burns hot against the shell of my ear. His tone is gentle, but there's no doubt in my mind that his words are a command.

Gather and present yourself.
This is the offering …

CHAPTER ONE

Grace

I can't stop staring at Lizzie. She's killing it with the look she's going for but the hot pink dress she's wearing is so tight her boobs are nearly popping out. I can't be too mad at her for that—if mine looked that good, I'd put them on display every chance I got. But the hem of her dress ends about an inch below her ass, and that's being generous. *It doesn't leave much to the imagination.* Not that I'm judging. I'm just worried other people will. If she bends over even the slightest, everyone's going to see all her goods. At that image, I scrunch my nose and a thought hits me.

"Are you even wearing underwear?" I try to keep my tone neutral so I don't sound like I'm being a prude, but I can't help asking since she goes commando all the time. Although I can't imagine her risking a wardrobe malfunction considering where we're headed.

She pauses her contouring and shoots me a naughty grin,

then rolls her eyes. "Yes." The self-assurance falters in her expression but only for a moment, and I think I may have imagined it. Confidence is practically her middle name.

"Thank God." I breathe out a sigh of relief and watch as she sprays something in her hair and smooths out the ends. Her hands tremble just slightly and this time I know I didn't invent what I saw. "You look hot," I say in an attempt to calm her nerves. It's not the dress that's gotten to her. It's what we have to do the moment we leave that's got her on edge. I know this is true, because it has me shaken too.

"You're just saying that," she says sweetly with a simper that doesn't look at all innocent on her. "It's the blond hair," she adds as she twirls a lock around her finger. "They have more fun."

With only a huff of a laugh in response, I shake my head and ignore the churning in my gut that's been bothering me all day.

She's really nailing the blond bombshell look. Honestly, she pulls off every color she's ever dyed it. Even last summer when she went purple. It looked fantastic on her, like she was made to have violet hair; I would've looked like a complete dumbass.

Touching up my makeup one last time, I stare back at the mirror before smiling and spearing my fingers through my natural brunette hair, giving it more of a relaxed appearance. Lizzie may have the sexy and seductive look down pat, but I've got more of a traditional beauty thing going on. I like my subdued look. It keeps assholes away. Lizzie can handle them, comically so … I cannot. Smacking my lips, all done with my lip gloss, it's time to decide on shoes.

I'm definitely wearing heels. It's a must when I go out with Lizzie. She practically lives in them since she's short, but so am I. It took me a little while to get used to wearing heels all the time, but now they're like slippers. For tonight, though … getting all dressed up makes the nerves at the back of my neck prick.

"New jeans?" she asks as she eyes the designer pair I bought the other day. I'm grateful for the distraction. No more thinking about that. The idea of being taken by anyone at all—much less the men who will stand on that stage today—is only a nightmare. It's not going to happen. Not a damn thing is going to happen this afternoon, and then we're *really* going out. That's the plan, and we're sticking to it. I need to stop thinking about the worst things imaginable. Sometimes my mind goes to the darkest places, but not today. Not now. Sure as hell not when Lizzie needs me to be levelheaded.

"Yeah, they're like the best pair I've ever owned." They fit my petite curves better than the rest of the jeans in my closet. I'm rubbing it in a little, but Lizzie knows I'm only teasing. Stretching a little in them, I turn to check out my backside. My curves are on the larger side, but I love it. I've got wide hips and small breasts, whereas Lizzie's got a full-on hourglass figure.

"When'd you get them?"

"Got 'em on sale last week. Should've stayed with me at the mall rather than taking off." I click my tongue at her and smile. She left me hanging when she went to go run an errand for our boss. His lazy ass does that kind of thing constantly. We basically run the bookstore ourselves.

She pouts and asks, "Did they have any more?"

I purse my lips and shake my head. These were the only pair on the clearance rack. If Lizzie and I wore the same size in jeans, I'd share them. But we don't. So she's shit out of luck. "Sorry, babe."

"Damn."

"We'll have to keep a lookout for more." I nod my head.

"We should look online too."

Her eyes shine brightly at the suggestion. "Hell yeah, payday is Friday," she replies in a singsong voice, swaying her head as she does. It makes the dangling earrings she's wearing chime softly. They're rose gold with moonstones. I gave them to her on her eighteenth birthday. Lizzie's allergic to silver, so I made sure to get pure rose gold. They cost a little more, but it was worth every penny to see the look on her face when she opened the gift box. She owns a lot of earrings, but she always seems to wear that specific pair.

The smile grows on my face until I realize I need to ask her the inevitable and it vanishes completely at the thought. "Are you almost ready?" She looks like she is but knowing her, she could spend another hour doing her makeup. I bet she could spend all day in here if I didn't remind her of the time. Her makeup looks perfect already to me, though, with her flawless cat-eye look and pink lipstick to match her dress. "And do you have a jacket?" I add comically, as if I'm her mother.

"Yeah and yeah," she says, rolling her eyes with the smile staying in place, "but we still have time to kill, right?"

I check my phone, which is sitting on the bathroom counter. Our small-town college, Shadow Falls, is only ten minutes away and we have forty minutes before we absolutely need to take off.

Nerves tingle down my arm and my throat tightens. There's not a trace of either when I answer her. "A little bit, yeah." I can guess exactly what it is that she wants. "Coffee run?"

"Yes!" she exclaims to the ceiling with dramatic flair. She's got a serious caffeine addiction. Shaking my head, I smile back at her and grab my phone. I could go for a chocolate chip cookie while we're there anyway. Something to calm my stomach.

"Let's go … like now … so we're not late then." I browse through our joint closet, which is crammed full of clothing, for only a split second before picking out my favorite clutch. Taking a moment to admire the pastel plaid print and soft tan leather, I drop in my phone, wallet, and cherry red lip gloss.

"You wearing the pink stilettos?" she asks as if she doesn't already know the answer.

With another smack of my lips, I tell her, "Duh." I wear them almost every day. They're neutral enough that they complement most of my wardrobe but they have a little more pep than nude heels. The dark red soles give them an extra bit of sex appeal, which I love. The additional two inches they grant me doesn't hurt either. It makes me feel like today isn't anything but ordinary and I'm going to kick ass … just like every other day.

Nothing at all to worry about.

"Unless you need them?" I say, offering them up.

"Nope, it would be too much pink." We're both a size six so at least we can share shoes, even if we can't share clothes. Lizzie has heels in nearly every style and color. She's a girl who likes variety. It's the one thing she really spends money on.

"I swear you never wear any of the others," she says teasingly.

"I like these," I say with a shrug, picking up my pale pink beauties. They make me feel in control and sexy. Why wouldn't I wear them every chance I get?

People say you can grow to hate your best friend when you live together but I can't see that ever happening to us. She's the yin to my yang, the peanut butter to my jelly. More than that, we were both grateful to get out of the shitholes where we grew up. The cherry on top is that we truly love and respect one another.

Always have. Always will.

I first met Lizzie in middle school, only a year after my mom had passed. We were both quiet loners and didn't really bond at first—not with each other, and definitely not with anyone else.

Summertime was when we actually started talking to each other. I approached her first, although I was deathly afraid of being rejected. It was worth the risk because I was more than tired of being so lonely. We were the only girls wearing long sleeves and jeans in the hot weather. That wasn't my first clue, but it was what I needed to sit by her at lunch. I finally gathered the courage to ask her about it, knowing I would be exposing my truth too. Her bruises were from her third set of foster parents and mine were from my father, who was always drugged up, drunk, or just plain angry.

She didn't tell me why she'd begged to leave the previous two foster homes. All I knew was that she was content to remain with the third even though they hit her for no reason. I asked her why she stayed, and she said it was the best she would get. Even as a twelve-year-old I had an idea of what she'd been through and I wasn't okay with any of it being true.

That night we had a sleepover at my house, not that my dad was home and not that her foster parents cared or knew where she was. It was nice to pretend it was a real playdate. To pretend like we had normal, loving parents who cared about us. I asked her why she'd left the last foster home, but she just shook her head and started to quietly cry. When I thought she was going to let up on the gentle tears that were falling down her face, I leaned in to hug her and she grabbed me fiercely, sobbing hysterically into my chest. Later that night she woke up screaming and I just held her until she fell back asleep. That was almost a decade ago.

Since then, we've been each other's rock.

I grab my keys in the living room and get ready to lock the door to our place. While I wait for Lizzie to grab whatever the hell she's getting, I smile at the sight of our secondhand sofa. Our apartment is finally starting to look like a home. We were able to get jobs at a bookstore after we turned sixteen and as soon as we could afford it, we moved in together. I shake my head, thinking about how we were constantly broke. Between the two of us, we finally had enough saved up just before high school graduation. It's been about a year of us living together in our small one-bedroom studio. I've loved every single second. This is what family is supposed to feel like. Plus we have an amazing shoe collection.

Minutes and more minutes pass of Lizzie not getting her ass to the front door.

"We're not going to be able to get coffee," I yell down the hall, knowing the threat will get her attention.

She shrieks and runs into the room barefoot, shaking out her blond hair with a huge smile across her face as I laugh. That's the thing I love most about Lizzie. She never lets anything get her down for too long; she refuses not to smile. Without that optimism and without her friendship, I don't know how I would've survived.

She meets me at the front door with a pair of spiked black heels in hand. "Let's do this shit."

CHAPTER TWO

Grace

As we pull into the line at the drive-through for our favorite coffee shop, I can't help but to feel anxious. So much so that my foot on the brake slips and the car jolts. "Shit, sorry."

Lizzie only lets out a short laugh, the worry I feel slightly reflected in her expression.

"What if they take someone this year?" My nerves are getting the best of me now. My tried and true pink heels aren't making me feel a damn bit confident. After we pulled away from our apartment, I could feel my hands growing hot and numb. My breath is coming in shallow and short, and it's starting to give me a headache. Deep, deliberate breathing isn't helping to calm me down; I just can't get rid of this uneasiness. I shake out my hands again and unsuccessfully try to swallow the spiked lump in my throat while Lizzie fidgets next to me.

Not much is known about shifters, not even the werewolves

who initially offered us the treaty. The different species stay to themselves, each in their own little group. Intermingling generally ends with a blood-bath and no one wants that. A few books have been published, but they've been proven to be unreliable. A recent news report even said one of the bestsellers on supernatural beings was put out by a vampire as a joke and that it was full of lies. Just thinking of vampires makes my skin crawl. The nonhumans have their own politics and territories, and we have ours.

All of us keep to ourselves ... except for days like these.

These are the shit days, but we don't have much choice. We're weaker. It's as simple as that. Humans have come to rely on treaties for protection. After all, we don't have their natural-born strength and our weapons don't do a thing to hurt them. I've even read about towns that have pacts with vampires, while others have allied with witches. Not in our town, though. Our treaty only applies to the werewolves of Shadow Falls. The other species know it and stay far away. Which I suppose I should be grateful for. I think I would be, if it weren't for the offering they demand.

Every year, Shadow Falls provides an "offering"—it's so fucked up they call it that—for the werewolves. All the women in town between the ages of nineteen and twenty-one have to gather for the shifters and present themselves. It's the law, so we have no choice. Once you're offered, you can't refuse if they choose you. You could leave rather than participate, but that would mean moving to a different town, leaving your family and forgoing the protection provided by the werewolves. My heart races just thinking about all the implications.

Refusing to participate in the rite or not providing an offering would lead to an end of the treaty. It's happened before every few years in various other locales. The news is always quick to cover any protesters who no longer want their treaty. Normally, those who want protection take off as soon as the debates start because they don't want to risk the fallout. Once a treaty is forfeited, all across the country people wait with bated breath to see the repercussions.

The werewolves never attack the towns that break their pacts. The shifters just leave them be. And when the other paranormal and vile creatures of the night show up at the vulnerable homes, there's no one to help. Sometimes it's only days after when people go missing, or worse. Other times it's years. I've watched on the news as fathers cry, begging for their daughters to be returned to them. I've seen pictures of entire towns burned to the ground, supposedly for nothing more than a witch's enjoyment. The attacks themselves are hardly ever captured but the resulting aftermath leaves enough evidence to determine what happened.

Vampires and witches are ruthless, taking without shame or apology. People say there are good ones and bad ones, just like every other species and race. But I've never seen or even heard of a *good deed* done by either vampires or witches. The only silver lining is that although they may wreak havoc, they don't touch what belongs to werewolves. History has proven time and time again that werewolves will win that fight.

It's been nearly one hundred and sixty years since the violence and tragedy that brought about our arrangement with the shifters of Shadow Falls. According to what Lizzie and I were taught in school, vampires came in the night all that time ago and abducted humans to hold captive for their own pleasure, leaving disaster in their wake. At the time the town had no help, no treaty, no one to beg for mercy. Shadow Falls put up a fight as best they could, but it was useless. Families huddled together at night yet in the morning, someone would be gone without a trace. Or they were massacred. Either way, it was hopeless. The vampires would swoop in, drink their fill, and leave their victims to die. Back then, those sharp-fanged villains were careless. Rather than snatching their victims and hiding like they do today, they'd remain on their hunting grounds and flaunt their kills.

It was only a matter of time before the werewolves came. The thick scent of blood that coated the air might have initially attracted them to Shadow Falls but with so many vampires around, the town was ripe for their picking. Desperate and out of options, the mayor at the time begged the werewolves for help. The wolves agreed, but on one condition— Shadow Falls would have to offer their women to them willingly once a year—forever. He agreed without hesitation, knowing there was precedent in forming treaties with shifters, but stopping the slaughter was his priority. Within days the vampires fled, and the ones unlucky enough to get caught by the werewolves were devoured without mercy.

That year, one woman was taken by the shifters at the offering. Since then, the wolves have upheld their end of the bargain to protect the town, but they haven't taken anyone else. Only that one woman at the first offering. She went without a word, without a fight. It's said she went into a trance of sorts and no one ever heard from her again. That's the story we're told and taught, anyway. And that's the reason we're headed to the local college to "offer" ourselves.

This is our first year and we'll have to attend for the next two as well. To put it mildly, I'm freaked the fuck out. I try to remind myself that the shifters haven't taken anyone in a hundred and sixty years. Maybe this is nothing more than an outdated tradition. *How the hell should I know?* But knowing they haven't taken anyone in over a century and a half only drops my fear down a notch, a very small notch.

The fact that I'll be presented to them gives me mixed emotions, but the overriding feeling is complete and utter fear. I finally have a home and safety and a life that I cherish. I don't want to leave. No one really knows what happens if they take you, but it's not hard to guess. If you're chosen, you don't come back. The very idea throws me into full-on panic mode.

With her lips turned down and her gaze looking off to nowhere, I know Lizzie's thinking the same things I am. My hand grips hers as fiercely as she held me that first night she cried in my arms, in my bedroom when we were only kids. "It's going to be fine," I reassure her, surprised my voice is even as the words come out.

A tight smile is my reward, followed by a shrug, then my Lizzie is back. "I'm fine, just ... remembering." It takes all my strength to simply nod, pulling ahead in the line for coffee.

Silence brings memories.

We came last year to watch, just to see what it would be like. It was Lizzie's idea. She was far worse than she is now. Just being around the werewolves made her tremble.

We nearly left, but we had to know what to expect so we could prepare ourselves. About a hundred girls were lined up single file and in al-
phabetical order, then they crossed the stage. If I had seen a picture of it
and didn't know the context, I would have thought it was a graduation. A
snort leaves me at the comparison. Unlike a graduation, the atmosphere
was ominous and grim with no speeches or sense of joy. The werewolves
came, the women walked in front of them, and then the shifters left. It was
somber and perfunctory, almost like neither party wanted to be there. I
know for a fact that was true on our end.

Even though the werewolves were mostly covered by their cloaks,
it wasn't hard to tell that they were pure muscle. Nothing but killing ma-
chines. I couldn't see much from the other side of the stadium but Sherri,
one of the cashiers at the bookstore, told me that they looked "scary as
fuck," as she so eloquently put it. She's a senior in college now, so her last
time to walk was last year. She told us she couldn't be more grateful.

I wondered why all the women walked quickly and quietly with their
heads bowed, but I guess that's why. Not that I can blame them. If someone were staring at me like they wanted to rip my throat out—again,
Sherri's phrase, not mine—I wouldn't want to look them in the eye either.
Especially knowing they could legally take me against my will.

So yes, head down and a fast pace.

"You okay?" Lizzie asks with a bravado I know is fake, but I love her
anyway for trying to be strong for us both. Lizzie licks her lips and then
pulls out a tube of gloss from her bag. She can barely look me in the eyes.

"Fine. We're going to be just fine." I pat her hand before pulling up
to get our drinks and then taking off. Time to face the music, so to speak.

"Of course we are." She smacks her lips after applying a thin, glittery
coat of gloss but I notice how her hand trembles. "And then we're going to
whoop it up at Jake's party." I force a small smile for her and try to shake
off my nervousness. If not for me, then for her. At least I'm concentrating
on the party tonight instead of the offering. Arriving at the college a few
minutes later, we park in the designated spots for "those participating in

the offering." I turn off the car and grab my stuff from the back seat, keeping my snide thoughts to myself.

"You think Mike's going to be there?" she asks as she opens her door. I follow her lead and walk quickly with her to the stadium entrance, trying to figure out what she's even asking. Right. Jake's party. We only have a few minutes left to get in there for the offering. If you don't make it, you're forced to leave town. *Supposedly.* No one ever risks being kicked out of a protected area, so I don't really know if that particular law would be enforced. Not that I have any intention of finding out firsthand.

"He told me he would." She's been trying to decide whether or not she wants to make a move on Mike. I don't think she should. He keeps coming into the bookstore just to flirt with her and never buys a book. He's worked at his father's construction company since last year when we all graduated. Whenever I suggest he buy something, he always tells me he has no need for any books, not that he has any time to read. He could use a book, though. He's kind of an ass and she deserves way better than him.

"Do you really have the hots for Mike?" I question, not bothering to hide my disdain. I'm all for blue-collar guys. Just thinking of those rough hands on me sends shivers across my shoulders in a good way. I'm just not into assholes. And Mike is way more ass than he is anything else. A shrug is all I get in reply while we both sign our names at the check-in station. After we're each handed a pamphlet, we make our way up the steel steps to sit in the back. I toss the handout into the trash as we walk. It's full of facts about Shadow Falls and how the treaty was formed. I read it last year and I'm not really a history type of girl. Even if I was, that's not the history I want to read about. It's basically designed to sugarcoat the one unquestionable requirement from the wolves. If you're chosen, you must leave with them that instant. No packing your things, no saying goodbye to friends and family. They take you. Plain and simple. I don't need a pretty piece of paper to brighten up that bit of information.

"I really want to get my cherry popped before college." The absurd statement brings me back to the present.

My gaze shoots over to Lizzie. She's practically the only virgin I know.

13

I wonder if she told me because she's looking for a major distraction right now since we'll have to line up soon. Even if she's not, I am, so I'll run with it.

We decided to only take a year off of school between high school and college to save up money, so that means she'd only have a few months to lose it. *If* she's serious.

"For real?" I can't help but to question her. She's never shown any interest before. She nods her head, but it's quickly followed by a bite of her lip. I know she wants my approval. Not that I'm an expert or anything, but I'm far more comfortable with sex.

"Why?" I ask in all sincerity. "It's really not what people make it out to be." We take our seats and stare at the empty stage as Mr. Horga, the gray-haired mayor of Shadow Falls, makes his way across the field with a wireless microphone. "Seriously, I have a better time with my vibrator." She laughs at me and goes back to sucking down her drink.

"I just feel like such an outcast, you know?"

"Yeah, I know how you feel." We've always been two peas in a pod, dancing to a different beat than everyone else. I clasp her hand with the intention of talking her out of pursuing Mike, but suddenly the whole stadium goes quiet as our gazes are involuntarily pulled to the entrance, waiting for the shifters to walk in and show themselves. Their authoritative presence is felt before anything else. My heart skips a beat and my blood runs cold. It's overwhelming. I swallow thickly. *They're here.*

"Oh shit," Lizzie hisses in a low whisper. She dropped her drink and what little bit was left is all over the floor in front of us. Her hands are shaking even harder now. "Sorry," she whispers and half the people around us give her a wary glance before turning back to the cloaked werewolves who are striding across the field toward the stage.

"Just come here," I say, begging her as if she's running away when she's still right here next to me.

"Did it get on your heels?" I look at her like she's lost her damn mind, silently willing her to be quiet, but when I look at her as she tries to clean up the mess, her expression is distressed.

"It didn't get me," I say quietly, focused on easing her worry. I wish I had something to help her wipe up the spilled coffee, though. She's only got the one tiny napkin that was wrapped around the cup so it's already soaked and useless. I give in and laugh a little bit before I look back up, which at least makes her grin in response. Her smile makes me feel like we're okay. Only seconds later, my own vanishes and my heart sinks. I try to swallow but my throat closes as three of the werewolves turn their heads in our direction. Their gaze on us feels like a cold blanket draped over my shoulders and my mouth goes dry. *Fuck.*

"All right, that's better." Lizzie's comment breaks the spell. I let out a small breath of relief when I realize she didn't notice the werewolves staring our way.

I reach for her hand and it feels hot in mine.

"Hey love, you're all right," I say to her.

She tells me back the same. It's what we've done for years when we're scared. Her voice is calmer and more comforting than mine. She doesn't seem to give a shit about their presence, which does wonders for my nerves. Thank God she's being strong when I can't. She squeezes my hand tight and smiles brightly at me. "We're going to walk up there then walk right back down." I force a small smile on my face and nod my head. Up and right back down. It almost sounds simple when she puts it like that.

"Head down," I add for good measure.

I look back at the four men who are now on stage, standing in a row. The voluminous cloaks cover their bodies entirely and their faces are mostly concealed by their hoods. Standing with their broad shoulders squared and hands tucked behind their backs, they emanate sheer masculinity and dominance. I breathe out deep.

"I got you, babe." She kisses the back of my hand, but doesn't release it. It's a good thing too because I don't plan on letting go either.

Mr. Horga has started calling out names. Lizzie and I make sure to go to the back of the line since both our last names start with W. We're dead last except for one older girl, a girl I recognize from school—I think she was two years ahead of us—who has the most vibrant red hair I've ever seen. She's supposed to be in between Lizzie and me. We've never spoken to her before, only seen her around school but this redhead isn't very talkative so we just keep to ourselves. Even though she keeps staring at our clasped hands like she's desperate to take her place in between us, I plan on waiting till the last second to get behind her. I'll be the final person to walk on the stage. My anxiety skyrockets.

"I wonder what they look like." Lizzie's curiosity knows no bounds, even if her voice is shaky. At this moment I couldn't possibly be more grateful for the diversion and I'm damn sure to ignore the tremor in her tone. I need something to get me out of my head and so does she.

"We're just going to be able to see their faces, and that's only if you look directly at them. Which you should not." I mutter my response. I'm not that bold. Glancing to the stage ahead of us, I see about half the girls have already filed through. Some of them approach confidently but all of them walk down the steps at the other end with their heads bowed, eyes glued to their feet. The stage is so long that there are at least ten girls on it at a time. The four shifters are spread out so that you're never more than a few feet away from one. They're just standing there like statues, not moving or saying anything. A chill runs down my spine. I'm no coward, but I plan on keeping my gaze down the entire time.

I can't stand how tense it is, so I blurt out the first thing that comes to mind. "Sherri said they all have a stick up their ass." We're getting closer to the stage and I swear my heart's trying to leap out of my chest and escape. Swallowing is useless; my throat is suddenly dry.

"Do their faces look different from ours?" the girl who's trying to get between us asks.

"I don't think so." I manage to get that out but then my chest starts heaving frantically as I see how close to the stairs we are. Lizzie finally takes her eyes away from the stage and places her hands on my shoulders while we continue to move forward.

"You're all right, babe," she says reassuringly. "Now tell me the same."

"We're fine, Lizzie. Nothing bad is going to happen to you, or to me.

I promise." I do a quick count and there are only four women ahead of us now.

"I love you, Lizzie." Tears start welling up in my eyes. I have to tell her. Just in case.

Now there are three.

"We're not saying goodbye," she whispers, sounding hopeful and I nod.

Only two ahead of us now.

"I love you too." She kisses my cheek as her name is called. I finally let go of her hand and immediately feel the loss.

Now one.

Breathe.

Miss Redhead walks up.

Breathe.

My name is finally called, marking the end of this year's offering. It's so close to being over. Just a few steps and it's done.

Although I hear my name ringing in my ears, my body falters and my fingers and toes go numb. I force my shaky legs up the four steps and try to control my breathing. Licking at my dry lips, I grip the clutch dangling from my wrist tight in my hands like it can protect me. My heels make loud clicks on the metal stage as I walk, and I concentrate on the sound. I remind myself that I just need to take one step at a time and then it will all be over.

As I let out a small breath at the calming thought, three things happen at once: the werewolf I just passed starts walking off the stage, I feel a large hand on my back, and I hear Lizzie scream. My eyes shoot up to locate Lizzie but before I can run to her I'm pulled against a hard chest by a strong arm made of corded muscle. I'm held firmly in place as a scream tears up my throat. My fingers frantically work to pull the werewolf off of me, my nails digging into the large hand splayed across my belly, but it's useless.

She's still screaming, and I can't even look at whoever's holding me, I can only stare as Lizzie struggles to free herself. "Somebody help her!" I scream. Slamming my elbow against the wall of solid muscle behind me doesn't do a damn thing. Panic turns my skin hot and chaos whirls around me. With all my strength I shove my weight forward, once again pushing away from the beast holding me while shouting her name.

"Lizzie!" I shout as my feet fly off the ground. The shifter restraining me has one arm wrapped around my waist, lifting me up as though I weigh nothing at all. His other hand cups the side of my head, bringing my ear to his lips. The forceful move makes my entire being instantly still.

"Calm her down," his baritone voice whispers, and his breath burns hot against the shell of my ear. His tone is gentle, but there's no doubt in my mind that his words are a command. My mind finally registers what he's said and I take in the scene as if in slow motion. The stage is now empty except for the shifter holding Lizzie, who's fighting like crazy with tears streaming down her red face, and me. Blocking the stairs on either side of the stage are the other two shifters, who act as guards.

Not a soul in the crowded stadium is moving from their position in the least. No one is coming to help her. It's only me. The only humans even remotely close to us are Mr. Horga, who's on the grass where I was just standing moments ago, an expression of complete shock etched on his face, and Miss Redhead. She's huddled in a ball on the side of the stage where she's been allowed to go and venture off. Everyone is silent from both terror and surprise while Lizzie is shrieking and crying, held tightly to the mammoth shifter's chest. Her fists beat against him, not doing any good, but the werewolf allows it, making no move to stop her. It's useless and he lets her waste her strength.

After repeating his command, I'm slowly released by the beast of a man holding me. I nod and the tears that had gathered in the corners of my eyes slowly trickle down my face while quiet sobs rock my body. Not Lizzie. Not my best friend. *They can't take her.* The realization finally hits me as I'm lowered. *They're taking Lizzie.* As soon as my stilettos touch the ground, I dart over to her, the trance broken. I wrap my arms around the part of her torso I'm able to reach, the part not restrained.

It's surreal. I would give anything in the world to deny that this is happening. That it's only a nightmare. The glare behind me sinks deep into my back and I remember his wish: calm her down.

"Lizzie!" I have to shout at the top of my lungs for her to hear me. When she doesn't respond, I yell her name again. It doesn't stop the wretchedness that wreaks havoc inside of me.

"Lizzie!" She stops shrieking for a moment and looks at me with frightened, glossy eyes as she grabs me with the half embrace that she can manage, yet with such force that I'm surprised I don't fall over. As soon as she's quiet, stifling her sobs in the crook of my neck, the shifter holding her gently places her feet on the ground. She nearly collapses as her spiked black heels scrabble to find purchase on the stage. I'm vaguely aware that the people watching us are a mix of emotions. Some are crying, while others have started screaming. But all I can really focus on are Lizzie's whimpers.

A force flows through me; I need to try and say something to calm her. It's like a wave, but I stop it. My body stiffens as I feel the werewolf from earlier approach me from behind. His hand comes down and lands on my shoulder. At first he squeezes firmly, causing me to go rigid, but then his hold loosens and his thumb starts rubbing soothing circles against my nape. I blink away the haze of fear and confusion to look up past Lizzie, who still has her head buried in the crook of my neck. She hasn't stopped crying hysterically.

"It's okay," I say. The words rush out of me even though I know it's a lie. My breath is warm in the air between us and my heart pounds in my chest so hard I can hardly hear myself.

I hold her tighter when I see the face of the werewolf behind her. He's staring at me with darkness in his eyes, like I've stolen his prey. I suppose that's exactly what I've done. His chiseled jaw is covered with dark brown stubble and his narrowed eyes are silver, but beyond that he looks human. He would look utterly breathtaking if he could turn his scowl into something less menacing. At his stern expression I take a step back, survival instincts warning me to take flight, but I'm prevented from escaping by the shifter holding me tight from behind. *We're trapped.* Lizzie looks up at me when I flinch at the thought. My eyes dart from hers to the silver stare of the wolf behind her. My body goes rigid as two hands grip my hips to steady me.

"Follow him and bring her with you," the dominating man behind me whispers and again I feel his hot breath tickle my neck as his lips brush against my ear. He releases me without another word and I try to walk while supporting the bulk of Lizzie's weight. We stumble and I almost fall, but the strong hands behind me reach out to steady us before forcing me forward. My chest heaves and my body shakes when I realize I'm going to lose Lizzie forever. They're using me to calm her down and lead her to some unknown fate.

"No," I whisper in defiance. "You can't take her." I try to protest, but the hand is strong and then something else, something I'm not able to fight, grips ahold of me.

My breathing falters and I immediately feel light-headed. I can't. I can't do that to her.

The last thing I hear before my vision goes black is Lizzie's scream.

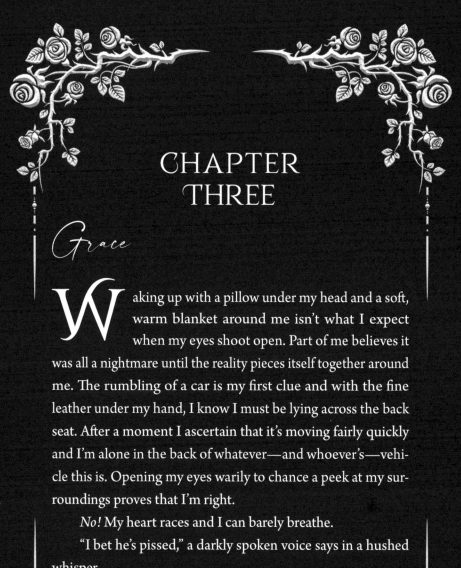

CHAPTER THREE

Grace

Waking up with a pillow under my head and a soft, warm blanket around me isn't what I expect when my eyes shoot open. Part of me believes it was all a nightmare until the reality pieces itself together around me. The rumbling of a car is my first clue and with the fine leather under my hand, I know I must be lying across the back seat. After a moment I ascertain that it's moving fairly quickly and I'm alone in the back of whatever—and whoever's—vehicle this is. Opening my eyes warily to chance a peek at my surroundings proves that I'm right.

No! My heart races and I can barely breathe.

"I bet he's pissed," a darkly spoken voice says in a hushed whisper.

"About not being in this car?" another male voice answers. There's a pause and then he continues. "The other one hurt herself. He had to stay with her."

Lizzie. Scrambling to keep still and not panic, I try to recount everything. *No, she can't be hurt, she can't be.* The need to scream out her name is suffocating as I choke on the syllables.

"Do you really think we should have split them up?" a gruff voice asks more casually from the front seat after a quiet moment. I go completely still at the sound. The other man merely snorts in response. Inwardly, I know I need to get a grip. *They took me.* My heart races. *Where's Lizzie? She can't be hurt. Please don't let her be hurt.* Tears prick at my eyes, but I will them away. I don't want the men to hear me crying. I need to be quiet.

"Fuck no we shouldn't have split them up." They both let out low, rough chuckles. My body shakes and it takes everything in me to stay still.

"At least we got the calm one."

"I hope she stays that way. They'll be settled in a bit and everything will be just fine."

Through barely opened eyes, I watch the dark figure in the passenger seat nod his head.

"You hear that back there?" My gut wrenches and my breath halts in my lungs. My eyes widen but I instantly shut them and pretend to still be asleep.

"Your heart's pounding so loud that I'm sure everyone in the car behind us can hear it, Grace." More rough chuckles follow this statement. I swallow and my sore throat protests the movement. My nails scratch slowly on the seat. They speak as if it's all a joke. Anger mixes in with the fear but still, terror overrides everything.

I reluctantly open my eyes and the man in the passenger seat looks back at me. I open my mouth to speak, but the only thing I can say comes out as a whisper. "Lizzie?" There's a pleading in my voice that's undeniable and I hate it, but I wouldn't change it.

"She's fine. She's in the car behind us with our Alpha. He had to calm her down when none of us could. You have a strong friend." The man looks at me kindly while he answers me in a reassuring voice. No, not man. The werewolf. I must look ridiculous to him, huddled under the blanket. I grip the fuzzy fabric tighter and break eye contact to stare at the floor.

It's been a while since I've felt like this, lonely and scared. Helpless and terrified. A while … but I remember how to deal with it. If I got through that, I'll damn sure get through this.

"I'm going to see my friend again?" I question in a staggered breath and then quickly add, "Soon?"

"Of course," he says. The answer is immediate, and relief weakens every bit of me. I struggle to keep it together as he continues, "I was going to sit back there with you, but I thought you might like some space." His tone is light, bordering on friendly. When his stare doesn't let up, I give a small, hesitant nod in agreement. Gratitude is a funny thing to be feeling at the moment.

"Thought so." He shifts in his seat, but from my periphery I can tell he's still watching me. If I wasn't so terrified, I could think. I could make a plan. As it is, I'm entirely numb.

"You must have some questions." This time it's the driver who speaks.

My heart beats once, then twice as the moment passes in silence. "Who are you?" Both of them laugh. Their relaxed manner calms me, if only slightly. If they plan on killing us, they're quite kind to their prey.

"I'm Lev," the behemoth riding shotgun answers with a wide smile, "and this is Jude." No matter how friendly he aims to be, his sheer size is chilling. With a quick motion to the driver, he goes quiet again but offers me a charming, yet tight-lipped smile. I nod my head again and look back at him steadily. Their easygoing manner alleviates my worry a bit more. I sit up ever so slowly, moving against the wishes of my racing heart and letting the blanket drop to my waist.

If they're going to play this game, this version where everything is just fine, I'll play along. Right up until they give me my friend back and pull the hell over so we can get back home. Somewhere deep inside me, I remember I have a backbone. I didn't fight this hard so early in life to have these assholes destroy it all. Whatever it is they're after, we'll give them something else. I'll find a way. I always do.

"Are you comfortable?" the first one, Lev, asks.

It's only then that I realize the cloaks are gone and the shifter staring back at me is gorgeous. Like the other werewolves, he has silver eyes, but he doesn't look like the shifter who held on to Lizzie back at the stadium. He doesn't possess nearly as hard of a look as her captor did. My heart races as my palms turn clammy at the memory.

"I'm fine," I say although my answer doesn't come out nearly as strong as I'd like. "Is Lizzie okay?"

"She's all right. Just scared." His answer is dampened by something and my stare implores him for more, but he gives me nothing.

Lev has a short beard and his dark hair is long enough to grab at the top, but short on the sides. It also looks like he's had his nose broken at least once, but the bit of imperfection on his otherwise classically handsome face only adds to his masculine appeal. I scoot around in my seat so I can get a good look at Jude. His black hair is short and he's clean-shaven. But I can't see much else of his face other than his full lips.

If it wasn't for their silver eyes and large shoulders, I'd question if they were even werewolves.

Their heads nearly touch the ceiling, and their broad frames look completely out of place in the car. It reminds me of sardines stuffed in a tin. They can't be comfortable. The two of them are almost polar opposites in the vibes they're giving off. Lev could easily be a badass biker and Jude a clean-cut military soldier. But they're not, they're werewolves. I can't let myself forget that, not even for a second.

"Are you all this big?" The question pops out of my mouth without conscious consent. Blaming it on passing out earlier and this odd light-headedness that won't quit, I let my head fall back and try to get my balance.

Lev's slow grin is sexy as hell as he says, "That's what they all ask and—"

Before he can finish, Jude lands a hard blow with his fist against Lev's chest.

"Shut it." Lev's only reaction is a deep, low chuckle that makes his entire upper body, and the entire vehicle, shake.

"I'm sure she's got a better sense of humor than you," he says and grins at me. "Did you want to hear the rest?"

My lips part, but words don't come out. I feel like I'm on the edge of losing it. "I'm not okay." The words are pulled from me and I hate that I spoke the sentiment aloud. The tears that prick my eyes and the coldness around me ... I hate that even more. This isn't real.

"Ah, shit." Lev runs his hands through his hair and then looks back at me apologetically. "You all right?" His face is the epitome of concern and his silver eyes shine with sincerity. It's been absolutely insane since we got to the stadium earlier and his kindness is my undoing. Ugly sobs start pouring out of me as I shake my head wildly. This isn't real at all. I wish I could just wake up.

Terror cloaks my whisper. "I'm not okay."

"Fuck." Lev turns and somehow manages to maneuver his massive body between the two front seats to join me in the back. I immediately feel claustrophobic as my personal space dwindles to nothing.

"This is worse," I blurt out, my response immediate as I shove a palm against his massive chest.

"I'm just going to hold you, okay?" Lev has his arms up but doesn't move them, waiting for me to respond. His voice is calm and his arms look so welcoming that I can't help but nod my head. His muscular arms wrap tight around me, practically consuming my body and making me feel like a small, scared child. I let go of my inhibitions and scoot closer to him, burying my head in his broad chest. Every ounce of him is pure muscle, so he's hard as hell. But at least he's warm and the gentle strokes up and down my back are soothing.

It takes a while with the rumbling of the car and the quiet drive, but I slowly feel myself calm down. Pulling my face away from him, I note the mascara smeared all over the white T-shirt stretched taut across his chest. Inwardly I cringe, but my breathing relaxes as I look up into his silver eyes and then back down immediately. Jude calmly tells me, "You're going to be all right, I promise." And Lev agrees, "You're going to be just fine." Their words and actions put me at ease. I must be in shock. There's no other explanation. The realization wakes me up, sobriety heightening my anxiety once again.

Lev's sharp silver eyes never turn from me when he asks, "You all right?" Without looking up or back at him, I nod slightly, biting my lip as I tuck a loose strand of hair behind my ear. I breathe in deep before I turn to stare out the window. There's nothing to look at but trees. I continue to nervously bite my lip. "Where are you taking us?" I question without having the balls to look either of them in the eyes. My heart gallops and the pitter-patter is almost too much. I feel like I'm going to faint. They're silent and neither seems to make an attempt to answer.

"Did you drug me?"

The quick no is followed by a sharp intake of breath and then he says, "We didn't drug you."

Up and down, my nerves climb and fall. All I can do is shove my hands between my thighs to keep them from trembling.

Lev's hand lands on my arm gently, just to get my attention. "I'm sorry. I really am. I'm not going to hurt you, I promise. No one is." I finally look at him. His brows are raised and his lips slightly parted. He looks as though he's trying to coax a wounded animal out from under a car or something. I nod my head and steel myself to ask the only question that matters right now.

"Why did you take us?" His silver gaze takes me in briefly and then his eyes shoot to Jude's in the rearview mirror. Jude is silent and Lev purses his lips. My breathing hitches at their hesitation.

"Well, I didn't personally take you." That's the only answer Lev finally gives me, placing his hand against his massive chest for emphasis. Jude snorts in the front and then shakes his head.

Anger creeps up, causing a deep crease in my forehead as my brow furrows.

Jude asks, "We heard your friend call you Grace. Is it okay if we call you that?"

"Yeah, that's fine." I'm surprised by how sturdy my voice is.

"Okay, Grace," Jude starts, "our Alpha is the one who ..." he hesitates and glances out the rear windshield before looking straight ahead again. "Um."

"Grabbed me?" I say to complete his sentence. My shoulders stiffen at the memory of their Alpha's hands on me. His thumb rubbing soothing circles on my neck as he commanded me to calm Lizzie down. With how tight my throat is, I don't know how I'm breathing.

There's no time for niceties. I need information. That's how we'll survive. It's how I'll save both myself and Lizzie. The constant thump in my chest reminds me of that. I eye Lev who's sitting back, taking up all of the room back here while watching me with an amused expression kicking up his lips.

"Yeah, grabbed you." Jude swallows hard and glances over his shoulder to the car behind us again. Lizzie's in that car. I know she is. She's safe. I'm safe. I'll figure out a way for us to be safe. I will. I'll be damned if I let anything happen to either of us.

"Okay." I drawl out the word in an effort to get him to continue. He clicks his tongue and meets my eyes in the rearview.

"He doesn't want me to talk to you about this, Grace."

"Why not?" I can't help getting pissed. I need to know. "I deserve to know."

"He wants to tell you himself." I let that sink in for a second before realizing their Alpha must have been at the offering if he's the one who grabbed me. Why take me and then ride in a different car in that case? A frown pulls at my lips and my hands fist in my lap. I don't have time to wait.

"Why isn't he riding with me if he took me?"

"Because of your friend, Lizzie," he says and my heart stops at the mention of her name.

"You said she was all right," I blurt out, cutting him off as I lean forward in my seat a bit to get closer to him. It's foolish, I know it is, but I can't help the note of anger that creeps into my tone at the end. I need to be calm; I know that much. Play along, get information. I can't let my temper get the best of the situation.

"She's fine. Don't worry," Lev reassures me, gently pushing me back against the seat. "Devin wants you to put your seatbelt on."

I stare at him like he's gone mad and snort. *Is he fucking kidding?* "Who the hell is Devin?" I don't care that my voice is raised. Completely ignoring Lev now, my head whips back to Jude. With quickened breaths and a tight throat, I say, "And what was that you were starting to say about Lizzie?" So much for keeping my calm ...

"Lizzie's perfectly fine, but she was extremely upset and got a bit physical with us after you passed out." I nod my head. That sounds just like her.

"But she's okay?" There's a threat hidden in my cadence. It's unmistakable and judging by their expressions, they don't miss it.

"She's all right, but that's why Devin, our Alpha, stayed with her and her ... guards." His eyes exchange a glance with Lev's in the rearview again. "To calm them down."

Guards? Calm them down? Rubbing my clammy palms against my thighs doesn't help to keep my head from spinning. I feel like I'm going to snap. I've lost all sense of sanity.

"Let me help you with your seatbelt." Lev tries to push me back against the seat, but I'm still worried about Lizzie and I don't want to just blindly do what they say. Anxiousness wreaks havoc in my mind and I'm getting increasingly upset with how secretive they're being. I push back against Lev's muscular arms, although I may as well be pushing on a brick wall.

"I don't want to wear it." I'm aware I sound like a petulant child but I'm losing it, quickly spiraling downward. I need something to grip onto. *I need Lizzie.* He looks like he wants to say something, but he clamps his mouth shut. "How exactly did he 'calm her down?'" I stare into Lev's eyes, urging him to answer me.

Finally, he says, "He really wants you to wear your seatbelt."

Motherfucker!

Staring down the beast of a man who, I do acknowledge is being kind at the very least, I bite back, "Well, Devin's not here, is he? So he can shove what he wants up his ass." Jude's loud laugh startles me and Lev covers his mouth with the back of his hand as he fakes a cough in an effort to hide his growing smile.

"Let me tell you a secret about werewolves, Grace." Jude pipes up from the front seat sounding very happy with himself. "As long as we're within a few miles of each other and concentrate, we can hear what the others are thinking and saying." I suck in a sharp breath and scrunch my nose. That's not something I've ever heard or read before, but I guess he did say it was a secret.

The car slows down, and the brakes slightly screech as the blur of trees lessens. Goosebumps spread across my skin and prick their way up the back of my neck.

Jude pulls over to the side of the dirt road and stops. *Thump, thump.* The beating quickens in my chest. I look over my shoulder through the back window to see the car that's been following ours pull up behind us. *Fuck.*

I bite the inside of my cheek and ask, "Does that mean he can hear me too?" *This is good,* I try to convince myself, giving myself a pep talk although my body is on fire with fear.

"Well no, he can't *hear* you," Jude starts as he puts the car in park and twists his body so he can look back at me. "But he can tell what we're thinking about what you're saying." I start to panic at the realization that the Alpha knows I disrespected him. That's probably like telling a mob don to fuck off.

Fuck. Fuckity fuck. My lungs still and I look everywhere around us to find no one moving yet. Maybe I should have just shut the hell up. My temper shouldn't be getting the best of me. My head spins with fear and desperation, my gaze shooting to the handle on the car door.

"Why ..." I want to ask why we pulled over since we seem to be in the middle of nowhere, but the words are stuck in my throat. Lev opens his door and gets out first, allowing a gust of cool air to filter into the car. My body starts to shake. Bracing his hands on the roof, he leans his head into the car and smiles at me.

"Relax, Grace, we're just switching people around. We're only a few minutes away, but Devin thinks it's best that you see him now."

I don't move. I don't say anything as the heavy footsteps come quicker than I'm prepared for.

Devin's faster than I can imagine. There wasn't a moment for me to will my body to move or to run. The car tilts slightly as he climbs into the seat next to me. His masculine, woodsy scent drifts into my lungs and suffocates every thought. He's tall, his jaw sharp and every inch of his corded muscles are showing with his sleeves rolled up. My chest rises and falls chaotically.

"You'll be quiet until we get home."

It's all he says, the words spoken in a deep low tone and anger pulses inside of me, but something else takes over with a force I can't describe.

"I'm scared," I say, whispering the truth although it's not for the same reasons I've been terrified throughout the day ... this is something completely different. As if my body, even my soul, knows my life has been irrevocably changed simply because this man looked my way.

"Don't be," he responds and that's when his gaze meets mine for the first time. It's sharp and silver and all-consuming.

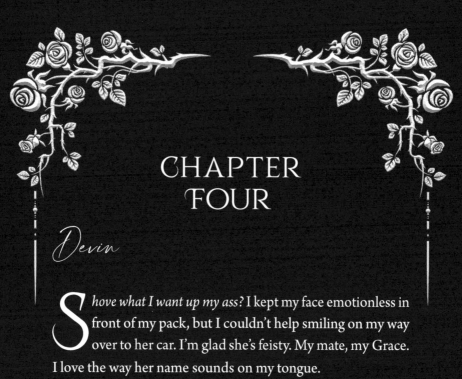

CHAPTER FOUR

Devin

*S*hove *what I want up my ass?* I kept my face emotionless in front of my pack, but I couldn't help smiling on my way over to her car. I'm glad she's feisty. My mate, my Grace. I love the way her name sounds on my tongue.

I stare at my mate from the corner of my eye. My mate is Alpha as fuck; the powerful force is rolling off of her gorgeous body in waves. If I was a lesser wolf, I'd feel the need to bow to her. It's unbelievably sexy and entirely unexpected from a human. She's subdued, though. At the realization, my grin vanishes and the impassive mask returns. Something's beaten down her Alpha, and I'm going to find out exactly what happened.

At least she's better off than her friend. Calmer, more in control. Something's very wrong with Elizabeth. I was two seconds away from putting her friend in the trunk. It really would've been for the best. She won't stop calling out for my mate and fighting, which is only causing her to hurt herself. But

Dom wouldn't have enjoyed that. Caleb wouldn't have liked it either. I feel so fucking sorry for my betas. Having to share your mate … that's a problem I'm not sure how to solve. Dom's already fighting an uphill battle. Liz denied him. Screamed at him, pushed him away and beat him repeatedly. It's unheard of for a mate to react that way. She didn't gentle in his arms like my mate did for me. Grace only pushed away from me to get to her friend, her pack. That's what an Alpha does. A chill runs down my spine; that better have been the *only* reason she pushed away.

Dom shouldn't worry, though. Liz's heat will come soon enough and she'll be begging for him … or Caleb. It's a damn mess. I'm going to have to figure something out before they kill each other.

The headaches don't stop there. Vince felt his mate in the stadium, just like I felt Grace last year. It's going to be hell keeping him off human territory. I should know.

In the meantime, I can't even tell Grace she's my mate. If I did, then Dom and Caleb would have to come up with a way to tell Elizabeth, or Lizzie rather, that she belongs to both of them. And that can't happen until they figure out their shit.

With the strongest members of my pack distracted over their mates, I should be concerned about us being prepared for the inevitable fallout from my old pack, but all I can think about is Grace. She'll be going into heat soon; I can smell it coming on and I can see it in the flush of her skin. All I need to do is get her alone.

PART II

The Alpha

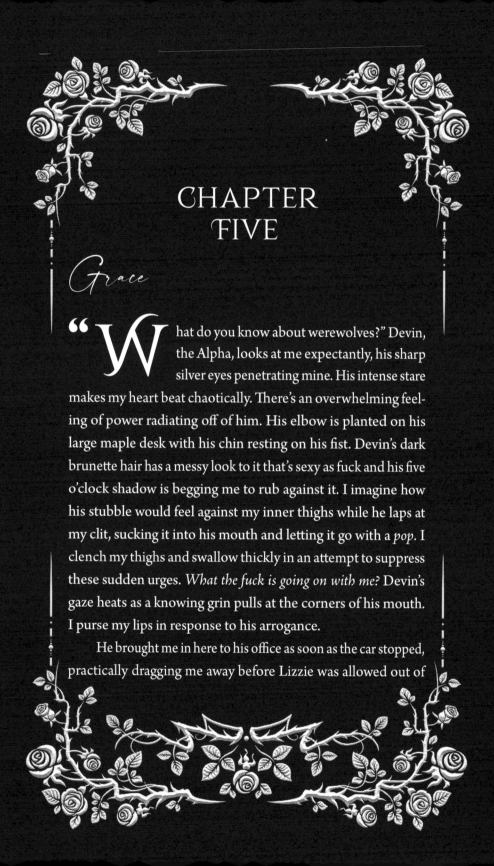

CHAPTER FIVE

Grace

"What do you know about werewolves?" Devin, the Alpha, looks at me expectantly, his sharp silver eyes penetrating mine. His intense stare makes my heart beat chaotically. There's an overwhelming feeling of power radiating off of him. His elbow is planted on his large maple desk with his chin resting on his fist. Devin's dark brunette hair has a messy look to it that's sexy as fuck and his five o'clock shadow is begging me to rub against it. I imagine how his stubble would feel against my inner thighs while he laps at my clit, sucking it into his mouth and letting it go with a *pop*. I clench my thighs and swallow thickly in an attempt to suppress these sudden urges. *What the fuck is going on with me?* Devin's gaze heats as a knowing grin pulls at the corners of his mouth. I purse my lips in response to his arrogance.

He brought me in here to his office as soon as the car stopped, practically dragging me away before Lizzie was allowed out of the car. I was only permitted to see her from a distance, her red-rimmed eyes staring back at me with her palm pressed against the window. My heart is a shattered mess.

I didn't want to be separated from her; she's a complete wreck. She shouldn't be on her own. Or left alone with *them*. Devin promised that if I behave and listen, we'll be reunited and left alone to process everything. It killed me to turn my back to her, to obey this werewolf.

But I pray I'm doing the right thing. Minding what he has to say, following his commands.

And that's how I ended up here.

The size of this "office" is ridiculous. It's larger than our entire apartment. I'm in awe of the sheer size and luxury of the werewolves' estate. I assumed werewolves lived in the woods, hunting down animals in their wolf form and basically behaving like savages. If it wasn't for their large frames and silver eyes, I'd have had no idea that these men were anything other than human. Not that I'd ever met a werewolf before. But I'd always imagined them to be … primitive. And nothing about them or this place is primitive.

If what Jude and Lev said is true, we're going to be fine. I keep reminding myself of that. But their version of fine and my version may be very different and I still don't know why they took us. The thought makes my eyes narrow. I don't like being kept in the dark.

"Why are we here?" My grip tightens on the armrests of the freshly oiled leather wingback chair. Every inch of my body is tight with worry and something else … something I cannot control. It's him. He's doing it to me and I hate him for it.

"I asked you a question first. Please answer it." I lift my head and square my shoulders, speaking calmly and politely, but with authority. His expressionless face gives nothing away. He sits back in his seat, letting his hand fall to the desk and taps rhythmically with his deft fingers as if he's waiting for something.

What do I know of werewolves? "Very little."

"Your tone leaves much to be desired." He slowly rises from his seat and stalks over to me. Standing directly in front of my chair, he leans against the desk as if it's a casual gesture but this close, his presence is suffocating. "That's something we need to work on, Grace." Just being this close to him is overwhelming and I shift in my seat as he crosses his arms. I love the way my name rolls off his tongue, although the fact that I love it makes me feel anxious.

I'm uncomfortable because I feel … I feel … I don't want to say it. Shame heats every inch of me. I shouldn't be feeling this at ease with him. I sure as hell shouldn't be fantasizing about him. Everything about this is just … off. Once again, I question if I've been drugged. I can't look him in the eyes. I try to, but I can't bring myself to carry through with the movement.

"There's plenty we need to work on," I respond, more menacingly than I'd like.

"I have to admit that I love your smart mouth," he states as he uncrosses his powerful arms and takes my chin in his hand, forcing me to look at him. Instantly, another pulse of desire races through me. His silver eyes mesmerize me. He rubs his thumb across my bottom lip and my body betrays me by sending a hot surge of need to my core. "Although I enjoy your boldness, you aren't permitted to speak to me like that in front of the pack. Is that understood?"

I nod my head as best I can with his hand still holding my chin. Although my head is clouded and it takes me much longer than it should for me to comprehend what I've just agreed to.

"Speak, Grace." Anger courses through me at the command and I rip my head away from his grasp. I don't care if I piss him off; I refuse to let him talk to me like that.

Blinking away the haze, I reprimand him by saying, "I'm not a dog!" I raise my voice in anger and stare straight into his heated gaze. He raises his brows in surprise.

"I didn't think you were." The light in his eyes dims and he crosses his arms again, stretching the gray Henley he's wearing until it's taut, making his delectable, chiseled chest all the more visible. "When I ask you a question, I'd like you to answer me verbally." I nod my head while I stare at the desk, avoiding his scrutiny once again. I can't stand looking him in the eyes. It's as if I lose myself when I do.

After a moment of silence, I glance up at him, but not directly into his gaze. His eyes are narrowed and his lips are pressed firmly against one another, forming a hard line.

"I understand." I do my best to keep the agitation out of my voice.

"Good. Don't speak to me like that in front of the pack." His hard, absolute tone makes me feel insignificant. For some reason it also makes my heart clench in agony.

Still staring at the desk, I respond dully, "I won't."

There's movement in my periphery, but I don't bother to look at him. I need all of my energy to calm down. Now that we're in here alone, my emotions are off the damn charts. I'm exhausted and inexplicably … sexually frustrated. I'm angry that he's talking down to me. I'm upset that I've been taken from the life I worked so hard to finally have. I feel like a shit friend for leaving Lizzie and every time I think about her, all I can see is her wounded gaze from the back seat of that car. It's all hitting me at once and it's on the verge of being unbearable.

"As far as answering your question, I'll tell you why you're here when the time is right. For now, you and Lizzie should focus on getting settled and making yourselves at home." My eyes fly to his and I part my lips to object. I want to plead with him to let us go, but he stops my appeal before it begins.

"You're a part of our pack now. There's no changing that, so you better get used to the idea of staying. The sooner, the better." I swallow my plea, but my mouth is suddenly dry. A hard lump forms in my throat, choking me. We're stuck here. They're keeping us. The tears prick again and this time I don't have the strength or energy to stop them.

I'm given a moment of reprieve when his cell phone vibrates on the desk. He doesn't speak as he answers, just holds the phone to his ear. I can't make out what the person on the other end is saying, but judging by the scowl on Devin's face, he's not exactly thrilled about the news.

"I'm sure it was a real fucking emergency." His anger lights a new sensation that flows down my arms, traveling lower until my nails dig into the leather of the chair. "I want to know as soon as his ass gets back. What about the paperwork?" He listens for a moment longer and then ends the call without another word.

Questions race through my mind.

He sets the phone on the desk and his silver eyes roam down my body before settling on my gaze again. His expression implies that he's contemplating what he should do with me. Which brings me back to my question. *Why did he take us?*

"What do you want from us?" I search his hard eyes for compassion or sympathy, but he's emotionless.

His jaw clenches. "I told you I'll tell you when the time is right." My eyes fall at his response. "Just know that you will be taken care of. You'll be safe and the pack wants nothing more than for you and Lizzie to be happy here with us." His voice softens some at the end. "It's Lizzie, right?"

I ignore his question and opt for a desperate plea over a response. "If you want us to be happy, let us go home," I beg softly to the wooden floor, unable to look him in the eye as my strength fails me.

"Enough." His hardened tone paralyzes me. "You aren't going anywhere. Get used to the idea of staying."

"I want you to come to me." I'm forced to peer into his gaze as he makes the declaration. It's hypnotizing, being caught in his heated stare. My entire body blazes.

It's too hot in here to even think.

"Come here," he commands and again his strong fingers grip my chin, traveling lower down, to my throat. I can't move. Not an inch.

My body trembles and I close my eyes, failing to gather my composure. I meet him halfway, ever so slowly, obeying.

I stiffen as his strong, muscular arms wrap around me, picking me up and pulling me into his hard chest. With only a gasp of protest, he lifts me as though I weigh nothing and settles me in his lap as he leans back in his chair. My breathing picks up and my entire body goes on high alert.

CHAPTER SIX

Grace

M y head is roughly level with his chest, so Devin speaks while peering down at me. My heart thumps loudly at feeling my chest pressed tight against his. My eyes stare straight ahead at the pictures on the wall in his office. The black and white images of wooded lands are actually quite beautiful and they center me slightly. Anything to keep my mind off of him. There's something about him that's like a drug. Like heroin sinking into my veins and luring all of my senses into some depth of perversion I've never felt before.

"I'll ask you again. Please be reasonable and answer my question, Grace. What do you know about werewolves?" With a rumble in his chest, my bottom lip quivers ever so slightly. Short breaths are all I can manage.

His thumb moves in slow circles over my thigh and I find

myself relaxing in his embrace. Something about him soothes me even if every bit of me is on high alert. He is the ultimate drug.

Exhaustion overwhelms me as my body eases from his touch. His hand at my hip releases me and he gently strokes up and down along the curve of my waist. I sigh at his soft touches, feeling myself slip deeper into comfort. Although he could easily run his hand up my shirt so we'd be skin to skin, he doesn't. I'm grateful for the restraint, but at the same time I crave his body against mine. For some unknown reason my anxiety seems to vanish and suddenly I can't remember what I was so concerned about. Everything just feels right and all I can think about is how good this feels. As if reading my mind, he gently pulls me into his hard chest and I allow it.

"Grace?" His voice is caressing yet still dominating.

"Yes?" I answer easily, rubbing my cheek against his chest.

"What do you know about werewolves?" he asks again, keeping his voice low and soothing. His chest rises higher with a deeper, longer inhale. I'm so relaxed that I hardly hear his words. Nuzzling into his neck, I have an intense urge to lick his throat and leave open-mouth kisses all over his chest.

As quickly as the urges come on, they leave me. *What the hell?* The realization of what I'd intended to do strikes me with a force that jolts me awake. I jerk out of his embrace and stand up so quickly I almost fall flat on my face. Devin doesn't move. He merely raises one eyebrow in question.

"Are you doing this to me?" I stare at him, meeting his gaze head-on. Of course he's doing this to me. *I'm not a damn toy he can play with!*

"Doing what?" he asks as though he has no idea.

"You know exactly what I'm talking about." I make an attempt to yell, but my cadence wavers and my voice cracks.

He stares back at me without any indication that he's even heard me. "Calm down."

Calm down? I want to cry at his response. What's happening to me? I need to get away from him. I search for the door, still disoriented and light-headed. I grip the edge of the desk to maintain my balance.

"Grace?" This time he sounds concerned and he gets up to try to steady me, but I push him away and nearly stumble into the wall, the push moving only myself and not him.

"You drugged me?" I say it as more of a statement than a question and I can't keep the sadness out of my tone. How the hell did I let that happen? I think back, searching for a moment when they could've slipped me something, but I haven't eaten anything. I haven't had so much as a single sip of water since they took us. It had to have been when I was asleep.

He approaches me cautiously, like the way one would approach a wild, wounded creature that's startled and backed into a corner. I don't blame him. I'm so unpredictable that I don't even know how I'm going to react. It's like I've lost my mind around him. He holds up his hands. "No one drugged you." He reaches for me, but I take a step back and round the desk.

"Grace, you're safe. It's okay." I shake my head at his words. The action makes me feel dizzy again. My skin feels heated and a tingling sensation takes over my limbs. He hasn't tried to grab me, but I take another step away from him to get closer to the door. My breathing is erratic and I don't know if it's from the drug or my anxiety. I try to swallow again, but I can't.

"Grace, I think you're going into shock." He stays planted where he is with his arms still raised. "Just try to calm down, okay?" I stare at him like a deer in headlights.

Shock? Is that what this is? No, that doesn't explain the urges. I bite my lip at the sordid thoughts. I've never felt this way before. My gaze travels over his body. He's absolutely gorgeous. He's got a vibe to him that lets you know he'd pin your legs back and fuck you until you begged for more and then some. My lips part and I let out a small moan as I picture it. My pussy clenches and heats.

A look of relief flashes across Devin's face almost too quickly for me to notice. I notice, though. I give him a questioning look.

"Calm down, Grace." His voice is firm now.

"No, not until you tell me what the hell is going on." I just barely get out the words while maintaining an air of authority. My body is begging me to bow to him. A hot sensation pulses through me, starting at my core and making me squirm. Something's wrong. I can't stop my facial expression from showing my desperation. My eyes plead with him to help as the tears fall.

"What did you do to me?" Any semblance of authority I had has vanished. I'm practically begging him to give me answers.

"I didn't do anything. I promise you." His eyes look so sincere, but I know something is wrong. "It's only because you're around me that you feel this way." His tone conveys his sympathy.

"Then I need to leave now!" His eyes harden and his fists clench.

"No." His stern reply offers no alternative.

My body crumples and heats, making me feel weak and light-headed once again. "I'm not okay. Please help me."

He nods his head and says, "I'll help you, sweetheart. Come here. Let me hold you." What other choice do I have? I can run, but how far would I get? I feel so weak right now. If he can help me, I'll let him. I've been told I'm independent to a fault, but I'm not stupid. My body is begging me to listen to him and obey. I cave and make my way back to him, sulking the entire time. As I near him, he sits down and opens his arms. He wants me to sit back down on his lap. I'm about to surrender to him but then I remember Lizzie, and it makes me hesitate.

"She won't be feeling what you're feeling. Not yet." His voice brings my focus back to him. I stare at his face as I try to comprehend his words.

"Why?" is all I manage to get out. He takes a deep breath, looking at the wall then back at me before he replies.

"She's not in heat yet."

"Heat?" I tilt my head in confusion. He just nods his head, maintaining eye contact. My eyes widen in shock and outrage. "Like a dog!" He grimaces and then a low growl barrels from his chest.

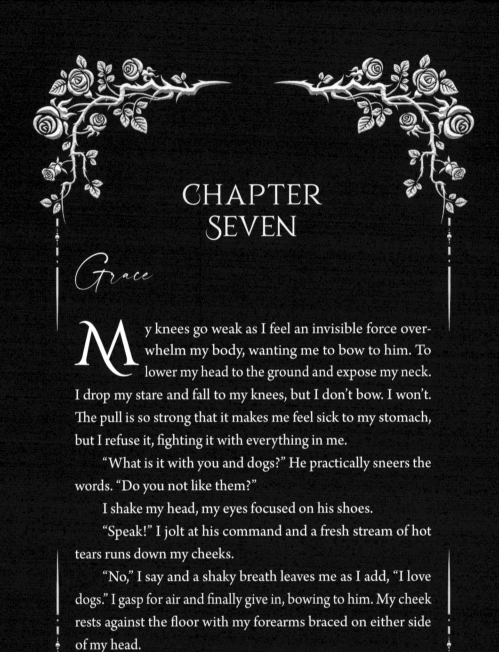

CHAPTER SEVEN

Grace

My knees go weak as I feel an invisible force overwhelm my body, wanting me to bow to him. To lower my head to the ground and expose my neck. I drop my stare and fall to my knees, but I don't bow. I won't. The pull is so strong that it makes me feel sick to my stomach, but I refuse it, fighting it with everything in me.

"What is it with you and dogs?" He practically sneers the words. "Do you not like them?"

I shake my head, my eyes focused on his shoes.

"Speak!" I jolt at his command and a fresh stream of hot tears runs down my cheeks.

"No," I say and a shaky breath leaves me as I add, "I love dogs." I gasp for air and finally give in, bowing to him. My cheek rests against the floor with my forearms braced on either side of my head.

He immediately lifts me up and pulls me into his chest.

"You don't need to bow to me, Grace. Not ever. Please don't." I sob against him, clinging to his powerful body as his hand cradles my head. Desperate for skin-to-skin contact, I move my hand under his shirt and up his back. I don't know why I need it, but I do.

Whatever's happening to me, I hate it. Make it stop.

"I don't mean to get angry," he says and his tone is gentle, but that doesn't take away a damn thing I currently feel. The belittling and weakness especially. I hate it all. "I don't like that you compare yourself to a dog." His free hand caresses up and down my back soothingly. He kisses my hair and I melt at his touch. I concentrate on taking deep breaths as he speaks, but at least my sobs have stopped.

"It's your cycle. You're ovulating. That's why you feel like this." I feel the rumble of his chest as he speaks and I push my body against it, loving the way the vibration feels on my skin. This is nothing like anything I've ever experienced. The need to brush my body against his is nearly intolerable. My entire being is pulsing with a desire to touch him and be touched by him.

I lick my lips and stare at his neck. There's dark stubble all the way down to his Adam's apple. I have the sudden urge to nip at his throat. I stir, trying to alleviate some of the hot ache between my legs and that's when I realize I can feel his stiffness against my thigh. He's huge. The image of him fucking me on his desk, riding me hard, comes to mind. I moan. Yes, I want him to ride me hard. I give in to the temptation and leave a hot, open-mouth kiss on his throat. My teeth pinch his skin and I pull back before letting go, knowing I'll leave a mark. Devin groans as I lean back to admire my handiwork. My chest rises and falls as I breathe heavily.

"Fuck, Grace, I'm trying to be good for you," he says as my gaze searches his face. His eyes are closed and his head is tipped back while his mouth is parted. It's so fucking sexy. I part my legs to straddle him. The move makes my hard clit throb. Resting my elbows on his shoulders, I spear my fingers through his messy hair before jerking his head to the side to bite his neck again. The move makes his dick twitch and it hits my sensitive clit. I let out a moan against his throat.

"Please." I don't even know what I'm begging for. All I know is that I need him. He can make this right.

"You want me to fuck you, Grace?" He breathes his words although they come out as a statement and not a question. I nod and faster than I can perceive, he's already moving. His fingers dig into the flesh of my hips as he lifts me up quickly, throwing my body onto the desk so that I land on my back with my legs spread wide.

"I told you to speak when I ask you a question." His tone is laced with danger as he takes a step back and backhands my clit through my jeans. *Fuck!* A fire ignites so hot in my core that my head thrashes and my limbs shake from the intensity. *Yes!*

As I come down from the overwhelming sensation, I realize he's undressing me, practically ripping my jeans off of me. With a snap and a rip, the jeans are torn halfway down my body.

Before the torn clothing even hits the floor, his tongue is on me. His rough stubble scratches against my inner thighs and it's even better than I imagined. Feeling his hot mouth on me is a dream come true. I arch my back on the desk and push myself into his face. Any sense of control is gone; I've fallen off the edge of a cliff. He growls with approval into my heat as he angles me so he can fuck me deeper with his tongue.

"Please," I beg him again. I *need* him. He continues taking his sweet time, but the sound of his zipper gives me hope. I wriggle on the desk, needing more. My body is impatient and my head thrashes from side to side. I need him now.

"Please!" I can't stand the torture any longer. I need my release. He moves from between my legs and hovers over my body while wiping my glistening arousal from his mouth with the back of his hand. His lips are swollen and his silver gaze doesn't hide his desperation to be inside me in the least. At least both of us are affected.

"You need me to fuck you, Grace?"

I don't hesitate in my answer. "Yes, I need you." As soon as the last word leaves me, his hands grab my hips and pull me to the edge of the desk while he pounds into me all the way to the hilt without a hint of mercy or shame.

"I promise it'll only hurt for a moment," he groans and I'm caught in his silver gaze. My breath is stolen, my nails digging into his forearms as he towers over me, fully inside of me. If I could speak, I'd beg him to move. It's too intense, too much.

The intense pain from being stretched begins to slowly ease as he moves inside of me.

My head drops back and I moan, the pleasure-filled waves riding up my body with every hard thrust.

"Fuck yes," he growls at the ceiling with his eyes closed and his mouth parted. He doesn't stop his steady pace, though. His head slowly drops and he opens his eyes to find mine. It's then that I notice his fangs and the hunger in his silver gaze. He is the epitome of power and lust. In this moment I am only his. I want nothing more than to bow down to him and give him every pleasure possible. My heart feels weak and raw. He has complete control of it. Sheer terror jolts through my body, freezing my hot blood. But in a flash, it's gone, leaving only the heat to scorch my sensitive skin.

My head drops to the desk and my eyes roll back from the intense pleasure radiating through my body. With one hand still on my hip and the other now wrapped around my throat, he picks up his pace and pistons into me with a primal need. I tremble as a numbness rises from the tips of my fingers and toes, threatening to overwhelm my body. I part my lips to beg for my release, but as I do he squeezes tighter around my throat and hammers into me as my pussy clenches.

"Come for me." His words are my undoing and I shatter beneath him. I *shatter* for him.

CHAPTER EIGHT

Grace

Devin leaves me for a moment, a chill draping itself around me as my body immediately notices his absence. I lift my head just enough to see him enter what looks to be a bathroom on the far side of the expansive office. As the aftershocks of my orgasm settle, my mind finally feels as though it's clearing. Like it's waking up from a fog. The realization of what just happened hits me with a force that makes me want to throw up.

This is why they took us.

My head shakes in denial. Shame immediately strips any sense of pleasure remaining from our bout of passion. They intend to use our bodies for their pleasure. *No.* I continue to shake my head, covering my face with my hands.

I couldn't even help myself just now. I wanted him to use me. Will I be like that around all of the other werewolves? Their very presence is a drug. It's hard to lift myself from the desk, the room spinning at the realization. Even if my body is begging for their touch, I don't want to be a whore available to them whenever they want. I want more from life. I *need* more. I push away my sadness as anger replaces it with a fierce need to rally.

Lizzie.

They will not touch her!

I push off the desk and land on my bare feet, my legs still shaking. Half-naked, I sprint to the door. The sound of my bare feet padding against the wooden floors is nothing compared to the screaming in my head. My camisole barely covers my ass, but I don't care. I need to get out of here. My limbs shake, but I run as fast as I can.

I make it to the door as Devin exits the bathroom and curses under his breath.

He's fast, but I'm at least able to grip the knob and rip the door open. I scream, "Lizzie!" Adrenaline races through my blood. There's no way I'm going to make it before he catches me. I'm going to fail her. *I already have.* As I run down the empty hall, I shout her name again. I don't make it more than a few feet before I hear the heavy thuds of men running toward me from both sides. I stumble as I realized I'm trapped and I start to fall. My eyes dart to a door on my left, but before I can open it Devin grabs me from behind, lifting my feet off the floor and spinning me around as I scream.

"What the—" a baritone voice starts to say but Devin cuts him off as I push against his hold and squirm.

"Leave us." His hard voice echoes in the hall and footsteps scurry away in the opposite direction. His arms are wrapped around me too tightly for me to escape. But I refuse to give up, fighting and straining against him. I work one arm free and slam my elbow as hard as I can into his face.

"Fuck!"

I doubt it hurt him but it shocks him enough that he drops me and I land hard on my ass; my palms hit the ground so hard that the resulting pain makes me think I broke my wrist, but at least I didn't smack my head on the floor. I try to get to my knees at the thought of Lizzie going through what I just did. When I glance up, breathless and weighed down with worry, two silver eyes stare back at me. Lev is wide eyed at the end of the hall with his mouth agape.

Devin's hand grabs the nape of my neck as he lifts me off the floor with one arm. "I said leave!" he screams at Lev with rage vibrating off the walls. I whimper in his grasp as he wraps one arm around my waist. My hands fly up to my neck and try to pry away his fingers.

"Calm down, sweetheart." His gently spoken words against my ear are at complete odds with his powerful grip on me. But my body obeys him without my conscious consent. My hands drop to my sides as I start to see white spots dance in my vision. My body may be willing to listen to him, but my mind isn't okay with any of this. He must know that on some level because he loosens his grip but doesn't remove his hold on me. As I try to come to terms with being trapped in his arms, he tells me again that everything will be okay and that I just need to trust him.

But I don't trust him. I don't trust any of them.

CHAPTER NINE

Devin

I leave for one fucking minute and she bolts? Rage courses through me but outwardly I'm doing my best to remain calm. Humans like controlled, collected behavior from shifters and typically I am. I have to stay composed for my mate. *My mate who doesn't even want me.*

A coldness settles inside of me, one I haven't felt in over a year. Not since I noticed her at the offering. I'll be damned if that thought doesn't hit me like a bullet to my chest. My wolf doesn't like it either. My pride is wounded. The only solace I have is that she's letting me hold her. Grace is finally settling in my arms. At least her body is. I can see in her eyes that she's resisting me. Struggling to find words to make sense of it all, I do my best to rein in my resentment that she ran right after she gave herself to me. How could she not feel our connection? How could she deny how perfect it   was?

"Maybe you shouldn't have fucked her the second you got her

in the house." Lev's words ring in my head. I grit my teeth to keep my irritation from showing. After all, Grace can't hear him. I don't want her to think my annoyance is with her.

"*Watch it, Lev.*" I manage to keep a low growl from rumbling in my chest.

"*I'm just looking out for my big brother. I really think it would have been better if you'd waited.*"

"*She's in heat … What the hell was I supposed to do? Let her suffer?*"

I wait a moment for him to answer. His silence pisses me off.

"*She was barely coherent.*" I sneer the words in my head, all the while staying relaxed on the surface for my Grace. Her body molds perfectly to mine. I've witnessed the heat before, in my old pack. I'm surprised it took me so long to realize that's what was going on with her. Especially with that sweet, intoxicating smell filling up the room. My head wasn't right with her looking at me like I was dangerous. Like I was going to hurt her. She shouldn't feel like that around me. With my touch though, she reacted like she should have.

Peering down at her small, huddled form, she presses against me with her eyes closed. She's so beautiful and serene, and now she's right where she belongs.

"*How about you give her some space? The farther away she is from you, the better she'll be till the full moon.*"

The young wolf has a good point. I'll be able to claim her then. There wasn't a part of me that thought I'd fuck this up like I just did. "*She'll still be in pain.*" The heat's a bitch. She'll writhe in agony once it hits her again.

"*It won't be as bad if you stay away from her.*"

Grace shifts in my lap, nuzzling into my chest as her breathing evens out and deepens. Just the thought of staying away from her makes the wolf within me whine in pain.

"*Easy for you to say. I've waited a year to have her. You haven't even met your mate yet. And the pull will only get stronger as the moon waxes.*"

I stroke her back to settle her and it seems to be helping. "*I should* explain everything to her. Maybe that'll put an end to whatever's going on in her pretty little head."

"How do you think Lizzie will react?"

I stifle a sigh. Lev makes another good point. My little brother has always been more logical than me. More empathetic, perhaps. Caleb and Dom aren't ready to tell her and Lizzie isn't in any condition to hear that news. As the Alpha of the pack, their needs come before my own. My heart hurts for my mate, though. She doesn't trust me or anything that she's feeling. For fuck's sake, she thought I drugged her.

"You could let them see each other. Caleb and Dom are going crazy because Lizzie won't come out of the bathroom and she's crying again. Something is really wrong with her. That'll give your mate something to focus on."

"Did you get their paperwork from Vince yet?" More silence from Lev answers my question. "He isn't back yet, is he?" I clench my fists and scowl before I can catch myself. Thankfully, Grace has fallen asleep on my chest. The last thing I need to do is to frighten her anymore.

"Not yet."

"When he gets back, I'm going to kick his ass." Motherfucker can't listen to orders for the life of him. I know him being MIA has something to do with finding his mate, but he could've waited until things were settled here. "What about Caleb?"

"Haven't heard from him yet. He's probably still packing up their stuff." I nod my head even though he can't see me. The fresh scent of Grace's hair wafts toward me and I breathe her in. She smells just like she tastes, like caramel apples on a crisp autumn night. My mouth waters at the memory.

"You want some privacy, alpha?" I can hear Lev's laugh.

"Fuck off." Even as I say it, I smile. I'll get my mate's worries worked out and then everything will be perfect. It has to be. My fingers twine with her brunette locks and I bend down just enough to kiss her temple.

"Where do you want all of their shit when it gets here?"

"I want it set up exactly as it was in their place. Put it all in the east wing."

"You don't think that will freak them out?"

"They need comfort and privacy right now. They want to go home so we'll give them their home to run to."

"That's fucking crazy, Dev."

A low growl rumbles deep within my chest, causing Grace to whimper. *Fuck.* I stroke her back until she settles again.

"I'm surprised she's bothered at all by your growl. I could feel those vibes you threw at her. It knocked Jude on his ass." I can hear him chuckle.

"Yeah? It didn't get to you too?" I know it had to because it took everything in me to get her to bow. The moment she did, though, I regretted it. She's my equal. My temper will be our undoing.

"Course it did. But I stopped doing my laps and bowed like a wolf. Jude fucking dropped like a pussy." I chuckle and the movement wakes Grace. At first she's content and almost nuzzles back into me. Then her eyes open wider and she stiffens.

Damn it. This isn't how finding your mate is supposed to be.

"Well, your mate is human." My lips form a thin line at Lev's words. I run my fingers through Grace's hair and she melts back into me, although her eyes don't close.

I sigh heavily, loving the added weight of her on my chest. This would be so much better if she were a shifter. So much easier if she knew what to expect. If Grace had witnessed a heat firsthand, maybe she would've recognized it. At least her body perceives me as her mate. That's more than I can say for Dom and Caleb's mate.

CHAPTER TEN

Lizzie

E very inch of me shakes and won't stop. The nightmares
come back, full force and with details that took years
to forget. I'm scared to death, huddled in the corner of
the shower with the curtain closed as though they don't know
I'm in here. It's only an illusion and one not a piece of me believes, but it's all I have. I wonder if they know I'm not human.
I pray they don't. I can't go back to what I once was.

   I'm not even completely sure what I am. Latent, maybe? My
old pack said I was useless and a waste. They sold me to some
assholes who beat the shit out of me, trying to force my wolf
to come out. Tears stream down my face and my body shakes.

   They're going to hurt me. Dom looks just like *him*. Like
the shifter who brutalized my body over and over again. I shudder and squeeze my eyes shut, willing the memories to go away.
I thought I'd escaped all this. I thought I was finally free. *How
could this happen?* My shoulders shake uncontrollably as sobs

wrack my body. I gasp for breath, but my throat dries and closes, suffocating me.

I remember the pain shooting through my back while they whipped me. Taking turns and betting on whether I would break or if the wolf would show. The small spikes piercing into my skin and gripping on before being ripped away, taking bits of bloodied flesh with it, leaving nothing but raw, broken skin and blood. Although my vision was blurred, I can still see the splatters of my blood as they hit the wall. So much blood. I can still hear their laughter as my wounds closed before their eyes, although the brutal pain remained. That's all the proof they needed. They kept at it, saying they would beat the latent out of me. That's how it works with latent wolves. They show eventually … but mine never did.

I prayed every night for the healing to stop. I begged any and every deity who might have been listening to have mercy on me. Some nights I prayed for them to let my captors kill me. And then one night, my prayers must have been heard. I stopped being able to heal. Their confusion gave me relief, but it was short lived. They continued to torture me. They brought me to death's door over and over again. Each day they invented new ways to damage me. To bring out my wolf, but she left me. Left me or died; I'm not sure which. I'm not sure if she ever even existed.

It took years before they gave up and tried to get their money back. They wanted to return me because I was broken. But my "pack" didn't recognize my scent. They denied me. I was thrown away and left in human territory for them to claim me. No one ever did. It took nearly two years of living at the shelter for the Henders to take me. They got a check for keeping me. It wasn't enough to stop them from the occasional smack and grab and push, though. Just like with everyone else, I was worthless to them. At that point I was so numb to the abuse I just accepted it as a way of life. At least they only struck me with their human fists, and I was grateful for it. They never tried to get "creative" like the shifters did.

I only started to heal when Grace took me in.

"Grace." I sob her name into the cold tile wall. *Please come help me.* I can't even speak the words aloud since my throat hurts too much. *Come hold me.* I wrap my arms around my shoulders and rock back and forth. She's the only one who's ever cared about me. I squeeze tighter as my head falls and rests on my knees. The only one who's ever touched me in a kind way. I won't survive here. I know it. This will kill me. With my last bit of energy, I whisper, "Please save me."

PART III

The Betas

CHAPTER ELEVEN

Dom

The sound of my mate crying is killing me. My chest feels hollow as I lean my forehead against the door to her temporary room. Her sobs never stop and my touch is useless to console her. I don't understand; it's not supposed to be like this. Her whispers echo in my head and my wolf whines in absolute torment. Rage replaces the agony … toward my wolf and myself. I should be able to soothe her, to be a balm to her broken soul. Instead, I'm the one causing her pain. The way she looks at me with sheer terror in her eyes shatters any hope I have at claiming my mate.

I need to do something, but how can I help her when she won't let me anywhere near her? I don't know what the hell to do. I pound my fist against the wall in fury. My only consolation is that our Alpha's mate can calm her to the point that she's still. I'll do anything to heal Lizzie, to have her whole and happy. But first she needs to let me the hell in. The sooner, the better.

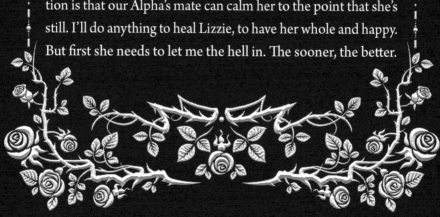

A scowl mars my face as Caleb approaches the door. I don't want to share her. Fate's a real bitch.

"She's not letting you in?" His voice is low, with more than a hint of worry.

"No shit." I practically spit out the words but he doesn't flinch at my tone. He's already used to my bitterness over this situation.

"We should tell her we're her mates."

I just barely resist the urge to knock him out. I'm worried about healing our mate and he's worried about fucking her. I grit my teeth but manage a response. "Do you see the way she looks at me?" I say. He ignores my words like the stubborn asshole he is.

"Let's just do it," he says and I shake my head. "It'll be like ripping off a bandage."

"I can feel the hate and fear radiating off of her all the way from here and you expect me to tell her she's my mate."

"*Our* mate!" I can't look at him so I just stare at the wall. "If we don't, then what's going to happen when her heat hits? What about three days from now when the full moon comes and we have to claim her?" He's out of his fucking mind.

"Have to claim her? We don't *have* to claim her."

"You don't want her?" Shock and disbelief are both present in his voice, but also overwhelming sadness. "How can you not want our mate?"

"Of course I want our mate!" His audible exhale is heavy with relief even though my words came out as a low growl. Caleb is truly out of his fucking mind if he thinks she'll roll over and let us claim her. Her terror is so thick it drenches the air around me. My next words come out easy. "We can wait till the next full moon. Or however long it takes."

"I'm not waiting. And I'm not risking her heat coming on and it fucking us over like it fucked over Alpha."

I finally meet his gaze, which stops him from pacing the hall. "How is he?" I heard him and Lev earlier but tuned them out to give my mate all my attention. Lizzie had been saying something in between sobs but all

I could understand was *Grace*. It's clear she loves her Alpha and it breaks my heart that she has so much love for her, but only hate and fear for me.

"Not looking too good. She ran from him."

"What the fuck?" My brow rises with shock. None of this is happening the way it should.

"Yeah, when he caught up to her, she knocked him in the jaw trying to get away."

Holy shit. The admiration in Caleb's voice is comical, complete with a cocky grin although the humor doesn't reach his eyes. No one's gotten a hit on the Alpha in years. Of course his own mate, a *human* mate, would get the best of him. It almost makes me smile. Almost. But I don't. So both of our mates have a bit of a violent streak? I can't help the fact that the Alpha's mate hitting him makes me feel a little better about my own mate.

"But she reacts to him." I saw her melt into him at the offering. Despite being petrified for Lizzie, she was perfectly fine in his embrace. "And that's the way it should be." Now I'm the one pacing as Caleb leans against the wall.

He comments, "Yeah and then her heat hit and it freaked her out."

"Why?" I don't understand how wanting her mate's touch could possibly hurt their relationship.

"According to Lev, abducting them, not telling them why, and then fucking them is not a good idea. Judging by how pissed off Devin is, I'm going to have to agree."

A grimace spreads across my face as I say, "You make it sound way worse than it is."

He raises his brows and says, "Not really. Anyway, she rejected him after they bonded."

Oh shit. I'm sure Devin's hurting after that. "But she's his mate."

"He hasn't told her yet and that's why I want to tell Liz."

"It's Lizzie." I narrow my eyes as jealousy creeps up on me. Shit, I don't even like him saying her name. There's no fucking way we're going to be able to share her.

"First of all, we need to tell her so he can tell Grace. He won't tell her because he wants to make sure Liz will be all right first. He's waiting for us to be ready. I know he's sacrificed for the pack before, but we're also hurting his mate. She's our new Alpha." He stresses the last bit and I feel my resolve crumble.

It kills me to admit it but I don't have any other ideas on how to get through to Lizzie. Maybe telling her will help; she can't get any worse.

"And second," he continues and Caleb's authoritative voice brings my concentration back to him. "Stop thinking like that. I hate that you're all pouty that we're sharing our mate." My brows knit together in anger.

"Get out of my head, Caleb."

"You know I can't." At least he has the decency to sound remorseful. "We'll make it work. Fate fucked us over for a reason, right?" He reaches out and pats me on the back, his black boot kicking off of the wall as he does. "Maybe we're both too messed up for her on our own," he adds and grins wickedly before continuing, "but together we'll be whole for her." I snort. *Real romantic.*

"The only problem with that theory is that we're the same kind of messed up."

He lets out a low chuckle. "No way, you're way more fucked up than I am." He smiles broadly at me and for the first time since I realized that we were going to have to share Lizzie, I don't resent him. "It wouldn't kill you to smile, you know?" And just like that, the urge to knock him out comes back. I shove him into the wall.

"I'm just screwing around." I know he is, but it really might make a difference for Lizzie if I could lighten up some. *Scary as hell* seems to be the most common description of me from the humans. I decide to change the subject. "Vince back yet?"

"Not that I've heard." I watch as Caleb's fists clench. He usually doesn't get his feathers all ruffled. Out of all of us, he's the lighthearted smooth talker. Vince is in for a world of hurt when he gets back. Nearly everyone in the pack is pissed at him. He was supposed to have Lizzie's background info ready for us. We already had Grace's since Devin practically stalked her this past year, but we didn't know Lizzie was ours until yesterday.

Instead, he hightailed it out of the offering and hasn't been back since. He felt his mate in the audience but he's going to have to wait until she's offered, just like Devin had to. He can't just take her. I have to believe he isn't that stupid. It's been nearly twelve hours since we last touched base with him, though. That's entirely too long for him to not be up to something that's going to fuck us over. He can't be hanging around in human territory; he knows better than that. I shove down my thoughts before they get the best of me.

"So you got all of their stuff in there?"

"Yeah, it's time to move them into their new home."

"It's weird."

He shrugs at my comment. "It's what Alpha wanted and I think it'll help them adjust."

Devin wanted the rooms set up exactly like their apartment. They have the entire east wing all to themselves. It has everything but a kitchen. Plus now they'll each have their own bedroom and bathroom instead of sharing like they were before. Although, given their dependency, I'm not sure they'll sleep apart for a while.

My wolf whines again, hating that fact.

"Honestly, it's not a bad idea. It'll give them a sense of home and safety." His words hit me hard and I scowl. "I know, man." He pats my back again, a firmer, harder pat that pisses me off but when he smirks, I smack him away. At least I know he's feeling the same way. "One day we'll be her home and safety." He nods his head as if he's reassuring himself. I can only hope he's right.

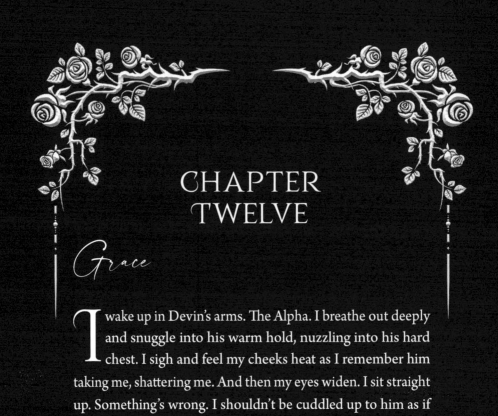

CHAPTER TWELVE

Grace

I wake up in Devin's arms. The Alpha. I breathe out deeply and snuggle into his warm hold, nuzzling into his hard chest. I sigh and feel my cheeks heat as I remember him taking me, shattering me. And then my eyes widen. I sit straight up. Something's wrong. I shouldn't be cuddled up to him as if he's the oxygen I breathe.

My heat.

That's what's wrong with me. I begged him, literally begged him, to fuck me. The shame and guilt washing over me make my heart clench and I have to close my eyes. My fingers go numb and my stomach sinks. *I can't do this. Where's Lizzie?*

"Calm down, sweetheart." Devin's words are accompanied by his arms around me, holding me there in his lap and I wish I could simply push him away. He traps me gently, but still it's against my will. He runs his fingers through my hair and pulls me back into his chest. I resist slightly but I want to lie against him. My body's pulled to him and I can't help it. It's as though my body and mind are two separate entities; I don't like the loss of control. It's disturbing.

He strokes my back and I feel myself relax into him. This power he has over me does nothing to ease my racing thoughts. A part of me thinks I should leave it be and give in. It isn't like I have a choice. But that's just not how I was made. He commanded me, fucked me, and now he's petting me like a prized poodle. I'm not going to sit back and be a good little pack-bitch.

"Why did you take us?" The words come out dead on my tongue. I already know the answer, but I need to hear him say it. Maybe then I can hate him. I can stop feeling this intense emotional and physical pull to him. His hand pauses as his back tenses for a split second, his strong muscles rippling.

"I wish you would trust your instincts." His comment is followed by a low and irritated sigh. Gritting my teeth, I shift in his lap so I'm facing him and stare up at his gorgeous face, ready to lay into him, to push him away and practically spit out every horrible thought I have. His silver eyes look almost sad. They soften my resolve to be combative. He rests his hands on my hips and says, "I wish you would trust me, Grace. I know you want to."

My mind is at war with itself to the point that I have to look away. He's right. I do have the desire to trust him, to let him hold me, to give myself to him. But that's not who I am. "Because of my heat." I frown and offer the words as a simple explanation. Once the heat is gone, I'm sure I won't feel this way about him anymore. It's only temporary. But I'll live with this forever … and Lizzie …

Devin's fingertips dig into the soft flesh at my hips. The possessive hold makes my body instinctively still. My heart races in fear. Once he registers my reaction, he loosens his grip and caresses instead, but I remain frozen in place as my heart tries to climb up my throat. I want to trust him, but I sure as fuck don't.

A moment of awkward silence passes.

"How long did I sleep?" I ask and peek up at him through my lashes only to find him staring at me. As though he's studying me.

"A few hours." Shock widens my eyes and I jump back a bit, as far as I can with his hands still gripping my hips, keeping me seated in his lap.

"Lizzie," I say her name in a breathy voice, not hiding my fear and shock. I can't believe I left her alone for that long.

"She's all right." I shift uncomfortably in my captor's grasp. Would he tell me if she wasn't? As if on cue, he speaks up.

"I'd let you know if she wasn't well. She seems to like her space and we're giving it to her."

I nod my head, but eye him questioningly. I almost ask him, promise? As if this man owes me anything or that I should trust him. But I don't have to ask. He tells me exactly what I want to hear.

"I promise nothing bad will happen to her. She's sleeping. Sound asleep and perfectly safe."

"She's not with—"

"She's not with a man, no. No one has ... touched her. Like I've touched you." There's a thrumming in my veins and mixed feelings that race through me.

Before I can whisper *promise?* yet again, he says it first. "I promise you, Grace."

Jude said they can hear each other's thoughts and now I'm wondering if he can hear mine. I purse my lips and narrow my eyes.

"What's wrong?" He seems a bit worried so I school my expression back to neutral. Still, I can't help but to ask.

"Can you read my mind?" At my question he chuckles, revealing his perfect, yet deadly white teeth. I find myself staring at his sharp fangs, mesmerized by them.

"No, I can't read your mind. Werewolves can communicate telepathically if we concentrate but that doesn't include humans." He runs his fingers through my hair and his silver eyes sparkle almost as brilliantly as his smile. "So unfortunately I'll never be able to read your mind, Grace."

His fingertips glide gently up and down my back, pulling at my cream camisole. It's then that I realize I'm only wearing my shirt. He's covered my lower half with a cashmere throw. I snuggle into it and shift my weight on his lap, feeling self-conscious. My eyes search the room and land on my ripped jeans and lace thong. Dammit. I can't help but frown at the sight.

"Those were my favorite jeans. I just got them." I can't conceal the disappointment in my voice. His eyes follow my gaze and he runs a hand through his gorgeous hair, looking guilty all the while.

"We'll get you more. The clothes from your apartment are here so you have plenty of outfits to choose from in the meantime. The betas are setting up your room." I perk up immediately.

"Our things are here?" I blink rapidly at him as my mind wakes up.

He smirks at my excitement and nods. I instantly glare at him. He'd better speak when I ask him a question. This shit's going to work both ways.

His eyes spark at the sight of my narrowed eyes. "Yes," he says teasingly.

"I swear to God, if you can read my mind, I'm going to beat the shit out of you." An asymmetric grin pulls at his lips.

"I told you I can't. I won't ever lie to you, Grace." The whimper that leaves me at the sound of his tender tone is … unexpected. As is the desire to lean in closer.

It's hitting me again … squirming in his lap, I close my eyes to will it away.

"I asked you one question and you still haven't answered it." The words rumble from his chest as I lean into him even more. I nuzzle under his chin and resist the need to nip at him. The temptation is nearly overwhelming and just the thought fans the low flames igniting my core.

"And what was that question again?" I really don't remember. I'm still tired and this day feels like one giant blur of raw emotion.

"What do you know about werewolves?" He leans back in his chair and I lean back too. A little distance is good.

Oh, right. I swallow and pick at the ends of the throw as I shrug against him. "Not much, really."

"And what is 'not much?'"

"Well, I know you shift into a very large wolf. You're good at smelling and hearing. You hate vampires." I bite the inside of my cheek and try to think of more. "I *now* know that you all have silver eyes and you're taller than average." I push the throw down and lean back into him. Staring at the black and white photographs on the far office wall I comment, "You have the ability to make unsuspecting women sleep with you."

A low growl rumbles up his chest as a warning.

"That's pretty much it."

"You're right; that isn't very much at all. And half of it's wrong." I scrunch up my nose and feel my forehead crease. I pull away from him, both my palms pressing against his chest as I stare into his piercing silver eyes.

"What did I get wrong?"

"We're not all *taller than average.*" He mocks me. "I don't like what you said about making women sleep with us." I'm forced to bite my tongue at that comment, so much so I'm surprised I don't bleed. "We don't all have silver eyes. And lastly, we don't hate vampires."

"Yes you do." The words come out accusingly. "That's why we have the treaty. You keep them away."

A slight frown mars his handsome face at my words, but he nods. "They stay away because we asked. But that doesn't mean that we hate them."

"You just asked them to stay away?"

"Well no, not exactly. We have an understanding." I raise my brows, willing him to continue. "They stay away or we kill them."

"But you don't hate them?"

He shakes his head. "Why is that so hard to believe?"

"I was always told you came to Shadow Falls to hunt them because they're your natural enemies."

He scoffs. "Not at all. A mate to one of the pack members was in danger. We had to protect her."

"A mate?"

"Yes," he says and his response is clipped.

"Whose mate?"

"The grandfather to the Alpha of my old pack."

"I don't understand. This is the same pack, isn't it? There's only one pack who we made the treaty with."

"We're part of that pack. I fought their Alpha for the territory after forming my own pack." The curious side of me itches to scoot closer to him. I need to know more.

"Tell me everything from the beginning," I say then cross my legs in his lap and watch him intently.

His grin in response is contagious. "I will, sweetheart." He shakes his head and adds, "Not today, though. It has to be two or three in the morning." My gaze wanders around the room, searching for the source of the ever-present soft ticking. Damn, he's right. The simple, sleek and modern clock on the wall directly behind me reads nearly 2:30 a.m.

"I'm happy you seem more relaxed now." His words are soothing as I hum a response into his chest. He smells so fucking good. Like a masculine, woodsy pine.

"You're like a drug." The words slip past my lips effortlessly. "It's not right and I don't like it."

He leans down and runs his teeth along the shell of my ear, causing a chill to run through me while his hot breath tickles my skin. He whispers, "I love that I'm your drug."

The shiver morphs into a spike of need and I rub myself against him, just barely containing my moan.

"Grace." His tone holds a note of warning.

"Yes?" My response is practically a purr and I don't recognize this person. With a desperate need riding over me, I lean forward just to smell him, just to get a small dose of that lust. The tip of my nose runs along his stubble and a warmth flows through me. It's like … like fate telling me everything is going to be all right. "I've never felt like this before," I confess to him.

"Grace," he warns me, but even his authoritative tone is weakened like I am. He feels it too. I steady myself against him, rocking slightly.

With his hands on my hips, he stops my movements. I murmur, "But I need you."

"Fuck," he groans to the ceiling as his head rolls back at my words.

"Please, fuck me." I have no shame this time. I'm throbbing against him with desire and I have no intention of being denied. My nipples are pebbled and all I can think about is him inside of me, thrusting and soothing every need I have. I splay my hand against his chest and push. With little resistance, he leans back into the chair, his hooded eyes finding mine.

With my chest pressed against him, I place my lips at his ear. "I want you. And you better not fucking deny me." He groans and takes my head in his hands as his lips crash against mine. His warm tongue runs along the seam of my lips and my mouth parts for him. My tongue dances with his as he struggles to release his hard dick from his pants. His movements beneath me make it obvious that he's stroking himself and that knowledge makes my skin heat even more with anticipation as I moan. I need him inside of me, filling me.

I position myself so that the head of his dick is at my hot entrance. He stares into my eyes as I gently glide down his massive cock. My bottom lip drops and I can barely hold his gaze. A strangled moan is torn from me as I move down his length, taking every inch of him. I'm still a little sore from earlier, but the fullness makes my body sing with pleasure. I move back and forth a few inches, whimpering as my limbs tremble slightly. My head falls onto his shoulder as the hot sensation overwhelms me. Devin takes my head in his hands and kisses me sweetly. I moan into his mouth as I glide up and down, my arousal making the movement effortless although his girth is still stretching me. I lean back and pick up my speed while my hands rest on his muscular pecs, riding him at my own pace.

He's good to me, I tell myself. Some part of me that sees this pathetic need as weak. I choose who I want to fuck and when. This is me, taking what I want. I won't be ashamed of that.

His hands stay at my hips as he takes my nipple into his warm mouth, bites down and pulls back. I arch my back at the spike of pleasure and wanton heat in my core. He relaxes against the chair, watching me with a hungered look in his silver eyes. Everything about him screams power and need. *He needs me.* The thought is heady.

His heated gaze of adoration sends yet another surge of arousal through me. My clit hits his pelvis with every downward stroke as I continue riding him and it makes my pleasure all the more intense.

I stop my movements and stare at him. He's letting me ride him. He's given me control. But it's false control. I find myself wanting him to fight for it. A moment passes before Devin looks up at me. He bucks his hips against me, causing me to moan as his eyes find mine. As we both catch our breath he asks, "What's wrong, sweetheart?"

I pause for a moment before admitting the truth. "I want you to fight me, to take me."

Before I can blink, he's lifted us out of the chair and he spins my body around, pinning me against the wall. It's cool against my flesh. I don't even have time to gasp until my cheek is pressed against the wall with his fist gripping my hair. My legs are spread wide and just the head of his hard dick is nestled between my folds. Both my wrists are captured in one of his hands and held above my head. *Holy fuck!* My heart races in my chest. His speed and strength are terrifying but somehow invigorating at the same time. His other hand loosens its grip in my hair, then slips between the wall and my body, moving lower and lower until he's able to circle my clit with heavy, unrelenting pressure. The feeling is so intense that I try to move away, but I'm trapped. I can hardly move any part of my body.

He whispers into my ear, "You questioning my dominance, sweetheart?" My pussy clenches at his words, feeling empty without him inside me. I shake my head slightly as best I can. "No," I murmur, my eyes barely open as the pleasure rocks through me.

Without warning, he slams his dick inside of me all the way to the hilt and I scream out his name while an orgasm rips through my body. He groans into my neck, "I know you love me destroying your cunt, you're so fucking tight on my dick."

His words bring me that much closer to yet another release as he starts rutting me from behind. I love every bit of what he's doing to me. I can hardly take it, but at the same time I want more. I want all of him. I need all of him. My heart clenches in agony as I find myself wanting to beg, but I don't know what for. His lips kiss over my shoulder and neck hungrily. I feel his fangs skim across my neck and I push myself into them. *Yes!*

He nips my ear and sucks on my neck, quickening his pace.

The sound of his hips slamming into me fuels my need to let go. I try to move away as the feeling becomes too much. I try everything to escape, but I'm pinned. I can't get away from the intensity of the need running through my body, heating and numbing every inch of me.

"I don't think so, sweetheart. You wanted me to fuck you like this, remember?" The danger in his voice is intoxicating. I was a fool to think I could fight him. "Take it, sweetheart." His low growl sends even more desire strumming through me and just as I'm about to find my release all over again, he pinches my clit, making me scream. My orgasm hits me like the rough waves of the ocean, crashing unforgivingly against the shore over and over as my body trembles uncontrollably. At the same time, I feel him release, heightening my own pleasure as his dick throbs inside of me.

"Tell me you felt that, sweetheart. Tell me you feel our connection." He breathes heavily into my neck and his words come out with desperation. I've had sex before. Plenty of times. But this is … it's more. He adds, "I'm not letting you go till you do."

Our connection. It's far too much. The violent crash is imminent and it's going to destroy me. Not even a day, and I already know Devin is going to ruin me. It's not fair. I never stood a chance.

I can't lie. "Yes." I answer him as quickly as I can and I feel his body relax against mine, but he still cradles me against him. I catch my breath and say, "I promise I felt it." Thankfully I stop myself before the next words slip out. My heart clenches and tears form in my eyes when I realize how close I was to blurting out three stupid words that should never be spoken.

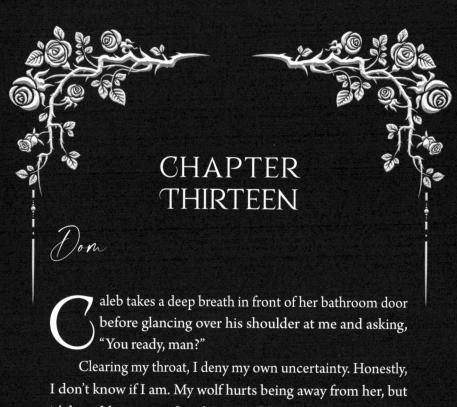

CHAPTER THIRTEEN

Dom

Caleb takes a deep breath in front of her bathroom door before glancing over his shoulder at me and asking, "You ready, man?"

Clearing my throat, I deny my own uncertainty. Honestly, I don't know if I am. My wolf hurts being away from her, but it's bearable compared to the pain I felt when she rejected me. The east wing is finished, every piece in its place, so we figured we'd get our little mate settled.

She wasn't in the guest bedroom. Not that I expected her to be in bed waiting for us; I'm not that naïve.

"She probably fell asleep in there." I nod at Caleb's assertion as he gestures to the bathroom.

It kills me that she's avoiding us, but I'm not going to lie down and just take this shit forever. She's my mate, and I'll be damned if she's going to refuse me without giving me a chance.

"Come on, stop dragging your feet. She's probably asleep

anyway." He reaches for the bathroom door before I'm even able to respond. It's locked. That's not surprising. He jiggles the handle and it pisses me off. He's being too loud. He's going to wake her up and I'd rather he didn't. If she's asleep I can at least hold her without having her attack me. That thought, that possibility, is the only thing that drives me to do this right now. Rather than just leave her be in peace until she's ready to come out. I grit my teeth and push him out of the way.

"Knock it off. I swear to God if you woke her up, I'm going to break your hand." He snorts and all out smiles at my threat.

"You may be a big motherfucker, but I can still take you, Dom." The idea of the two of us going at it puts a wicked grin on my face. Not many in the pack like to spar with me anymore. I take a credit card out of my wallet and slip it between the lock and the doorframe. I'm not as good as some, but I'm sure I can jimmy this lock.

"Put your money where your mouth is, pup."

"Pup? I'm six months younger than you." I chuckle at the indignation in his tone that rings in my head.

"Still younger." As I whisper the words, I hear the lock clear and I twist the knob. We're in. Holding my breath, I push the door open as quietly as possible. I silently step into the room, but she's not here. My brows furrow and Caleb pushes past me. I take another glance around the large bathroom, but she's nowhere to be seen. Adrenaline spikes through me and my heart beats frantically, pounding against my rib cage. My throat closes and I struggle to take in a breath.

As I'm having a goddamn breakdown, Caleb pulls open the shower curtain. The sound of the rings sliding along the metal bar steals my attention.

"Calm down; she's right here." I release a breath I didn't know I was holding and walk silently, but quickly to my mate.

She's curled up on the bottom of the deep soaking tub, lying awkwardly against the cold cast iron so that her neck is at a weird angle. That's got to fucking hurt. She could've at least grabbed a towel for a makeshift pillow. That now familiar pain creeps up in my chest. She'd rather stay hidden and cold than to attempt any kind of comfort. Shit, we left her alone in the bedroom; she could've slept there. I breathe in deep, letting the disappointment and guilt run through my body. She doesn't trust us.

I lean down to sit on the edge of the tub and brush her soft blond hair away from her face. Her cheeks are tearstained and black mascara is smeared under her eyes, but she's still impossibly stunning. Her petite frame only takes up about half of the tub, making her look even more fragile. Her deep, even breathing confirms that she's out cold. She's still in her skimpy dress; I can't help it as my eyes linger on her upper half that's very much in danger of being exposed. The bottom of her dress doesn't even come close to covering her ass. I tilt my head and I can see a bit of a cream-colored lace thong. I close my eyes and bite back a groan. She's fucking gorgeous. I sure as hell don't deserve her.

I consider undressing her and putting her in something more comfortable but nix that idea as soon as it pops into my fucked-up brain. She doesn't even want me to hold her hand. There's no way she'll be all right if I undress her.

Caleb picks up her heels on the other side of the tub and looks them over. "It's a wonder she hasn't broken her damn neck wearing these things." I snort. Her toenails are painted hot pink and match her dress perfectly.

"You think pink's her favorite color?" I don't know why I ask. The thought slips out.

"Judging by all the pink shit we just brought here, yeah." I nod my head, idly wondering what else she likes. I want to know everything about her. My eyes drift down her luscious curves.

"I grabbed this to cover her up," Caleb says. I turn around to face Caleb although I have to look up at him since I'm still seated on the edge of the tub. He's holding the comforter from the bed she could've easily slept in. I nod and exhale deeply while I stand. I didn't even realize he'd left the room.

"All right, let's wrap her in it so we can get her to her room." I move out of his way. *"You think Alpha's going to have Grace sleep with him tonight?"* I'm still debating on sleeping next to Lizzie. I'll wake up before her, so I

can slip out before she has a chance to freak out. He huffs, giving me a look like I should know better.

"I think he'd like to, but he's not going to have much of a choice." I tilt my head and give him a side-eye. He just shakes his head and reaches down to collect our mate. *"You really think Grace is going to want to sleep with him tonight?"* I frown and shrug. I don't understand why our mates are so difficult.

Caleb stands in the tub, draping the comforter over her body. I bend down with him to help gather the blanket around her tiny body. As I tuck the blanket under her arm, her blue eyes spring open and stare straight into mine, scaring the shit out of me. I stumble back a bit, caught off guard. My action halts Caleb and he follows my gaze to our mate's eyes. I hear her heartbeat pick up, instantly racing, but outwardly she shows no signs that she's coherent. Her body is frozen in place and her face is devoid of emotion. She reminds me of an animal playing dead, hoping a predator will go away and leave her alone.

I raise my hands to show her that I don't mean her any harm. "You all right, little one?" I keep my voice as reassuring as I can, trying to calm her. She doesn't answer. Her eyes dart to my hands then back to my face. The sound of her heart beating chaotically fills the small room it's so damn loud, but she remains rigid and tense. Something about her expression has changed, though. She's no longer a wounded animal; the hint of silver in her eyes sparks in a way that makes me aware she's waiting to strike. She wants to fight me. As much as that thought makes my dick hard, this isn't her challenging my worthiness as a mate. I wish that were the case. I'd pin her ass down so fast and fuck her ruthlessly till she had no doubt who she belonged to. But that's not what this is. The smell of fear, not arousal, permeating the air is so strong it's practically suffocating.

"Liz, you fell asleep in the tub, baby; we were just going to move you so you would be more comfortable." Caleb slowly steps out of the tub as he talks to her, but Liz's eyes don't leave mine. She shows no sign that she's heard him. I part my lips to say something, but I don't know what the hell to say. She's obviously scared out of her mind. She's looking at me like I'm her worst enemy. What the hell did I do to put her on edge?

"Lizzie, you okay?" Still no response. If I could just touch her, then I could calm her down. I know I could. I could make her *feel* this connection, this electric pull between us. My thoughts give me the push I need to move toward her. Swallowing thickly, I slowly reach down with the intention of stroking her arm, but she silently rears back and scrambles to get away from me. I pull back and put my hands up again, showing her that I won't reach out to her. The comforter restricts her movement as she struggles to get up. Her feet slip, caught up in the blanket and I'm too damn slow to stop her from bashing the back of her head against the spout.

She winces as both of her hands shoot up to cradle the wound on her head. The distinct smell of blood reaches me instantly. I reach down for her again, wanting to help her, *needing* to help her. I know that had to hurt. But as my large hand palms her chin she screams, kicking furiously against the comforter as her nails dig into my forearm and her teeth sink into the flesh of my hand.

"Fuck!" I pull back before her teeth release me, spilling more blood than necessary. Blood seeps from the two large scratches she left on my arm. I stare at them in surprise before turning my eyes back to her. My blood glistens on her lips and her sharp blue eyes stare back at me full of hate. My gut drops and I swallow the lump forming in my throat, which feels too tight to breathe. I can only hope that the look on my face conveys how torn up I am.

"Hey now, baby girl, you're all right." Caleb moves in front of me to catch Lizzie's eye. She ignores him, continuing to stare at me with utter hatred. "Dom's just trying to help you, baby." He kneels on the tub without reaching for her. "It's okay. I promise we aren't going to hurt you."

Her small voice hisses her words dripping with venom. "Don't let him touch me."

At her statement, I feel my soul shatter into jagged pieces as my wolf howls in agony. And then I hear something I shouldn't. It takes me a moment in my despair to realize that it came from my mate. Caleb looks at me with disbelief, giving me confirmation that he heard it as well. I stare into those icy blue eyes and will her to speak again. She doesn't, though. Her wolf is silent. But I know I heard her whine in pain.

Our mate's a werewolf.

I scent the air, but I can't smell her wolf at all. If Caleb hadn't heard her also, I would be doubting my sanity.

I push Caleb to the side to stand in front of our mate. He doesn't resist at all. He's looking at her with a look of pure confusion. "Where'd your wolf go?"

A look of dread crosses her face. I see her swallow as she pushes her body as far away from us as the tub will allow. All traces of anger have dispersed, leaving only fear.

Staggered breaths leave her parted lips, and tears well in her eyes.

"Why are you so scared, little one?" I hold up my arm for her to see. "It's okay. I'm not mad." Her shoulders start rising and falling as her breathing becomes erratic.

"It's okay," Caleb finally speaks up. "What happened to your wolf?" She shakes her head violently. Why is she so terrified of us? More importantly, how the hell is she hiding her wolf like that?

"I'm not a werewolf." The rushed words barely have any sound as they leave her lips.

My eyes narrow at her. "Don't lie to me, little one." I try to keep the threat out of my voice, but it's still there. The moment I hear the admonishment, I regret it. She's fucking terrified. I shouldn't be giving her more reasons to fear me.

"She left me," our scared little mate whimpers. "I'm not latent anymore, she won't come back." She gasps for breath as her body shakes. "Please, she won't come back." I feel my heart hollow as my wolf whines in distress.

"Please what, little one?"

"Please don't beat me." Her sad blue eyes burrow into mine as she begs, "Please don't hurt me again. I swear she won't come. She's dead. I can't shift. I swear I can't shift." Her words are barely coherent, but I've

80

heard enough that I understand her terror. I close my anguished eyes. Now I get why she hates me and it shreds my insides.

If I could bring my father back to life, I would.

When I killed him, it was for me but if I could do it again, I'd torture him first for her.

"It wasn't me." I choke the pitiful words out. I was just a child, just a pup, but I knew what my family was doing. I knew what my father did to those kids, but it took years for me to gather the courage to fight him. Years of listening to their tormented screams. He recorded everything as proof of their identity when he sold them on the black market. As I grew older, he made me watch. First the videos and then in person. I'll never forget their haunted eyes as my father and uncles beat them mercilessly, forcing their animals to the surface. His large hand on my shoulder kept me pinned in place as he made me watch. Even as I vomited in revulsion, he insisted I needed to see it to be a man.

The day he handed me a weapon to do as he told me, as my Alpha commanded, was the day I fought back. I bludgeoned him with the bat he used to break his victims' bones. By the end of our battle, we'd both shifted and he lay in front of me coughing up blood with what little life he still had left. Before he could heal, I ripped out his throat; his hot, sticky blood gushed into my mouth before spilling onto the floor. The only regret I've ever had in my entire life was not stopping him sooner. If I hadn't been so scared of dying, I could've saved nearly half a dozen children. I never once had any remorse over killing him. Not until today. I wish he were still alive so I could kill him for her. So she could watch as her tormentor took his last breath.

"It wasn't me. It was my father."

"Just stay away," she cries and I swear my heart breaks.

"It wasn't me," is all I can answer, the words only a whisper.

Caleb's consoling hand on my shoulder brings me back to the present. Back to my sobbing, shattered mate. She's so fucking damaged. My heart aches for her. I reach out my hand to her unable to stop myself, but she backs herself into the corner like a scared animal. Her rejection is deserved as I drop my head in shame. I take a deep breath and square my shoulders.

Now that I know why she's been acting the way she has, I can make this right. I'll fix this.

I meet Caleb's eyes. "Bring her to the bedroom."

PART IV

Their Mates

CHAPTER FOURTEEN

Dom

"**W**hat the hell, Dom?" Even though he's screaming in my head, Caleb looks back at me with a neutral expression.

"She's scared. I'm going to fix it."

"By tying her up?" His shocked tone is laced with disapproval. *"She's scared out of her mind, you sick asshole!"*

"Knock it the fuck off," I sneer with disdain before calming myself and adding, *"you know I'm not going to cross the line."* He presses his lips into a thin line, his hands clenching into fists before quickly relaxing and then he looks back at our mate. She's still huddled in a ball shaking uncontrollably, intently focused on ignoring us. As though we don't exist if she can't see us. She's got the blanket cocooned around her like it's going to protect her. I shake my head at the sight of her. *Nothing's coming in between us, little one.*

"Tying her up is crossing the line." His low growl is fortified with an unspoken threat.

"Bring it on, motherfucker." The low growl I thought was inaudible awards me with a small whimper from our mate. One that shreds me. *"I'm doing this for her."* I leave him with anger pouring off of him in waves. With long, determined strides, I make my way to the other side of the estate. I need to gather rope from the dungeon. I couldn't care less if Caleb doesn't like it. She may be both of ours, but that isn't going to stop me from doing right by her on my own. She needs to be subdued and reconditioned. Now that I know what she's been through, all bets are off. Our mate isn't a scared little human afraid of the big bad werewolves. No, she's an abused, latent wolf in desperate need of being given a kind, devoted touch. Except she's shown she'll fight us tooth and nail before she lets that happen. She'll do anything to keep us away because she's petrified. All of her past experiences have her on edge and frightened.

I scowl thinking of what she's been through. My chest tightens and my throat constricts. My poor mate. Fate's one cruel bitch. She's scared of me and by extension all of us, simply because I look just like my father. Just like the man who bought her and tortured her. She's been taught to fear the very sight of me. I know just as well as her what he's done and seen how his victims look at him with sheer terror in their eyes. That's how she looks at me. I clench my fists and grip on to the rage and resentment; better that than the sadness threatening to destroy the last bit of hope I have of claiming my mate.

She may have learned to fear my presence, but I can retrain her. I'll have to tie her down at first so she can't hide from me. That way she won't be able to ignore me or run from me anymore. I nod my head as I collect what I'll need. I'll soothe her and relieve her of her agony. Instead of the pain and fear she's used to, I'll condition her mind to crave my touch and her body to want me. She'll let go of the past once she can see her future with me.

Then there's the issue of her latency. Her wolf was there. I heard the poor broken creature whimper in pain; she reached out to our wolves. But somehow Lizzie held her back and hid her. She vanished; there one split second and gone the next. We couldn't hear her or feel her or even scent her. It doesn't make any sense. I should know, since latent shifters were my father's main perversion. You can't hide your wolf. They're always able to be heard, felt and eventually seen. Even if you're latent and can't shift, there's always something that will bring your animal to the surface. Lizzie, my sweet, haunted mate, is not *latent*. She's something else and I have no fucking clue what. But her wolf is in there somewhere and my own wolf is chomping at the bit to get to her. He knows she's hurting and he claws at me to protect her.

If only it were that easy. If only you could protect someone from their past.

My strides pick up as I get closer to my mate. I've only been gone a few minutes, but I don't want to miss a thing. If her wolf comes back, I want to be there for her. I want to be there for Lizzie every step of the way.

First thing we have to do is tell her we're her mates. I don't know if she'll know what that means or what she remembers from her pack, but I'll figure it all out in time. I've got forever with my mate and today is just the first day. There's no way I'm going to let her deny me. I'm not going to let her, or her wolf, hide from us anymore.

"You tell her yet?" I silently question Caleb as I push the door open. The room looks just like the kind of room I'd expect any typical twentysomething to have. Caleb made sure to get everything set up exactly how it was for them back at their apartment. These girls really love the color pink. It's everywhere with splashes of yellow and the occasional pale shade of teal. Lizzie is still huddled in the cream-colored damask comforter from the guest room. She's right in the middle of her bed with her head resting on her knees, nuzzled into the blanket. She's got her arms wrapped around her legs and she holds on to them like they're her anchor. When she hears my boots thud against the wooden floors, she lifts her head slightly and her red-rimmed, blue

eyes peek through her dark, thick lashes at me. The soft movement of her shoulders becomes rigid with fear.

Her eyes dart to the rope in my hands and terror flashes over her face. Her kissable, pouty lips release a small gasp and she quickly backs away from me, crawling on her hands and knees to the headboard and pushing her side up against it. She wraps her arms around her bent legs and hastily rocks her body, resting her cheek on her knee so she can keep her eyes on me. Her big doe eyes are drenched in panic and tears fall carelessly down her reddened cheeks. She sniffles before swallowing and saying in a small voice, "Please don't."

With his arms crossed, Caleb stands in the corner on my right; the corded muscles in his neck and arms make him look like a rock-solid beast. At least he has a tight smile on his face. Although that's obviously not doing anything to calm her.

"*Nah, I figured you'd want to be here.*" I glance at him and then walk slowly to the edge of the bed. I sit my massive form down and feel the soft bed dip. Our little mate lets out a squeak. Caleb follows me but doesn't sit.

"*I tried to sit when you left and she freaked out.*"

"*This'll help her.*" I see him slightly shake his head in my periphery. "*Just don't get in my way then.*"

"*Don't fucking make me.*"

I clench my teeth and ignore him. Our mate hasn't heard a single word of our silent dialogue and I don't want her to think I'm pissed at her. At least I don't think she has.

"I want you to come sit by me." It's a simple request. My words come out as soft as they possibly can. She stops rocking and stares at me for only a moment before burying her head between her knees as she shakes her head in denial. I resist the urge to growl, not at her disobedience, but at the former pricks who did this to her. Instead I pat the bed next to me and calmly repeat myself. "I want you to come sit by me." I look at Caleb and then back to our scared little mouse. "We have something very important to tell you and I want to be able to hold you when you hear it." Caleb's lips turn up at the corners. I don't know if he's try-ing to force a smile onto his pretty-boy face or whether he's trying to hold one in.

Caleb stalks closer to her and slowly drops to his knees at the foot of the bed. His tall frame hovers over the mattress as he bends to offer his upturned hand to Lizzie. "Come on, baby girl, I want to hold you too. Let's go sit with Dominick." She doesn't even lift her head to meet his eyes. Her blond hair swings across her back as she shakes her head, adamantly refusing our requests.

"Let's just tell her." I hear Caleb's words in my head, but instead of responding silently I continue to speak out loud so our mate can hear.

"I don't want to tell her until I can hold her."

"Stop being so fucking stubborn." He continues his silent conversation.

"I'm not being stubborn; when I tell her that she's my mate, she needs to be listening. She's not listening to anything we say."

"She is listening; she doesn't want to obey. There's a difference, Dom."

"I know there's a difference. She's hearing us, but she's not really listen-ing." I glance back at our terrified mate before looking Caleb in the eyes. *"You want to claim her on the full moon?"* He squirms uncomfortably.

"You know I do. But I don't want to scare her."

"Too late." I speak out loud, but he doesn't follow suit.

His shoulders slump in defeat. *"I don't want to give her a reason to fear us."*

"She already has one." Frustrated with all this pussyfooting around, I question him, "Are you going to help me?" He grits his teeth and clenches his fists, but then he gives me a slight nod. I take a deep breath and crack my knuckles before turning to fully face our mate.

"Hey, Lizzie," I say and stare at the back of her head. She stops moving but doesn't turn to me, and she doesn't respond. I know she's terrified, so it doesn't make me angry—in fact, it's exactly what I expect.

I sigh and say as casually as I can, "If you won't listen, I'm going to have to tie you up, little one." Her breathing hitches, but other than that

I get nothing. I'll give her one last chance. "Come here. Come sit next to me so I'll know you'll hear me." I pat the bed and continue to stare at the back of her head.

"How are we doing this?" Her lack of a response gets Caleb to finally relent.

"Well, do you want to get your eyes clawed out or have your nose kicked in?" A small grin plays at his lips.

CHAPTER FIFTEEN

Devin

I place featherlight kisses along Grace's bare neck as she sits perched on the granite countertop of the large island in the center of the kitchen. I don't want to let go of her, but I know she's dying to get back to Lizzie. I breathe out deep and resign myself to feeding her and then taking her to her room. I'm vaguely aware of Dom's and Caleb's anxiety. They must be going to Lizzie, which means our mates' room is set up.

Dom's feelings are more of a painful anxiousness whereas Caleb's are hopeful but tinged with apprehension. I block them out. They don't need me interfering. They'd better come up with a plan soon to tell her that she's their mate. I don't think I can wait like I'd planned to. Keeping this from her is tearing me up inside. It's easy to see when she's overthinking it all. I know the moment I explain it to Grace, everything will fall into place for her. Our bond is already strong, as it should be between mates, but she's still holding back and that's a problem I'm unwilling to allow to go on much longer.

She pulls my shirt down her thighs, covering herself from me, and glances around the large kitchen. I could tell she was shocked by how modern her new home is. She probably expected to live in some shack in the woods. I reach for the cheese and butter in the fridge. After spending a year watching her, I know she makes grilled cheese whenever she's stressed. I made sure to stock up on groceries before we went to the offering. I want her to indulge in anything that will offer her comfort. Once she's settled, she'll have all the comfort she's always wanted.

I set the ingredients by the stove and glance back at her as I reach for a pan. She avoids my gaze and bites her lip, nervously looking around the room again. Her eyes linger on the doorway to the hall. Doubt filters into my mind each time her attention focuses on an escape route. I swear to God if she runs from me again, I'll lose my shit. As long as I'm touching her, she seems fine but the moment I step away, it's like our bond doesn't exist. That's an indescribable pain. Doesn't she feel that as well? There's so much I don't know … all because she's human. This is the first instance in nearly a century for our kind to mate with humans from what I've heard in the whispers from other packs. It's not common, but it's not completely unheard of either.

"What are you looking for, sweetheart?" I keep my voice even. As if I don't know she's thinking about bolting even though it's written all over her face. She peeks up at me through her lashes and meets my gaze head-on. Well that's a good sign at least. I see her noticeably swallow.

"I was keeping an eye out for the … others." The jealousy is unexpected. My nostrils flare and my breathing picks up in anger. I can't school my expression fast enough. Her gaze drops to the floor and she hunches her shoulders. She doesn't realize it, but she's trying to shield her neck from me. Yet another thing I don't like. It takes far too much effort to compose myself. This isn't what we're told to expect. Especially for an Alpha's mate. Again, doubt lingers.

"Why are you waiting on … *others*?" I can't say anything else without giving away how pissed off I am and this level of aggression is not for her. Imagining someone else walking in on her like this, and her attention being given to them ... a pack member and not her mate ... dressed as she is ... The fact that Dom and Caleb are sharing their mate has gone to my head. I turn my back to her and put the pan for her goddamn grilled cheese on the stove to heat. I have to work hard not to slam the drawer shut after I grab a butter knife.

"I ... I ..." Her stammering isn't helping to calm me down. "I don't want to see them." My shoulders relax at her admission.

"That's a hell of a lot better than what I was thinking."

I turn back around to face her before I ask with all seriousness, "Are you afraid of them?" She shakes her head "no" while her beautiful hazel eyes meet my gaze. Nodding, at least I know I chose well for who would accompany her when I couldn't. Lev, even if he is younger and less experienced—he's soft where the rest of us aren't, charming and easy to talk to. He has patience where I don't, and more importantly, he'll protect her.

Satisfied, I nod, letting my gaze drift down her body.

She's so fucking gorgeous covered in just my white T-shirt. I have a perfect view of her pale rose nipples through the thin fabric and I'm not sure if they're hard because she's aroused or if she's cold. Maybe it's both. Her bare feet dangle from the counter and her ankles are crossed. She looks so sweet and innocent. The blush that rises to her cheeks proves she's not so innocent as her gaze lingers on my chest, then moves lower. I watch her lick her lips before her eyes meet mine again. My sexy, knowing smirk makes her roll her eyes.

Damn, I love her confidence.

Her eyes dart to the far edge of the counter as the small smile on her lips fades. I follow her line of sight and my brows pinch. I'm not sure if it's my laptop or something else that's caught her attention, but I'd be willing to bet she would do anything now to tell the people in her hometown that she's all right. Which can never happen. Never. There are laws in place and her silence is required.

I flip her grilled cheese before striding across the room and bringing the laptop to her. I don't care if she uses it and I want her to know I trust her. That she has access to everything she desires.

"Go ahead and order those jeans." I smirk at her shocked expression and then give her a stern look so she knows I'm serious. "No social media, though." Focusing again on the sandwich I turn my back to her, but she nods before she leaves my view.

Her buttered bread is perfectly golden and crispy, with the melted cheese dripping down the sides. I smile inwardly. It's just the way she likes it. I'll never admit to her that I practiced making them as soon as I noticed her obsession. The first week, I burned all the ones I tried making. After that, I had to actually study her while she cooked and realized she kept adding butter. No wonder her ass has that tempting curve to it. My dick hardens at the thought of pounding into her against the wall. I stifle my groan.

"I don't have my card ..." Her sweet voice brings me back to reality. Nervousness echoes in her worried statement.

The ceramic plate clinks on the counter and I slip the grilled cheese onto it before taking it to her. Her hazel eyes light up and the most beautiful smile I've ever seen plays at her lips, exposing her perfect white teeth as she immediately picks up her comfort food, not hesitating for a moment. Sometimes she adds salt, so I grab it from the cabinet and set it next to the empty plate. The sandwich occupies both of her hands. "I love grilled cheese." She practically moans the words through a mouthful of sandwich before she realizes she's talking with her mouth full. She blushes and puts a hand up to her mouth. "Sorry," she chokes out once she swallows.

Fucking adorable.

Shaking my head, I admit, "I don't mind." I glance at the screen and see she's picked out her jeans. They're only fifty bucks and I'm honestly shocked. I thought women's clothing was more expensive than men's. "Those are what you want?"

She hesitantly nods her head. "I know Lizzie wants a pair too." Although it's a statement, her meek voice makes it a question.

"Go ahead and order them, choose the first card that comes up, or any of them. Get as many pairs as you'd like." I turn back to the stove and take a look at my own grilled cheese. I burned it. Motherfucker. I don't really care about the damn thing.

"It's important you only use the computer for shopping ... you know that?"

She nods, midbite and drops the late-night meal to the plate. "I imagine there are rules."

All I give her is a nod and then say, "We'll discuss them later." I take a large bite of my sandwich and gesture to the last bit of hers.

"I didn't know werewolves ate real food." I chuckle at her comment and take a bite with my back leaning against the sink so I can face my mate.

My curiosity is piqued. "What did you think we ate?" Even with as much as I have to tell her, I'm curious to hear what the humans think and say. I've heard things, but the truth is always hidden and less obvious.

She shrugs noncommittally. "No clue. I figured since vampires drink blood, and witches eat organs and nasty shit that you would eat ..." she trails off and scrunches up her nose before concluding, "I don't know, raw meat or something."

From the corner of my eye I watch Lev pause at the doorway when he catches sight of Grace perched on the counter. I nod at him, acknowledging his presence and giving him permission to enter. He walks into the kitchen and yawns audibly, obviously in an attempt to make her aware of his presence before he says, "You two are up early." He eyes Grace on his way to the fridge, no doubt wondering what kind of a mood she's in ... and probably wondering if she's struck me again. "Good morning, Grace." He turns his attention to me and says, "Alpha."

The entire pack knows that she hit me and tried to get away from me. Part of me is delighted because I can feel their admiration for her strength and courage; the other part of me wants to sulk at the fact that she denied me. It's embarrassing at the very least, and alarming at the worst. There's so much she doesn't know, but the wolf of a denied mate can't lead a pack. She doesn't realize how much control she has and how much is at stake.

So, striking me ... it's a precedent that can't be set. Lev got to see it firsthand and I still feel ashamed for making her want to run from me. His presence reminds me that I need to talk to her about why she bolted the moment I left her. And more importantly, how it can't happen again. No matter the circumstance.

"You consider this early to be morning?" she asks Lev like he can't be serious. My lips kick up into a smirk at her response. She's confident and relaxed. She fits right in as the Alpha mate.

It was shocking when I found out my mate was human. When I felt her, when I was drawn to her. Having to leave without her at last year's offering was … excruciating. The pain is inhumane. We're the strongest pack on this side of the country. I thought having a human mate would make me weak and waiting for her certainly held its challenges, but I can already feel the power she's giving me through our bond. I'm honored to be her mate even if she's younger and has so much to learn. I hope one day she'll feel the same way.

Lev smiles at her response after taking a swig from the jug of orange juice. "Well, it's the morning shift." He wipes his mouth with the back of his hand. Lev is … Lev. A fucking animal. "I've got to go do my laps and get shit in order before Jude checks out."

Grace tilts her head in confusion, her brunette hair slipping from her shoulder and falling behind her. The curve of her neck is … tempting.

"We have to do rounds to ensure the estate is secure," he explains to Grace and her expression falls just slightly, a flicker of uncertainty present. As she swallows, her fingers grip the edge of the counter slightly.

"You think … you think someone would try to come for us?" she questions and Lev keeps his laugh to himself, although I hear it.

"She doesn't need to know yet," I warn Lev and although he doesn't respond to me, he tells her, "No, it's just a good habit for a wolf to be in." We share a glance and Grace's shoulders lose some of their tension. She offers him a tight smile.

"Already lying to her?"

"I'll tell her soon," I answer Lev but then doubt myself and my

decision. Never in the years since we've formed a pack have I doubted so much. She brings questions and unease, but it feels right and just.

My pack's on high alert now that the old Alpha has threatened to return. I should've killed him rather than shown mercy. I shake my head and silently tell Lev to shut the fuck up. She doesn't need to know about all that shit. Not after the day she's had.

Grace yawns although it's obvious she tried to hold it back, and then says, "Well, I call this bedtime." Her shirt rises up as she stretches her arms above her head. The hem tickles her upper thighs, and with the small movement and realization she's only in a top, her eyes widen with a hint of embarrassment. She grabs the fabric and pulls it down as a rosy blush of embarrassment brightens her cheeks. I let a chuckle rumble through my chest. We're shifters, so we don't give a fuck about nudity. I want her to feel comfortable, though.

Lev smirks at her response so I have to silently scold the little shit. *"Have some respect for her modesty, Lev."*

"Sorry, Dev." I hear his humorous remark in my head. He turns on his heels leaving the juice on the counter and heads toward the hall while calling out, "Good night, Grace. See you two later."

Grace calls out in a strained voice, "See you, Lev," while pushing her knees and thighs together and staring at the floor. She whispers, "I'm sorry. I forgot I was only wearing a T-shirt." Her eyes peek up at me, searching for something, and I reach out to cup her chin and run my thumb along her bottom lip.

"It's all right, sweetheart. You don't have to worry about that. Lev doesn't mind." My words don't have the effect I thought they would. She pulls away from my grasp and I let my hand fall to my side. She noticeably swallows.

"I want to go to bed," she speaks quietly to the floor. I can tell she's trying hard not to say something and I have no fucking clue why.

"What's wrong?" She shakes her head, still not making eye contact and I'm not going to stand for that. That's not what this is between us. I should be able to hear everything. Frustration is … so unexpected. I take her chin in my hand again and force her to look at me. Her skin is hot against mine, sparking from the small contact. My gaze bores into her hazel eyes, willing her to answer. She squares her shoulders before shrugging.

"I'm fine. Really. It's just been a long day." I stare at her lying ass for a few seconds before releasing my hold on her. It only takes a second of debating whether or not I should drop this. She's keeping shit from me, but I'm guilty of doing the same to her. Her hands cover her face for a moment before she lifts her hair off her shoulders, breathes in deep, and exhales slow and steady. She twists the hair at the nape of her neck and pulls her brunette locks over her shoulder.

My eyes focus on the sight of her exposed neck; it's a welcome distraction. There are a few tiny scrapes on her delicate skin from my fangs and it makes my dick hard remembering how I fucked her earlier. The marks call to me to bite her. Hard. To claim her by sinking my fangs deep into her tender, pale flesh. I lean down and run my tongue over the most prominent mark, torturing my wolf. She leans into me and hums in approval. I grin into her neck. I may not be able to justify scolding her for keeping secrets when I am too, but I can give her a merciless, punishing fuck. I nuzzle under her ear before nipping her lobe. Her thick thighs clench together as I smell her arousal.

My intentions were to feed her and then take her to bed, but I can't let her go without satisfying all of her hunger, and my own. I run my fingers down her neck to her collarbone then trail back up as I plant small kisses on the other side, up to that tender spot behind her ear. She shivers at my touch. I fucking love it.

"I know you're tired, sweetheart, but I'm not going to leave you while you're in need." I take her bottom lip in between my teeth and bite down hard enough that it'll leave a bruise. She yelps and her little whimper makes my dick swell with desire. I swiftly pick her up off the counter and lay her on her stomach across the barstool so she's at the perfect height for me to fuck her greedy cunt with long, hard strokes.

Brushing her hair over one shoulder, I grip the nape of her neck. With my chest pressed to her back, I listen to her unsteady breathing pick up.

Nothing but lust settles in the warm air between us. She moans my name and arches her back just slightly. This is the obedience I've craved. She's a dream come true. Letting my lips tickle the shell of her ear, I whisper, "Hold on, sweetheart." Her hands instantly grab the legs of the stool while I slam my dick into her.

Fuck, she's even tighter than she was earlier. She's got to be sore to be this swollen and I've only taken her twice so far, but I know that the pain will only heighten her pleasure. The barstool wobbles on the ground, struggling to stay balanced as I hammer my dick into her, pulling almost all the way out and then slamming back in over and over. My grip tightens on her hips as she bites down on her bottom lip, attempting to quiet her sounds of pleasure.

I groan as the feeling of her tight walls stroking my length sends a heated rush through my body, starting at my toes and working its way up in long pulses. She feels too fucking good. I keep my pace slow and steady, knowing how intense it is for her. Hard and fast is right around the corner, but she needs to get off first.

It only takes a few more strokes for me to push her to the edge of her release. Her body trembles and she bites her arm to quiet her moans. I slam my hips into her, forcing her to take all of me and hold it there while she screams out my name and arches her back as her orgasm rips through her body. *Fucking perfect.*

I ride recklessly through her orgasm. My fingers dig into the tender flesh at the front of her throat as I grip her harder. Her arousal makes pistoning into her easier and I pick up my pace, brutally pounding into her welcoming heat. The sound of me fucking her, with her sweet low moans muffled in the background, fuels my need to find my own release. With my left hand gripping her nape to steady her body as I rut into her swollen cunt, I use my right hand to roughly rub her throbbing clit. She struggles beneath me to get away from the intense pressure building in her so soon after her first release. But I want it. I want more of her and all of her.

There's a very sick desire I possess for her to feel me inside of her every second she's away from me.

My hands go numb as a cold sweat breaks out on my skin. The need for release creeps up on my body, slowly building in intensity. I growl into her ear with a primal need, "Come for me." Being so close to her neck makes my fangs ache with the desperate need to mark her and claim her as mine. I let them skim along her sensitive skin, causing a shiver to run down her barely clothed body. My words and the gentle touch of my sharp fangs send her over the edge and I come hard with her. I ride through both of our orgasms as the pleasure numbs my toes and makes my legs tremble.

It's only once she's sated, panting, and limp beneath me that I can breathe again. I lay my chest over her back to plant small kisses over the marks on her neck as my breathing slows with my dick still hard inside her. My arms wrap around her small, limp body and I effortlessly pick her up. I slip out of her as I sit on the barstool and nestle her into my chest then tenderly kiss her forehead. I take my time soothing her, wanting to stay in this moment as the time ticks by. She sighs, happily satisfied, and snuggles against me as she slowly drifts into sleep. I debate on waking her up and fucking her until I've had my fill, but it's late and the sight of her relaxed body in my arms is enough to temper my appetite. For now.

CHAPTER SIXTEEN

Caleb

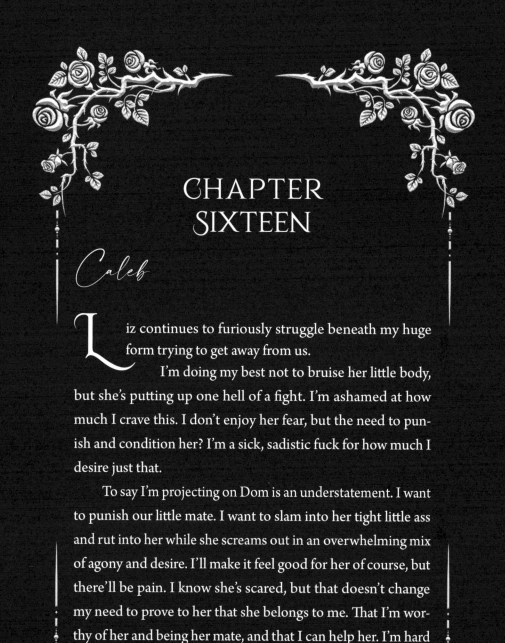

L iz continues to furiously struggle beneath my huge form trying to get away from us.

I'm doing my best not to bruise her little body, but she's putting up one hell of a fight. I'm ashamed at how much I crave this. I don't enjoy her fear, but the need to punish and condition her? I'm a sick, sadistic fuck for how much I desire just that.

To say I'm projecting on Dom is an understatement. I want to punish our little mate. I want to slam into her tight little ass and rut into her while she screams out in an overwhelming mix of agony and desire. I'll make it feel good for her of course, but there'll be pain. I know she's scared, but that doesn't change my need to prove to her that she belongs to me. That I'm worthy of her and being her mate, and that I can help her. I'm hard just thinking about it. Like I said, I'm a sick fuck. I only hope my little mate has a beast in her that wants to come out and play just as much as mine does.

Dom's plan of action only fuels my desires. Tying her up is our next move. She's going to fight us every step of the way and I desperately want her to challenge me. Knowing she's not human puts me on edge, but in a way that gives me relief. If she were human, I'd have to go easy on her and be careful. I can't hurt my mate. Physically or emotionally. I don't want to either. But fucking her within an inch of her life, I'm dying to do that. Knowing she's got shifter blood in her means she could take more punishment than a human can. I know it's going to be hard to control how rough I am with her. I'll try, but I'm dying with need. Need to let out my inner demon and thrust into her with unforgiving, deep strokes. Need to have her writhing beneath me, trying to get away from the pain yet at the same time needing more of it. It's a cruel, twisted need, but it's a need nonetheless.

And she needs to know she's mine, she's safe and she is wanted more than she could possibly imagine.

I've always had these desires. Slow, sweet, and passionate has never interested me. I need it hard and savage. I've never given my perversions free rein. I've never spoken them out loud or let anyone sense these urges. Seeing my mate refuse me, that makes me want to let loose on her. Let my beast out to ruthlessly claim her for himself. Maybe that's why fate gifted me a mate I'm destined to share with Dom. He's frightening to look at, but he has control where I am lacking. I'm a slave to my beast. I should tell Dom what I want to do to her, but he's so wrapped up in having her forgive him for shit he didn't even do that he hasn't noticed my lust for her body.

I have the look of her tearstained face memorized. I love the way fear and anger look on her because it's evidence of how much she needs me. I want her to scream and cry, letting her tears run freely down her gorgeous face while I punish every inch of her body for denying us. For thinking for one second that she doesn't belong to us. More than that, I desperately need her to fight me. I want to feel her sharp nails dig into my back as I draw out every orgasm I possibly can from her body. The only regret

I have is that she won't be able to leave scars. That's a damn shame. I want her marks all over me. And mine all over her.

Liz's nails scrape across my neck while I tie one of her wrists to the headboard and I have to stifle a groan. I can feel her squirming beneath me to get out of Dom's grasp. For being so small she's got a hell of a lot of fight in her. It makes me hopeful. Whatever she went through didn't kill her spirit. All of a sudden, her fist swings out of nowhere and lands square on my jaw.

"Fuck!"

I wrap my hand around her throat knowing her natural reaction will have her hand flying to my fingers to try and pry them off. I lean back and flex my jaw. It actually hurts. A touch of pain makes me smile inwardly. I tighten the rope on one wrist, making sure it's properly secured while my other hand presses against her small, fragile neck. It's enough pressure to feel the blood pumping through her veins, but I'm not pushing hard enough to actually cut off her breathing. I just want her other hand busy while I make sure I have her where I want her.

"Baby girl, that hurt." I admonish her while grabbing her other wrist in my left hand and the rope in my right. Her eyes widen as she realizes her struggling is useless now. The shadow of Dom standing up behind me catches my attention; he must have secured her legs. She screams out un-intelligibly, but within seconds Dom shoves something in her mouth. I glance at her to see what it is. She's shaking her head and trying to spit out his shirt that now acts as a gag. I tug on the rope and fasten it tighter to the bed to restrict her movements as much as possible. I finally breathe out and climb off the mattress to have a look at our gorgeous mate all tied up.

No longer able to fight us, no longer able to hurt herself.

Her dress is bunched up around her waist revealing a cream thong that's begging to be torn from her. It takes every bit of self-control I have not to shove my face in between her legs and leave a languid lick. Her breasts are covered by a simple white strapless bra and I want to rip it to shreds. It's not sexy enough to grace her skin. Our mate is anything but simple. She should be covered in skimpy but expensive lace. My dick hardens at the thought. Or leather. Fuck, she would look so hot with a thin leather strip draped over her breasts, just wide enough to cover her nipples, to tease me. I resist the urge to palm my dick; now is not the time. Not when she's still as scared as she is. Her long platinum blond hair is spread out under her in a messy halo, making her look wild and recently fucked. Damn shame the last part isn't as true as the first. Wild perfectly describes our mate.

That's when I notice the small bruises around her wrist, hips, thighs, and ankles. I stare at them waiting for the purplish blue to slowly fade. They aren't bad, but she's pulling against the rope and it's going to rub her skin raw or give her welts, or both. She needs to knock that shit off and let them heal as wolves do.

"Stop struggling." I give her the command with ease but worry filters in as the bruises appear to darken. "You're going to hurt yourself, baby." She yells something incoherent through the shirt stuffed in her mouth and I have to suppress a grin. The happiness sneaking up on me at seeing our mate spread out for us vanishes when I look back at her bruises. They look even darker. *What the fuck?* I hear Dom thinking the same; she should be healing by now. Concern for our mate rapidly kills any desire I had.

"We hurt her." I shake my head in disgust. Yeah I want to fuck her and bring her to the edge of pain while I pleasure her delectable body, but I don't want her injured in any other way. She's a wolf. I heard it. Dom heard it. She isn't supposed to be bruised. I don't want to mark her unless she can look at them and remember the pleasure that came with it. This isn't what I want. A deep regret settles in my chest. *"Why isn't she healing?"*

"She's not a werewolf." My neck whips around at Dom's blunt statement.

"The hell she's not; you heard her wolf!" My breathing becomes erratic and adrenaline starts pumping through my blood, making my fists tremble with the need to thrash against something. And right now, Dom's face is looking like the best option.

"Calm down, Caleb. She's going to be fine. Her wolf is in there, but she's something else."

"She needs to heal. Why isn't her wolf healing her?" I don't understand what's happening.

He ignores me, which only intensifies my alarm, speaking his next words aloud so Liz can hear. "Little one, you okay?" I'm pretty sure the two syllables she shouts into his shirt are "Fuck you!" A grin threatens to pull at my lips, but I stop that shit; she's not okay. And I don't know how to handle her if she can't heal herself. How can I be rough with her then? How can I be who I am with my mate if she's unable to take something as simple as this?

"Baby girl, bring your wolf back so she can heal you." I focus on the one thing all of us need. "I don't like seeing these marks on your body." I'm surprised by the absolute truth in that statement. I never thought I'd want her marks to go away but then again, these weren't given to her in the way my wolf demands. She shakes her head violently at my command. My brows knit together in anger at her insolence and Dom's hand comes down on my shoulder in an attempt to placate me.

"Calm the fuck down."

Dom crawls on the bed, making it dip and groan, and straddles her tiny frame while he talks. "I want to talk to you. Are you going to be good so I can take your gag away?" Her eyes travel over his body and I scent the air; there's nothing but fear and anger. My wolf snarls in my chest. I want her arousal. Taking a seat on the edge of the bed, I rub soothing circles on her calf. She flinches at first, but soon resigns herself to my touch. It's not like she's in any position to stop me. Dom looks back at me and his eyes light up as he watches me caress her tender skin.

"Maybe we should keep your gag in until you're more relaxed." He stares into her piercing blue eyes and she stares defiantly right back.

"Baby girl, we have something important to tell you." I trail my fingers teasingly up and down her calf before taking her knee in my hand. I want to kiss her leg, but she'll probably just knee me in the face and break my nose. The motion would take all the slack these ropes have for her to do it, but there's not a doubt in my mind she would, so I hold back.

I share a glance with Dom before continuing to talk to Liz and he nods his head in agreement. Now that she can't ignore us and can't run from us, it's the perfect time to tell her we're her mates. Even if she is spitting mad. Beggars can't be choosers. "Baby, when you were with your pack, did you learn about mates?" I'm reaching here. She may have wolf in her, but I don't have a clue whether or not she was ever in a pack. Her body tenses at my question. I press my lips in a hard line. Damn it. I want her to relax.

"You shouldn't have brought up her pack." Dom silently scolds me.

"Then you fucking do it." I answer him in my head so that she doesn't hear my irritation.

"Lizzie, we're your mates." Dom makes the matter-of-fact statement while he bends down to pick up more rope. I scrunch up my face and hang my head at his nonchalance.

"What the fuck, Dom?"

"What?" He looks at me like he's confused as to why I would be aggravated.

"Women want romance, you dumb fuck." I hiss the words in my head.

"Does she look like she wants romance right now?" I take a look at my doe-eyed mate. She's still scared to death and furious, looking at Dom like he just smacked her across her pretty little face. *"She's not even listening. Look at her."*

"Do you know what that means, Liz? That we're your mates?" I ask her evenly, making my voice as soft as I possibly can even though the words choke me. I expect her to shake or nod her head, but she does nothing. I school my expression to keep my anger under wraps.

"She really likes being difficult, doesn't she?"

"It'll take time, but we'll break her habit of ignoring us."

Dom's words ring clear in my head. I don't respond because truthfully I want her to be difficult so we can let our beasts out to play. But not right now. Not when I'm telling her that she's my one and only for as long as I live. That she is my everything and every choice I make will involve her and prioritize her. My heart clenches and my hand stills on her calf. Fuck. Maybe fate knew how fucked up I'd end up being so they gave me a mate who can't love me back. I have to clear my throat and stop those thoughts. I'll *make* her love me.

"Nod if you understand." She stares back defiantly although some of her fight has waned.

"We're your mates. You belong to us and we belong to you." Dom's statement means more to me than anything else I've ever heard.

She hears, she knows. I know she does from the way her breathing picks up and her chest rises and falls heavily. It's sinking in and I pray she can feel the pull and how much stronger it's gotten in only seconds.

"Do you understand what that means? That we're both your mates and you are our only?"

"Little one, answer Caleb." Dom's voice is level, but full of authority. Our stubborn mate continues to ignore the two of us, refusing to nod or attempt to speak. But I know she heard; I know it's dawning on her. Dom sighs as though he's not looking forward to what he's about to do and I watch as he crawls on the bed to wind rope around her knee that's farthest from me. After he knots it, he pulls it to the edge of the bed, forcing her legs to spread apart. He secures the rope to something under the bed and I can't help but wonder where he came up with this idea. My dick pulses in agony at the sight of her legs being forced open. She's completely exposed with no way to hide and I fucking love it.

"You're my mate, Lizzie. *Our* mate." He glances at me and I nod my head while keeping my eyes on Liz. She looks downright pathetic as she struggles against the rope at her knee. I use a little force to bring her other knee up while Dom secures it. I can't take my eyes off of her pussy. The skimpy lace has shifted from her struggles and she's partially exposed. My mouth waters at the sight. Dom moves between her legs then gently pets her pussy, and the smell of her desire nearly makes me lose all control. Between fear and lust, a being will cling to lust. It's just a matter of offering it, and letting them choose it willingly.

"We're going to relax you, Lizzie," he says as he rubs his thumb along her clit. I see him press down as he looks back up at Liz to gauge her reaction. "I won't fuck you until you beg me." She moans and throws her head back at his touch, making my dick struggle for release in my pants.

"You'll snap your fingers if it's too much," he says, allowing her a safe signal and Liz's only response is to breathe in deeply. "Do it once for me," he commands her. When she doesn't answer, he pauses his ministrations. I nearly repeat his demand, desperate for this to continue, but she looks him dead in the eye and her fingers come together, although there's no crisp snap. She makes the effort and that's good enough for him.

I watch as two of his thick fingers slip past the lace material and dip into her heat. His thumb continues to rub circles against her little nub while he strokes the front wall of her pussy, hitting that sweet spot that has her nearly begging for more.

"Fuck, you're tight." He finger fucks her harder. I groan at the sight of her writhing helplessly at his touch. I lean down and kiss the inside of her knee as a reward for her. I grin as I realize even if she wanted to bash my nose in with her knee, she couldn't. She can barely move any part of her body. Liz moans and rocks her pussy against Dom's hand as she gets closer and closer to her release. She's pulling at her ropes, but this time it's not to escape.

"Caleb asked you a question, little one." He stops all of his movements and looks expectantly at her. Her eyes pop open, revealing dilated pupils and she hisses something at him through the shirt.

"Do you know what it means to be our mate?" he asks her calmly.

She nods vigorously. "Good girl." He starts hammering his fingers into her cunt, adding a third, and leans down to suck her clit into his mouth. Her moans of pleasure fuel my need to be inside her and I struggle to keep my eyes from closing in ecstasy. I don't want to miss seeing any second of Dom coaxing her orgasm out of her. All I can smell is her arousal and it's suffocating me. I give in to my need to find my release and stand up, unzipping my pants while watching my gorgeous mate writhe with pleasure.

"I want to fuck you, baby. Tell me I can fuck you." Although it's meant to be a command, I'm practically begging as I pant out the words. Even as she's approaching her climax, she shakes her head, refusing my need for her welcoming heat. I groan out in agony as I climb on the bed. "That's all right, baby. I understand." I stroke myself over her and breathe heavily as my spine tingles and my toes go numb. The gag is muffling her sounds too much and I need to hear her just a little more clearly as I race for my own release. I rip the shirt out of her mouth and she screams out in ecstasy, thrashing her head as she comes all over Dom's fingers. Just the sight of her screaming in pleasure pushes me over the edge.

As my breathing calms down, I hear Dom's pick up.

"Eat her pussy, Caleb." I only pause for a second at the command. Then I see the desperate look of lust in his eyes and I don't hesitate to scoot down her body. I got mine. Now he needs to get his.

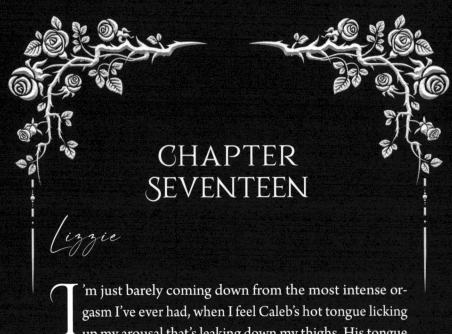

CHAPTER SEVENTEEN

Lizzie

I'm just barely coming down from the most intense orgasm I've ever had, when I feel Caleb's hot tongue licking up my arousal that's leaking down my thighs. His tongue dives into my heat, causing me to arch my back with what little freedom I have to move.

"Yes!" I buck my hips, pushing myself into his face, needing more. He ravishes me like a starving man. I'm vaguely aware of Dom kneeling over my stomach. I'm able to glance down and my eyes widen as I watch him pleasure himself. His large hand is barely able to wrap around it. He's far too large. I start to shake my head, but before I can think too much, Caleb bites my clit. Hard. I cry out in a mix of intense pain and pleasure.

"You want more, baby girl?" I don't waste a single second to nod. *Yes!* Yes, I want more. He sucks my clit while his fingers thrust deeper and deeper inside me, stroking my front wall each time. Hitting that rough spot that has me begging for his touch.

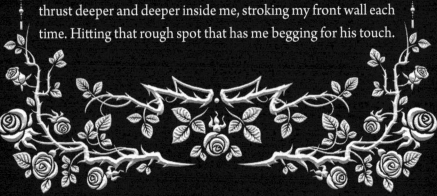

I'm so damn sensitive to every small movement he makes. My body is pulling to get away, but at the same time pushing to get closer.

"Fuck, Dom, she's still got her cherry for us."

Dom leans back and I watch him stroke himself to climax at the realization that I'm still a virgin. He spurts his release all over my chest while he groans a rough, low moan. It's the sexiest fucking thing I've ever seen. I can't look into his eyes, though. I can't bring myself to do it.

Mates. They are my mates. It's cruel really. Fate is cruel.

I watch as Caleb licks my arousal from his lips while staring at me with the forceful hunger of a brute. I can't deny I'm attracted to them. My body absolutely is. And my mind is soothed hearing the word *mate*.

Still, if I weren't tied down, I would run. I can't help it.

"Are you more relaxed now?" Dom asks and I nod once, letting my eyes close. Betrayal seeps into my veins. So much of it, for so many reasons.

I don't know which one of them is sexier. The rough savage who's kneading my breasts and plucking my nipples crudely between his knuckles, or the skilled huntsman who's flicking his tongue along my throbbing, hot clit. I writhe and moan as they attack my body in unison.

"Come on Caleb's tongue like a good girl." Dom's dirty words bring me to the edge of another release. "Come for your mates."

My mates. My pussy clenches and another orgasm tears through my body. Waves of heat run over my skin as I scream out my release, lighting a flame that I didn't know existed inside of me. I breathe heavily, my chest rising and falling sporadically. I'm barely able to lift my head to meet Dom's. His soft, smooth lips crash onto mine. His tongue dives into my mouth and I run my tongue along his. Caleb nips my collarbone, leaving a hot stinging pulse where his teeth marked me and I break away from Dom's kiss to meet Caleb's waiting lips. Blood rushes loudly in my ears as I struggle to stay awake. *My mates.*

I hear a door creak open and my mates shift their attention from me to whomever just came in.

I can't look at them. Whoever it is ... I can barely deal with myself. Let alone my mates ...

PART V

The Claiming

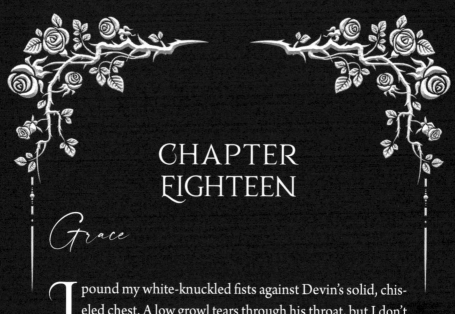

CHAPTER EIGHTEEN

Grace

I pound my white-knuckled fists against Devin's solid, chiseled chest. A low growl tears through his throat, but I don't care. A small part of me knows this is stupid because I'm pissing off a beast who could easily crush me. Another, much larger part of me knows it's stupid because I'm only going to hurt myself; his body isn't reacting at all even though I put every ounce of strength into each blow.

He swore to me. He promised. And what I just saw is horrific. How fucking dare they! I would scream but his hand is over my mouth, his arm wrapped around me, trapping me, preventing me from going to her.

They tied her up. They took from her. I swear to God I'll kill them.

I ignore the voices screaming in my head for me to stop.

My breathing hitches as I recall the sight of those two monsters hovering over her small body. My body is weak and my

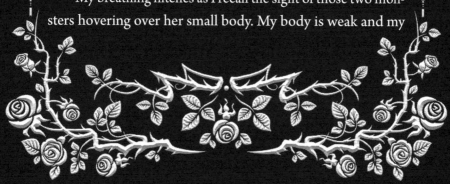

efforts useless. Tears stream down my hot red face in wretched anger as I put every bit of energy I can muster behind what little resistance I can manage. My breathing is shallow and desperate. I'm vaguely registering his command for me to stop, but I don't pay his words any attention. He saw and did nothing! I hear him yell louder but again, I ignore his demand. My only need is to get back to Lizzie.

I swear I try. I do everything I can, including scratching and biting, the last resorts I have. Nothing seems to affect him.

I attempt to push past his massive frame to get to her. I scream out her name, but Devin's large hand covers my mouth again, silencing my call for her. A growl of my own rumbles in my chest as I open my mouth in an attempt to bite him. He sees my attack coming and forces my head back causing me to stumble, banging my shoulders and back against the wall. One hand pins my wrists above my head and the other has a firm grasp on my chin and mouth, effectively silencing me.

"This isn't the first time I've let you hit me, sweetheart." Devin's sneered words at the shell of my ear are dripping with menace. His warm breath on my neck sends a wanton heat rushing through me. Tears well in my eyes. I hate my treacherous body; I hate him. I hate all of this. "But it's the last time I'll let you get away with it."

"Fuck you!" I scream at him, unbothered by his tone. My body shakes with tremors from fear, but I don't care anymore. I thought … I can't even say out loud what I thought I felt for him. How could I be so stupid? My body pleads with me for his touch, to rub against him and beg for forgiveness. I won't do it. I won't lower myself to this pathetic "heat." I'd rather die than let them hurt her.

His hard erection digs into my stomach as he presses his body against mine. A whimper is forced from my lips and I wish I could take it back. I don't want him to affect me. I don't want to give him the pleasure of knowing he can affect me. A sob heaves up my throat. *Lizzie.* My body goes limp in his hold. I've failed her. Another sob wracks through me. There's nothing I can do to help her.

How could they hurt her? How could they do that to her?

"They're her mates; they won't hurt her." His authoritative declaration echoes in my ears. I'm overwhelmed with self-loathing and hatred that I fail to register his words. I let the tears fall freely and stare at the rug lining the wood floors of the hall.

"Look at me!" His demand shoots through my body with an inhuman force. Immediately my eyes find his. Sadness grips me harder than he does. If he fails to see that, it's his own demise.

His silver eyes penetrate mine with a power that makes me want to bow to him, but I won't fucking do it. I stare back with hatred and defiance. He breathes in deep as he relaxes his hold on my chin. I don't take my eyes off of his, and somehow the piercing silver of his gaze softens. It's subtle. He's still a dominating brute, a powerful force not meant to be denied, but somehow diminished. The sickening churning of my stomach lessens slightly, but his eyes still hold a command.

"Listen to me." Although his words are harshly spoken with barely restrained anger, I hear desperation in his voice for me to obey him. I continue to stare into his eyes, relaying my decision to give him my attention. Even if my fists have yet to relax, the skin tight across my knuckles.

"They're her mates. They love her and won't do anything to hurt her." I part my lips to utter my disagreement with his explanation but his eyes narrow, warning me. I'm tempted to push him. *Go ahead and hurt me; show me who you really are!* My heart clenches in agony and my throat closes at the thought. His hand gentles against my throat and his thumb rubs against the line of my jaw. I close my eyes and enjoy his touch for a moment. Just one. Only one moment to feel his caring devotion.

"Come watch, but you *will* keep your mouth shut." He growls his command in my ear and it cracks the bit of peace I'd hidden behind in that small moment. My anger comes back with a heaving breath. As I part my lips to berate him, Devin jams his thumb into my rebellious mouth, scraping his skin along my teeth, once again silencing me. The force of his hand shoves my head against the wall. A snarl forces its way past my lips and I sink my teeth deeper into his flesh while my eyes narrow in a threat.

"Go ahead and bite me." His eyes meet mine. "I won't interfere with the way they handle their mate. For the first time since she's been here, she's relaxed and content." His words settle in me as I let them burrow into my head.

Mates.

"They are devoted to her. Caleb and Dom will be by her side however she needs. And if this is how it had to happen … then it's how it happened and you will not harm them."

My pulse flickers. Harm them? But more than that, mates? *Mates.* The word resonates deeply.

It's hard to weigh the truth in his statement. The moment I saw her tied to the bed with Caleb and Dom surrounding her, Devin snatched me away, leaving only a blip of an image rattling in my memory. I shake my head. She wouldn't do that. There's no way she would've wanted it.

"If she'd seen us earlier, do you think she would've realized what was going on between the two of us?" he asks as though he read my mind.

"If she walked in on us while I had you against the wall, would she have known how much you fucking loved it? How you wanted me to pin you down and hammer into your hot cunt to prove you belong to me?" My breathing hitches as his dirty words are whispered into my neck, just before he gives it a gentle kiss. The softness of his touch is at odds with his tone, but I cling to it.

"Look at me." His command is softly spoken, nearly a whisper. I tilt my head as he removes his hold on me altogether and steps back. My body instantly misses his warmth, his touch. I want what he's saying to be true. It means they didn't hurt her. Please, God, I want that to be true.

"I want you to see." It takes a moment for me to register his words and I have to blink away the hazy desire clouding my vision, my thoughts, my self-respect. I hate this. I hate this damned heat. I hate the effect he has on me. Anger rips through me. Devin pinches my chin, forcing my eyes to focus on his. I clench my teeth but stare back into his heated silver gaze.

His eyes search mine for a moment before he releases his hold. "Come with me." He walks toward the door without waiting for my response, leaving me to watch his hulking frame take long, confident strides to the door before quietly opening it. My feet hesitantly follow without my conscious consent. I swallow thickly as I realize I'm not sure I want to see. As I come up behind him, he angles his body toward me and opens his arms for me to stand at his side. I glance up at his stern expression and question whether or not I want to be in his embrace. I'm not given the opportunity to deny him as my body continues to behave of its own accord, moving next to him. I close my eyes as his strong arm wraps around my body. His hand rests on my shoulder and his thumb kneads soothing circles into my tense muscles. He peers into the room with me. I close my eyes, reveling in his comforting touch. "Stay quiet, I don't want to interfere. Do you understand?" I nod my head slightly and whisper yes before focusing my gaze on the sight of the three of them. My eyes slowly adjust to the darkened room, illuminated with only hints of daylight whispering through the curtains.

My body stiffens as I watch Dom wipe Lizzie's lower half clean. Before getting off the bed, he places a small kiss on her inner thigh. Caleb is lying next to her on her left but leaning his massive chest over her small frame, loosening a knot on her wrist. He tosses the rope onto the floor and then massages her arm. She turns so her chest is beside his and he responds by pulling her small body against him. My breathing slows and I relax slightly into Devin's hold.

Thump, thump, my heart pleads for this to unfold in a way that will make it all okay.

Dom walks to the other side, releasing her other wrist before climbing onto the bed to lay behind her, his chest to her back. He gently kisses her shoulder and runs his hand over a bruise on her hip. My lungs halt as I see the marks on her body. Her ankles are red and look raw. I shake my head and try to back away, but Devin holds me steady. "Just listen."

"Please bring your wolf out. You're hurt." Dom's whispered plea is almost too soft to hear. *Wolf?* My brow furrows in confusion. Before I can whisper that she's not a wolf, she speaks.

"I can't." I hear Lizzie for the first time and naturally I try to step forward to call out her name, but Devin's strong grip keeps me by his side. My instinct is to push him away so I can go to her, but he holds me in place.

"Could you try?" Dom's words sound wounded and desperate.

A small sob escapes her as she shakes her head into Caleb's chest. "It's okay, baby girl. We'll take care of you. Just relax. You're safe now." Caleb places his head on top of hers while Dom nuzzles into her neck before kissing her sweetly.

"Hold me." I can barely hear her.

"We're here, baby girl." I watch as Caleb strokes her cheek with care before wrapping his arms around her.

"Sleep, little one." Dom covers their bodies with a cream-colored damask comforter before getting back into position, molding his muscular body against hers.

I can't stop staring at the three of them. Even as Devin closes the door, I continue to stare straight ahead, unable to blink away the sight of their loving touch.

"She's their mate. I told you they wouldn't hurt her." He turns me to face him and stares into my hazel eyes. "They may have to push her. She's in a lot of pain. But they aren't going to hurt her. I promise you."

As Devin leads me away from their room, I steady my breathing and try to come to terms with his words. So many thoughts and emotions threaten to overwhelm me. Relief and confusion are the two winning out.

"She's a werewolf?" I don't even realize that I've spoken until Devin stops at a massive door at the far end of the long hall and forces my body to turn to face his.

"She's the same woman you grew up with. She's your best friend. Don't think too much on what you heard. You'll have a chance to talk to her tomorrow." I nod my head in agreement and blink my sore eyes.

"And they love her, like really love her?" Devin gives me the most handsome, genuine smile.

"They do. She's their mate." His eyes are soft and his smile lingers on his lips. I can practically feel his happiness and it warms my heart. "They would die for her."

His hand spears into my hair and I lean into his touch. "And Grace?"

"Hmm?" I open my eyes and find his soft, yet heated silver gaze on me.

"You're my mate." Hearing those words on his lips awakens something deep inside of me, numbing every pain and settling every doubt I've clung to, lighting them to fuel a fire of need. His lips find mine as he walks me backward into his room and kicks the door closed without breaking our contact. His hands fondle my ass before lifting me up into his chest. I wrap my legs tight around his hips and moan into his mouth as he deepens the kiss.

"Mate." He growls the word before nipping my bottom lip, fanning that fire in my core and sending desire pulsing through every inch of me.

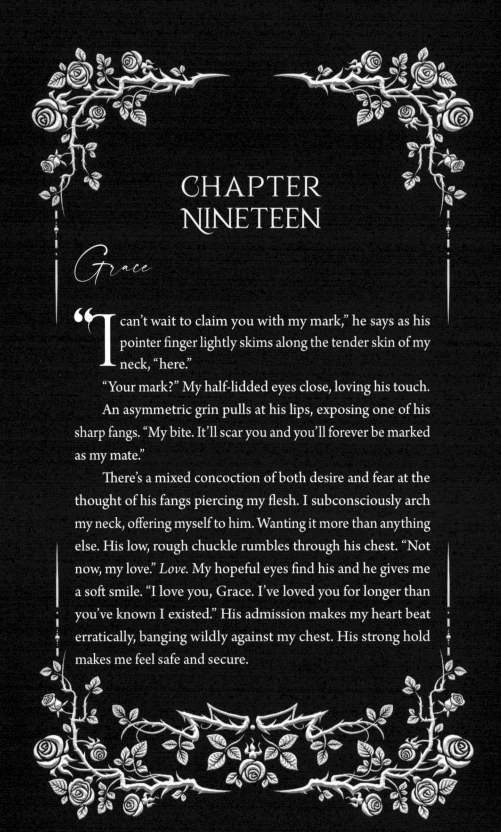

CHAPTER NINETEEN

Grace

"I can't wait to claim you with my mark," he says as his pointer finger lightly skims along the tender skin of my neck, "here."

"Your mark?" My half-lidded eyes close, loving his touch.

An asymmetric grin pulls at his lips, exposing one of his sharp fangs. "My bite. It'll scar you and you'll forever be marked as my mate."

There's a mixed concoction of both desire and fear at the thought of his fangs piercing my flesh. I subconsciously arch my neck, offering myself to him. Wanting it more than anything else. His low, rough chuckle rumbles through his chest. "Not now, my love." *Love.* My hopeful eyes find his and he gives me a soft smile. "I love you, Grace. I've loved you for longer than you've known I existed." His admission makes my heart beat erratically, banging wildly against my chest. His strong hold makes me feel safe and secure.

It's a feeling I'm not used to, but it feels like home.

"I love your Alpha spirit." He gently tucks a strand of my hair behind my ear before setting me down. "You have no idea how proud I am to have you as my mate." He takes both of my small wrists in his large hands; seeing the difference in size makes me feel fragile and easily breakable. He kisses the underside of my right wrist and says, "I love your strength and courage." He moves my hand so that my palm rests against the stubble of his strong jaw as he closes his eyes and rubs into my soft, warm touch. "When it's just the two of us, I don't want you to hold anything back from me."

I nod my head and say, "I won't." My immediate agreement makes him smile and he closes his eyes, then leans down to nuzzle his nose along mine.

"I have no doubt of that," he comments.

He breathes in deep before straightening his shoulders and looking down on me with those piercing silver eyes. "It's a different story when we're with the pack, or anywhere that's not private." My eyes instinctively narrow. "If you question me, or if you fight me, then others will target me and the pack. My dominance will be challenged. For the most part, you won't have to worry about anything; just be yourself. But sometimes I'm going to need something from you, sweetheart." His soft, calming tone slowly takes an authoritative edge.

"What's that?"

"Your complete and immediate obedience."

I part my lips to object, but he shakes his head and narrows his eyes. His expression is one of absolute authority. He will not be denied. I struggle with the need to fight him.

"When we're in public, you will listen to me." I hold his gaze with mine, tasting his words on my tongue and not liking them. His brow arches, pushing me for an answer.

"I will try to listen." He immediately narrows his gaze at my honest response.

"No, you *will* listen to me." He gently wraps his hand around the nape of my neck and rubs his thumb over the front of my throat in an unexpectedly soothing way. There's not an ounce of threat in his touch. "There will be times when you're confused, when you don't understand what's going on." His eyes travel from my throat to my eyes. "Even if you think you do, you won't. You'll want to question me, but you won't." There's a finality in his statements. "Do you understand?"

"Yes."

"I'll never do anything to break your trust." His voice softens as his hand caresses my sensitive skin. "Your safety and happiness are at the forefront of every decision I make." I nod my head in the silence between us, acknowledging his words. "Do you believe me?"

His question catches me off guard. My eyes fall to the floor beneath us before reaching his gaze again.

I look deep into his silver eyes; I remember his touch, his words, his looks of devotion. *Mate.* I'm reminded of the shift deep in my soul when he told me I was his mate. I feel an innate sense of comfort and protection with him. He will be my downfall regardless. My soul is very aware of that.

"I do."

He leans down and I push forward, seeking his mouth. Licking and kneading his soft lips with mine. When I pull back, all I can see in his eyes is lust.

"I want you on your knees," he says as his fingers tease my sensitive skin, slowly playing with the hem of my shirt, "now." His commanding voice forces my legs out from under me and I land hard on my knees in front of him as my heated core begs for his attention. *Complete and immediate obedience.*

"Do you like it?" His deep voice is one of control, but he can't hide his desire.

"Do you like me like this?" I try to keep my voice even and leave out my distaste for being wanted to submit as I turn his question on him.

He takes my chin in his hand and tilts it upward, so I'm forced to look into his eyes as he says, "You have no idea what seeing you on your knees does to me." He kisses my lips, licking along the seam and nipping at my bottom lip for me to part for him. I obey, loving his touch and wanting more of it. I feel his passion as his hand fists in my hair and he pulls to cause a hint of pain. I open my mouth to gasp, but I'm silenced as his tongue finds mine in a dark, heated dance. I moan into his mouth as a shot of craving heats my core.

"I have no desire to control you." He breathes heavily as his forehead rests against mine. "Never. I don't want to tame you. But the idea that you'll do what I say simply because I ask? I don't even have the words to describe how much I fucking crave it. Only because it's you." My breath leaves me as I revel in his confession. His lips find mine again and I lean into him, tasting him. His hand fists in my hair again as he takes control of the kiss. He worships my mouth with his tongue.

He slowly stands, leaving me panting and wanting to claw at his pants to get to him. But I know not to. I'm on my knees for him. I wait with bated breath for his instructions as he palms himself.

It's the first time I get a good look at his cock. It's fucking beautiful. I lick my lips at the sight of the thick veins running along his length. He's so big I'm surprised he fit inside me. "Open." My lips part and I open wide to accommodate him as he slides the head of his dick into my mouth.

The feel of his soft, velvety skin on my tongue makes me moan. I run the tip of my tongue along his slit, and he responds by letting out a low hiss. He pushes more of his hard length in my mouth and I greedily accept. I suck him down eagerly, hollowing my cheeks. "Fuck, you're so damn gorgeous," he groans as he pushes his cock deeper. I moan around him as I hear his breathing pick up. I pull back slightly and his silver eyes penetrate mine with a force that makes my pussy beg for his touch.

"I want to touch you." I barely breathe out the words as my desire for him numbs my body.

"Then touch me." My hands instantly wrap around his thick cock and my lips seal around him as I take his length all the way. He fists my hair and shoves himself down my throat.

"Look at me." My eyes instantly find his lustful gaze and the moment they do he releases his hot cum in the back of my throat as his legs tremble, and all the while his silver eyes stay locked on mine. I keep my eyes open, not wanting to break the contact as I swallow him down. He pumps in and out of my mouth in short, shallow thrusts before pulling away from my lips.

His strong arms lift me off the floor and he effortlessly carries me to the bed and tosses me down on the mattress, stalking on his knees toward me. "Open your legs." I obey his simple command, parting them wide as he pushes my thighs apart and he positions himself between them. His hot tongue runs between my legs, lapping up my arousal before flicking my swollen clit.

My back arches and my hands grab his hair, pushing him into me as I moan at the teasing touch. He sucks my clit into his mouth, massaging his tongue against it. "Yes!" I scream out as the pulsing heat runs through my body. My heels dig into the mattress and I push myself harder against him, searching for my release. He pulls back as his fingers continue to tease me, and his eyes focus on my wanting heat.

"Please fuck me," I moan into the hot air.

"You're too sore." He curls his thick fingers, finding that rough spot along my front wall and strokes it mercilessly before leaning down to nibble at my clit.

I claw at his shoulders and scream in desperation for him to pound into me. I feel so empty without him; I know I need him inside me. He smacks my clit with his other hand, causing my body to jolt off of the bed. I scream his name as waves of heated pleasure pulse through my body. Wave after wave keep me trembling as he continues his rough strokes. He slowly pulls out as the aftershocks dim and my breathing steadies.

"Watching you get off is the most beautiful thing I've ever seen," he says then climbs up my body, leaving kisses on my heated skin as he travels to my neck to suck the spot he told me he would bite when he claims me.

"Mmm," is the only response I can manage.

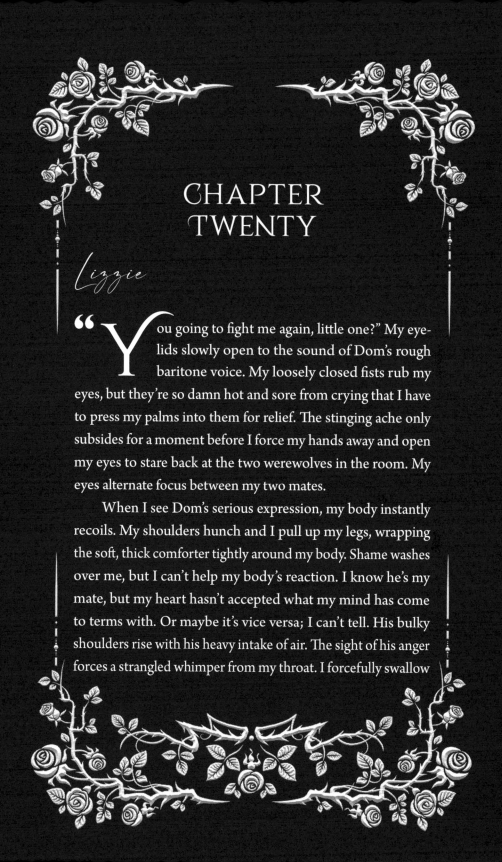

CHAPTER TWENTY

Lizzie

"You going to fight me again, little one?" My eyelids slowly open to the sound of Dom's rough baritone voice. My loosely closed fists rub my eyes, but they're so damn hot and sore from crying that I have to press my palms into them for relief. The stinging ache only subsides for a moment before I force my hands away and open my eyes to stare back at the two werewolves in the room. My eyes alternate focus between my two mates.

When I see Dom's serious expression, my body instantly recoils. My shoulders hunch and I pull up my legs, wrapping the soft, thick comforter tightly around my body. Shame washes over me, but I can't help my body's reaction. I know he's my mate, but my heart hasn't accepted what my mind has come to terms with. Or maybe it's vice versa; I can't tell. His bulky shoulders rise with his heavy intake of air. The sight of his anger forces a strangled whimper from my throat. I forcefully swallow as I remember his question. "No," I whisper. I won't fight him anymore. Not intentionally, but I can't stop my defensive reactions.

"I'm not going to hurt you." My chest aches at his soft words.

I keep my head hung low as I reply, "I know." He's my mate, and I know everything that the word means. I used to dream of the day, but that was before my life turned into a nightmare.

I listen to them both approach and feel a dip as they sit on the left side of the bed. I lift my eyes to find both of them watching me expectantly. My handsome hunter and gorgeous savage are an intimidating pair. I smile weakly at them, feeling both unworthy and grateful. In truth, I'm relieved to find my mates, but sadness overrides that relief. I'm all too aware of how hollow my chest feels. I know that as their mate, I'm supposed to feel a pull to them. I'm supposed to desire their touch. And I do, but it's subdued. It's so weak I can barely feel the gentle pull. Dom slowly reaches for me with his hand turned upward. I breathe in deep and put my hand in his; it's so small in comparison. His large fingers wrap around my hand and pull me to him. I willingly prop myself up on my knees and silently crawl in between my mates.

They must hate that they're stuck with me. That fate gifted them such a fragile and broken mate.

I wish I could be better for them. If I could change, I would.

"You going to let us claim you, baby girl?" I nod at Caleb's question as my eyes focus on his gorgeous body. Both men are only wearing jeans. My mouth waters at the sight of their broad bare chests. I may not feel the electric pull I'm supposed to, but I'm still a hot-blooded woman. My eyes roam their bodies shamelessly as my own heats in desire.

"Are you going to accept our marks and both of us as your mates?"

I nod my head and let out an easy sigh. "Yes." I watch as Dom shifts under my gaze and palms his growing erection through his jeans. I love that my gaze of lust is enough to make him want me. It brings a heated blush to my cheeks and a small smile to my lips.

"You know we have to take you to claim you? We have to fuck you and scar you with our bites." Caleb's words draw my attention to him.

I swallow as my thighs clench at the thought and nod my head. "Yes." I never thought I'd be claimed. Why would I, when my wolf has never showed herself. Until last night, when they told me they were my mates, I hadn't realized how badly I wanted it still.

"Come here, I want to taste you." I scoot my body closer to Caleb, my hunter, and offer my mouth to him. His soft lips press against mine. His tongue licks along the seam and I instantly part for him. His strong hand grips my hip and pulls me closer to him. I feel Dom's hand run along my shoulder and slowly grip my nape. As his fingers close around my neck, I break my kiss from Caleb and turn to Dom. Caleb nestles his head in the crook of my neck and gently sucks my sensitive skin.

I moan from Caleb's sweet touch as Dom's teeth nip my bottom lip. My blue eyes find his silver gaze and I nearly crumble from the look of utter devotion. I lean into his lips and his tongue dives into my warm mouth, exploring and tasting with his savage hunger. I hear Caleb unzip his pants as his teeth bite down on my tender earlobe. I moan into Dom's mouth as Caleb climbs behind me on the bed before pulling me away from Dom and into his naked lap, his hard erection digging into the curve of my backside.

My breath comes in short pants as I crane my head to look into Caleb's hard silver eyes. As I do, his hands travel to my breasts, roughly kneading them before pinching my nipples. His gaze holds mine the entire time and I gasp as the pain shoots a heated pulse to my core, dampening my entrance with arousal.

"You like that, baby girl?"

I whimper as his deft fingers pinch my nipples again and let my head fall back onto his shoulder in desire. I barely whisper to the ceiling, "Yes." Dom kisses the front of my exposed throat as his naked body settles in front of me on the bed. My eyes travel from his massive erection up his bulky muscles, to his heated gaze. I swallow as my body starts to shake, overwhelmed with a mix of fear and lust. I fail to steady my hands as Dom reaches for them. *Fuck.* Adrenaline spikes through my blood as my breathing hitches. I wish I could stop this. I wish I could stop my body from fearing him. It's all too obvious he's not the man who haunted my dreams. But the scars are just too deep. Even the smallest hints of the past cripple me. I let him take both of my hands in his and try to steady my breathing. He kisses the knuckles on each hand while rubbing soothing circles against my pulse.

I close my eyes as stray tears travel gently down my cheeks. I'm ashamed at my response to my mates. Caleb licks away the tears. He kisses my hair and whispers, "You're all right. You're here with us. We'll take care of you." I choke out a sob as my forehead lands on Dom's chest. Caleb's strong arms circle tightly around my waist as Dom's wrap around my shoulders. They both whisper calming, loving words, but I can barely hear them. My blood rushes in my ears and the sound drowns out everything else. Caleb and Dom lay me down on my side, keeping their hot, hard bodies pressed against mine.

"Please love me," I gasp.

"We do, little one."

I shake my head against his chest and rock my pussy against his thigh. "No. Like this. Please. Please take the pain away," I beg helplessly into his chest.

"No." He denies me, saying, "Not like this." My tears fall recklessly onto Dom's chest.

"Please. I need you two." A warmth flows through my body as Caleb nibbles my neck and Dom's hand cups my bare pussy. "Yes."

"We'll take care of you," Dom whispers at my lips before taking them with his own. Caleb's fingers travel along the curve of my hips as I rub my sensitive, hardened nipples into Dom's chest and push my ass into Caleb's hips.

I moan into Dom's mouth, "Please." I need this from them. I've never dealt with the past. I've never wanted to. I don't have a choice now, but I just can't take the overwhelming sadness crushing my chest. I need their touch. I need to *feel* something other than fear. Their desire can be that something. I want to feel all-consuming pleasure. Caleb nestles his dick deeper against my ass and gently rocks into me. I moan louder, feeling it vibrate in my chest as Dom rubs the head of his cock on my clit before burrowing it against my folds, grinding into me at a steady pace.

The feel of both of them taking pleasure from my body, both dangerously close to taking my virginity, makes me dizzy with desire.

"Please," I beg as my head spins with a hot, burning need for release. My arousal eases their movements as they rock faster. Even without either of them in me, I feel unbelievably full as Dom's dick assaults my clit and Caleb's rubs against my forbidden ring. They thrust faster, as if they're fucking me, yet I'm achingly empty. Feeling their need to reach their own climax steals my breath. I breathe in hot, heavy air as a cold sweat breaks out along my skin. Dom grips my hip harder and Caleb pulls my thigh tighter to him as they thrust in unison. Caleb kisses my neck while Dom does the same to my breasts, sucking my nipples before pulling them between his teeth.

Their hands roam over my body, gripping and caressing and pulling at me with a desperate need. It's all-consuming, as if they're everywhere at once. I arch my back and wrap my arms around Dom's neck, screaming my pleasure into my bite, while Caleb nearly slips inside of me, and I come violently in their arms. My body trembles with waves of heat burning through me as they both find their release, the three of us peaking in unison. I breathe heavily as the tremors subside.

"I love you, Lizzie."

"I love you too, Liz." They declare their love for me into the hot air between us before leaving kisses in my damp hair and on my forehead.

I hear their words of devotion and I desperately want to feel the same way, but in this moment, I can't say the words back, because I refuse to lie to my mates. A piece of my heart is gone and I just can't let them in to something that's so broken.

"One day you'll say it back to us, but before that day comes, I want you to cry for me, Liz. I want you to pour yourself out to me completely."

"And I want you to shift for me. I don't want any part of you hidden from me."

I nod into Dom's chest while squeezing Caleb's strong hand, silently praying for that day to come.

GENTLE
SCARS

PART I

Lost Puppy

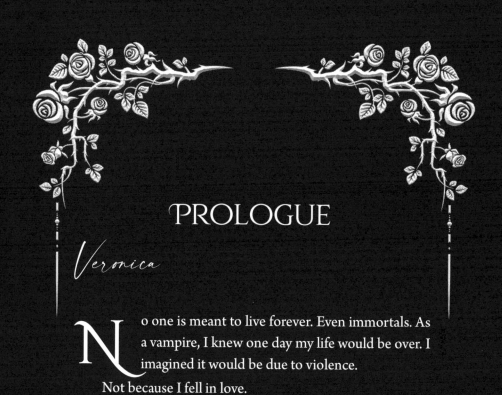

PROLOGUE

Veronica

No one is meant to live forever. Even immortals. As a vampire, I knew one day my life would be over. I imagined it would be due to violence.

Not because I fell in love.

"Promise me you won't take the drug anymore." Vince's voice is tight, his plea desperate. The bloodied tears that stain my cheeks fail to stop.

I chose this. I did it for him. For us. If there's a chance for us to have a real life together, one where I won't grow old … One where I could possibly have a child … it's for love. I never asked for a mate. In all my decades, I never felt this deep need.

Just as I never asked to be immortal, and now …

"Promise me, Veronica." All I can do is slowly nod my head.

I've turned into a fool for him. Become weak for him. I would do anything for him.

"I promise." I whisper the words I know are a lie. No one is meant to live forever and this had to be done.

"I will give you everything you need. I promise you, my love. It could kill you." I sniffle and kiss the crook of his neck. His gentle embrace brings a warmth to my chilled blood. "I would die without you."

He says that, but expects me to live when he's gone from this world. He'll understand. He must. He's my mate and he'll forgive me.

"I love you, Veronica."

"I will love you forever, Vince."

Our forever.

CHAPTER ONE

Vince

Weeks before
The first moment I felt my mate

How the hell did Devin do it? How could he leave his mate after feeling *this*?

My fingers ball into fists as I stand on the stage, stiff and all but snarling.

A burning shock lingers in my blood, chilling my skin with a cold sweat and willing my limbs to go to her. *To my mate.* My heart races, adrenaline coursing through me as the pull to go to her is overwhelming. By order of my Alpha, I'm ignoring the instinctual demand, just as he did last year. With every second my feet stay planted on this damn stage, the pit in my stomach grows larger, twisting and churning. My dry throat closes, threatening to suffocate me. The aching need devours me. I'm practically fucking weak and useless.

I *need* her.

How the hell did he ever wait for the offering? How could he resist when she was so close and he felt *this*?

"You will wait." Devin's command rings loud in my mind.

My wolf whines, but settles. *"It hurts."* My teeth grit as another wave of stinging heat rolls over my body, punishing me for disregarding her. My neck arches, straining against all reason. With my muscles coiled, I fight my instincts. I have no intention of going against my Alpha, but this is fucking torture.

"I'm trying."

Our telepathic conversation pauses as the young women hesitantly walk across the stage. They reek of fear and anxiety, and the awful stench is a slap in the face. The reverberation of their shoes clicking against the metal stage continues to get faster and faster as more of them scuttle past us. The Authority demands the humans be deathly afraid of the paranormal species. Given my urge to howl in utter agony at this moment, I imagine I could reduce them all to nightmares and lasting trauma if I openly struggled to control myself.

Containing this visceral reaction is brutal. The fear it creates will be rewarded by the Authority, so perhaps there's a silver lining. The humans' fear is good for us; not so good for the Alpha's mate, though. I can smell her dread from here. They call her Grace. Although I can barely focus on her, I'm proud to welcome her into our pack. If she knew more about why these treaties exist and what it means to be chosen, I'm sure she wouldn't be so damn terrified. But then again, neither would any of the other humans.

A smirk pulls my lips up; I can faintly hear Dom and Caleb's mate telling Grace something about us having sticks up our asses. The humor relieves the agony for a moment.

"She must've met Dom." I stifle my chuckle at Lev's comment. Grace's friend, Liz, isn't as scared as she should be. Either that or she's putting on a front. I barely resist the urge to turn my head toward Dom to gauge his reaction.

Caleb snickers and says, *"Our mate's a little firecracker, isn't she?"* I can practically feel his grin. Ever since the two of them felt their pull to her, Caleb's excitement has been radiating through all of us and his wolf won't stop panting for her. If he were in wolf form, he'd be drooling with his tongue hanging out of his jaws. Dom's enthusiasm is dampened by his reluctance to share his mate. I'm sure as hell not jealous of those fuckers. Especially not now that I've found my own mate.

Goosebumps spread along my skin. *My mate.*

"Which one is she?" Jude's excited so many of us are finding our mates. Perhaps all of our mates are human. It would be a rarity, but then again, so is the continued existence of our pack.

I search the crowd in the direction of the intense pull I've been denying. My eyes lock on my mate and travel down her body, appreciating every inch. She's wearing a black, pleated leather skirt that ends mid-thigh, making her long legs appear even longer, along with her sheer thigh highs. Her high heels add even more to her height. Still, she's got to be a few inches shorter than me. My gaze longs to strip away each button on her sheer white blouse. Her tanned skin and long black hair, along with her large dark eyes, inform me she's new to the area. We come to this town for the offering every year, and I've never seen her or anyone like her; she must've moved here recently. A few strands of iridescent black pearls are settled over her cleavage. Filipino, maybe? I've yet to hear her speak. She drips of sex appeal … the only thing I'm certain of is that she's mine.

"Mine," my wolf echoes with a growl.

It's evident she was made for me. Her black hair is pulled into a simple bun, exposing her slender neck that's tempting me to bite her. To sink my fangs into the tender flesh and claim her. I stifle my groan as my dick twitches. My hands flex once again before fisting, my blunt nails digging into my skin.

My mate's dark brown eyes are focused on the far right of the stage, then they wander, studying every inch of the stadium and failing to follow my direction. A low growl forms in my chest, scaring the fuck out of the poor girl in front of me.

Shit, I didn't mean that. I'm too damn desperate for her attention. The need for her to see me nearly overrides my logical side. I need her to watch me like I'm watching her. Just the thought of her locking her eyes on mine makes my cock harden. I can't wait for this damn offering to be over.

My eyes narrow as I continue to stare at her gorgeous body. There's no way she's younger than nineteen. It's not that she looks older; it's something about her poise and the confidence she exudes. She's a woman in every way. My mate should be up here. She should be in line, waiting to offer herself to me so I can take her. Even if she's only just moved here, the terms of the treaty are clear. My heart speeds up with angst pumping through my veins.

What if she'll never be offered because she's older than twenty-one? What if she doesn't live in Shadow Falls at all and she's only visiting? The thought of never seeing my mate again sends a pulse of panicked heat through my body with a force that almost brings me to my knees.

"Calm down, Vince." Devin's stern voice grounds me and I place my hands behind my back.

"I cannot. I cannot lose her, Alpha." Even in my mind, his title is emphasized, both pleading with him and warning.

There's a second of hesitation. Only one, that's tense and severe, before he answers.

"You may stay behind only to find out why she wasn't offered."

"Yes, Alpha." My heartbeat slowly stops hammering in my chest as I continue to watch my mate. As soon as Grace and Liz are collected and safe in the cars, I'm hunting down those sexy, long legs. *"Thank you."*

"Shut the fuck up; our mates are here." Dom's threateningly low voice makes my lips kick up into a smirk.

"If I didn't know any better, I'd think you were pissed." I can practically feel his rumbling growl.

"Knock it off. Dom, you handle your mate; I'll handle mine. Grace is last, so we won't have to wait. Any questions?"

"No, Alpha." We answer Devin in unison. This should be easy enough. Then I can track down my mate. I've never been so eager for an event to be over in my entire existence. My skin heats with anticipation as Grace walks past me. I can hear her breath steadying as she walks toward Devin.

The presence of her mate is already soothing her nerves. *Good.* This will be over soon and then I can stalk my sexy little vixen.

As I walk down the steps, knowing their mates are in place, chaos ensues on stage. It happens far too fast and unexpectedly. With rigid discipline, I don't hesitate; I react. Moving to my position as ordered, I'm calm on the outside, but inwardly there's an equal amount of chaos as there is on stage. Dom's mate is screaming. Her cries are hysterical and they elicit a knee-jerk, involuntary reaction from the onlookers. Her fists pound with violent thuds against his hard body and it feels like a damn bullet to my chest. She's fighting him. She's resisting her mate. It's shocking; it's soul crushing. It takes everything in me to keep my expression neutral and not react.

I can't even imagine how he must feel.

It's not supposed to be like this. I've seen offerings before in my old pack. The women are meant to be calm and go willingly. The bond, even if they don't know a damn thing about it, is strong. It's unbreakable. It's captivating. The touch of a mate is comforting. The only times there are problems at the offerings is when some asshole wolves take what doesn't belong to them. That doesn't happen much now that the Authority has taken over inter- and intraspecies relations.

She doesn't stop. Their mate fights for her life against them.

"Are you sure she's your mate?" Several growls vibrate through me in response. *"I didn't mean that. Shit, I apologize."*

Caleb's voice reaches me through the deafening snarl still coming from Dom. *"Don't worry about it. She'll be all right. She'll be fine."* Even though his words are laced with positivity and confidence, I can feel his apprehension. Those poor fuckers, Dom and Caleb. Their pain permeates through us. The cries of outrage pick up now that the crowd is no longer shocked and other emotions are surfacing. *Double fuck.* If we don't act fast, things are going to get messy.

I'm vaguely aware of Devin's aura pushing down on my shoulders, steadying me. Holding all of us in place and settling our nerves. I'm grateful for it.

Devin's mate fights against his hold as she screams her friend's name, the trance broken. She pushes off of him in a futile attempt to free herself, but in her struggle against him, she's radiating dominance. I flinch at the Alpha waves overwhelming me and look to Devin. He's calmer than still waters, not even affected by her innate influence. I know he felt it, though. We all felt it.

Our Alpha mate.

"Calm her down." Devin finally gives the command to Grace, the words spoken low, gently and she immediately composes herself as if they were a balm she needed. A soothing wind pacifies my nerves, even though Dom's mate is still battering her fists against him. The effect of our Alpha mate's emotions is overwhelming. It's clear she was made for Devin. Together, the two of them exude power. I've been told that an Alpha finding his mate makes him stronger and his pack closer, but to feel it, to be a part of such a strong union—it's all-consuming.

As Grace holds Liz, Dom's sadness and anger creep in. But typical of the beast he is, on the surface he's furious. Grace's powerful force is weakened when she sees his scowl. She's terrified, gripping Liz tighter, protecting her small pack of two.

The air is bitter with their fear.

Devin's hands settle on Grace's shoulders; it does little to assuage the anxiousness rolling off her in waves. It's so strong it's practically choking me. But in an instant, the surges cease and my breath returns. I turn just in time to see Devin catch his mate as she faints. The crowd erupts in outrage and screams of terror. The Authority requires the humans' submission and for us to reinforce it. This is not how I envisioned the day's events. Every second is more somber than the last. My brow furrows in anger, but Devin continues to hold us in place. A fierce growl bursts forth from his throat, carrying through the stadium and silencing the humans.

"Move." He snarls his command and we all walk forward in unison. Devin cradles his unconscious mate in his arms while Liz cries helplessly, weaker by the second, flailing her fists against Dom's back as he carries her over his shoulder like a caveman. The tension pours from him. I can't help but to wonder what's wrong with her. Something is very wrong. Dom's grief ricochets through me as he releases a shaky breath; it's the only indication he's anything other than furious.

"She'll be better once we're back." Caleb's words almost sound like a hopeful question. His panting wolf is whining in agony. I feel nothing but pity for all three of them.

As I lead our pack to the parked cars, my gaze roams the stadium for my mate. But she's gone. The hammering in my chest speeds up as I frantically search for her.

Before panic takes over, I'm given my leave.

"Go, Vince. Do not approach her. You have two hours."

Two hours.

I don't waste a second once Devin grants me permission. My limbs push forward with determination and my wolf claws at my chest to get to her. *I must find my mate.*

CHAPTER TWO

Veronica

A moment before the chaos that is the offering at Shadow Falls

My lips purse in annoyance listening to these foolish mutts snickering as they formulate a shit plan of retribution. I've never felt such a snarl of distaste overwhelm me. My eyes narrow and I bet these wolfish pricks waiting behind the stadium can't even spell the word they chant in unison: *retribution*.

Bitter cold envelops me at feeling the depths of my desire to rip them apart. It's sudden and not welcome. Lifting my chin, I shut out their conversation. It takes more effort than it should, though.

With an uneasy exhale, I return my attention to the stage. My intention was to discuss a proposition with the Alpha on behalf of the coven, but that's not going to happen.

I didn't anticipate his pack finding mates. From what I've heard of Shadow Falls, it hasn't happened in quite a while. So

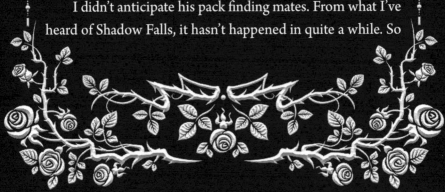

color me surprised by the change of plans. My nails tap impatiently on the metal seat in front of me as I watch both girls struggle against the massive beasts. Fear permeates the air around me and it reminds me of my youth.

For some reason I have a soft spot for the petite blond wolf. Lizzie, if I heard her friend right. I don't know how they can't hear her wolf whining. Someone needs to let it out of its cage. My nose scrunches and my tongue clucks. If they'd calm the hell down, I may still have a chance to speak with Devin. That's all right, though. I'm sure I'll be meeting him soon when my big bad wolf comes to fetch me.

My smirk is at odds with the screams around me, with the humans who cower in terror in their seats. Yet all I can focus on is the beast of a man who dares to stare me down as if I'm his. As if it's his right to take me.

He's so obvious. A small smile plays at my lips while my heart beats with lust. He's fucking adorable. Well, maybe adorable isn't the right word. *Sexy as fuck.* Yes, that's a better description. I could feel his eyes on me ever since he got here, willing me to stare back at him. My smile morphs into a wicked grin. He's going to have to learn that it's not so easy to earn my submission. Hell, I'm used to being the one giving the orders.

"Let's run them off the road," one wolf murmurs beneath his breath just outside the stadium, grabbing my attention once again. Three are certainly werewolves, and one must be something else. Otherwise they wouldn't have needed to speak aloud. Irritation runs through me.

This time I'm even more displeased; they've interrupted the little fantasy I was concocting of my strong, handsome wolf on his knees for me with his tongue between my thighs. Holy hell, I can't wait to enjoy him, play with him. I may even allow him to toy with me.

The four assholes have finally gotten out of their cars to witness the spectacle on stage. It's far too easy to hear the doors shut. They're so fucking reckless. If we weren't bathed in chaos, every soul in Devin's pack would hear them with how loud they rush around the stadium's perimeter. I've been listening to them rant incessantly about taking back this town for the past half hour. Their voices picked up with excitement when they realized

Devin and the hulking doom-and-gloom were taking mates. That's when I went from bored to pissed.

With what they joked about doing ... I'll enjoy making them suffer.

"You two go in the first car and we'll follow. As soon as we get a chance, we'll grab whichever one we can. We only need one to bring to Alpha." My eyes roll at their piss-poor plan. Haven't they seen the size of the werewolves they're so desperate to fuck with? They truly are idiots.

I don't know much about the pack of Shadow Falls, but I know enough. Devin, the current Alpha, has always belonged here. A few years ago, he left before returning with a new pack to reclaim this territory as his. He had the backing of the Authority, and he's the one the coven wants to deal with. So the "rightful pack" can piss off.

The wolf girl shrieks yet again and it pierces my eardrums, making me wince. She needs to get her shit together. I look to the stage to see the Alpha mate passed out in Devin's arms. My perfectly plucked eyebrows arch in surprise. I didn't take her to be one to faint.

"I hope we get the blond one; she looks like fun." My attention is drawn back to these four dumb fucks. Devin doesn't need to deal with this.

As I right from my seat, I imagine he'll be thanking me if I intervene and our negotiations will start out with the coven having the upper hand. He'll owe us greatly for ensuring the safety of his mate and her friend. His pack will be more willing to hear the wishes of my coven.

And from the way these dogs have been talking, it'll be my pleasure to handle this minor mess for Devin. My lips curl up into a fiendish smile. Pride flows through me as I stride toward the parking lot to take care of this little problem. Taking one last glance over my shoulder, I'm certain my wolf will search for me. He's eager and if I'm honest with myself, so am I.

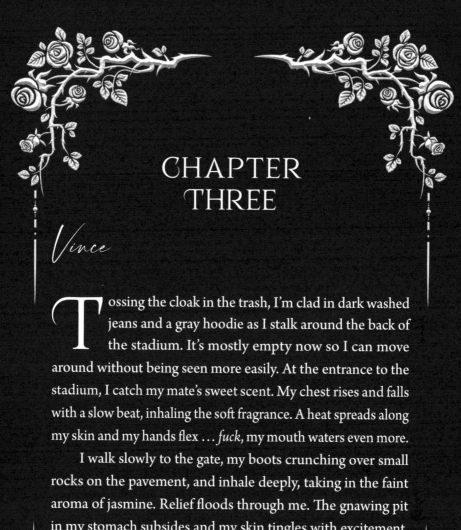

CHAPTER THREE

Vince

Tossing the cloak in the trash, I'm clad in dark washed jeans and a gray hoodie as I stalk around the back of the stadium. It's mostly empty now so I can move around without being seen more easily. At the entrance to the stadium, I catch my mate's sweet scent. My chest rises and falls with a slow beat, inhaling the soft fragrance. A heat spreads along my skin and my hands flex ... *fuck*, my mouth waters even more.

I walk slowly to the gate, my boots crunching over small rocks on the pavement, and inhale deeply, taking in the faint aroma of jasmine. Relief floods through me. The gnawing pit in my stomach subsides and my skin tingles with excitement. A wolfish grin graces my lips; the hunt is on. Unfortunately, the relief is fleeting as I follow the floral breeze to the parking lot. My heartbeat picks up once again. The thought of her getting into her car and leaving me forever is a real possibility. With my inner wolf howling in protest, my pace quickens. Staying quiet and crouched in the shadows of the building, I need to stay inconspicuous. There aren't many people lingering, but I don't want to draw any attention.

I'm already too tall, my eyes not quite right. I don't fit in but I don't stand out too much either. Still, I'm careful to stick to the shadows and remain quiet.

The scent trail takes me to a few parked cars, but then it continues past the lot and toward campus. Her sweet smell cuts off to the right down a sidewalk between two dorms. My head tilts as I eye the large brick buildings. Maybe she's a student. My lips kick up into an asymmetric grin. Stalking past campus and toward Main Street, I'm eager to learn more about my mate. There are a few shops just now closing down, but there's a bar and a nightclub at the end of the street. I follow my tantalizing mate and that's when I go on high alert. Scenting the air, I fight the urge to growl.

Wolves are here. And they sure as fuck aren't from my pack. Adrenaline floods my veins knowing the trail to my mate and the trail to the unknown werewolves lead in the same direction. Both panic and anger consume me.

"Devin, we have problems." Not waiting for a response, I continue along the path. My focus narrows; my pulse accelerates. They better not fucking touch her. I'll kill them. They will die slow deaths if they dare to approach her. Woods to my left offer a modicum of cover, allowing me to sprint. No more of this plodding human pace. I'm barely able to keep my composure until I'm safely hidden in the shadows of the forest.

I try calling for the pack again, but it's too late. They've traveled too far and can't hear me. *Fuck!* Rushing past the trees, branches snap loudly under my boots. I don't care about stealth, only speed. I need to get to her as fast as I can. If they're after my mate, I'll rip their throats out. I refuse to fail my mate. To hell with that shit about waiting until she's offered. I'm taking her with me and Devin will just have to deal with it. It only takes minutes to reach the end of her scent but with each second that passes, the growl deep in my chest gets louder. The trail cuts past the bar and through a deserted alley.

Veronica

Time passes far too quickly as the pack trails me, and the sun sinks into the night's embrace. I almost lost sight of my little wolf stalker. The other dogs call him Vince. His name sends a chill down my spine in the most unexpected ways. The shiver of delight, of intrigue even, perks up my lips into a pleasant smile.

I love the way his silver eyes follow me, just like the lost puppy he is. My smile widens, threatening to expose my sharp fangs if I don't contain myself. How could I resist this, though? How could I resist *him*? Especially given that I've been so damn bored scouting out this Podunk town for the coven. Hearing him pant with lust dripping from his desperate whimper for me to be his has my cold, dead heart beating with scalding hot blood.

The other werewolves shadowing him have put a damper on my intrigue. Just the thought of them, of a pack, forces the pull I feel toward Vince to quiet itself. I wonder if he knows they've been tracking him all night. Probably not, considering that he hasn't stopped following my every step in these gray suede pumps. The dogs may have a better sense of smell than us vamps, but their hearing is shit.

Every pump of their hearts, every swallow, every murmur and whisper ... I hear it all. My eyes narrow with contempt at the pack following the lone wolf who's set his sights on me.

Tapping my sharp nails against the railing to the nightclub, I admire my bloodred manicure as I wait for Vince to catch up. I've done this all day, allowing the hours to pass and standing by for the sun to slip away. What's about to happen shouldn't be done in the daylight with humans out and about. The scant two hours Vince muttered about possessing have long since passed.

I could play this game of cat and mouse all day, but now that the humans have mostly dispersed, the time has come to end this charade.

The club is the only place open this late, and even it's going to close down soon. Aptly named Allure, music blares from the doors every time they open and patrons pour in and out. Tipsy women who dared to wear heels pass me with slurred speech and an unsteady gait.

I keep mulling over the words whispered by my pup's predators: *rightful pack*. The wretched creatures were planning on stealing the Alpha's new mate. Devin's mate. My crimson lips that match my nails kick up into a smirk once again. Their plan went to shit when their cars wouldn't start and they ended up stuck in this boring-ass town. Reaching into my studded black leather clutch, I pull out two spark plugs and toss them into a dingy trash can on the deserted sidewalk. The clunk ricochets down the alley, almost in rhythm with the sound of their steps coming closer and closer.

Initially I thought about cutting their brake lines, but they were planning on following my pup's pack and I wasn't sure how that would turn out. I wanted to play with him, after all, and I wasn't about to let some rent-a-pack pricks wreck my night.

Wiping a touch of engine grease down the side of the brick wall, I walk slowly, not stalking, simply waiting. Control is divine. And tonight, every bit of control is mine. My heels click against the broken asphalt beneath me as I wait, my pace turning slower and slower.

I perk up as I hear the sound of the "rightful pack" to my right. A sarcastic huff leaves me as they say it again. "Rightful pack." My long lashes flutter shut as I listen close. My pup's shuffling somewhere behind me, maybe a mile back on my left, no doubt following my scent. It seems his enemies have a new target. My smirk morphs into an all-out grin. All their muttering makes it sound like they've set their sights on me this time.

"He must be following his mate."

"Get her first."

"We'll use her to get to him. And then him to get to the pack."

Oh, those sweet foolish men. My fangs peek out ever so slightly as I bite down on my bottom lip, grateful they've finally put two and two together. How adorable that it only took them hours and not days. I can only hope Vince's pack, the one Devin has sovereignty over, isn't full of idiots like this one is.

Humming, I tap absently at the railing before piercing my nail through the metal and gouging a long scratch into it as I walk to the end of the bar. The odds are low they know I'm a vampire. Their hastily arranged plan is careless. With the element of surprise on my side, it'll be easy for me to take each one of them on my own. It's been too damn long since I've been able to release this pent-up energy. And so much longer since I've been able to drink my fill. My tongue grazes the sharp fang slightly puncturing my bottom lip.

To my right is a dark alley. The pack waits there, the ones who are determined to get revenge by scooping up their enemies' mates. My eyes roll at their pathetic plan.

To my left is a winding dirt road sheltered in a dense forest. My panting pup chose to take that route so I wouldn't see him following me around, the silly little thing. Well … not so little.

When these werewolves meet up, I'm sure blood will be shed. Four on one isn't the best odds for my pup, although I'm interested in seeing how he'd fare. We're in human territory, though. My lips purse at the thought; the coven will be pissed if I allow it. Not to mention the Authority.

I've never been much for the outdoors and seeing as how I'm in heels, I think I'll head to my right. I wanted to have a little fun tonight anyway.

The only thing I'm not quite sure of is how much fun I'll get to have before my pup catches up to me.

Vince

The alley is narrow and my clothing snags on the rough brick as I rush through to the other end. Hastily emerging from the shadows, my hoodie's torn to shreds so I rip it off and leave it. The white Henley stretched tight across my chest has a small tear running across my abs and is stained with blood. That's what I get from running recklessly through the wooded trails. I've already healed, though, and I don't give a fuck. The scowl on my face, clenched fists, and white-hot anger pouring off me in waves complete the image of a pissed-the-fuck-off werewolf. If I could contain my anger to avoid scaring my mate I would, but I can't. Four large frames are arranged in a loose semicircle at the end of the alley.

They have her surrounded.

I've never felt fear like I do now. Even more so, I've never felt rage as I do now.

My fists clench so hard that the skin on my knuckles tears and blood seeps from the self-induced wounds. A low growl of warning rips through my chest, reverberating in the air. All four of them lift their heads immediately, their eyes widening and mouths parting in either shock or an attempt to speak.

I don't give the fuckers a chance to say a damn thing.

As I hurl my body toward them, I release my wolf, morphing into a beast of violence. Bones contort; fur emerges. The burning sensation and cracking in my ears fuel my desire to destroy. I'm fully wolf before all four paws land on the cold, hard ground. Snarling, I'm only vaguely aware of how this may frighten my mate. This isn't how I'd planned on meeting her, on telling her who I am and what she means to me.

Regret doesn't have a moment to linger. For now, I allow the fury to consume every thought and action, consequences be dammed. One of the four assholes attempts to shift, but he's too slow as I immediately go for his throat. His claws dig into my shoulders, slicing through the tender flesh and scraping at the bone as my jaws sink into his throat, piercing his jugular and causing hot gushes of dirty blood to fill my mouth. I barely feel a damn thing. A low snarl leaves me as his body goes limp and I turn to the other three.

My eyes flicker with shock and then pride as I take in the scene. My sexy mate's knees are crossed with her thighs wrapped around the neck of a man who must be human, judging by his inability to shift. I don't have time to question what a human is doing with these werewolves as she flings her body toward the ground, silently and effortlessly. Tossing his large frame in the air, he lands hard on his back with her sitting on his chest. The crack of his bones echoes in the alley as she peeks up at me.

Holy fuck.

My gaze is locked on her as she lashes at his throat, slicing it with a small knife nestled between her knuckles. Her expression is that of a ruthless predator. Her perfectly pinned bun has fallen, leaving her black curls to cascade gently down her back. Confidence and power radiate from her small frame as she turns, still crouched on his chest. Her dark red, plump lips part as she lifts her head and hisses at the remaining shifters, revealing long white fangs that reflect the light of the moon.

The shifters stumble back, mouths gaped, but before they're able to turn and run she quickly flings her hand outward, sending two blades flying. The first lands in one man's back, effectively paralyzing him and his limp body instantly sinks to the ground, crashing against the cement. With nothing to break his fall, blood flows freely from his broken nose, pooling around his face. The other blade is lodged in the last shifter's neck. As his hands fly up to his neck, my mate, my *vampire* mate, sends more blades darting through the air in a rhythmic dance, pinning his hands to the base of his throat. Blood spurts from his jugular. The sight is violent and bloody, brutal and efficient. As the shifter struggles to breathe, landing hard on his knees and coughing up blood, my mate saunters over casually and twists the knives while ripping them out. His dead eyes stare at nothing as blood forms a puddle around him and his face flattens against the brick.

Noticeably catching her breath, her chest rises and falls and I'm given a moment to admire her. A vampire. My mate is paranormal, not human. There will be so much less to explain.

With dark red blood splattered on her blouse, her heels click as she strides to the other shifter, who's limp yet conscious. With my hackles settling, I prowl closer, but give her the room she obviously desires. Squatting, my gaze is captured by her leather skirt sliding up her leg, revealing a black lacy garter belt holding up her thigh highs. She is the sight of deadly beauty. Still in wolf form, I groan with lust and desire. I move to shift, but her dark eyes find mine and her lips part as she says,

"Stay. I want to feel you … like this. I want to see you up close."

If I could grin, I would. She'll know damn well how much hearing that pleased me the moment I shift. Pride flows through me and I huff in agreement as I pad over swiftly to be closer to her. Her delicate hand grabs the knife, but before retrieving it she looks back at me. "I thought we could keep him for Devin." Although it's a statement, it's clear she's asking me. My hackles raise, realizing she knows more of me than I know of her. She waits for my nod and then she removes the knife. It's a silver blade. He'll heal with time, but we'll deal with him before he has a chance to come to. I watch her skilled moves while coming to terms with the situation. My mate is a vampire and she knows of Devin. Numerous questions pile in my mind, but in wolf form I'm unable to speak. Standing, she places the bloody blade behind her back and tilts her head as she takes me in.

Her dark eyes travel down my body. Although she's shorter than I am, we're the same height while I'm standing on all four paws in my wolf form.

"Lie down." Her command makes me grin inwardly. I'm so fucking turned on it hurts. I need to shift so I can play this game with her. Obeying my mate, I settle on the ground in the brick alley. A low rumble vibrates my chest as she spears my fur with her small hands, petting me. She moves in front of me and takes my large head in her grasp before gently scratching my chest. Her touch on me is a heaven I didn't know existed. I resist the urge to close my eyes so I can stare back at her while enjoying her touch. A small smile plays at her lips as she watches her fingers disappear in my thick, soft fur. All too quickly, she stops. Her smile vanishes as she glances at the bodies around her.

She purses her lips and looks behind us at my tattered and shredded outfit. "You ruined your clothes." I sit up, making me about a foot taller than her so I tower over her, but she maintains eye contact. "What are you going to wear now?" Is she admonishing me? "I'm going to need help moving these bodies and storing him in the trunk." Her thumb points to the incapacitated shifter. "I have silver rope in the back of the car, but how the hell am I going to carry him?" Her tongue clucks as she surveys the scene. "You need clothes. Do you have any?" I shake my head, causing her dark eyes to narrow. "Shift."

My mate is ... testing me. I allow a moment to pass, observing her and she stares back at me, her confidence disappearing for only a moment. "Please," she adds, dragging out the word as if she's not used to saying it.

That's better. All I can think before I shift back is that my mate is going to challenge me, push me, command me even ... and I'm eager to play and to do the same in return.

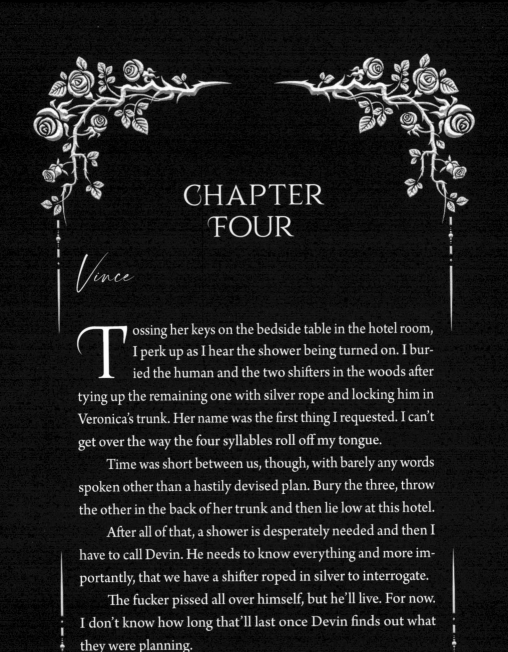

CHAPTER FOUR

Vince

Tossing her keys on the bedside table in the hotel room, I perk up as I hear the shower being turned on. I buried the human and the two shifters in the woods after tying up the remaining one with silver rope and locking him in Veronica's trunk. Her name was the first thing I requested. I can't get over the way the four syllables roll off my tongue.

Time was short between us, though, with barely any words spoken other than a hastily devised plan. Bury the three, throw the other in the back of her trunk and then lie low at this hotel.

After all of that, a shower is desperately needed and then I have to call Devin. He needs to know everything and more importantly, that we have a shifter roped in silver to interrogate.

The fucker pissed all over himself, but he'll live. For now. I don't know how long that'll last once Devin finds out what they were planning.

I strip out of the jeans and simple white T-shirt my mate

got me. The shirt barely fits, but I think she likes seeing it stretched tight across my broad shoulders. She knew damn well I needed a larger size.

So far I've learned my mate is opinionated. She likes what she likes, and I'm hard as a fucking rock for her. Every little detail about her seems to scream to me to pay attention. From the way a soft accent lingers on a few of her words, to the way she tucks her jet-black hair behind her ear to accentuate her slender neck. I crave every inch of her.

Every step I take toward the bathroom makes my dick harder as I imagine my gorgeous mate wet and naked, waiting for me to ravage her. Palming myself, I stroke a few times.

The bathroom door opens with a soft creak, allowing the steam to billow out and I find her wrapped in a towel. Her hair's dry and she's rubbing some balm that smells like honey into her shoulders. There's a large dark bruise covering the crook of her neck and the sight of it makes me growl deep and low.

They hurt her. I was right fucking there and they laid hands on her. Weakness and anger war within me. I was right there and I didn't protect her. The bastard in the trunk is lucky that she wants to give him to Devin. If it were up to me, he'd be dead like the rest of them. I know vampires heal, but obviously they don't heal as fast as we do.

"Vince." My name on her lips pulls my attention from my dark thoughts.

"Don't be so upset, pup. It's just a little bruise." Her dark eyes twinkle with mischief when they meet my silver gaze in the mirror.

Pup. If I wasn't feeling as if I've failed her already, only hours into meeting my mate, I'd smirk at her nickname for me. *Pup.* I imagine once she discovers what I can do to her, she won't be using that word anymore.

As it is, my gaze falls back to the bruise. "I don't like to see you marked."

She smiles devilishly before turning around and unwrapping her towel. The white cotton falls to form a puddle around her feet, revealing her light brown skin that looks flawless.

Peeking over her shoulder, she toys with me. "You don't want to put your mark on me then?"

I groan in approval. My dick gets impossibly harder and lust rages in my blood at the sight of her gorgeous curves. *My mate.* I part my lips to speak as I walk toward her, but she stops me by putting one slender finger against my lips. "Uh, uh, uh. I want my big bad wolf on his knees." Smirking, I obey my mate. I love this little game. Just the thought of her putting a collar and leash on me makes precum leak from my slit. She can do what she pleases as I learn her boundaries.

"You want me to lick you first?" I question.

I kneel in front of her and gently place my hands on the back of her thighs, petting her smooth skin and testing my limits. She allows it and I smile up at her in gratitude before nuzzling my nose between her thighs and inhaling her arousal. She's wet already. Wanting me as much as I want her. My groan matches the desire in her moan. She leans back against the counter, spreading her legs a little wider. "Good boy. Enjoy your treat."

I can't help but to grin against her pussy. *Pup. Good boy. Kneel.* If she wants to be in control, who am I to turn down a good time? Besides, it's enticing. I've never met a woman like her. I've never craved this like I do now.

A rough chuckle vibrates through my chest and I smile into her heat before taking a long, languid lick through her lips. *Fuck.* She tastes just like honey too. Moaning into her heat, I suck on her clit. I massage her with my hot tongue and pick up my pace as she mewls louder and runs her hands through my hair. My tongue dips between her folds and I lap up her honey. I pull back to look at her glistening opening before shoving my tongue deep inside her and she bucks against me. I'd smile at her arousal but I don't want to let up tongue fucking her.

My hands grip onto her thighs to hold her tighter as she starts to tremble, already close as her breathing picks up, my fingers digging into her skin. I pull away to run my tongue along her length and suck her clit back into my mouth before she can protest. Her small hands push me against her.

I slow my movements as she gets closer to her release, her thighs tightening as she holds her breath. I want to hear her beg me to get her off. I want this sexy-as-fuck, dominant woman to beg me for her release. She moans my name and pushes me into her harder. My name. My name is what she pleads for.

She may be greedy, but I'm full of pride. I suck her clit back into my mouth but slow my movements as her hands shake in my hair and her pussy clenches. Imagining her body shuddering in my arms while her orgasm rocks through her makes me leak more precum onto the bathroom floor. Impossibly hard, I want nothing more than to push her against the wall and fuck her so I can feel her come on my dick. I stop my movements as she moans my name louder. I grin before taking another languid stroke against her wanting heat.

Her heavy breathing slows and her hands grip my hair tighter to the point of pain. She forces me to look up at her. Her narrowed gaze is heated. "Do you enjoy teasing me?"

"I want you to beg me." My simple statement makes her grin.

"I don't beg." She releases my head and walks to the shower, which is still running. The shower is filled with so much steam she nearly vanishes as she steps into the glass stall. She doesn't shut the door, though, and the steam flows out into the room, giving me a better view. "Come here."

My gaze narrows but I immediately oblige.

"Everyone begs," I tell her. My head tilts, waiting to see if she's serious. Her hand reaches out and her splayed fingers push against my chest before I can join her. The hot sprays of water splash against her chest, reddening her skin. "Knees." My brow furrows, but I do what she says and kneel on the small white bath mat.

"I don't take it lightly that you didn't let me get off." Her admonishing tone sends a pulse of nervousness through my chest. She closes her eyes and lets the water hit her face and hair before streaming over her lush curves. "Now you'll have to watch." She opens her eyes and faces me before cupping my chin in her hand. "I wanted to let you pleasure me ..." Her pitying voice turns stern as she continues, "... but I don't need you to get mine."

Her cold words crater my chest. My lips press into a hard line. I don't fucking like this. "No." It's the only word that will escape my lips, my growl of contempt barely restrained as I speak.

"You did this to yourself." She watches me through her thick lashes. "Take your punishment like a good boy and I'll reward you." She pats my head before adding, "I'm willing to believe you didn't know any better."

My fists clench at my sides to hold back from grabbing her waist, pushing her small body against the wall and pounding into her tight pussy. I could easily take her however I wanted, and she knows it. She's taunting a beast, trying to tame me.

The moment is tense between us and I know she feels it too from the way her expression changes. A second passes and then another. "A good boy?"

"I need to be the one in charge, Vince," she tells me with her voice tight. "If that's not going to work, you—"

"Fine." I cave before she can say another word. There's something off about her, something ill at ease and frightened. But more importantly, she wants me. My mate, the only soul I'm meant to be with. "You want to call the shots?"

"I want you to do everything I say and nothing more." With a second passing in silence, her long black hair slicked to her tan skin, her breasts taut and this dangerous woman vulnerable before me, she adds, "I'll be good to you but this is how I need it."

There is more. I'm certain of it. But for now, I ease her worries. We have a lifetime to spend together. And I don't mind playing the part of whatever she needs in this role.

I grin and sit back on my heels, then say, "Yes, ma'am." She smiles brightly, looking down at me with delight in her dark eyes that fills a void I've held in my chest for all my life.

"Call me Mistress." I nearly come on the damn rug at her words. Stifling my groan, I regain my composure.

"Yes, Mistress." My obedience makes her sharp fangs sink into her pouty bottom lip. The sight makes me want to beg her to bite me. Shit.

Maybe some part of me wants to be her submissive. I want her to pierce my skin, marking me just as I plan on marking her.

Her fingers dip into her heat and she throws her head back, moaning at her own tender touch. She tilts her head to look at me with her fingers strumming along her clit. "You got me so close." Her cadence is soft and full of yearning.

"Can I taste … Mistress?" My question makes her lips kick up into a smile. Her happiness fills my heart with pride. She offers me her fingers and I reach out a hand to hold them steady, but she pulls them away before I can touch her.

"Only taste." She shakes her head, sending droplets of water down her breasts to the tips of her dark brown nipples before landing on the rug. "No touching." Her mouth is parted slightly and her breasts rise and fall with her deep breaths. The smell of her arousal floods the bathroom. I place my hands on my thighs and lean forward. Giving her a wolfish grin, I stare into her dark eyes as I take her fingertips into my mouth to taste her honey. I let out a groan at the taste and sit back on my heels.

"Fucking delicious."

She smiles with satisfaction and returns to touching herself. Her head leans back against the stall as she moans and squirms. Her pace picks up as two fingers brush along her clit and dip into her entrance over and over. I watch her in rapture as she brings herself to the edge of her climax. Her mouth gapes and her shoulders spasm as she finds her release. She screams out my name before sagging against the wall of the shower.

My name.

It's the most beautiful vision I've ever seen. Sitting patiently on my heels with my hands firmly pressed against my thighs, I wait for her to come down from the aftershocks. I wish I was holding her and she had gotten off on my tongue. Next time. Her next orgasm will be mine.

As if she read my mind, she backs up against the tiled wall and beckons me into the shower with a playful smirk. Rising slowly, I carefully navigate my large frame into the shower, crowding the space and hovering over her tiny body. She takes my face in her hands and I lower my lips to hers. My tongue brushes along the seam of her lips and she parts them for me, her hot tongue massaging mine. I growl into her mouth and rest my forearms on either side of her head against the wall, caging her in as I kiss her with every ounce of passion I have. Her arms wrap around my waist, her fingers splayed against my ass, pulling me closer to her. She breaks our kiss and moans a contented sigh as my erection digs into her soft belly. Ducking her head and stepping under my arm, she reaches for a small bottle of body wash.

"Have you learned your lesson?" She lathers the soap in her hands before massaging it over my body. Her fingers linger over my chiseled chest and play in the small bit of hair below my abs, trailing down to my cock. I nod and tell her, "Yes."

She makes a sound like she's pleased and stands on her tiptoes to kiss the crook of my neck. "Good boy." Her hot breath tickles my throat as her sharp fangs skim along the sensitive flesh. She hastily turns away from me and applies more soap to her hands. Twirling a finger, she commands me to turn. Her hands knead my muscles as she lathers more soap onto my skin. Every little touch from her is heaven. My mate. I'm still in awe.

She hums as she washes every inch of my body *except* my raging erection.

My mate is a fucking tease.

At that realization she commands, "Turn."

I obey slowly, turning to face her. She gets onto her tiptoes to wash my hair, her breasts pressing against my hard chest. Fuck, I love it though. My arms wrap around her small waist as she massages my scalp with her nails. Her touch relaxes me.

"You like calling me pup?" I ask her, planting a small kiss on her temple.

Her smile is soft and playful. "You're at least a foot taller than me ... I think I love calling you pup."

Love. She's demanding, controlling and there's a reason for the way she is ... but she wants to be with me. To be my mate. She offers no protest at all and I know damn well she knows what this means. "Do you like it?" she questions in a whisper.

"Mmm." I murmur into the crook of her neck as I grind my dick into her stomach, loving the skin-on-skin contact. The touch reminds me how much I fucking need my release. She lets out a small, feminine snicker, but otherwise ignores my not-so-subtle hint.

She steps toward the back of the shower and instructs me to rinse. I chuckle, loving the way she orders me around like she owns me. She really fucking does own me. What's worse is that she knows it. I let the hot water hit me and rinse the suds from my body, but I don't linger. I want my mate. I need more of her touch. With a single stride toward her, I cage her in like before. I move to kiss her soft, supple lips, but her finger at my mouth stops me inches away from her face. "Bedtime, wolf." *Bed.* Absolutely.

"Yes, Mistress." My response is paired with a grin and I lean forward to kiss her cheek. A blush runs through her chest and up to her face. The slight pink hue looks beautiful on her olive complexion. I dry off as quickly as possible and the soft cotton against my still-hard dick is enough to have me on my knees. God, I can't wait to get off. Hopefully it'll be in her tight little cunt. I lick my lips, remembering the mouthwatering taste.

She seems to be taking her time towel drying her hair before she reaches in a small floral bag on the counter and pulls out lotion. When my silver eyes catch her dark gaze in the mirror, I cock a brow. "I'll be there when I'm finished." I nod my head, not trusting that my mouth won't demand she come with me if I open it. Fuck, I'm tired of waiting. Tired of being teased. I lie on top of the covers with my hands behind my head, looking at the bathroom. I left the door open and I keep getting hints of her honey scent mingling with the sweet, floral fragrance of jasmine.

She saunters to the bed completely naked and it makes my dick snap to attention. She smirks at the sight of my bobbing erection before climbing into bed, pulling up the covers and crawling underneath. "Get under here. I want you to hold me." I move as quickly as I can to get my hands on her lush body. My arms reach around her waist and pull her small, delicate frame to my hard chest. I rock my dick into her ass, and even that feels like heaven.

"Stop it. I don't want you to do that." Her softly spoken words shock me, but I immediately stop. My brow furrows as she nuzzles her head into my chest, drapes her leg across mine and settles her forearm across my abs. She's getting into position to sleep. "Good night, pup." *What the fuck?* My lips part to protest but that damn finger comes up to silence me yet again. "Uh-uh. No complaining. You kept me from my release to tease me … for your own pleasure. Bad boys don't get to come." She settles back into my chest as I contemplate her words.

A tic in my jaw spasms, but then a thought comes to mind. "Are you challenging me?"

Her gentle snicker tickles my chest hair, then she says, "No, not in the least. I know if you wanted to, you could take from me. I don't want that." I didn't think she was, but I had to make sure. Tapping my fingers on her arm, I try to figure out what the hell I should do. A fucking light-bulb goes off in my head.

"Do you want me to beg?" Of course she does. I wanted her to beg, so this is my punishment. "I'll beg on my knees. I'll plead with you. Whatever you want." I whisper my words into her hair, meaning every word. Shit, just the thought of me begging her to suck me off has precum flowing down my shaft.

She snickers again and I know her answer before she says it. "No, I don't want you to beg."

"I don't like this." I know I sound like a petulant child, but really, what the fuck?

"That's the point of a punishment." She lifts her head to give me a kiss on the cheek before settling back down beside me. A moment of silence passes. I stare up at the ceiling with a raging erection that won't die, next to my sated mate, who doesn't seem to have any intention of returning the favor. *Motherfucker.* I close my eyes and try to sleep, but there's no fucking way that's going to happen.

"Vince, I'm thirsty." Her sleepy words register slowly.

"You need to drink? Do you have any blood here?" Vampires don't drink directly from beings anymore. At least they aren't supposed to; it was bad for *relations*. Her head shakes gently, ruffling her hair before she nips at my neck. Her little bite shoots a wave of heated desire down my body.

"Will it hurt?" If I'd known my mate was going to be a vampire, I would have given more of a shit about their species.

"Only a little," she says and hesitates before adding, "at first." I nod once and arch my neck, offering it to her without thinking twice. She straddles my body and her naked, hot core presses down on my tortured erection, making my eyes roll back in my head. *Fuck yes!*

"Drink it all, baby." The lustful words slip past my lips as she licks my neck, telling me where she's going to bite.

"Stay still." She breathes into my neck. "Just feel it." I barely register her words before her sharp fangs pierce my flesh. It stings and I have to fist the sheets to keep my hands from instinctively going to my neck. And then she sucks. *Holy fuck.* I can feel the pull of my blood through my veins. The intense rush is accompanied with a heated pulse of pleasure hovering over every inch of me. I groan and tighten my grip on the sheets. She rocks gently on top of me while sucking harder and I almost come from the heightened sensation. My legs stiffen with the need to release.

"More." It's not even close to a command, but before I can add *please* she digs her fangs in deeper and sucks harder. And I erupt. The tingling in my spine travels through every inch of my body, starting at my toes and fingers and numbing its way through my quivering body. Waves and waves of cum leave me as she continues to suck on my neck, intensifying my release. As aftershocks flow through me, she gently licks the bite wounds. The soft touch sends a satisfied chill through my body. She shuffles onto the bed beside me and kisses me tenderly on the lips before grabbing something off the nightstand. Wiping herself with a damp cloth, she then scoots over to clean off my stomach and thighs.

"You made a mess." Her voice is teasing, as is her side-eye.

Her weak admonishment makes me grin and I tell her, "You knew I would." She gives me a soft, small smile and continues wiping me down before tossing the rag on the floor.

"Did I taste good?" I have to ask.

"Delicious." She answers with my own words before nipping at my neck and settling beside me.

"Did you even drink enough?"

She hums into my chest while molding her soft warm body to mine. "Sleep."

"Yes, my little mate."

"That's not how you say Mistress." I feel her smile as her deep breaths even out and she nods off.

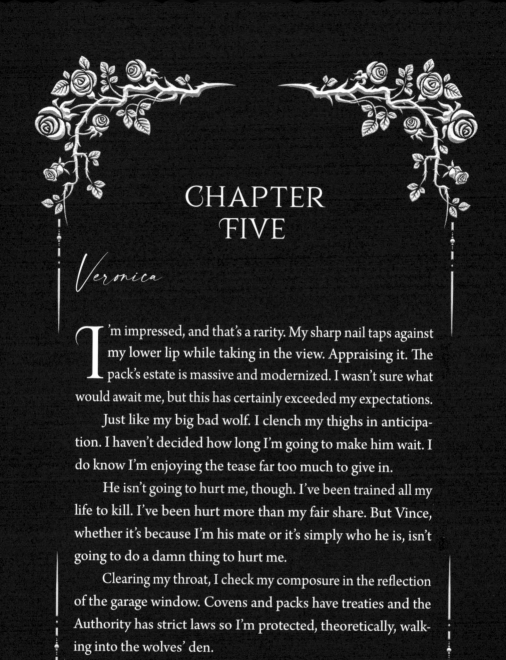

CHAPTER FIVE

Veronica

I'm impressed, and that's a rarity. My sharp nail taps against my lower lip while taking in the view. Appraising it. The pack's estate is massive and modernized. I wasn't sure what would await me, but this has certainly exceeded my expectations.

Just like my big bad wolf. I clench my thighs in anticipation. I haven't decided how long I'm going to make him wait. I do know I'm enjoying the tease far too much to give in.

He isn't going to hurt me, though. I've been trained all my life to kill. I've been hurt more than my fair share. But Vince, whether it's because I'm his mate or it's simply who he is, isn't going to do a damn thing to hurt me.

Clearing my throat, I check my composure in the reflection of the garage window. Covens and packs have treaties and the Authority has strict laws so I'm protected, theoretically, walking into the wolves' den.

I would have felt more secure on human territory, but now

that I know what I mean to Vince, that certainly changes things. I don't appreciate the anxiousness it offers me.

As my patience wanes, I hear my pup hurl the limp body of the shifter bound with silver rope onto the paved driveway with a loud thud.

A wicked grin spreads across my face as I listen in on the heated conversation flowing from the windows as two sets of footsteps come down the stairs. It may be faint to these mutts, but I can hear just fine. "I need it, Devin." The Alpha mate is practically seething. Usually I try not to eavesdrop, but I can't help the fact that the angry human is fighting with her mate. Although she's whispering, she's furious. I wonder what her wolf has done to piss her off.

"You're my mate. You're meant to carry my pups." My eyebrows shoot up at his response. I can feel the low, threatening growl barreling from his chest. His mate's response is even and firm. "I need my birth control." Pursing my lips, I listen more intently but am unfortunately interrupted.

"What's wrong?" My sweet pup looks devilishly handsome as he wraps his arm around my waist and kisses my cheek. I lean into his touch slightly, but hold back.

"Have you already told them?"

"Yes, they know everything. They're gathering now to meet you." I nod in acknowledgment. An odd sense of discomfort settles through me. It's been a while since I've felt this way, but I think I'm genuinely nervous. I huff as the realization hits me. Shaking my head, I shut that shit down as I strut in my suede pumps toward the entrance with my pup following closely behind. When I get to the door I pause, waiting for him to open it for me, which he does easily.

My big bad wolf is such a gentleman. He leads me through the expansive hall toward the eat-in kitchen with his large hand resting on the small of my back. I square my shoulders as I enter the room and see the other seven members of the pack staring back at me.

"Veronica, this is my pack. Caleb, Liz, Dom, Grace, Devin, Lev and Jude." He motions toward each of them as he says their names and they nod in turn. Both Liz and Grace look uncomfortable at my presence and it causes a chill to go through me. I restrain myself from sneering at their obvious distaste for my species. Or maybe it's just a dislike for me. Either way, I don't care for the immediate judgment. Although I'm used to it. I offer them a curt nod each.

Caleb and Dom are on either side of their mate on the left side of the table with the Alpha mate, Grace, next to Dom. Her small muscles are corded as she eyes me. A knowing smirk pulls at my lips. The little human is balling her fists under the table. It's difficult not to laugh. I have to remind myself that she knows little of vampires. Whatever small bits of knowledge she's been given have almost certainly been designed to cause fear. Devin is seated next to her at the head of the table and the other two pack members are on his right.

"Hello." I greet them all at once, making eye contact with each of them as I take a seat at the opposite end of the table without hesitation. Vince pulls out my chair and scoots it in as I sit before joining me at my right. His affection toward me gives me confidence I wasn't expecting. I'm growing rather fond of him, far too quickly. So much so that I don't trust it. I know of mates and werewolves, but this ... these feelings are uncontrollable. I don't care for them.

The large wolf to the right of Devin smiles at me and asks, "Do you know the difference between ooh and aah?" The wolf next to him smacks him in the back of the head.

"Shut it, Lev." The large wolf chuckles, unaffected by the hit.

"About ten inches," I answer effortlessly with a straight face. I rather enjoy crude humor. Most of the pack laughs and Lev gapes, though there's a twinkle of camaraderie in his eyes. It earns him a small smile in return. Grace's cold gaze narrows and Liz continues to shy away, hiding behind Caleb. I make a mental note to mention a coffee run and a trip to the pharmacy before the conversation is over. They'll be begging me to come along. A wicked grin curls up my lips.

I'm not the monster here; they'll learn that. Monsters and evil exist, but that's not who I am.

"I welcome you to our pack," Devin begins, although I hear an unspoken *but*.

"Thank you."

"Why were you in our territory?" Devin's baritone voice is even and disrupts my thoughts.

"I respect your straightforwardness." Meeting his silver eyes with a professional gaze, I begin. "As you know, with the new laws, our food source is now scarce. We're doing our best to respect the Authority's wishes, but the blood banks are hardly providing enough to sustain us."

"Your coven sent you?"

"Yes."

"Just you?"

"Yes; there are no others. I was hoping to talk after the offering on human territory, for obvious reasons."

The pack nods in unison at that comment. They wouldn't dare cause a scene in front of humans. Not when it means facing the consequences of the Authority. "I didn't anticipate the ..." I pause and tap my bloodred fingernails along the table thinking of an acceptable word. "... distractions."

"What distractions?" Grace speaks up. It seems her curiosity is greater than her fear. There's hope for us after all.

"Well, you fainting for one." She pales at the reminder. "And Liz screaming certainly wasn't conducive to holding a business meeting." I eye the petite blonde, who has yet to smile. "It seems you're both much more agreeable today." There's only a thin veil of sarcasm over my words. "And then of course ... the dogs."

"Vince has informed us. You have my sincerest gratitude." I can't help but to smile at the Alpha's warmth.

"He's in the shed." Vince leans back in his seat. "All set up for questioning." I eye my pup with envy. He's laid back and easygoing.

How fate has matched us, I have no idea. I don't know what he did in some other life to be stuck with a woman like me. Guarded and quite honestly, vengeful. I almost feel sorry for him that I'm the woman who's meant to love him. I think I've long forgotten how to do such a thing.

"What dogs?" A tic in Devin's jaw spasms at Grace's question.

"We'll discuss that matter later."

The little human's discontent is palpable. Judging by the bags under her eyes, it doesn't appear that she's slept much. Poor thing. Absently, I wonder how she's taking all of this in. Glancing to Liz, I gather Grace is faring better, seeing as how she's at least speaking her mind. "I want to know what you're talking about." Devin faces his mate with a hard glare, but his voice is soft when he speaks. He gently takes her hands in his. "Later, sweetheart. I will tell you later."

Her lips purse before she parts them several times without speaking. Finally, she nods her head and repeats, "Later."

He places their clasped hands on top of the table. "So you came to discuss business matters on behalf of your coven?"

"Yes. As I was saying, the blood banks aren't enough. Our research indicates that the overwhelming majority of the Shadow Falls residents do not give blood. We're willing to pay them substantially for their donations."

"The Authority has approved this?"

"Only on the premise that it's run by humans and that they are not privy to any information involving vampires."

I pause, picking up the sound of tires on the long, winding driveway. Someone is coming. I listen closer.

"What does the coven—" I hold my hand up, interrupting Devin's question. I shouldn't have disrespected him, but I act without thinking.

"Are you expecting company?" I ask.

"No." His silver eyes narrow.

I barely hear the voice, but I instantly recognize it. Yet another distraction. Chills trail down my spine. I may not have feared a den of wolves, but I certainly fear who's coming next.

"The Authority is here."

PART II

Wolf in Pain

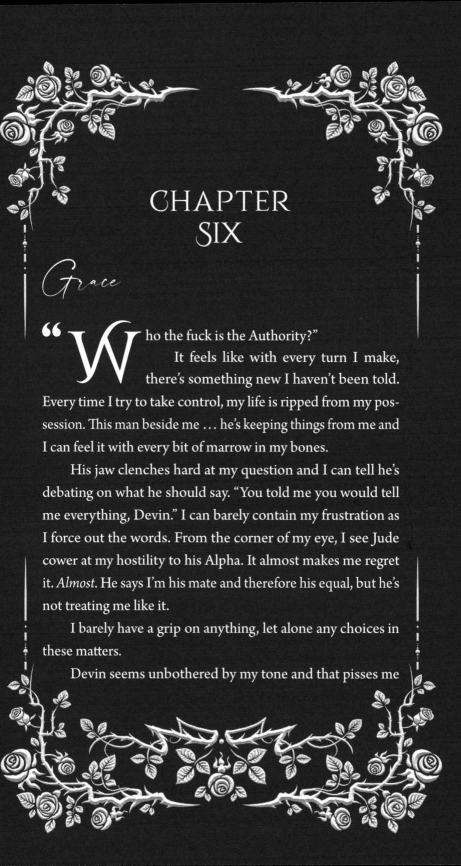

CHAPTER SIX

Grace

"Who the fuck is the Authority?"

It feels like with every turn I make, there's something new I haven't been told. Every time I try to take control, my life is ripped from my possession. This man beside me … he's keeping things from me and I can feel it with every bit of marrow in my bones.

His jaw clenches hard at my question and I can tell he's debating on what he should say. "You told me you would tell me everything, Devin." I can barely contain my frustration as I force out the words. From the corner of my eye, I see Jude cower at my hostility to his Alpha. It almost makes me regret it. *Almost.* He says I'm his mate and therefore his equal, but he's not treating me like it.

I barely have a grip on anything, let alone any choices in these matters.

Devin seems unbothered by my tone and that pisses me

off even more. "The Authority is in charge of communications between and within species. They formed an alliance with the humans and enacted laws to prevent certain instances from occurring." I narrow my eyes at his sanitized response.

"Instances such as the one that occurred yesterday at the offering." Veronica elaborates, her bewitching voice demanding my attention, the faint accent only adding to her beauty. Her tanned skin is flawless, while the way she carries herself is both demure and yet superior. I still don't know what to make of her.

She's a vampire and that alone sends up red flags. I hardly heard a word out of her mouth because every time her lips moved I could only stare at her fangs. She's provocative and the embodiment of female strength; both things I value highly, yet I find myself on guard. She has a seductive aura I don't trust.

Although she's not the only one I hesitate to trust.

"So they're like the werewolf police?"

Veronica's feminine laugh echoes in the kitchen. She smiles, revealing those sharp fangs, and tells me, "The Authority looks out for themselves, first and foremost. Very little of what they do involves justice."

"They can be very just in their actions, Veronica." Devin's response is slightly reprimanding.

"Just because they can be doesn't mean they have been. They often choose a route that will instill fear and maintain their position in power. Would you not agree?"

Vince cocks a brow at his mate and her tone. Rather than overriding her, as Devin's done to me, he smirks, nodding slightly and waiting for Devin's response.

"At times." He concedes as his hand finds mine under the table.

That feels far more like equality than "hush now, I'll fill you in later."

The fact that she is Vince's mate is the only reason I'm not terrified of her. Devin assured me. Hell, maybe I do trust him. I don't know what to think about anything anymore.

"I'm certain they're here because of last night." Veronica nods her head in agreement and runs her fingernails lightly along Vince's upturned hand, almost as if she's not aware she's touching him. My heart skips a beat. I wonder if she feels this too? This overwhelming need to be with her mate like I do with Devin.

It's heady and confusing. It feels like something else is taking over my body and, if I'm being honest, it's terrifying. The word "fate" has lost the comfort it used to hold.

"What do you mean?" I'm sure he's referring to the offering, but I don't understand what it has to do with them.

"Generally speaking, there isn't any resistance at the offerings. Mates go willingly. Humans hardly fight for those who don't mind being taken. You fainted after fighting me and Liz had to be carried out while she resisted and screamed."

I can feel the blood drain from my face. "Oh." I bite the inside of my cheek. They're here because they think we aren't their mates. Lizzie sulks in Caleb's arms.

"I'm certain the response to the scene has been less than pleasant on the human side of relations, which will piss off the Authority. They prefer to keep the masses content."

"They're discussing it now." Veronica stares at Vince's hand and continues running the tips of her fingers along his wrist as she speaks. "They're planning on taking them back." Her words send a jolt of anxiousness through me. I can't go back. I belong here, with Devin. Everything in me knows I'm meant to be with him. Even if we are struggling to find stable and common ground. I've barely been given a chance.

"Well, the Authority can go fuck themselves." Dom's seething baritone voice startles me, making me flinch. Devin's arm wraps around my waist and pulls me closer to him.

"There's no need to be hostile. I'm sure once they see Grace and Liz, they'll leave in peace."

"It might not be your intention, but it will end up being hostile." Veronica's eyes are still fixed on her playful touch. If she wasn't consistently speaking, I wouldn't think she was listening.

I dare to ask her, "Why's that?" I'm not leaving. The thought of never seeing Devin again makes my chest feel hollow. I won't let it happen.

Her dark eyes find mine and she gives me a small smile with her fangs digging into her full bottom lip. "Natalia's a bitch."

"How do you know Natalia?" Vince asks with curiosity. I fucking loathe that everyone knows everyone else except for me. With my complete attention, I glance between the two of them, determined to find my place and the confidence I used to have.

"She's the one who trained me." Her smile falls slightly.

"Trained you for what?"

"To kill werewolves." Devin's serious response, answering for Veronica, makes my blood run cold, causing goosebumps to run down my arms. I stare with wide eyes down the end of the table. *She kills werewolves?*

My breath leaves me and I feel light-headed.

"Times were much different back then." Her lips tilt down into a small frown before she schools her expression. "I don't participate in the sport anymore."

Vince's eyes smile with humor at the knowledge; he has no fear of his mate. He doesn't seem affected at all. He relaxes into his seat and takes her hand in his before sweetly kissing her knuckles. "Ain't fate a bitch." A soft smile plays at her lips, but her large eyes are full of pain and torture.

"You had your reasons." Devin's words are spoken with compassion and it eases my discomfort marginally. She nods slightly at Devin as a loud, melodic chime echoes in the room.

Devin inclines his head in silence and remains seated. At his nod, Jude stands up to answer the door. I watch as Dom positions Lizzie on his lap and Caleb angles his body so he's directly in front of her with his chest toward the entrance after giving her a small kiss on the cheek. He's still smiling faintly, but his silver eyes have a lethal look to them. Their defensive act puts me on edge. Devin pulls my chair closer to him and kisses my forehead before nuzzling his nose in my hair. "Everything is fine, sweetheart. They will not touch you."

"Promise me."

"Everything I tell you is a promise. My entire existence is a promise to you," he tells me and his confession is a balm, a drug. It's everything I didn't know I needed.

I close my eyes, enjoying his tender touch and when I open them the Authority, comprised of three foreboding figures, is staring back at me. My body tenses and my lungs still. The bit of soothing from Devin is powerless when I take in the intimidating trio.

There are two men and a woman, all three in black cloaks like the ones from the offering. The woman is obviously a vampire. She radiates seduction and power just as Veronica does. But her eyes are a shade darker than bloodred and there's no hint of the mischievousness that twinkles in Veronica's brown eyes. Only wickedness exists in her gaze. Her thin lips curl up at one end, revealing a sharp fang. Her pale skin and sunken cheeks make her appear older than Veronica. Much, much older. The sight of her sends an unwanted chill down my spine.

The men are both large, similar to Devin, but not as bulky or muscular. The man on the right, carrying a large black duffle bag, has silver eyes and the crooked smile of a man not to be trusted. The one on the left is devilishly handsome with a smile that seems charming and inviting, plus the lightest blue eyes I've ever seen. The skin around his eyes wrinkles when he smiles, giving away his older age. But his dimples pull you in with a boyish charm. His presence is instantly calming, negating the fear the other two instill.

"Good afternoon." Devin is short, but cordial. His hard voice snaps me out of my daze.

"I suppose the blood on the driveway doesn't belong to your mates?" The silver-eyed man speaks first.

Every bit of me feels cold from his words. It's not a traveling chill; it happens all at once.

A low growl rumbles from Dom's chest, but Devin remains unaffected, merely cocking a brow. "We would not harm our mates. I'm sure you could smell that it's shifter blood."

"So they do in fact belong to you?" His choice of words makes me snort. They may be intimidating as all hell, but I can't help my reaction. It doesn't go unnoticed. When the cloaked fucker eyes me, I just smirk. It's slightly forced, but still. With Devin's possessive hold on me growing tighter, a sense of confidence spreads through me.

"Grace and Lizzie, meet Natalia, Remy and Alec." They each nod in turn and I give them a tight smile while they take seats at the far end of the table. It's quiet as the legs of the chairs drag across the floor. Alec and Devin seem to engage in a quiet conversation before Alec's eyes settle on Dom and his lips press into a firm, hard line.

"I see. We'll need them to give a statement. The *humans* want it to be done live," Natalia speaks with annoyance thick in her tone. "I'm so glad they rightfully belong to you. It would've been a shame to start off on such poor terms."

A nervousness pricks at my skin and the thinly veiled admission of violence brings an anger out of me, one that seems intensified. Every emotion seems to swing back and forth like a wild pendulum.

"We have an issue that needs to be attended to. Also, as you know, we've just met our mates and the claiming is only two days away. So the sooner we can get this over with, the better."

"Eager to throw us out, old friend?" Alec smiles with a light dancing in his eyes.

"I'd like to tend to my mate's needs. I'd throw out my mother if she were still alive." Caleb's humorous response gains a laugh from Alec and a huff of humor from Lev. Dom is still obviously on edge, but then again, his hard glare and scowl never seem to leave him.

"We've all had a long night getting acquainted with our mates, and familiarizing them with their new lives. We'd like to continue getting them settled as soon as possible."

"Of course. Where would you like to set up?" Devin stands. He looks down at me, still seated and offers me his hand. I place my small hand in his, taking his lead and having faith that all is well. A trace of a smile graces his lips for just a moment. The rest of the pack follows suit as he leads us to a large front room. A single pane of glass lines the side wall overlooking a forest. The view is spectacular and the sight of it reminds me that I haven't even had a tour of my new home.

I barely know anything at all.

I search the large room for Lizzie to gauge her reaction and find her small frame molded to Caleb's body. Her shoulders are hunched forward and the familiar smile I'm accustomed to is nowhere to be found. She looks utterly lost. My heart shatters at the sight of her. My bubbly, spirited best friend is shadowed by a dark cloud.

I hate this. I hate how all of this happened. Somehow, it feels as if it's my fault. Every bit of it.

"Lizzie—" I start to say as I take a step forward to go to her side, but Devin's grip tightens, halting my movement. He leans down to whisper in my ear.

"Not now." I grit my teeth and prepare to shove him away, but Lizzie catches my eyes and smiles at me. It's not a weak smile, but not quite a happy smile either.

She mouths, "I'm all right." I tilt my head and she adds, "I promise," with a brighter smile that reaches her eyes. My heart squeezes in my chest. I haven't had a single moment alone with her yet. She was already sitting with Dom and Caleb when I came into the kitchen with Devin. I didn't get to say a damn word to her before Veronica arrived.

"As soon as we're done, you can have some alone time, all right?" Devin whispers, tickling my ear.

Staring straight into his stunning silver gaze, I tell him, "I swear to God I'll kill you if you can read my mind."

His low chuckle makes me smile. It doesn't go unnoticed that the three members of the Authority watch every interaction like hawks.

There are three dark gray sofas in the room. One long, high-back sofa serves as a focal point, facing a large brick fireplace on the back wall. The other two are smaller and on either side of the first, loosely forming a U. Remy sets up a camera and microphone in front of the fireplace and positions them toward the large sofa.

"This is already going better than expected," Remy comments offhandedly as he does.

"Have a seat." Alec motions toward the longer sofa and I sit close to the middle while catching Lizzie's eyes so she'll know to sit next to me. She follows my lead and takes my hand in a firm grasp as she gets comfortable. Devin sits to my left and places a firm hand on my thigh.

"Maybe it's best if only one of you accompanies your mate. Perhaps Caleb?" Natalia purrs as Caleb and Dom both prepare to sit next to Lizzie. The two of them share a look for a moment and then Dom nods, giving Lizzie a small kiss before stalking to a smaller sofa.

"Your statements will need to be genuine. You cannot mention anything about being mates." Lizzie nods as Alec gives his instructions.

"What exactly can we and can't we—" I start to ask, but the bitch in the corner interrupts me.

"Do you think you could control your mate, Devin?" Natalia asks with a devilish smirk.

"He doesn't need to control me," I practically snarl.

"She'll be fine." His large hand finds mine, but I refuse to take it. I didn't ask for this. It's not right and perhaps I am bitter I've been lied to my entire life before being plucked from my existence and thrown into a world with entirely new rules. Even worse, I'm given no grace in that fact.

"I don't believe it." The vampire turns away dismissively and faces Remy. "She's going to ruin everything. It can't be live."

Remy responds as though we aren't in the room. "We should just give them back; it's not worth the risk."

"There's no risk. Grace will follow my lead."

"I don't believe you. It's obvious you have no control over her." Remy dips his chin toward Devin's hand on my thigh and adds, "She can't even follow simple commands."

"I listen to my mate." My nostrils flare slightly as I try to get a grip on my composure. I hate that this prick is getting to me.

"I want to see you bow to him then." A smug smile crosses his face and I have an intense urge to smack it off.

"My mate is only concerned with what pleases me." Power and anger radiate from Devin. Remy noticeably cowers and Natalia narrows her eyes at him, obviously displeased by his reaction to my mate's harsh tone.

Devin's dominance suffocates the room and it's a heady feeling. Devin's silver eyes pierce mine. His aggravation lingers in his words, but I know it's not intended for me. "Do you think it would please me to have you bow to me simply because *he*," he sneers the word, "wants you to?"

Pride flows through me as I relax my shoulders and lean into him to stare into his gaze. "I think it would please you if I sucked your dick in front of them." I purr with a flirtatious smile as my hand gently strokes his inner thigh. I must still be in heat because the idea turns me on. I hadn't intended for the comment to be taken seriously, but as I picture myself on my knees between his legs, taking his cock into my mouth in front of everyone to see, a warmth flutters in my lower belly. So much so that I almost drop to my knees in front of him. My aching core clenches in need as I lick my lips.

"These are the mates that gave you so much trouble? A broken wolf and a bitch in heat?" Natalia's words break the haze of lust clouding my judgment. Alec looks between his two companions with obvious revulsion.

Dom snarls and Caleb's smile slips as he glares at Natalia.

"Enough!" Alec reprimands his colleagues.

My heart hurts for Lizzie. *Broken wolf.* She blows off the comment with the joyful laugh she's known for, all while shrugging and rolling her eyes. I know it hurts her, though. I can see it in her expression.

"Carol will be here in five. Then we'll get this press conference done and over with." Alec walks to the window to study the forest with a stern look on his face. I don't understand how he's aligned with the two of these pricks. I'm also not sure who he is. Or *what* he is.

"I see you have a new pet, Veronica." Remy's eyes travel along Veronica's body with obvious desire. It surprises me since I figured he was *with* Natalia. Even more unexpected is Natalia's heated gaze at his comment.

"I'm her mate." Vince's strong voice is relaxed. He's not threatened in the least. The lack of offense seems to take the wind out of Remy's sails.

"You let the dogs speak for you now?" Natalia picks up where Remy left off. *What a fucking bitch!* All eyes turn to Veronica for her response. She tilts her chin up slightly and leans into Vince's embrace, which makes him smile. She kisses his cheek and then turns to face me.

"Don't mind the bitch in heat comment," she says and I meet Veronica's dark eyes. "You can't help the heat, and there's nothing wrong with being a bitch." She turns in Vince's arms and starts to lead him toward the hall.

"You're turning your back on the Authority, sweetheart?" Natalia casually calls out with a cocked brow.

Veronica offers up the same threatening smirk in return and answers easily. "My back, no, but I've been known to turn a blind eye. Wouldn't you agree, darling?" The older vampire pales and her thin lips press into a hard line.

"Come, pup, this doesn't concern us. You need to show me around." She grins deviously and takes his hand as she waltzes to the doorway. "Start with your bedroom. I have a treat for you."

He flashes her an asymmetric grin and says, "Yes, Mistress." Watching the massive, rugged beast allow his small, feminine mate to lead him away from us makes me smile.

CHAPTER SEVEN

Dom

The sofa groans as I sit back in the seat, but then I immediately lean forward, the nervousness refusing to let go of me. Fuck, I hate that I'm not sitting next to her. Carol bursts through the door in her typical melodramatic fashion. She pops a stick of gum in her mouth and removes her earbuds. The noise flowing from them fills the room. It's a wonder she's not deaf.

Clearing my throat, I attempt to relax but it's next to impossible. The only piece of this situation keeping me steady is that Caleb is right there. Just like I would, he'd give up his life to protect her if anything happened. It offers little relief, though.

Carol smiles brightly as she enters. "So, where are my humans?" Her singsong voice bounces off the walls. She reminds me of Lizzie as she waltzes across the room with confidence. Back before I got ahold of my mate, she had the same carefree air. The thought makes my scowl deepen.

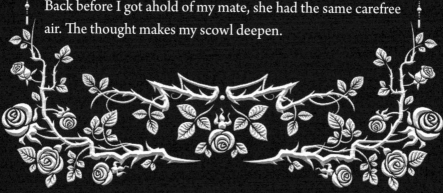

She stands in front of my mate and gasps looking between Caleb and myself. Pointing her finger at the two of us Carol says, "Well, well, congrats to you, lovely lady. A ménage à trois mating; now that's something you don't see every day." Lizzie's cheeks blaze and that faint change in her makes me long for her. To touch her, to run the back of my hand down her cheek and nip the curve of her neck playfully.

Instead, my fingers steeple together in my lap and I sit with this emptiness on my own.

"Fate has certainly blessed you, little human." Her eyebrows raise and she takes one of Lizzie's small hands in both of hers. "Good luck taming these two." Caleb bellows a laugh and Lizzie smiles shyly.

"She's wolf," I say, correcting Carol. "Latent." I say the words with pride; nonetheless Lizzie's smile falls, and she recoils into Caleb. I wish I'd kept my stupid mouth shut. I can't do a damn thing right by her.

"Oh." Carol perks up even more and says, "Well that's wonderful, dear." She purses her lips and taps her heel. "But it's a PR nightmare." My brow creases and Carol answers my unasked question. "A latent wolf on human territory?" She shakes her head. "It'll be called a conspiracy, of course. That we set her up as a spy of sorts." She tsks. "It's a shame, but we're going to have to stay with the human version."

"We're on in five." Alec positions a chair angled toward the sofa and turns the camera on, extending a screen and flipping it so we can view the human newscasters.

"All right, Daddy," Carol answers him easily.

"Daddy?" Grace's curious look almost makes me smile. Devin is going to have his hands full answering our Alpha mate's questions after this morning. She truly has been thrown to the wolves.

"He's not *really* my daddy." Carol winks at Grace and takes a seat, fixing her skirt and tucking a strand of hair behind her ear. She flashes her pearly whites and asks, "No lipstick, right?" She sucks at her teeth while Grace shakes her head, grinning at Carol. A warmth settles through me as I watch Lizzie relax. Carol and Grace are good for her.

Maybe Grace doesn't realize it, but she set the mood the moment we walked in here. Devin's appraising gaze tells me he's aware of it as well. It provides an unexpected comfort.

"She'll be all right." Caleb's words sound in my head as he pats Lizzie's knee and kisses her forehead. A faint blush appears on her cheeks. I love the look of her flushed skin.

"Okay, ladies and gents, I'll field the questions. You just play along." Caleb and Devin nod slightly as Lizzie fidgets with her fingers until Grace takes her hand and squeezes. "Any questions? It's now or never." Grace shakes her head and Lizzie follows suit.

It seems just then that Grace looks down at her outfit and realizes she's going on camera in sweatpants and a simple gray T-shirt. Lizzie is just as casual in worn, faded jeans and a blush tank top. Both of their faces fresh, without an ounce of makeup on.

From one event to the next, they're thrown into it with no warning. Grace's unease comes and goes quickly as she squares her shoulders. I don't miss Devin's hand squeezing hers either.

Alec hands Carol a mic that she immediately turns on and taps lightly. The sound vibrates through the room, making her smile. There's an innocence in Carol that hundreds of decades of violence have yet to break.

"There's a five-second delay in case we need to cut the feed." Alec speaks only to Carol as he gets behind the camera. "We're live in three, two ..." He finishes by mouthing *one.*

"Hello, Carol." We hear a woman's voice from the screen.

"Hi, Amber. How are you this evening?" Carol's sweet voice takes on an edge of professionalism. It's her mask for the humans. Far less theatrical. She's the Authority's PR dream.

"We're all a bit anxious over here to see the state of Elizabeth Weatherly and Grace Windom. I can see they're sitting with you now. Is that right?" The news anchor's dress shirt remains stiff when she leans in slightly, as if she could get a better view. Her anxiousness is more than obvious and the back of my neck heats with a tingle.

"They are. I can assure you that I was just as anxious watching the offering of Shadow Falls as it aired on the news and saw the clips that were shared on social media. The Authority was prepared to take action and mete out justice had the werewolves of Shadow Falls violated the law. We will always honor our pact with the human nation. However, we have no desire to interfere in this case. As you can see, both humans are doing well. The Authority's investigation has determined that no laws were broken."

"Carol, I have to ask. Why is it that there was such a difference at this offering? We're given so little information that the sight of the Shadow Falls incident was very disturbing for the human population." The anchor drops her tone, matching the somber expression on her face when she adds, "It reminded us all of much darker times."

"As we promised years ago when we formed our alliance, we will not allow supernatural beings to harm humans that reside in areas of treaties." Carol answers with an air of authority and confidence. "Unfortunately, this offering was different due to the mistraining of a wolf. The werewolf collecting Elizabeth Weatherly was given poor advice on how to handle humans. As you can imagine, a paranormal being's touch can be intimidating and forceful." Carol turns in her seat to face Lizzie and tells her, "I can only imagine how scared you were." Her eyes and tone turn sympathetic. "Would you like to tell us how you were feeling during the offering?"

A chill spreads through me and I swear my heart stops. The gulp of Lizzie's swallow is audible.

Lizzie's arms wrap around her midsection as she answers, nodding her head. "I wasn't so much scared as I was shocked when he grabbed me. I wasn't expecting it and then ... Without knowing what would happen, I reacted without thinking." Her voice is small but firm. She tacks on an apology. "I'm sorry." The shock I feel in this moment is genuine.

It takes everything in me not to comfort her, not to tell her she has no reason to be sorry.

"*Stay still.*" Devin's command comes with a force that bows my head. Gritting my teeth, I shut down every emotion. *"We're live,"* he reminds me.

"And how were you feeling, Miss Windom?"

The attention moves to Grace, all of our eyes on her. "I was startled and genuinely scared for Lizzie. She's been my friend for as long as I can remember. She obviously wasn't okay." Grace's eyes find Lizzie's and she squeezes her hand. "My reaction was purely one of trying to help a friend."

"How are the two of you feeling today? Now that you've had time to adjust."

Lizzie and Grace both smile sweetly into the camera. "Oh, much better," Grace answers with a hint of comedic flare that seems to resonate with the anchor. Her lips turn up slightly. "We're much better today." Grace answers for them both.

"I can't tell you two enough how much the nation is relieved to see that you're happy and well." Carol faces the camera again. "Do you have any more questions for us, Amber?"

The woman on the screen doesn't hesitate to ask, her words rushed, "What is the purpose of the offering? For what reason were they taken?"

Carol's smile slips and she turns solemn. "Unfortunately, I'm unable to divulge that information at this time." I cross my arms and lean farther back in my seat. That's the Authority's game. Keep us separated and divided with a lack of information. "I know that you're aware of those limitations, Amber. Any final questions?"

"Are we going to see these two young women again? Can we be updated on their status?" The newscaster sounds hopeful.

A moment passes, a beat in which Carol doesn't immediately respond, providing me with the thought that someone in this room is speaking to Carol silently.

"That's a possibility, Amber." My eyes flash to Carol. That would be a first. She must be lying. "We understand there is unease in the unknown, and we are doing everything we can to dispel your fears of our species." She smiles so sincerely at the camera. She's such a fucking liar.

I watch my mate force a smile for the camera as they wrap up this charade.

"I need one of you for the fucker in the shed." Devin's words sound in my head. Apparently he's over this and already making plans for the soon-to-be-dead shifter. I'd nearly forgotten about him. My hands form fists at the memory of what Vince told us the rival pack had intended to do to my mate.

I nod. *"I'm all yours."*

"You want me to take care of Lizzie on my own?"

My lips turn down even further at Caleb's question. *"I'm sure she'd rather it just be you."*

"Knock it off."

I don't respond. It's obvious she reacts differently to his touch versus mine. *Why wouldn't she?* Caleb doesn't look like the prick who tortured her. I do. I don't know how to make it right. I can't change the past. I'm just grateful she's going to let me claim her.

That simple fact is proof there's no justice in this world. But I will care for her every way I know how until she feels how much I love her, and until she knows she's safe with me in every sense of the word.

After the niceties have finished, the screen turns black with a loud click and the members of the Authority are quick to move about. That prick Remy starts packing up the camera and Devin stands.

"We ask for a moment," Devin speaks and doesn't wait for a response. Instead he gestures for the pack to head back to the kitchen, leaving Carol with an arched brow. Alec acknowledges Devin's request with a nod before moving beside him as the rest of us continue forward.

I walk behind my mate with my hand on the small of her back. When she leans into my touch slightly, I wrap my arm around her waist. She molds her body to mine with a small sigh. And then she looks up. The small smile vanishes and she noticeably withdraws. It takes all of my effort to remain holding her. She'll get used to it. It fucking hurts, like a damn punch to my chest, but both of us will get past this.

Thankfully I'm distracted. I overhear Alec and Devin's conversation.

"I'm sorry, Dev. I hope you know that I was truly hoping you'd found your rightful mate."

Alpha nods and slaps a hand on Alec's shoulder. "I hold no ill will against you, Alec. I understand how it looked."

"I'm pleased we can part on good terms." Alec pauses before adding, "I may need you soon." This catches Devin's attention and he stops in the hallway as the rest of the pack files into the kitchen, while Remy and Natalia remain in the front room. I stay behind to listen in, making sure my presence is known. Devin gives a slight nod and I get comfortable, leaning against the wall with my arms crossed over my chest. As I listen, I watch Caleb lead Lizzie down the hall to our new room. Jealousy races through me as she takes his hand easily.

"Have you heard about the attacks?"

Devin inclines his head slightly, keeping his expression emotionless.

"The vampires are not faring well now that we're limiting their food supply."

"Then lift the law. It seems simple enough." I agree with Devin. It was a stupid law to begin with.

"Unfortunately, the Authority disagrees. The majority are against it. They don't see a need to drink from a vein when there are other options available. Especially when taking blood from an untested source is the number one cause of sickness in the vampire population."

"Veronica mentioned her coven wanting some changes made to the way the blood banks are run in Shadow Falls."

"Did she now?" Alec's tone holds a curiosity that hints at something I can't quite place.

"She made it clear that the humans wouldn't be privy to any information regarding vampires." Devin's quick to defend Veronica. I nod in agreement again. Not that it's needed. She's Vince's mate and we will support her. Given what happened last night, with the other shifters and their attempt to kidnap Grace and Lizzie, I consider myself personally in her debt.

"That would be paramount."

"Is this the way of it now, donations from humans?"

"Perhaps. But the few that have been running have had disturbing results," Alec confides in Devin and the hairs on the back of my neck stand up.

"How's that?"

"Several vampires have gone missing."

"Surely humans aren't abducting vampires?" Natalia and Remy pause their conversation in the other room as Natalia's wicked eyes drift to Devin and Alec.

"It's not certain what is occurring."

"I see."

"I just hope that if I need to call on you, you'll be at the ready."

"As always, Alec." The two men brace their hands on each other's shoulders. "Next time it would be beneficial for you to come alone." Devin stares at Natalia as he says the last word, startling her. I stifle my grin. Alec chuckles and signals for the two vile beings to leave with him.

It's not until the front door closes that Devin meets me at the threshold of the kitchen.

"Good riddance." I don't hide my disgust for that bitch who called my sweet mate *broken*.

"Agreed. But he had to bring backup in case we had …" Devin trails off as his eyes find Grace. Clearing his throat, he murmurs so his mate can't hear, "We'll take care of the issue in the shed in just a moment." I remain at my spot on the wall as I watch my Alpha take his mate in his arms. She noticeably relaxes in his embrace the very second he touches her. One day. One day soon, I will have that with my mate.

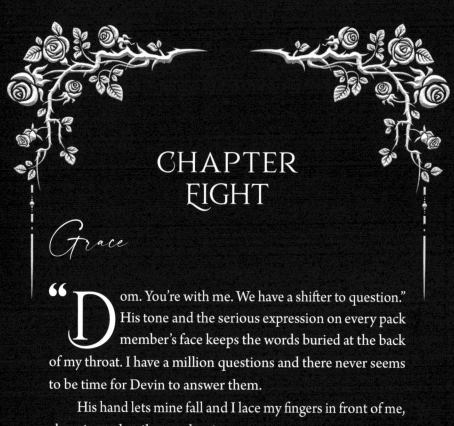

CHAPTER EIGHT

Grace

"Dom. You're with me. We have a shifter to question."
His tone and the serious expression on every pack
member's face keeps the words buried at the back
of my throat. I have a million questions and there never seems
to be time for Devin to answer them.

His hand lets mine fall and I lace my fingers in front of me,
choosing to be silent and wait.

I watch Devin and Dom walk out of the kitchen. His broad
shoulders and corded muscles ripple as he stretches out his back
and cracks his knuckles.

I have no idea who the hell they're going to "question" but
I'm certain they'll be getting whatever information they want
out of him. There's a thick tension that can't be denied in the
room. Dom's almost as tall as Devin. The sight of the two of
them is intimidating. Just watching Devin move with the skill
of a predator sends a chill down my spine. But knowing what's

underneath that white T-shirt has butterflies fluttering deep and low in longing. I stifle my moan. I am, without a doubt, still in heat.

I hope he isn't long. I notice Lev and Jude smirk at each other before Lev opens his mouth.

"You're drooling a little there." His response makes me huff and with Devin and Dom gone, I'm given a bit of relief. The first bit of it I've felt all day actually.

It's one thing after another, and at that thought, I remember the vampire.

"I'm just a bitch in heat, remember?" I can't help the insecurity from slipping out. In an instant, the two shifters tense.

"She's a bitch and she *wishes* she could go into heat." I smile a little at Jude's flat remark. Patting his hand in thanks as I get up from the kitchen table, I go to search the cabinets. Lizzie's going to need coffee. She's a pain in the ass when she goes through caffeine withdrawal and given everything that's happening, her coffee fix is the last thing on her mind and her mates won't know what hit them. I wish Caleb hadn't taken her the second the interview was over.

I need my friend. I need to know she's truly okay and that everything will be all right. My throat gets tight, but I simply swallow and busy myself.

"Where's the coffeepot?" I ask as I stand on my tiptoes looking into the upper cabinets searching for some kind of coffee maker.

"We don't have one." I accidently slam the door shut in shock at Jude's words.

"How do you not have a coffee maker?" *Seriously?* They have granite counters and top-of-the-line appliances, but no coffee maker?

"Easy," Lev says, shrugging his shoulders, "we don't drink it."

"Well, that's not going to work. Then you'll really see me be a bitch and Liz will top that. I can guarantee you that." Opening the fridge, I grab the orange juice, but then my nose scrunches and I put the bottle back when I remember Lev drank from it. We're going to have to set up boundaries. I tap my foot while looking through the fridge. Maybe

I'll write my name on my groceries. I have to take a deep breath and remind myself that this is my home. My new home. A mix of emotions comes over me and it's hard to keep my composure.

"I need to buy some things I think …" Instantly, I'm reminded of something I've lost.

"Lev, do you know where my clutch is?"

"Clutch?"

"The little purse I had at the offering." I point to my wrist and shake it as if that'll give him a clue.

His forehead creases. "I don't think he'd like it if you called someone, Grace."

"I just need to run to the store. Whatever store you all go to, I assume it's like any other grocery store?" I question, careful with my words. Lev nods easily enough. Thank God. I need some sort of normalcy.

"Good. I need to get a few things. You can keep my phone. It's not like I'm going to see anyone ever again." The thought makes my heart sink a bit, but I just sigh and shake it off. There are things you can control and things you can't. I learned that a long time ago. There's no use in pining over something I can't have.

"If you want to see someone, Devin will make it happen. You know that, right?"

"No, I don't know that." My words are tight as I whisper. I don't know nearly enough. It feels like I'm falling aimlessly and it's not a feeling I'm used to. There's nothing to grab onto or steady myself with. My gaze drifts to the door. I already miss Devin.

"The Authority likes to monitor interactions between species. But he'd move the world for you. You'd just have to keep it on the down low, you know?" I let his words sink in, but then brush them off.

"It's fine, really," I reassure them both and lean against the counter. I huff a humorless laugh. "Who am I going to call anyway? Shadow Falls is a small town full of asshats." It's still nice to think that Devin would piss off the Authority if I wanted to break their laws.

I give him a small, tight smile. "I don't need my phone; I doubt anyone will miss me anyway." Their eyes turn sad and they need to stop that. "Knock it off. The one person I give a shit about is here with me." I point my finger at them. "And you better believe if she hadn't been Dom and Caleb's mate, then we would've smuggled her here." A smile pulls at my lips. I would beg Devin to move heaven and earth to make that happen if she wasn't here with me.

Reaching back into the fridge, I settle on lemonade. There's only a little missing from the top so, at most, only one set of lips has been on it.

"Anyway, I need my clutch so I can grab some stuff from the store. I don't have much cash, but it's enough." I have almost a grand in savings. "Do you guys use banks?" Jude gives me a sexy grin that makes his clean-cut marine look turn bad boy.

"Which bank do you use?"

"S and N." I tilt my head and frown. "What's so funny?"

"Devin owns that one. And Union Trust." My eyes bulge. *Oh shit.*

"How did you think we make money?"

"I hadn't really thought of that." His words start to sink in as I set the lemonade down. Glancing around the kitchen, it's obvious the pack is wealthy. But ... my mate owns banks? Never in a million years would I think the banks were owned by shifters. "That's odd."

They both grin at me. "How's that odd?" I shrug. I suppose it's not that abnormal, seeing as how the powerful are the ones who control wealth, aren't they? And Devin is quite powerful. "Well, you don't need to worry about money; Devin got you a card to use."

"So what am I supposed to do here?" I fidget uncomfortably before crossing my arms and leaning against the counter. A small voice in my head whispers, *"Be the Alpha's baby maker."* The thought makes me shiver with delight, but at the same time, I long for more.

I barely know him. Yet I feel as if I know him more than anyone. I need far more time to get a grasp on this life before I can even think of bringing another into this world.

"Whatever you want." A stinging sensation travels down my body and my heart slows. *Whatever I want.* It's surreal. Tears prick at my eyes and I don't even know why. Wiping them away, I try to compose myself. What the hell is wrong with me? Lev gets up from the table with a concerned look on his face. "You okay, Grace?"

I nod as he places a hand on my shoulder. "Yeah, I just … I just don't know what to say." I can do *anything* I want. I sit with those words for a beat. *I can do whatever the hell I want to do.*

I worked so damn hard at too many shit jobs just to escape my dad. I doubt he even cares that I'm gone. I'll never have to work for a lazy asshole again and smile at pricks who come in just to complain to someone. I'll never have to get up at the break of dawn because my irresponsible coworker has a hangover and can't work their shift. I don't have to worry about money. No shuffling payment dates around just so we can make it through the month. My grip tightens on the counter just to stay upright. I never really thought much about any of that. It was just something I had to do. Day in and day out. It was one more thing to survive. Everyone has to do it. And now I don't. I can do anything, yet I have no idea what I should do. I don't even know what I *want* to do. I don't think I've ever dreamed beyond what I could reasonably attain.

Once, Lizzie and I talked about opening our own bookstore; we practically ran the place ourselves anyway. But it wasn't anything that could be a reality. I knew better than to dream for something I'd never have. Hell, I'd just barely been able to escape the shit hand I'd been dealt. I absolutely loved my tiny apartment with Lizzie and making the best with what we had. Other than Lizzie, I had nothing. Nothing worth anything. Thank God I had her.

At least I knew who I was, though. I was the tough bitch with her shit together. I knew life would get better one day and that as long as Lizzie and I were together, we'd survive and make the best of every situation. But who am I now? Devin just bulldozed his way through my life and I don't know what's left in the rubble. I should be grateful; I *am* grateful. But other emotions rage through me. Surprisingly, fear is the overriding one. Am I just supposed to lie down for him and let him knock me up? Which brings me back to my scare this morning. I need birth control.

"I need to get some things." I bite the inside of my cheek, making a mental list. The morning-after pill is listed at the very top. "I know Liz is going to want coffee. Do you have, like, a werewolf coffeehouse?" They grin again.

"You can order whatever you want and have it delivered."

"What if I want to go out and go shopping?" I'm sure as hell not staying here like a prisoner. Even if it is a gilded cage.

"There are a few shopping malls a few towns over. Right now may not be the best time for you to go alone with everything going on."

"What exactly is going on?" All I know is that this morning the werewolves talked to one another silently. And I sat beside Devin with him reassuring me that I would be told everything later.

"It's a bit of a drive but if you want to get out of here, we can take you."

"Way to dodge the question," I retort.

Lev throws his hands up in defeat. "Just name someplace," he suggests and his tone is nearly pleading. "We'll take you."

"What about the nearest coffeehouse?"

With an uncomfortable demeanor, he tells me, "Sorry, Grace, you'll have to order it and have it delivered, but I can take you to one of the malls after?"

I nod. That's not a bad option.

"Let's order Lizzie's coffee and head out so I can pick up some stuff. Which room is hers?"

As I ask the question, Vince strolls into the kitchen wearing sweats, no shirt, and has a belt draped around his neck. The buckle of it hits him in the chest a few times while he walks and a look of irritation crosses his face before he swings it over one shoulder.

"Yo, what're you guys talking about?" He grins mischievously, heading to the fridge.

"Shopping trip." Jude gives a clipped response.

"Ah, I think Veronica said she wanted to go out and get coffee." My lips purse at the mention of Veronica.

"Do you like it when she calls you 'pup?'" I blurt out but the question is riddled with my judgmental tone. Shit. If I could suck the words back in, I would. There's no doubt in my mind the fact she's a vampire has colored my opinion of her. And every detail of what she does. I immediately regret asking, but Vince doesn't take offense. *Thank God.*

"Like it? I love it." He smiles like a proud kid who just won a spelling bee and grabs a soda. Lev snorts a laugh and Jude chuckles.

"Seriously?"

"Yeah. I fucking *love* it when she calls me pup."

"Isn't it like … a little degrading?" I can't help but to ask.

"What's your favorite color?" A broad smile spreads across his face as he leans against the granite counters.

"What?"

"What's your favorite color?" He repeats his question with strained humor.

"Purple."

"Why?"

"Why what?"

"Why is it your favorite color?" A smug look crosses his face.

I nod as I pick up on the point he's making. "There doesn't have to be a reason."

"Exactly." He claps his hands loud in front of him.

"Don't you feel disrespected, though?" His brow furrows and a small frown pulls his lips down. Maybe I pushed too far. Damn my stupid mouth. He finally shakes his head.

"Not at all. I'm earning her pleasure." His smile returns. "And she's earning my trust. Fuck, she has my trust. I know she's going to take care of me." Lev and Jude choke out a laugh again as he tosses the belt back over his shoulder. "Fucking thing keeps getting in my way, though."

"It's just like you and Dev. Isn't it?" Lev asks. My eyes narrow. Fuck no, this isn't like us at all. "He's earning your trust, isn't he?"

"Yeah, but not like that." Vince lets out a bellowing chortle and his silver eyes brighten.

"It works both ways, sweetie. Just because our kink's a bit different from yours doesn't change anything. He's gaining your desire to please him, isn't he? And proving that you can trust him to make sure your every desire and need are met?" I let out a small hum in contemplation.

His words sink in as he strides out of the room, but I end up focusing on a single question.

How can Devin be ensuring my every need and want are met, when I don't even know what I want or need anymore?

CHAPTER NINE

Lizzie

"She called you a broken wolf." The cool air slips against my heated skin at Caleb's words.

He said he would take my pain and turn it into pleasure. We decided together… but this is different. If only I snap my fingers, it all ends. I know that much and hearing him repeat the words, *broken wolf*, has the thought at the forefront of my mind.

I'm naked, on my knees with my head and chest lying on the foot of our bed. I hear Caleb unbuckle his belt and a flood of mixed emotions dries my throat and makes my hands tremble while simultaneously heating my core. "You didn't defend yourself. You hid your emotions and blew it off as though it doesn't matter." He bends down with his mouth at my ear and whispers, "It matters. Don't hide your feelings from me. I'll ask you again and this time there will be consequences if you lie to me. I refuse to let you hide." He straightens his back and runs the leather down my spine, tickling my skin and sending goosebumps down my body. "Tell me how you felt when she called you broken."

My heart races and emotions swarm up my throat.

I don't want to talk about it. I don't want to admit how much pain it caused, how many memories resurfaced ... I don't want to think about it and make it all real again. I lived in happiness for years, avoiding the truth. It doesn't have to be real. I don't have to acknowledge it. Caleb's wrong; it doesn't matter.

"I don't care." I can barely give him my answer. It's the same answer I gave him last time and the time before that. The answer I know will push him to punish me. He'll take care of me after. And I want that. I crave it in a way that drives me to keep this going. I don't know how to explain it. I want this over and over, because in the end, he's going to make it better. He has to. He's my mate.

Smack! I jump as the belt whips through the air and lands hard on my bare thighs, just below my ass. I breathe through clenched teeth, hissing at the pain. Tears cloud my vision. But I'm used to them. Just like I'm used to the pain.

"They called you broken and you don't care?" My head is so dizzy, it takes me a moment to realize he's waiting for an answer as he rubs the swollen, red marks. His cool touch soothes my heated skin. Caleb's fingers are dangerously close to slipping between my legs. I'd rather he touch me there, but he'd rather whip me. Punish me for not admitting I'm damaged. *Fuck him*. He's not getting that from me. He can beat me until I'm black and blue. Just like all the others. Just like Dom's father. Burying my head into the sheets, I tell myself that's not true. My head thrashes and the splinters of pain deepen. I know all I have to do is tell him it hurts, not the punishing blows, but the fact that I'm broken.

"You care, don't you?" This question is spoken in a softened voice. Staring straight ahead, I don't want to tell him I do, because then what? Is he going to make me face the past?

"No." I brace myself, preparing for the blow that's coming. *Smack*! The belt lands across my ass, making my blood rush violently in my ears.

"Why do you lie to me? Why do you lie to yourself?"

"I'm not lying!" Tears prick my eyes and I let them fall. *Smack!* My skin burns from the repeated strikes of the leather. I find myself pushing against the sweet sting. My pussy clenches in anticipation.

"Stop lying. Tell me how you feel." His tone is tortured. I shake my head as tears fall down my face. Why am I lying again? I can make this stop. I can stop this by just admitting the truth. I shake my head harder. I don't want it to be real.

"She called you broken. How does that make you feel?" I keep refusing to answer. My body trembles as he gently runs the leather across my tender ass. "Answer me!" He's going to belt me again. But I don't want it anymore. I don't want this anymore. My skin is hot and sensitive, each smack bringing me closer to the edge of something else. That's all I want. I want to fall off the edge.

"Caleb," I plead with him.

He lowers his lips to my ear after kissing the crook of my neck and says, "Tell me, tell me."

"Worthless. It makes me feel like a failure." I sob, gasping for air as the pain of my admission flashes through me. It's out. The words flew out of my mouth without my conscious consent. I'm so worthless. A wolf who can't shift. I don't know what's wrong with me. I don't know if I can ever be fixed. "I'm useless. Like I shouldn't be alive." The belt falls to the floor with a loud thud and in an instant Caleb is on me, pulling me up and cradling me in his arms.

"You're none of those things. You're perfect." The words rush out of him and then his lips devour mine. Everything ceases to exist.

I cling to him as he pulls me into his chest and rocks me. There's a sweet sting of pain and pleasure as my ass settles against his thigh. "Look at me." I stare into his silver eyes as he kisses my nose and rests his forehead on mine. He whispers, "You're not broken." My lips part to object. Of course I am. "You were made with perfection. Including your latency." The word makes me flinch. He takes my chin in his hand with a firm grasp. My eyes are caught by his fierce gaze. "You are a latent wolf.

205

And you are fucking perfect." The sincerity and love are undeniable in his admission.

Hot tears prick again and this time I welcome them. His adoration heats my core. Slamming my mouth against his, I push him against the mattress and climb over his hard body. He moans into my mouth. I rock against him and grind into his throbbing erection. My blood heats and races through my body.

I want to thank him for loving me. I'm desperate to please him. Making my way down his body with openmouthed kisses, I nip at his hip bones as he takes out his cock for me. I stroke his thick length as he throws his head back. My lips wrap around the head of his cock and I can barely fit it in my mouth. My teeth scrape lightly against his hardened flesh.

"Open your mouth wider." I do as I'm told, stretching my jaw to accommodate his size. I lick at the bead of precum at the head before bobbing along his length. His hands run through my hair before pushing his length into the back of my throat. I swallow and his girth is almost more than I can comfortably take. My eyes sting and water before he pulls back, allowing me to breathe again.

"Bite me." I look up at him wide eyed. *Bite him?*

"Come on, baby girl … Bite me." His voice is breathy but still full of authority. He's close to his release. My teeth close around his dick and I bite down, digging into the velvety steel of his flesh.

"Harder." Clamping my mouth shut again, I push my teeth into him. If I bite any harder, I know I'll break skin. I pause, waiting for his next direction. He fists my hair and pulls my head back, causing a small bit of pain. "Bite me like you want to hurt me. Bite me, baby." He's breathing hard and barely able to get the words through his clenched teeth.

It's obvious he's right on the edge. He wants this and I'm failing him. I can give him the pain he needs. He releases me and I seize the chance to sink my teeth into his hard cock. I take half his length into my mouth and bite down as hard as I can. The second my teeth clamp down he shoots his release into the back of my throat and I quickly swallow, moaning around his dick. His head falls back on the mattress as his legs stiffen and tremble with the shock of his orgasm. Once he's no longer pulsing, I pull back and dip my tongue into his slit to get the last drop, making him shiver. My lips curl up into a smug smile as I crawl up his body. *My mate's a freak.*

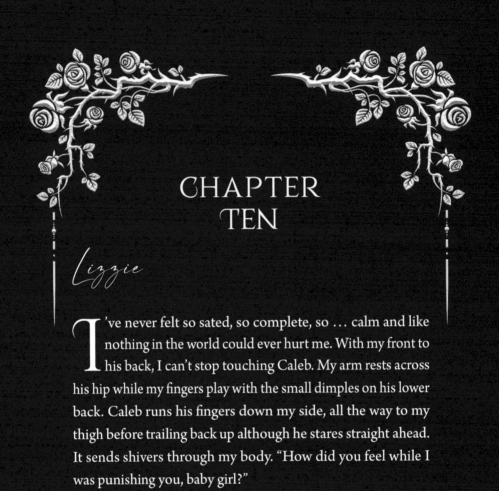

CHAPTER TEN

Lizzie

I've never felt so sated, so complete, so … calm and like nothing in the world could ever hurt me. With my front to his back, I can't stop touching Caleb. My arm rests across his hip while my fingers play with the small dimples on his lower back. Caleb runs his fingers down my side, all the way to my thigh before trailing back up although he stares straight ahead. It sends shivers through my body. "How did you feel while I was punishing you, baby girl?"

My eyes pop open and I tense a bit at his question. My ass still stings, yet the reminder of his belt brings on another wave of desire. *As if I could take any more today.*

"It hurt." I answer simply, not wanting to divulge the fact I wanted the belt to sting across my aching heat.

"Is that all? I thought you may have been angling your ass so I'd hit a certain area." My face flushes beet red and I duck my head into his strong, muscular chest. Caleb laughs low and

deep, causing his chest to vibrate. I love the feeling and the sound. "Did you like it?"

"Only a little bit." That's the truth. I wouldn't be afraid of it happening again, but I don't *want* him to whip me. I don't *want* to be punished.

"What part did you like?"

"I don't really know. It's hard to explain. I just know that I wanted it ... across me there ..."

I lean back so he can see my sincerity. "I don't want to be whipped again, though. I don't like it enough to want it again." He nods his head and closes his eyes while he kisses my forehead.

"I understand, baby. I won't do it again unless it's needed." I settle into his chest again while his hands run down my back. "Do you want to try something else? Something for pleasure?" His question piques my interest and I pull back to look at his curious expression.

"Like what?"

"Like a spanking." My cheeks heat and I nod eagerly. Maybe I'm a freak too. Although I should have known that.

Caleb's bright smile makes my chest fill with pride. In this moment I would do anything to please him. He gets on his knees and smacks my ass. Fuck! The sting is immediate and as it wanes, pleasure builds and every nerve ending lights aflame.

He commands, "Up!" I quickly oblige, getting on all fours for him. His hand rubs my ass, grabbing and pulling at the flesh, forcing me to moan. It takes everything in me to hold still for him. "All right, baby. The first few times will sting, but you'll feel it when you get there." His hand comes down hard, causing my body to fly forward as I let out a yelp. I stop myself from falling, fisting the sheets beneath me, and his hand comes down on my shoulder to keep me steady. "Head down, baby." His hand rubs the tender, reddened flesh and then disappears. Bearing down, I hold my breath waiting for the blow. This time it comes down hard on the other cheek. The stinging pain shoots through my body and my eyes water.

"Is it normal to cry?" It doesn't feel right that I want the pain, but can't help the tears.

"Only if you want to. I can go easier on you if you want, baby." I shake my head. No, the heat and the stinging are just right. I need more of it. *Punish me.* As if reading my mind, his hand comes down hard between my cheeks with his fingertips grazing along my pussy.

"Fuck!" My neck arches back and I push my ass higher in the air as he comes down hard again and again and again. The numbing, stinging pain heats my core. My pussy clenches around nothing, the absence making me moan in frustration.

"Good girl." His fingers run through my slick folds and I hear him suck his fingers into his mouth. "You're soaking, baby." He rubs his hands over the sensitized skin. "You want more?"

"Yes," I tell him, moaning out my response. I'm so close, the pleasure building like waves approaching the shore. Slowly but surely, each wave larger than the last. His hand comes down on my upper thighs, causing me to jump. Then he moves back on my left cheek, then the right, followed by my thighs, then finally my aching center. The tears fall easily with each blow. "More," I plead with him, pushing my hot, tender flesh into his hand as he kneads the growing soreness.

"Uh-uh." He pushes two fingers knuckle-deep inside of me and curls his fingers to hit that sweet spot. His thumb rubs my clit while finger fucking me and I know I'm going to unravel on his hand as my body starts to tremble. A hot wave of pleasure rolls through my body as I hear the door open. Turning my head, I see Dom striding forward. I moan his name. His eyes find Caleb's quickly before looking back at me with his brows raised.

"You want to come, little one?" I nod my head vigorously. I'm so close. He watches for a moment while Caleb continues to finger fuck me. Dom's large hand splays against my ass and rubs it gently, soothing the tender skin. I look up at him through my thick lashes and moan at his sweet touch. Caleb removes his hand, leaving me reeling in the immediate loss. Before I can object, Dom's other hand slides down to my sticky wetness. His fingertips brush along my clit, sending a wave of chills down my spine while simultaneously heating my core. I groan in pleasure into the mattress.

My mates. The pleasure mixes into a concoction of lust to cloud my vision.

I vaguely hear Caleb pick up the belt. He puts the leather against my pussy, trailing the cold, metal buckle along my clit and up to my entrance, while Dom's hands come back to my ass. My eyes shoot open at the feel of his belt. Propping myself up, I turn to look back at Caleb. My heart races. He said he wouldn't unless it was needed. Fear spikes through me. *What did I do wrong?*

"Relax, baby girl. It's not what you think."

Dom massages my shoulders and pushes my upper body back down against the mattress. "I'm going to make you feel so fucking good." My heartbeat picks up and the flood of adrenaline makes the pulsing need between my thighs pound even harder. I trust him to do whatever he wants to my body. He gives me pain I didn't know I needed, and pleasure I didn't know existed.

"Please." It's the only word I can manage. After I speak, Dom's hands move lower, spreading my lips and exposing my throbbing clit. I hear the swing of the leather and then it smacks against my hard nub, sending a jolt of pleasure through my body. There's hardly any force behind the blow, but the feeling is so intense that my body stiffens and shakes uncontrollably. Dom holds me in place as a shock races through my body, making me cry out in ecstasy. I'm paralyzed with wave after wave of pleasure as Caleb strikes my clit with the leather again and again, extending my orgasm. My body shudders in Dom's grasp, overwhelmed with the mix of pleasure and pain. As the last aftershocks subside, I collapse into Dom's arms and he pulls me close, kissing and nipping my neck.

After I come down from the intensity of everything, I find myself between my two mates, held tightly by both of them under the covers. I hum my satisfaction into Dom's chest. "Mmm, I liked that."

"I don't think I can hit you." His sad eyes tell me he thinks he's failing me. That he won't be able to sate me.

"I don't want you to. I just want you to love me." The truthful words are voiced easily. His lips find mine before the last word is fully spoken, kissing me with passion.

"Isn't she perfect." Caleb's comment is a statement, not a question. I would smile, but my lips are being forced open by Dom's tongue.

"She's so goddamned perfect." My eyes shoot open at Dom's words and my heart pounds. I can hear his muted reply, yet his mouth is still on mine, his eyes closed in ecstasy. Even so, I heard him loud and clear. His eyes stay closed as he leans his body into mine. I shut my eyes quickly as Dom rolls me onto my back and settles between my legs. He pulls back, biting my bottom lip before kissing along my neck and nipping my collarbone. All the while I listen in on their silent conversation.

"I love the marks you leave on her."

"Everyone who sees her will know she's taken."

"I feel like an asshole." Caleb's words are almost a whisper.

"Why?"

"She's not healing because her wolf is hurting, yet I'm enjoying the marks."

"Don't think like that." It's quiet for a moment while Dom lies down beside me, pulling me back into his chest. Caleb kisses my shoulder and spoons me from behind while his hand runs along my tummy. Both of their erections dig into my flesh.

"You smell her heat?" My heat? Oh my God, I'm going to be in heat during the claiming. The thought makes my pussy clench and a small smile plays on my lips, but I bury it in Dom's strong, hard chest.

"Just barely."

"I can't wait to knock her up." My smile widens at Dom's admission. I nuzzle my nose into his chest to hide it as he looks down at me and kisses my hair.

"You think our pups will be latent?" Dom's question shocks me and my smile vanishes. Latent.

"Don't know, I've never met a latent wolf before." His words are easy, no judgment, no fear.

"She'll love them just as much, won't she?" And with those words, Dom melts my heart. His only concern is how I would react.

"Of course she will. Why wouldn't she?"

"She thinks she's less of a wolf because of it." His words fuel me to push my body into his, wanting as much of him against me as possible. Tears prick again. Fucking tears. I wish I could just stop crying. At least these are happy tears.

"That's all right; she'll learn she's perfect. We'll teach her." The tears stream down my heated face as the realization of how much they love me hits me with a force that makes my body want to bow to them.

Dom's strong hands run along my ass and thighs.

"Do you hurt at all, little one?" His words are clearer and louder now. They were spoken out loud. I don't want him to see that I'm crying so I just shake my head without looking up at him.

"You're lucky I didn't kill your ass." I stifle my laugh at his silent statement.

"I'm a lucky sick fuck. You should've seen how she was dripping from using the belt." There's a pause before he adds, *"It was a punishment, though."*

"What set you off?"

Caleb huffs in the same muted tone as their words. *"Blowing off her emotions like they don't fucking matter. And then she lied to me. I'm not going to let her hide from us. She's denied who she is for too long."*

Dom nods slightly and kisses my hair again.

"Can you hear me?" I think the words as hard as I can. I would concentrate on finding his wolf but I don't know how to.

Lifting my head and searching Dom's eyes, I find nothing but confusion. "Little one, are you all right?"

I look deep into those piercing silver eyes. Why can I hear them, but they can't hear me? As his mouth parts slightly with his brow furrowed in concern, I press my lips to his, gently sucking on his lower lip and pushing my breasts against his strong, hard chest. For the first time, my heart fills with devotion, my hot skin needing his touch.

My wolf can hear my mates. A warm calm runs through me as I feel her against my chest. *My wolf.*

PART III

Broken Heart

CHAPTER ELEVEN

Devin

Gritting my teeth, I attempt to keep the anger at bay. This is exactly why I left that shit pack. We let him sit for hours, alone and in the pitch black while he came to… but he's still high. "What are you on?" The stupid fucker just grins and lets out an unhinged laugh. The blood on his teeth and his bloodshot eyes make him appear even more deranged.

My wolf presses against my chest, eager to be released. I grimace as the man's foul breath lingers in front of my face. The shifter is bound to the chair in the middle of the shed with silver rope. Trapped and undoubtedly in pain. His left arm is hanging out of the socket. That's going to take a while to heal, but the rest of him is covered in only faint bruises and blood from wounds that have already healed. Dom cracks his knuckles, preparing for another round.

The disadvantage to being shifters is that this could go on forever since we heal so damn fast. I don't have time for this. I

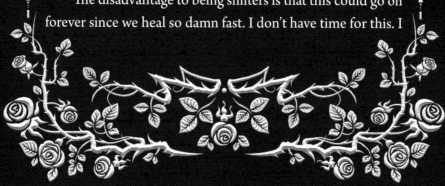

need to get back to my mate. My hand flexes as I tilt my head, judging this prick and finding him lacking.

"Fine, I don't really give a fuck anyway." I move back as Dom steps in front of the mangy shifter and takes his anger out on his already fucked-up face. I let him destroy the poor fucker. It's not doing a damn thing, but Dom can't get past the comment from earlier about "the blond one" looking like she'd be fun. A chill runs through my blood remembering what Vince told us about the pack. We've got all the equipment we need in the back of the shed to get answers.

Answers on where they are and how many are left. I had mercy the last time. I won't the next. They'll all die a slow death. Their fate is sealed.

"Did you know Dom's an expert in torture?" I question casually as Dom lands a fist square on the shifter's jaw. Bloody spittle flies out of his mouth onto the ground as his jaw shatters and hangs off his face. "He didn't want to be, but you could say it came with the territory he grew up in." Pain flashes in Dom's eyes and I immediately regret my comment. That was a poor judgment call, but I continue and apologize telepathically. He nods slightly in acknowledgment before continuing to land punch after punch on his victim's face. The force behind the flurry of blows has the chair that's bolted to the floor shuddering.

I head to the back of the shed and wheel out the IVs and O negative blood. I have to go to the other side to get the key ingredient.

Holding the bag in front of the stupid bastard's face, I tell him, "Liquid silver." I toss the bag back and forth between my hands as my words register on his face. A hint of worry passes through his eyes. Apparently he's not too far gone.

It'll scorch every inch of this bastard's flesh from the inside out. Constantly. No relief will be given as his heart continues to pump the tainted blood throughout his system. "We'll start off with a low dose, just to give you some pain and the motivation to be forthcoming to end the suffering as quickly as possible. You'll be able to answer our questions easily. But if you don't talk, we'll up the concentration until all you can do is scream. We'll let you go for a few hours, maybe a day before we give you some of this." I grab the IV stand. "Fresh blood. Then we'll ask you again. If you don't answer, well ... rinse and repeat."

Kicking the IV stand back, I grab a syringe. I stab the bag in front of him and let him watch the silver flood into the chamber before injecting it into his bloodstream. The fucker immediately screams and thrashes in his restraints. I can practically see the silver flowing in his blood as each part of his body trembles in agony.

"Are you going to talk, or should I give you some more and let you think about it?"

He snarls and grits through his clenched teeth, "Fuck you!"

"Have it your way." I stab the bag again as he writhes violently in a shit effort to get away from me. His pathetic attempt makes me laugh. There's no doubt we have to kill him. The sooner I get the information I need out of him, the better.

"Wait, wait, wait!" he yells as I stick him with the syringe. I leave it there dangling out of his arm as he seethes, staring at the injection site like it's on fire. His breathing is heavy as he scowls, seeming to reconsider.

"Are you ready to talk?" I keep my face expressionless and voice even.

"I'll tell you everything if you let me go." My lips kick up into a smirk and I huff a humorless laugh as I push the plunger down. His screams hardly register as I think about how he may have taken my sweet mate away from me.

My everything. She *is* my life. So his is no longer relevant.

I speak slowly as the silver leaves the barrel, disappearing into his arm. "You'll die after you give me answers. Whether that's right now, in a couple of hours, days, or weeks even, is up to you. I can promise you that I will make sure you are in pain every second that you continue to breathe." His breathing becomes chaotic as he starts to hyperventilate. "Unless you're ready to talk."

"I'll tell you everything," he barely gets out as he writhes in agony.

"Talk." I peer down at him with my arms crossed over my chest.

"Make it stop! Please, I'll do anything!" His eyes plead with me, but I don't give a fuck. I know what they were planning to do to Liz and Grace. He has no sympathy from me.

"Talk." My hard command is repeated without an ounce of emotion.

"It's the vamps. They want the blood bank." His hurried words rush past his cracked lips. "Stop it! Stop it, please!" I keep my expression calm, but his words make my blood pump faster and fists clench harder. I grab the IV and let fresh blood flow through him.

"Vampires?" Dom's question fills my head. Our captive won't be able to hear our conversation because he isn't a pack member.

"I have no fucking idea what he's talking about. They never dealt with vampires when I was a part of the pack." I slowly drain the tainted blood into a bucket.

"Remind me to keep some blood to test. I want to know what the hell they're on."

"Yes, Alpha."

The shifter slowly stops shaking as the silver leaves his system. "Talk." Tears fill his eyes at my simple command. "They're going to kill me." He swallows hard, then looks between Dom and me. "They'll kill me if I talk."

"You don't have to worry about that." Crouching in front of him, I tell him, "I'm going to kill you first. I can make it painless and fast. It's up to you." His eyes fall and sobs wrack through his body. "I don't have time to listen to you cry." I grab the bag of silver and pierce it with the syringe.

"No! No!" He tries to back away from me while shrieking, "I'll talk! I'll talk."

"Then talk!" I let my irritation show. I want him to think I'm ready to pump him with silver and leave him in unrelenting agony.

"They want to taint the blood. They're testing different drugs."

"Taint it with what?"

"I don't know. I swear!" His fear is evident as he pisses himself.

"Why?"

"So they can be the only ones. The drug ends their immortality. They'll be the only ones."

"Who is 'they?'" The words leave me in a growl.

"I don't know. We never saw her. She leaves the drugs. All we have to do is get the territory and make the deal with the coven. That's it, man. That's the deal. I swear!" Rage bristles through me. It must be vampires in the Authority.

That explains why they made drinking from the vein illegal. It ensures the others will use the blood banks. This is fucked. My thoughts fly to Veronica and what she knows about all this. She did come on behalf of her coven to make a deal with the pack. I shake my head at the thought. There's no way she could've known. I wonder how eager her rulers are to build the bank. And whether they still drink from the vein.

I'm vaguely aware the fucker in front of me is now silent apart from his pathetic sobs.

"Nothing else? Is that all you have to say?" He shakes his head as his body trembles with the fear of his imminent death. Turning to Dom I ask, "You want the honors?" He nods once as he picks up a crowbar that's hanging on the wall. I walk out, the sound of the shifter's panic ringing in my ears as I close the door behind me.

CHAPTER TWELVE

Veronica

What is the claiming like? The unspoken question plays on the tip of my tongue as I take a seat in the high-back, black leather chair in the corner of Vince's room.

Yesterday was nothing more than fun. It was the first time in a long time that I've felt alive. Perhaps that could explain why I'm riddled with emotions that pile on top of one another.

"You were right; it ended quickly," Vince states.

Burying down the unwanted emotions, I nod. "It was much better without me there." Taking in the modern furniture that's quite masculine and not at all to my liking, along with his king-sized bed, I comment, "We'll have to add an addition if you expect me to stay here."

There's a darkness of worry that stretches in Vince's gaze. "I can't leave my pack."

"I'm aware, but I can't store my shoes in your closet, so …

addition?" I offer him, again feeling a war brewing inside of me. The air feels lighter even, as if it threatens to dizzy my thoughts. In a quick motion, a flash of a second, I rid myself of my dress.

"We can build on whatever you'd like," Vince agrees easily, his gaze moving to my bra that I quickly undo and toss in his direction.

"You're insatiable," he comments and I ignore it, other than to smirk. I'm not usually, but him ... inwardly I remind myself that vampires are not susceptible to the "heat" of a mate's desire. Yet ... I feel this unyielding pull.

"I'd like you to tell me everything about this pack." In another quick movement, one I'm not certain Vince can even register, I rid myself of my lace garter and panties, leaving myself bared to him. "The coven knows very little ... other than the basics filed with the Authority."

Vince grins back at me. "About *your* pack, you mean."

My grip tightens on the armrest. I am his mate. There's a fluttering in my heart that wasn't there before.

Cocking my brow, I correct myself. "Yes, my big bad wolf." I spread my legs, exposing my cunt to him and with a single finger I motion him to come to me. "Let me come on your tongue first and then you'll tell me everything about *my* pack."

His asymmetric grin does something awful to me. It pulls something from deep within and heats my body from head to toe all at once. As he crawls to me, his hulking shoulders flexing and his silver gaze never leaving mine, I feel more vulnerable now than I can ever remember.

His touch is hot as his hand grips the inside of my calves, spreading my legs wider for his broad shoulders. In between kisses up my leg to my inner thigh he tells me, "I'll get you off."

Kiss. "And then tell you about our pack." Kiss. "Our history." Kiss. "The claiming that will happen tomorrow." Kiss. "And anything else you want to know."

My fingers splay through his hair as my head falls back and his lips find my clit. He sucks gently and then his large hands take possession of my hips, pulling me closer to him. My legs wrap around his shoulders as I lean back, getting lost in his touch.

He pulls back, staring at my slick folds, and whispers, "We only have one night together, and then we have forever."

Forever. My heart stirs in a way it's not meant to at the word. Before it can take command of my thoughts, Vince devours me and delivers me pleasure like I've never felt before.

CHAPTER THIRTEEN

Grace

I mpatience is my sole companion as I stare at the bedroom door, waiting on Devin. We need to talk. I'm still coming to terms with everything that's happened and I'm sure as hell not ready to be a mother.

Pups? Do I give birth to a wolf? I'm on the verge of a nervous breakdown as I pace the length of Devin's massive bed. My only identity is his mate. That's who I am. He's taken control of everything and left me with only his plans for our future. I feel backed into a corner and yet I keep thinking if only he didn't leave me alone with my thoughts, I'd be fine. I know deep down I can trust him and I'm very aware that I love him with every part of my being. But the idea of submitting and not knowing what his plans are … it puts me on edge in a way I'm certain changes my life. I don't want to be a baby factory and that seems to be exactly what Devin's plan entails.

It's too much. Too soon.

The door creaks open and I turn stiffly to see Devin. The sight of him causes me to take in a sharp inhale; his shirt is stretched tight across his broad shoulders and it's covered with blood. His stern expression softens as I run to him with concern.

"Devin." I can barely do anything but whisper his name. "Are you—" He takes my hands in his, keeping me from reaching out to him.

"Don't touch, sweetheart." He gives me a small smile, seemingly pleased with my worried expression. The worry is all-consuming. "I'm all right."

"What happened?" I clasp my hands together in front of me to pre-vent myself from running my hands over his body in search of the wound. All the while my heart races.

"It's not mine." I take a hesitant step back.

"Don't worry. Everything's taken care of," he says, his tone casual as he walks past me to enter the bathroom, stripping down as he goes. I'm left speechless at the door.

I'm stunned only for a moment before anger creeps in.

This is exactly what I'm talking about. I need to know what the hell's going on and Devin doesn't tell me a damn thing. Gritting my teeth, I stalk after him and shove the already cracked door open. It bangs against the wall, which gets Devin's attention as he steps into the shower. *Good.* He glances back and raises his brows, but continues to walk into the stall.

"Why don't you tell me anything?" Tears prick at my eyes and I wish they didn't. It's not fair that I get so damn emotional and he seems com-pletely unaffected.

"Why are you upset?" He motions for me to join him after he lets the spray flow down his hard, tight body. My eyes glance down involun-tarily to his thick cock and I close my eyes, wishing this godforsaken heat would leave me. The sight of his naked, wet body makes my core heat. I stifle the moan threatening to rise up my throat.

"You don't play fair," I murmur with my eyes still shut. He gives a low chuckle, and it's followed by the sound of him walking toward me. His large hands gently tug my shirt up and I help him accomplish his task by raising my arms. With a sigh I open my eyes to find a small smile playing at his lips. His silver eyes are full of devotion as he leans down to kiss me chastely. I part my lips and lean into his touch, but he nips my lower lip, causing me to gasp as he pulls back.

"What did I do to upset you?" After a moment of letting his words sink in, I shake off the lustful haze and square my shoulders.

"You don't tell me anything." As the words leave me, I realize I sound like a petulant child. I wish I could take them back and start over. It seems I've been thinking that far too often recently.

"That's not true. I answer every question you ask." His brow furrows in confusion at my statement.

I stop myself from yelling in an effort to have a civilized, adult conversation. "Then whose blood is on your shirt?"

"You don't need to know that."

Well, fuck the adult conversation. As I step closer to him, I shout, "This is what I'm talking about, Devin."

"If I don't want you to worry about things, then I'm not going to tell you. That's final." His voice is even and full of authority. Power radiates around him, but I ignore it as my heart clenches in denial.

"I can't do this. I can't be in the dark about things and stay shut away pumping out babies for you."

His forehead pinches. "Is this about having my pups? Do you not think I'm a good enough mate? That I won't be a decent father to our children?" His eyes betray the emotionless mask he wears. They're full of pain and doubt.

I second-guess my conviction at his obvious insecurities.

"I never said that, Devin." I try to ease some of his hurt before I realize he's changed subjects. "And that's not what I'm talking about. You don't tell me things unless *you* think I need to know them. Which isn't fair. I know nothing about all this. It's even worse because I was led to believe lies before." My hands wave chaotically in the air and I huff in frustration. "Why the fuck is there blood on your shirt?"

"Why don't you trust me?" He steps closer to me and I instinctively take a large step back. My back hits the wall, making me jump at the sudden contact. "Are you afraid of me?"

I shake my head and answer evenly and immediately, "You intimidate me, but I know you won't hurt me."

He steps closer and gently lifts my chin to kiss me. His forehead rests on mine as he closes his eyes and whispers, "Never. I'll never hurt you."

"I really don't care for being kept in the dark." His silver eyes open and stare into my own. He seems to be searching for something and I don't know what. "It makes me feel uncertain and like I can't control anything."

He sighs heavily before turning his back to me and getting in the shower again. The water runs down his gorgeous naked body as he says, "I'd prefer for you to trust my judgment, but if you insist …" He sighs again and catches my eyes roaming his body. I can't help it. He gives me a knowing smirk, which makes me blush. "The blood is from a shifter who came to the offering." His words ground me.

"What kind of shifter?"

"A wolf. From my old pack." I stare at him, willing him to explain. After a moment, frustration grips me as I realize he has no intention of telling me any more info. It's like pulling teeth with him.

"Why was the shifter from your old pack at the offering?" Devin stops shampooing his hair to look at me. His eyes travel down my body and back to meet my gaze. Foamy suds drip in heavy dollops.

"Strip and get in." He steps under the hot stream of water to rinse. My lips purse at his short command, but I obey. Only because I was going to anyway. At least that's how I justify it.

His hands find my hips as soon as I enter and he pulls my body close to his, resting his chin on my shoulder. "They were there to take you and Lizzie. Or at least that's what they decided when they got there." My body stills in fear. A million questions threaten to burst from my lips, but he continues to talk as he reaches for the body wash. "They want their territory back." He lathers the soap and then massages my body, starting at my shoulders. His strong hands feel like heaven and his touch brings a sense of ease that's at odds with what he's telling me. He kneads my tense muscles and I lean into his warm, expert touch. "Apparently they had a deal with some vampires."

"Veronica's coven?" I'm barely able to make the words coherent as a blissful moan takes over my body.

He chuckles at my effort. "No, sweetheart." He kisses my cheek before adding, "I don't think so. I'm not sure who yet." He turns me in his arms and I rest my forearms on his chest. "Have I told you enough?" I look up at him through my thick lashes and try my best to think. His touch is so soothing and comforting that it's hard to remember why I'm angry.

"You were upset that I keep you in the dark. Are you still mad at me?" How does he do that? My brow furrows.

"Are you sure you can't read my mind?" He laughs and leans down to kiss me, which I more than welcome.

"I'm sure. But that doesn't answer my question."

"I'm not mad. But I don't like having to pull information from you. I wish you'd just tell me."

"And I wish you'd trust me. When I say you don't need to worry, I wish you'd believe me and stop pushing me." I step out of his hold, not liking his response, and reach for my conditioner. I coat my hair and step farther away to gather my thoughts.

"It makes me feel weak when I do that." I nod, agreeing with my own words. That's really what it comes down to.

"When you do what? Trust me?" I shake my head.

"When I put all my faith in you and submit to whatever you want." I lean my head back to rinse my hair but maintain eye contact as I tell him, "It makes me feel weak."

"Do you think our pack is weak?" His question catches me off guard. "Of course not."

"They all submit to me. But you don't think they're weak?"

"That's not the same." I rinse off and step out of the shower.

He follows, but reaches for a towel before me and wraps it around my small body, pulling me into his hard, wet chest. Our naked bodies touching make me arch my neck, wanting him to kiss, lick, and bite the exposed skin.

"It is the same. They trust my judgment, knowing that what I decide is what's best for everyone. They're each strong and worthy of being Alphas themselves. But they choose to let me lead and have faith that I'll ensure their safety and happiness above all else. Yet you," he says and rubs the towel along my body, drying me off, "you don't have the same faith. And you're my mate." The last sentence is thick with emotion. "When I met Caleb and Dom, I didn't say a word. I kept walking and they followed. They never questioned my authority or judgment. Never. Yet you've consistently questioned me."

"Really?"

"Yes, at every point you seem to enjoy fighting with me."

"No," I say and let out a small laugh. "I don't *enjoy* fighting with you. I was asking about Caleb and Dom. I don't understand why they would just follow."

He hesitates, searching my eyes again. "Come, I'll tell you more. Maybe hearing how easy it was for the others will help you." I doubt that, but I'm eager to hear any information he's willing to share with me.

"Can you tell me about your old pack too?"

"What do you want to know?"

"Everything." I want to know *everything*. I feel like I'm the only one who's clueless and I'm tired of it.

"Okay. Well, for starters, I hate my old pack and they are worthy of my contempt." I crawl on the bed and wait for him to sit. Patting the spot next to me, he side-eyes me before lying on the bed. With his arm wrapping around me, he pulls me in and I don't object to his touch in the least. Even if it is distracting. "My father was Alpha." His hand runs through my damp hair as he talks. "I was a pup when he died and I hardly remember anything about him. I know a little of my mom, but when he died, things changed quickly and got out of hand so suddenly." His hand stills as he takes a deep breath.

"I was too young to take over; it was my right, but I was only about ten or so. No one fought for the position. A shifter by the name of Sarin took over and started changing things." His brow furrows and he stares straight ahead as he continues. "The pack started dealing drugs. My mother became addicted. I remember more of her than my father. I know I loved her. I did. But I was angry with her. It felt like she may as well have died with my father the way she ignored us." His fingers pinch the bridge of his nose and he heaves in a deep breath. "She died a year or two later and that's when things got worse."

I rub his chest in encouragement. Placing small kisses on his shoulder, I tell him, "I'm so sorry, baby." He kisses my hair, acknowledging my words.

"One day, the day I left, I heard them at the fighting ring." He swallows before adding, "They used to make money by betting on the fights and taping them to sell on the black market." A chill goes through my body. Suddenly, I don't know if I want him to continue. "I heard Lev. He was crying. They threw him in with two wolves. Not shifters, just animals. Starved and angry animals."

"Oh my God." I let out a gasp as tears prick my eyes.

"I knew he'd heal, but only if he could fight them off. I was able to get him out and run before they killed him. No one stopped us." He finally meets my eyes. "Did you notice the scar on his nose?"

I nod and whisper my admission. "I thought he broke it."

"It's scarred from the wolves. I didn't realize the bones had to be placed together to heal right. I've offered many times to break it," he says and chuckles, lightening the mood. "But he wanted to keep it. To remember." His hand gently tucks a loose strand of hair behind my ear. "He may joke and smile, but he's still hurting. They would've let him die. All for entertainment and a bit of money." I bury my head into his shoulder, wiping my stray tears on his warm body.

The urge to cry nearly overwhelms me but I fight back the tears, eager for Devin to continue. Pressing my skin against his, I nestle as close as I can and wait for him to continue.

With a deep breath, he does.

"We left that night and I was determined to start a new pack. I wouldn't ever go back. By then I was fourteen and just coming into adulthood. We met Vince first, only a few days after leaving. He was out hunting in wolf form, alone after his parents died. A bear had ventured into their den at night. It was just the three of them. His dad eventually killed the bear, but his wounds were too deep and he bled out before he was able to heal." I swallow hard and try to get rid of the knot in my throat. I hadn't expected all this heavy information.

Each one of them damaged in a way I could never know.

"Vince was hurting and in deep need of comfort and companionship. He was a bit older, but when I led us toward the river, he followed. A few weeks later, we found Dom and Caleb. They were fishing, two rogue wolves who'd fled their shit pack together. I found out eventually that Dom had killed his father and uncle, then taken Caleb with him before the rest of the pack went looking for them. When we saw them, I said nothing. I simply acknowledged their presence and continued to lead my small pack south, to warmer lands before the winter storms would cause us too many problems. They followed us. At first they kept a few miles behind. But one night when we set up camp, they came and sat around the firepit as though they belonged." He smiles down at me before lying on his side and trailing his fingers down the curve of my hip. "And they did belong. I knew they'd come so I'd cooked extra meat and left it to the side for them. For whenever they decided that they could trust us."

"I love hearing all of this. Don't stop." He chuckles at my soft words and kisses the tip of my nose.

"Jude was more difficult. He's more reserved. We noticed him while we were hunting down south. Like Caleb and Dom, he followed. But he stayed in wolf form and didn't approach us for nearly a week. A few times I thought he'd changed his mind and decided we weren't the right pack for him."

"Why?"

"I'm not sure. I never asked and he hasn't offered his thoughts. It's not my place to question his hesitation." My lips part to object, but then I decide to keep quiet and let him continue.

"When he did finally confront us, he came to me in human form and asked who we were. I told him and offered him a place in our small pack.

We were all just barely men, but we were a strong pack at that point. He nodded and asked, 'When will you be taking your home back?'" Devin lets out a heavy sigh. "I looked at my small pack and knew it was enough. I decided that day to turn around and take my home back. Well, I burned it to the ground actually. It was too easy to take over. Most of the children were dead or sold. Half the pack was unconscious or strung out from whatever drug they'd taken. I challenged the Alpha, but the coward ran. We torched everything to the ground and started over." A somber expression takes over. "When the Authority heard, they came and agreed that I had the right to challenge for the territory. I was young and naïve to think there wouldn't be consequences. Thankfully, they were less interested in the laws I'd broken and more interested in discussing other terms. Alec helped us financially until I got my footing in stocks and a few startups. For years, making our pack a stable home was my only objective, until we had far more than enough. And then I started dreaming of you. I started living for the day that I'd meet you."

My heart clenches at his words as his strong hand tilts my chin up and he leans down to softly kiss my neck. "I want sons and daughters, Grace. I want a family. A strong, healthy family." His silver eyes find mine. "I understand that you're young and haven't fantasized of this like I have. But it's all I want." The bed groans beneath us as he gets onto his knees and trails warm kisses down my body to my stomach. "I would trade it all just to see you swollen with my pups." He kisses just below my belly button and the sight makes my body heat. I can see him holding me, rubbing along my body as he listens to our unborn child growing inside of me.

"I—" I don't know what to say. I speak without thinking, "I want that too. I do. But not yet. I don't think I can be a mother yet." My voice pleads with him for understanding. He closes his eyes and kisses my stomach sweetly.

"I understand." He nods his head and lies next to me again, rubbing soothing circles on my back. "I do, sweetheart. And it's all right. In fact, it may be for the best that we wait. I may have to leave soon. I need to talk to the Authority about this new development."

"What does that mean? I don't understand." I'm overwhelmed with concern. "Leave for how long?"

"I'm not sure yet, sweetheart." He rests his forehead on mine and smiles. "But as soon as I know, I will tell you. I promise." I can't help the pleased smile that grows on my face. *Progress.*

"Thank you." I breathe out the words before finding his lips with mine and pushing my body against his. He chuckles at my lack of subtlety.

"You'll be too sore for the claiming tomorrow." I shake my head, but refuse to leave his touch. Nipping his top lip, I rub my thigh over his hip. He groans as my heat rubs against him. "Once more." He breaks away and waits for me to meet his gaze. "But then you'll have to wait. I don't want you to be hurting."

"It'll be a good hurt." I rub my cheek against his chest. He laughs again and rolls me onto my back, caging me in with his strong, hard body.

"One more time, sweetheart." My head falls back against the mattress in incomparable ecstasy as my mate makes love to me, with long, gentle strokes until we peak together, finding our release in each other's arms.

CHAPTER FOURTEEN

Lizzie

"Baby girl, wake up." Caleb's words barely register as I groan in displeasure. I was having such a wonderful dream, but for the life of me, I can't keep a grasp on it and it leaves me without permission. I push against his hard chest.

"Five more minutes." Both he and Dom huff a masculine laugh at my reluctance to wake up.

"Wake up, little one. Do you feel your wolf?" My eyes shoot open at the mention of my wolf. She came to me. I *felt* her.

"You healed while you were asleep."

"All my hard-earned marks are gone." Caleb pouts playfully, but I can see the overwhelming happiness in his eyes.

With disbelief, I quickly throw aside the bit of blanket remaining on my body and turn to look at my ass and thighs. Tears prick my eyes when I see that she healed me. *My wolf.* She came back to me. I close my eyes and try to feel her, try to talk to her, but I feel empty and alone. My lips pull down and a sadness flows through me. I don't want to hope that she'll come back. I can't take the disappointment.

"Hey, don't be upset." Caleb tugs my bottom lip with his teeth and kisses me.

"Do you think she can hear us?" I nearly react to Dom's unspoken words. The muted voices in my head ask, *"Can you hear us, little one?"*

"Can you hear me, baby?"

Keeping my eyes shut, I will them to hear me, admitting the words I'm afraid to say aloud. *"I love you. I love you both so much."*

"Give us a sign if you can hear us." I hear Dom's voice and those damn tears threaten again.

"I can hear you!" I nearly yell in my head. *"I love you! Listen to me!"*

"Are you all right, baby?" Caleb asks out loud and tears form in my eyes. They still can't hear me. I shake my head and let the tears fall as I sob in his arms.

"It's all right; it's a good sign." I try to speak, but give up when I realize it's no use. For so long I thought she'd left me. I thought she'd died. And now she came back, but left me again. She didn't give me a chance to heal her.

"We need to talk to her about the ceremony." Dom's voice echoes in my head and I do my best to settle down. Caleb's right. It's a good thing. It's a good sign that she came out at all. Shaking out my hands, I take in deep, steadying breaths before brushing my tears away.

"Baby, we need to talk about how you want us to claim you tonight." My eyes open at Caleb's words.

"What do you mean?"

"Well, there are two of us so we're not quite sure how we're going to handle each other. We don't want to be rough with you or fight over you." He runs a hand through his thick hair and looks past me at Dom before continuing. "When the moon is at its peak, we may be difficult to deal with. It brings out our wolves and our primitive side." He glances at Dom again and opens his mouth, but closes it.

Dom places a gentle kiss on my shoulder and says, "We weren't sure if you wanted us to take you like that for our first time."

"Oh." Surprised but also intrigued, a rush of arousal dampens my core. The thought of them sharing me, taking turns giving me pleasure and taking theirs from my body, makes my entire being heat with anticipation. Licking my lips, I arch my head to look at Dom over my shoulder. His eyes are drawn to my exposed neck before he meets my blue-eyed stare. "Were you thinking it would be better to ..." I say and hesitate. *Fuck me* doesn't sound appropriate to use when referring to me giving them my virginity. I don't have to finish my question, though.

He swallows, holding my gaze. "We may be gentler."

"The sooner, the better. Your heat is coming on strong now. It's fucking killing me to wait." My lips curl up into a smile at Caleb's impatience. I glance between my two mates.

"How?" They share a look before Dom answers.

"We want to break your hymen together." My eyes widen with disbelief. Both of them? Together? "No, no. Sorry." He chuckles, looking down at the bed before looking back at me. "With our fingers." His smile broadens at my obvious relief. "We don't want to hurt you. And I think we can all agree that, for your first time, that may be a bit much." The words *for your first time* linger in my head as I stare back at my beast of a mate. My body heats and cools at the same time as I remember him stroking his huge cock over my stomach. I lick my lips again with anticipation.

"Do you want to do it now?" My teeth sink into my lower lip. I'd be lying if I said I wasn't nervous. "It's going to hurt, isn't it?"

"Only for a little bit." Caleb gets on his knees and leans down to the crook of my neck. "We won't leave you in pain, baby girl."

"We'll take care you."

I nod and settle on my back, between my mates. Looking between my savage beast and skilled hunter, both of them hold expressions of longing and desire. I run my hands along their chiseled abs and watch as Dom shivers and Caleb leans in for more of my touch. I bend my knees and part my legs for them as another wave of heat flows down my body, pooling in my core, causing my clit to throb. Caleb's fingers travel down my tummy, leaving goosebumps in his wake. He gently presses on my clit, rubbing small circles on the sensitive nub.

My nipples harden instantly as my head falls back in pleasure.

"It'll only hurt for a minute. Dom will take you first and then me. Okay, baby?"

I nod with my eyes closed as numbing tingles flow from my core to my limbs, making my body stiffen with the need for release. He dips two fingers inside of me and the slight stretch is welcomed. My pussy clamps down on his fingers, needing more of his movement to get me off. Dom joins with two fingers and the added girth stretches me to a point of slight pain. My mouth drops open, forming an *O* as the sensation leaves me feeling full already. Wincing, I wiggle involuntarily as I relax around their shallow movements. They slowly finger fuck me, moving together and putting pressure on the sweet, rough spot on my front wall. The pain quickly subsides. I arch my back and moan as my skin heats and my toes go numb. My heels dig into the mattress as I push myself into their hands.

Dom's other hand moves to my clit and he rubs my own arousal against the throbbing nub in strong, unrelenting circles. I buck against the overwhelming sensation. "Yes!" *Fuck, yes!* Caleb's free hand holds my hip down as they finger fuck me harder, no longer in unison as my need to cum has me thrashing against their hold. The building waves threaten to overwhelm me. It's then that I feel a pinch of pain, followed by the enormous weight of pleasure coursing through my body. The waves crash against me as Caleb kisses my shoulders and Dom moves between my legs.

There's a slow, stinging pain as he pushes his thick cock inside of me, stretching my walls. *Thump, thump,* my heart hammers. It's happening. I'm giving myself to my mate. My heels dig into the mattress as my eyes close and I try to relax around his enormous size. I'm so full and so hot; the heat is nearly unbearable. With my chest rising and falling, my breathing comes in chaotically. He pulls out slowly, not all the way. At first there's relief, but my body immediately misses his touch. He rocks into my body, pushing more of himself into my aching core. His head falls onto my shoulder as he groans, "You feel so fucking good." He leaves an openmouthed kiss on my collarbone before slowly sliding in and out of me again. The heated sensation pulsing through my sensitized body makes me moan.

"You're doing so good, baby." My head lazily rolls to the side so my hooded eyes can focus on Caleb and the sweet kisses he's leaving down my shoulder and on my breasts. He sucks a nipple into his mouth while pinching and kneading the other. Dom's fingers pinch and circle my swollen clit. My two mates work together to overwhelm my senses with undeniable pleasure. My body bucks off the mattress as Dom pushes inside all the way to the hilt and stills. My walls pulse around his cock and arousal leaks down my thighs as I come violently and unexpectedly, trembling beneath their touch. The sensation is paralyzing. Dom's hips push against mine as he thrusts into my aching heat, prolonging my release. A strangled cry leaves me in pleasure as he picks up his pace. His massive frame hovers over mine before he reaches around me and lifts my small body off the bed. His large hand grips the nape of my neck, helping him to fuck me with ease. Each forceful pump of his hips sends my body into a heated shock. White lights dance in my vision and my voice is stolen as I silently scream my pleasure.

He pulls me to his chest as he lies down on his back. His strokes slow as Caleb approaches behind me. My numb body sparks to life as Dom stills deep inside me and Caleb presses the head of his dick into my ass. I push off of Dom's chest, but he holds me still. "Shhh, push against him. It will help." I whimper at the foreign sensation, but do as Dom tells me. As Caleb slowly pushes himself into me, the slick but cold lubrication from his arousal quickly heating, I feel overly stretched and full. And hot. So damn hot and full.

I shake my head on Dom's chest and tell him, "Too much."

Caleb pauses and then kisses my shoulder. "Try again?" he questions and I can only nod, my head laying weakly against Dom's chest. I want them both. At the same time. Even if it is too much.

He's gentle and slow, encouraging me to take all of him. All the while, Dom nips and kisses every inch of my skin he has access to.

He holds my hips steady and kisses me with a tenderness that soothes my nerves. My body shakes and a cold sweat covers my body as they move, first Dom and then Caleb, in and out of my body. I tremble as another wave of heated numbness overtakes my body, starting at my toes and building in the pit of my stomach. Caleb's fingers rub my clit and his other hand pinches and pulls roughly at my nipples. Their pace speeds up as I pulse and come brutally from their unrelenting touch. My hands fist in the sheets, my body tensing.

Wave after wave of intense pleasure hits me, each greater than the last as they continue to use my body, claiming it as theirs, thrusting ruthlessly, taking their pleasure from me. It feels like an endless orgasm shocking my numb body over and over again. Time loses all meaning as my orgasms flow together. At last they finally find their release, each buried to the hilt inside of me. I drift off as they each kiss me, their touch warm on my lips, my neck and my shoulders, whispering soft words of love and devotion.

CHAPTER FIFTEEN

Grace

I can't help but to compliment her. "Your car is really nice." In reality, I fucking *love* Veronica's car. It's an Aston Martin. *Holy shit, I'm riding in an Aston Martin.* I'm freaking the hell out! But not on the surface. Nope. Staying cool and calm and collected. Even though she can probably hear my heart racing with excitement.

"I fucking love your car!" Lizzie offers no pretense, bursting at the seams with excitement. It's the first time I've seen her genuinely smile since we got here. Her schoolgirl level of enthusiasm makes my lips kick up into a grin. It's contagious. The two of us are in the back with Vince riding shotgun. And of course Veronica's driving. My fingers run along the expensive leather and I take in every little detail.

She's loaded. Is every shifter dripping in wealth?

Her gaze meets mine in the rearview.

"It's pretty fucking awesome." I cave. At least I'm not drooling.

Veronica gives us a small, knowing smirk and says, "It's a guilty pleasure." Her eyebrows raise as Lizzie sucks on her drink. "Don't you dare spill that in my car."

Lizzie shrinks back slightly but doesn't lose her smile. "I won't, *Veronica*." She drawls out her name and adds, "Can I call you V?"

"V?" The smooth skin on her forehead pinches.

"Yeah. V for vampire and Veronica." Lizzie's simple explanation has Veronica grinning broadly with those damn fangs on full display. I suppress my shiver and keep telling myself it's just fine she's a vampire. As Devin insisted this morning, she's part of our pack now.

"Call me whatever you want, little wolf." She slaps at Vince's hand as he tries to change the station on the radio. Her admonishment earns her a wolfish grin from her mate.

Lizzie starts mouthing the words to the song before going back to her favorite pastime: sucking down her iced coffee. I desperately need to talk to her in private, but I just can't wait any longer.

"You seem happier now than you were earlier." She takes another sip and nods.

"I'm feeling a lot better." She looks toward the front seat at Vince before making eye contact again. "It's just a lot to happen at once." Her words are soft, but the twinkle in her eyes is still present.

"So you're a werewolf?" It's odd that I still think of her as the same Lizzie. My bubbly partner in crime, yet there's a side of her I didn't know existed.

"Sort of." She twists the hem of her shirt between her fingers. She keeps her voice low, and thankfully Vince and Veronica don't pry although I'm sure they can hear. "I've never shifted or been a part of a pack that I can remember." She breathes in deep while her lips pull down. "What I do remember I'd rather forget."

"I can't believe you never told me." I take her hand in mine.

She shakes her head and squeezes my hand tight. "I never would have. I've never thought of myself as a wolf." She squirms uncomfortably in her seat and glances at Vince again before adding, "I felt her, though." Her eyes light up and she holds back her smile. "It's been years, way before I met you. But she's back."

"How do you feel her?" It's shocking; exhilarating. All of it is overwhelming and I can't help but to want more. "I want to understand."

"I just can. It was only for a second and then she vanished. I don't know how to control her." She sucks the straw back into her mouth.

"That's good that your wolf is coming back, Lizzie," Vince states simply and nods. Then he smirks and teasingly adds, "She must've found something she liked." Veronica smacks Vince on the chest. "What?" he asks in that voice a kid uses when they've been caught stealing cookies.

"You know what." Her eyes find mine in the rearview. "So, where are we going first?"

"Pharmacy, please?"

"You got it, Alpha." I blush at her comment. My eyes dart to Vince to see his response, but he doesn't give anything away. His hand brushes along Veronica's thigh as he lifts up her skirt.

She gives him a side-eye. "What the hell do you think you're doing?"

"I want to see if you've still got that garter on."

"I took it off. No panties either this go-around."

His eyes bulge. "In this scrap of a skirt!" She smiles at his outburst and the tip of her tongue plays with her fangs.

"You're too easy, pup."

"So you *are* wearing something?"

"Hmm," she hums noncommittally.

"Is that a yes?"

"Hmm." He frowns at her response, but his eyes hold nothing but desire.

Finally he settles on, "That's fine." Veronica's lips curl upward in a pure female expression of triumph. He relaxes back into his seat. "I have ways of finding out." He turns to look back at the two of us. "So, *ladies,* how's everything going?" Lizzie blushes slightly at his question, which makes that wolfish grin return. "Are you ready to be claimed?" Veronica stiffens a little, but Vince doesn't seem to notice. I notice, though.

"I want to get something pretty to wear." His brows raise and he chuckles.

"You know you won't be in it for long ... and it'll probably get destroyed." Lizzie laughs and hits my thigh at his response.

"I know, but I want it to be special." She fidgets a little, obviously giddy. I stare at my best friend in wonder.

"You're in love?"

She bites her lower lip and blushes before she gives me a small nod. My heart swells with happiness as I take her hand in mine and squeeze. "With both of them?" I whisper, and I didn't realize how much I need the answer until I've spoken the question.

Biting down on her bottom lip, she meets my prying gaze and nods. "Both of them."

The relief is unexpected but so very welcomed. For the first time, it feels as if everything is going to be all right.

"So tonight they'll," I hesitate to say it but spit it out, "*both* claim you?"

Lizzie nods and for a flash of a second, I feel like she's holding something back.

"Do you have any questions about it?" Vince asks, distracting me from my thoughts.

"It happens under the full moon tonight, right?"

"At its peak," Vince adds with his nod.

"Not all of us at like once, right?"

"It's not an orgy. If you were hoping for that, you're going to be disappointed," Vince jokes and Lizzie laughs, sucking the last bit of her drink down and then shaking the cup to reach the whipped cream at the bottom. Vince's attention turns to Veronica, his voice softening. "We'll each go our own way, and enjoy our mates, biting down and claiming our love for them forever."

His gaze stays on her, but she fails to look back at him. Unease flows through me, but again Vince doesn't show concern.

"You two as well?" I question him.

He looks over his shoulder to nod again. "We'll run errands, get you two all settled and then," he says, peering back at Veronica and settles in his seat, "the night will come and the full moon will guide us."

CHAPTER SIXTEEN

Veronica

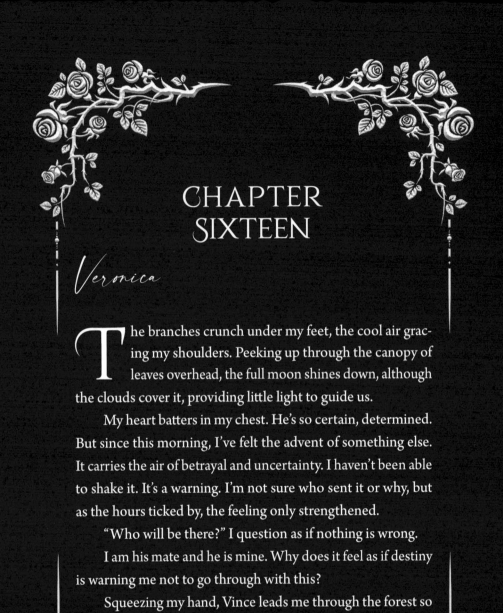

The branches crunch under my feet, the cool air gracing my shoulders. Peeking up through the canopy of leaves overhead, the full moon shines down, although the clouds cover it, providing little light to guide us.

My heart batters in my chest. He's so certain, determined. But since this morning, I've felt the advent of something else. It carries the air of betrayal and uncertainty. I haven't been able to shake it. It's a warning. I'm not sure who sent it or why, but as the hours ticked by, the feeling only strengthened.

"Who will be there?" I question as if nothing is wrong.

I am his mate and he is mine. Why does it feel as if destiny is warning me not to go through with this?

Squeezing my hand, Vince leads me through the forest so he can claim me. On the surface I do what I can to remain calm, but I'd be lying if I said I was unaffected. Fate has given my hard heart a mate. One mate to love with everything I have, and he's going to claim me as his. My nerves make my fingers tremble and I yank my hand from Vince's grasp before he has a chance to notice. Under a denser gathering of trees, it's dark and I can't see as well as he can, but I'll manage.

"Just us and the others with new mates. There's no need for anyone else to be there."

"So we'll all be witnesses to everyone else's claiming?" My pulse pounds, anxiousness climbing. I knew this would happen. I knew this was coming. I should have said something before now. A heat lingers on my skin, daring me to turn around.

Vince lets out a low laugh. "No, there's no need for witnesses. My bite will mark you and scent you as mine. You won't really be able to see anyone else anyway. This is the best spot for the moon, though. It's better for our wolves."

"I see." My mouth dries as we near an area with much more light than the surrounding forest. My heart races in my chest. One mate for all eternity. This is the beginning to a bittersweet end. I shake out my clammy hands and will away my tears. I'll outlive him by hundreds of years; I'll watch him grow old and die. And there's nothing I can do about it. The realization weighs heavy on my heart. But, as always, I shove my emotions into the depths of my cold heart and move forward. I've accepted my fate. It would be far too cruel to stop.

Even if destiny is warning me to do just that.

As we step into the clearing, the light from the moon provides a slightly better view, but it's still too dark to see more than a few feet in front of me. It takes a moment for my eyes to adjust, but I can hear what's going on with absolute certainty. Dom, Caleb and Lizzie are to the left, and Devin and Grace are to the right. No one seems to notice anything except their mates. Both women are obviously in heat, mewing and rubbing against their mates.

"What all does the claiming involve?" I quietly ask Vince as he unbuttons my blouse with deft fingers.

"We bond in the most intimate way possible and at our peaks, I scar you with my mark." His little fangs gleam in the moonlight as he leans down to nip my collarbone. It sends a shiver of want through my body. As my blouse falls to the cold, hard ground a chill hardens my nipples. His eyes focus on my breasts and he leans down to suck a nipple into his hot mouth. I moan and lean back, pushing my breast forward as the heat of arousal flows through me. A tingle of need flows through my blood. I'm obviously affected by the full moon, though not to the extent that the wolves and humans are.

As I open my eyes, they widen even further. I watch Grace on her hands and knees, pushing against Devin as he thrusts behind her, slamming his hips against hers. She meets every blow, moaning her pleasure into the ground. She arches her back as her body jolts over and over again. She whimpers as her body trembles, "I love you, Devin."

He presses his chest to her back and kisses frantically along her skin, never slowing his pace. "I love you too." His whispered words cause her body to shiver and convulse as he brings her to the edge of her release. He groans in satisfaction before biting into her neck.

My eyes shift to Caleb as he moves on top of Lizzie with Dom beneath her small body. "Please, please," she begs them, but I don't know what for.

"We've got you, little one," Dom murmurs in her ear.

"We'll take care of you, baby girl." Caleb slams into her welcoming heat. She screams out in pleasure as tears fall down her cheeks. Caleb kisses away the tears as he pumps into her, his hands roaming her lush body. Dom's hands squeeze her full breasts and strum along her clit as he moves in time with Caleb. Her head thrashes as the intense pleasure overwhelms her.

"I love you; I love you both so much." Her moan is nearly incomprehensible.

Caleb kisses her with undeniable hunger as they both pump faster into her. Her nails dig into his shoulders as they kiss, lick and nibble each side of her neck, preparing to mark and claim her.

My heart clenches as I watch them make love to her. They may be beasts and they may be rough, but their love is unquestionable.

Vince's hand brushes along my back as he whispers into the shell of my ear, "It's time." His hot breath tickles my neck and I lean into his hard chest. Turning to face him, I trail my nails along his muscles. He rumbles a hum of encouragement.

I press my lips to him and push my breasts against his chest. "Take me, then." In an instant, Vince throws me to the ground, bracing my impact with his forearm. His ferocity takes me by surprise, but I allow his lips to crash against mine, and he kisses me passionately with frantic need. He growls into my mouth as he tears apart my skirt, baring me to him. My lips part to object and taunt his primitive behavior, but he shoves his hot tongue into my mouth, devouring mine with a fierce hunger.

Instantly, my worries are gone. I crave him. I ache for him. Is this the heat? Is this a part of being his? Succumbing to this desperation?

I've never felt a sensation so all-consuming. It's too much. Peering past him, the clouds clear from the moon, and the light brightens. Everything comes into focus with sharp clarity.

My breath quickens as he parts my legs and slams into me. I throw my head back in ecstasy as hot pleasure races through my body. He takes my exposed throat with his teeth, raking them along the tender flesh. My heart beats wildly, slamming against my chest as his pace picks up and my back scrapes across the ground with each forceful pump of his powerful hips. This is not my pup; this is my big bad wolf.

"Vince," I whisper as fear creeps in. It's a fear I haven't felt in a long time and for good reason. The beast of a man doesn't pause. It's as if he didn't hear me.

Vince's hand closes around my throat and pushes me down to the ground as his thick girth slams into me, stretching my tight walls, sending a pinch of pain through my body. I squirm in his grasp, but he doesn't relent.

My eyes widen as I comprehend, in this moment, that he owns my body. I'm completely at his mercy. Instinctively my hands fly to my throat and try to peel his fingers away. My sharp nails dig into his skin, scratching and scraping in a furious effort to pry my throat from his hold.

He roars as he continues to slam into me. Tears form as the memories flood me and I scream. The shrill cry brings a coldness that dampens everything else. His grip instantly lifts and I scramble to get away from him, stopping just feet from his hulking form. Landing hard on my forearms, I struggle to catch my breath. I close my eyes tight, willing the painful memories to go away.

This is Vince. My mate. This is Vince. My mate. I repeat the thoughts over and over, trying to calm myself.

When I finally turn around, my fingers brushing along my throat, I see Vincent's massive form on the brink of losing control. His silver eyes pierce mine with an intense, primal need and his fists clench tight. His shoulders and chest heave with every breath as a low growl rumbles through his chest. He's a beast in need. He needs me. I brace myself and swallow thickly. I can do this. I need to give him this. I get down onto my knees and face away from him before lowering my shoulders and head to the ground and parting my legs for him.

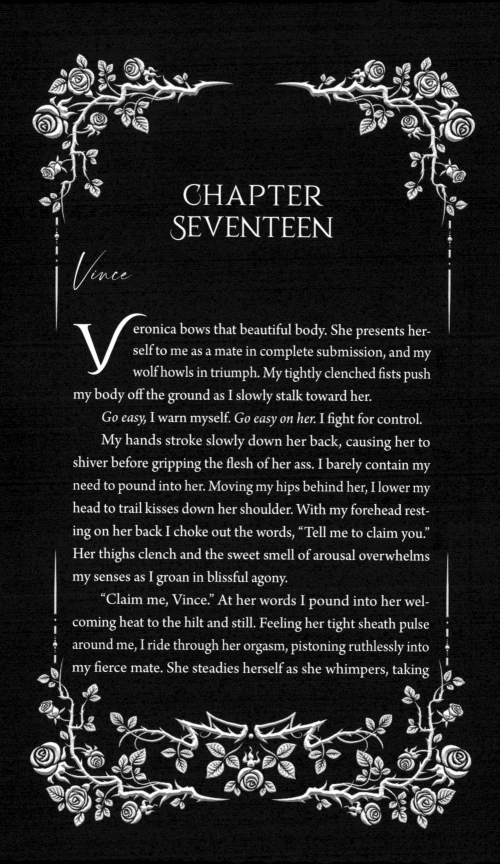

CHAPTER SEVENTEEN

Vince

Veronica bows that beautiful body. She presents herself to me as a mate in complete submission, and my wolf howls in triumph. My tightly clenched fists push my body off the ground as I slowly stalk toward her.

Go easy, I warn myself. *Go easy on her.* I fight for control.

My hands stroke slowly down her back, causing her to shiver before gripping the flesh of her ass. I barely contain my need to pound into her. Moving my hips behind her, I lower my head to trail kisses down her shoulder. With my forehead resting on her back I choke out the words, "Tell me to claim you." Her thighs clench and the sweet smell of arousal overwhelms my senses as I groan in blissful agony.

"Claim me, Vince." At her words I pound into her welcoming heat to the hilt and still. Feeling her tight sheath pulse around me, I ride through her orgasm, pistoning ruthlessly into my fierce mate. She steadies herself as she whimpers, taking every forceful blow of my body. My fingers dig into the soft flesh of her hips as I pound into her, over and over. A cold sweat forms over my body. Her moans and trembling body have me growling and my spine tingling. But I'm not ready to come. I'm not ready to give this up. I flip her body over and immediately bite into the tender flesh of her breast, never letting up the brutal pace of our fucking. Taking her nipple into my mouth, I suck while my other hand digs harder into her hip as I slam into her welcoming pussy.

I savagely kiss up her throat and lick that delicate, pulsing spot in the crook of her neck. My claiming spot. Mine. My mate. Ecstasy is all I can feel.

My fingers find her swollen nub and I wait for her body to tremble and her pussy to throb with need. The tingling settles low in my spine and my limbs go numb as I near my climax. She shouts out my name with her release and I slam into her and still as I fill her with cum and clamp my teeth over her flesh. The tang of her blood fills my mouth, but I don't release. I feel myself pulse as her pussy milks every drop of cum from me. Cum drips down her thigh and onto mine. My wolf howls in victory of claiming our mate and it fills me with pride and a sense of completion. My heart settles with deep satisfaction. My mate, my other half—she's truly mine, now and for forever. After a moment to calm my breathing, I lift my heaving chest off of her small body and smile down at my mate. But the sight of her is nothing like I expect and concern quickly fills my now hollow chest. Her eyes are red with bloodied tears and her body is shaking.

"Baby?" I lean down to pick her up to soothe her panicked body, but she flinches and stumbles back, scrambling to put distance between us. My blood heats and my heart drops as I swallow thickly, trying to understand. Her chest rises and falls chaotically as her dark eyes penetrate mine with fear. "What's wrong, baby?"

She shakes her head, but doesn't break eye contact. "I'm not okay."

"Okay." Kneeling in front of her, I gently place a hand on her leg. She jolts from the contact, but I keep rubbing back and forth, letting our mating bond soothe her. After a moment, she calms and I scoot closer to her. "Can you tell me what's wrong?"

She swallows and her eyes dart left and right before she lowers her head. "Baby, just tell me." Tears threaten to prick my eyes like a bitch as I realize I was too rough with her. "Did I hurt you?" She adamantly shakes her head and my brow furrows. "I don't understand. Tell me what's wrong."

Her dark eyes finally find mine. "It reminded me." Her gaze drops to the ground again as shame washes over me. "It—it reminded me." She doesn't have to finish. My hand falls as my world collapses, crumbling into an unrecognizable mess.

"It reminded you of—"

"Of why I started hunting wolves ... after what one did to me."

My breathing nearly stops as dizziness overtakes me. Our mating bond. Our claiming. The moment that was by far the most memorable experience of my life, reminded her of ... her assault?

"You were raped?" I don't know how I get the question out.

"Yes."

My hands on her body brought up traumatic memories of her past. Overwhelming nausea hits me, but I suppress it. Stumbling back, I fall on my ass. She moves to her hands and knees and crawls over to place a hand on my back, telling me, "It's okay."

"No. It's not." How could I let this happen?

I attempt to cradle her, but she recoils. Shame and guilt overwhelm me. With the pull of the moon, my mind whirls. Barely able to focus.

"What did I do specifically?" I question, and again attempt to comfort her, but she scoots back, avoiding my touch. "I will never do it again."

"I just can't. I can't be held down." It takes me a moment to feel grounded enough. Did I hold her down? When did I hold her down? I can't think, I can't control the shaking.

"How?"

"It's okay, Vince," she whispers, not answering my question. It's okay? None of this is okay. How could she say that?

My stern, hurt gaze finds hers as she tries to comfort me. *She's trying to comfort me?*

"Why didn't you tell me?" If only I'd known. I never would've held her down. I would've restrained myself.

"I thought you knew. That's why I need … I have to be in control and it's okay." Her voice is soft and full of agony.

What the fuck? "That's why?" A twisted sickness fills my chest. I thought it was a game. I thought she was just playing with me. I need to leave. I've failed my mate in so many ways. I need to think. I need to make this right.

"You should have told me that." Anger swirls in my mind. I could have … if I had let the pull take over … the things I could have done … the damage that would have been done …

As I stalk into the woods clenching my fists and breathing hard, I barely hear my mate's soft plea. "Don't leave me." The need to take her again vies for control. My wolf begs me to claim her again, to prove that she's mine. To care for and to love, to have in every way.

I can't control it. This need to take her again and the fear that comes with it that I'll hurt her again presses down heavily, making me hate myself all the more.

My mate felt pain by being mine. I did that to her. Peeking up from where she sits, the red streaks on her face are evidence of that and I take another step backward.

"Vince, don't you dare leave me," she threatens and she doesn't know what it does to me. Every instinct in me wants to unleash the needs of the claiming. To pin her down and—

Fuck! I can't. I can't hurt her again.

I would rather die than hurt her again.

I snarl as the tearing and cracking overtakes my limbs, morphing my human form into the beast taking over. She thinks I'd leave her?

Anger consumes me. She's everything to me. I would never leave her, never hurt her.

And yet I have. I just did. Because she withheld from me. Controlling me rather than confiding in me.

Her veiled threat echoes in my head. *Don't you dare leave me.* Never in my life have I felt so lost and conflicted. My mind reels with the intensity of the moon seeping into my consciousness, wanting nothing more than to take Veronica.

I shake my head as my paws collide with the hard ground, hurling me forward through the brush. All I know is I need to be away from the moon, away from my mate, before I hurt her again. The cold air already has my lungs aching, struggling for breath. Good. I want to feel that pain. I push my limbs harder, wanting to feel the aching soreness throughout my body.

This isn't real. Denial seeps in. It can't be real. And yet, when she calls out again, commanding me to go back to her, I know damn well it is real.

Commanding me. Because she doesn't know my wolf is threatening to take control. He doesn't think. He only acts. A menacing growl erupts from my chest.

At war with myself, I force myself farther away from her. Only to protect her, and yet she cries out that I'm her mate and I can't leave her.

How could she think I'd leave her? It's because she thinks she controls me. That if she falters, I'd run. I push faster on the ground. Barreling between trees and ducking under fallen limbs.

She needs to learn. She needs to learn to trust me like I trust her. I thought she did.

The moon threatens to wane as I approach the edge of the forest, breathing heavily and far too aware that the claiming is broken. I did not lick the wound clean. I did not lie with her after the deed, under the light of night.

How could I? With her in pain and our trust broken, that wasn't ever an option.

I will heal her. I will take away her control and give her true security. I will teach her to trust me. I've failed her as a mate until this point. I've let her hide her pain under the guise of control. No more. My silver eyes narrow as I sprint back to her. I'll take her away from the moon, away from any danger and I'll fix this. I'll make it right.

Veronica, my mate, I promise I'll make it right.

My conviction is firm: I won't rest until I've truly claimed my mate. Every bit of her. Her past and her future.

Only when I get there ... she's already gone.

PRIMAL
LUST

PART 1

Scarred Mate

CHAPTER ONE

Grace

My palms and knees roughly scrape back and forth against the grass, my nails digging into the dirt as my body pushes forward with every pleasure-filled thrust. Every nerve ending in my body is sensitized and even the moans that slip from my lips seem to add to my insatiable desire. My head hangs low, then rises with a desperate need to cry out as I take the punishing fuck. Devin's grip on the curves of my ass is so powerful that I wouldn't be surprised to find bruises later. His sharp fangs graze the tender skin on my neck, causing my blood to heat and rush through my veins with intense need. Arching my neck for him, I give him easy access to bite me, to claim me as his.

Every move is achingly natural and primitive; dark and seductive under the full moon.

"More," I say, whimpering my plea. His hips pound against mine as his pace quickens. Devin's thick girth stretches me fully,

giving a hint of pain to the waves of pleasure crashing through me. It's instantly forgotten as overwhelming heat builds in my core. It spreads slowly through my body as my toes numb. *Yes, yes!*

As he slams into me, the force of his powerful thrusts pushes my body forward, nearly knocking me to the ground. Strangled moans escape me as he continues to pound into me without holding back, the beast in him taking over, fueled by the full moon. It's all so intense and my head thrashes as I fight the urge to pull away.

Too much. Too much.

I almost cry out for him to stop but I hold myself back, clenching my teeth and submitting to the overwhelming and all-consuming haze of passion, loving his fierce desire to claim my body with his.

Devin gently kisses my back, a move that's at odds with his forceful motions. Again his fangs glide across the skin of my neck, threatening to pierce me, to mark me and scar me forever as his. I groan in approval at the thought. I desperately want to be his. I *need* to be his. I moan my pleasure into the chill of the air, knowing I'm his to claim.

He owns me: my body, my heart, my future.

The unrelenting heat threatens to burn me as he pistons his hips harder and faster. I whisper the words "I can't," as he nips my ear, sending a fresh wave of pleasure to my throbbing core. Refusing to slow his pace, a low growl rumbles in his chest. I gasp for air as my body gives out and he slams into me to the hilt. His fangs finally give me what I've been wanting. They pierce into my sensitive skin, and I let out a scream at the agonizing sensation.

A sharp pain attacks my body, making every inch of me shake violently. Fire courses through my veins, blistering my skin and threatening to choke me. Just as I register the pain, a soothing wave of unmatched pleasure rocks through me, easing the burn and forcing me to tremble with sated desire.

"Mine." Devin licks the deep marks on my neck. Devin's hot tongue soothes the claiming bite. The intensity subsides as the cool wind caresses my exposed skin. "Mine."

"Yours. I'm yours." I say the words quickly as I try to catch my breath. His long, warm exhale against my skin causes goosebumps to flow down my shoulders as he licks his mark again and then nuzzles into the crook of my neck. His strong arms pull my feverish body into his muscular chest.

"I love you, Devin." My eyes refuse to open as I nestle into his embrace and sigh with contentment. I am his mate. Feeling overwhelmed with the emotion consuming my every thought, I leave kisses on his chest, his neck—every inch of him. I don't know how it's possible to feel this kind of love so quickly, so assuredly.

"I love you, Grace." Hearing the tender words spoken in his deep voice has my heart swelling in my chest. My limbs continue to tremble as he holds me tighter.

A small smile pulls at my lips until the heat in my veins slowly returns, demanding attention. I struggle not to pull away from my mate, my Alpha.

The sensation tightens my throat with a fire that's unsettling.

"It feels like I'm choking." I murmur the words, writhing in his grasp. He doesn't react except to pull me closer to him. As if he didn't hear at all.

I need air. I need this burning to stop. Every inch of my body feels superheated, growing hotter and hotter with every passing second. Fear latches on to me as I push away from Devin. The cold ground calls to me, promising me respite from the unrelenting heat. His arms tighten rather than loosen and I struggle against him. "I'm too hot." I can barely push out the words. The feeling of my breath against my face is too much. It's too hot. My hands shake, and my muscles tighten all at once. I try to push away again, but a dizziness overwhelms my body. Anxiousness washes over me. I'm not okay. Something's wrong. Something's very wrong.

"Shh, sweetheart. It'll be over in a minute. I've got you." His words are a soothing balm, and paired with his dominance, I'm able to settle for a moment. It's a much-needed reprieve. Devin rubs soothing circles on my back as he licks his mark. His touch calms me and his tongue soothes the burn. I manage to take one deep breath, and then another. The burning slowly wanes, starting at my neck and cooling in small waves down my body. The cold sweat that's left makes me feel even more tired. I lie limp in his arms, knowing I'm safe. Knowing he can comfort me and heal my pain.

It's only then my racing heart seems to steady and beat in tandem with his.

"Why?" I don't have the strength for more words, but I know he won't need any more. He'll tell me what I need to know.

"The essence of my wolf is claiming you. It will scent you as my mate." Devin gently pulls away from me to look into my eyes and I whimper from the loss of his calming touch. "Everyone will know you are mine. Only mine. Forever."

With his hand around my throat, he lowers his lips to mine and kisses them lightly. Before he says the word, I feel it, I hear it even, just a moment before. "Mine."

Exhausted, I lie in his arms, feeling the heat turn to warmth as my body slowly comes down from the high and adapts to the effects of his mark. My eyes close as he kisses my hair, murmuring words of love and devotion.

At the sound of a sob, my brow furrows and I pick up my head, immediately on alert. *Lizzie?* Brushing Devin aside, I whip around to my right to find her somewhere in the dark. "Lizzie?" I whisper as I try to creep from Devin's lap. His stubble gently scratches the shell of my ear as he shakes his head.

"It's not her, sweetheart." His voice carries a hint of anguish. Oddly, I feel it. That worry, that knowing concern, in a way, is present deep in the pit of my soul. I glance up at him and then follow his gaze to the gap in the tree line where we entered the clearing. Off to the left I make out the tall form of Veronica. She's alone and another sob rips through her as my eyes focus in the dark. She's hunched on the ground and crying. I scan the area for Vince, but he's nowhere to be found.

"He left her?" First disbelief, then anger runs through me, awakening my senses and energizing my limbs. How could he leave his mate crying? She must be in pain! The very thought she's suffering from his bite, from that unbearable heat, has me nearly in tears. *How could he leave her alone to suffer?*

"It's not what you think. She's not in pain. She's not human, so she won't be feeling the same as you. She may not even feel anything at all."

"How could she not feel anything? How could she not feel *that*?"

He chuckles and my instinct is to strike him for it. A member of our pack is broken down and alone. "She needs us." He must hear the insistency of my comment because his grip tightens and his voice lowers to a serious timbre.

"They're working through other things right now. It's best to leave them be."

My head shakes of its own accord. "She needs someone." My whispered plea begs him to understand. Regardless of whether or not she felt the pain of Vince's mark, she's obviously hurting from something. "I want to go to her." I've already started to stand as I make the statement, but Devin's powerful arms constrict around my body.

"It's best not to interfere." His words are hard and his tone is absolute.

How can he be so cold? A moment passes and she sobs again, crying out for Vince.

"I can't sit here and do nothing. She needs someone." His eyes soften at my words and his grip loosens. He doesn't say anything, merely gazing into my hazel eyes before nodding his head and releasing me.

As I step out of his hold and walk toward her, I'm suddenly very aware of the fact that I'm naked. Cold and naked, to be exact. With my arms crossed in front of me, I gather my courage and set the thought aside. They're shifters, they don't care.

Well, she's a vampire, but I doubt she'll mind.

Another soft cry for Vince is barely heard in the distance and any thought of modesty vanishes.

She needs me. I feel a pull to her. A pull to my pack as I get closer to her. It's a strange sensation that I haven't felt before, almost like a pressure in my chest is pushing me forward, urging me to comfort her. My hand rubs at the hard knot growing in my chest as the pain becomes impossible to ignore.

I approach slowly until I'm able to see her more clearly. Streams of blood leak down her face. Tears? She blinks and the whites of her eyes return to normal before clouding with the dark red liquid yet again.

The terrifying sight is both shocking and frightening, and I gasp while taking a hesitant step back. At my reaction, Veronica's head pulls up in a nearly violent fashion. My heart pounds and I can't control the natural instinct. When her eyes catch sight of me, she immediately rises, and in a blink, she's gone. Nothing but a blurred vision.

She vanishes so quickly, I don't believe it at first. I question my own senses. Did she run? *Holy shit.* How is that possible? I'd heard that vampires were fast, but to see it is something else entirely. Something eerie and startling.

I swallow a scream as Devin's hand comes down on my shoulder. My beating heart slows once I realize it's him.

"She ran." I don't know what else to say.

"I saw. I thought she would. Like I said, it's best not to interfere. It's complicated, Grace."

My head shakes at his words. "No. She's not okay. She needs someone. I need to help her. I felt a pull to her."

His tone changes at my admission. "You felt a pull?" He turns me in his arms to look at me. "You felt a pull?" he repeats. I nod at his question. That's exactly what I felt. I rub my chest remembering the slight pain and growing knot. That's all but gone now. "I felt a physical need to go to her."

Devin lips turn up slightly into an asymmetric grin of pride.

"You were meant to be an Alpha, sweetheart. Fate has given me a strong mate."

"An Alpha?"

He nods his head. "An Alpha feels the needs of his pack. And sometimes those who aren't even his responsibility. You," he says as his hand cups my chin and lifts my lips to him for a sweet, soft kiss, "you are an Alpha." I smile against his lips, his words warming me with satisfaction.

Pulling back slightly, I manage to remember Veronica through the needy haze of my heat returning. "Where do you think she went?"

"I'm not sure. Vince is going to her now, though." My confusion at his knowledge dissipates as I remember their ability to communicate even at long distances.

"But how will he find her?"

"He'll always be able to find her. She'll never be able to run from him. Not now that he's claimed her."

I look back at the direction she ran. "But what if she doesn't want him to find her?"

He shrugs. "I suppose she'd have to keep running. Vampires are much faster than werewolves. She could outrun him forever, but she won't." I look back into his silver gaze questioningly. He gives me a small smile and a peck. "She may want to run now, but she needs him. And she knows it just as much as he does."

CHAPTER TWO

Grace

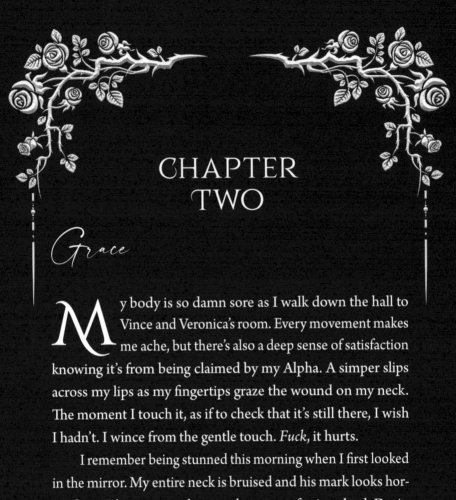

My body is so damn sore as I walk down the hall to Vince and Veronica's room. Every movement makes me ache, but there's also a deep sense of satisfaction knowing it's from being claimed by my Alpha. A simper slips across my lips as my fingertips graze the wound on my neck. The moment I touch it, as if to check that it's still there, I wish I hadn't. I wince from the gentle touch. *Fuck*, it hurts.

I remember being stunned this morning when I first looked in the mirror. My entire neck is bruised and his mark looks horrendous. It's going to take a week or more for it to heal. Devin spent most of the morning licking and kissing it. A familiar heat rolls through my body at the remembrance and the pain is so easily forgotten.

The sigh of contentment is met with regret as my gaze settles on Vince and Veronica's door. Taking a moment to shake out my hair, I wipe the grin off my face. This isn't what Veronica needs. I can already feel the venom she would give me if I were to prance in with puppy love, no pun intended, written across my expression.

An image of her disheveled and broken appearance last night flashes in my mind and my heart drops, although my pace doesn't slow. I have no business going to her with my happiness so damn evident. I clear my throat and compose myself before knocking hesitantly on the door.

Thump, thump, my heart is only given a single second before the doorknob turns.

Veronica opens the door slowly and raises her brows when she sees me. Given how well vampires hear, it's obvious she's not surprised to see me. Just surprised at the sight of my condition judging by how her gaze travels over my plain white V-neck tee and dark gray sweatpants. I was a bit too sore for jeans.

"Well, that beast didn't take it easy on you, did he?" She steps away from the door, holding it open and allowing me to walk through.

My eyes widen at the sight of her in a deep burgundy satin robe. I nearly gape at her appearance. She looks just the same as she did yesterday—not during the ceremony, but before. The way she always looks, which is stunning. Her tanned skin is completely unmarked with the only exception being a very faint silver scar along her shoulder. I have to squint to make it out. *Seriously?* I look like shit, like my mate mauled me, and she gets to go back to looking like a runway model? *Not fair.* Swallowing the petty thought, I enter the room and feel slightly uneasy as she shuts the door behind me.

It's only when I clear my throat to speak that I notice how sore it is. If I had to put money on it, I'd bet Veronica's throat isn't hurting either. As I part my lips, I note how casual she appears while she makes her way to the window. She doesn't seem to be in distress like she was last night. She's entirely composed. There are so many questions that beg to be asked. So many thoughts filled with compassion and empathy that stay lodged in the back of my throat. Nothing is as I thought it would be.

Devin was right when he said it's complicated, and that's in addition to the significance and difficulties Veronica being a vampire already brings.

Before I can speak, she gestures to a high-back chair in the corner of the room by a desk. "Sit."

A brow of mine cocks up of its own accord. I hesitate and narrow my eyes, not liking her tone or the use of the word "sit." Flashbacks of my first night with Devin run through my mind.

With a corner of her lips pulling up, she adds easily, "Please," while gracefully lowering herself into the desk chair. She crosses her long legs, which causes the slit of her robe to fall open slightly, exposing even more of her. I glance around the room before taking my seat.

"Where's Vince?" My posture mirrors hers, both of us resting our hands on the arms of our respective chairs. Suddenly, it feels claustrophobic in here even though it's just the two of us.

I'm alone in a room with a vampire ... although Veronica's lips perk up again, no doubt at the sound of my racing heart, her dark eyes contradict her countenance. Her gaze holds a sense of mourning in them that I wish I could ease.

"I heard you were coming, so I asked him to get us coffee." I don't miss how she relaxes her posture, appearing far less dominating.

"You must've heard Lizzie and I are practically caffeine addicts." I grin, but Veronica simply stares back without any trace of humor. "Thank you, though." I'm quick to add, "That's really sweet of you." At the word "sweet," her crimson lips curve upward and a small huff of a laugh leaves her.

"Yes, I can be very *sweet*." The way she speaks makes me uneasy. Any semblance of ease vanishes. She stares back at me as though I'm her prey. I shift uncomfortably. She doesn't seem to want my company, and I find myself regretting my decision to comfort her. She obviously doesn't need it. I start to get up, but then that knot in my chest forms again. My hand flies to the center of my chest and I press on it to try to ease the discomfort.

"Are you all right?" There's a trace of concern in Veronica's voice.

Nodding my head, I plant my ass firmly back down in the seat. "It's funny you should be asking me that, because I came here to ask you the same question." As the words leave my lips, the hard pain dissipates, granting me freedom to breathe normally. Rubbing the spot, I'm amazed at how quickly it left me. I make a mental note to talk to Devin about what the hell just happened.

It's similar to the pull from last night. Something has changed and it demands attention.

In the silence, my eyes find Veronica's dark gaze. Her lips are pressed in a hard line.

"I'm fine. I was mistaken about something last night."

"Mistaken?"

Her eyes narrow and I hold my ground as a flare of anger passes through me. She was more than shaken last night, so beat down, yet she refuses to acknowledge it. It's none of my business, except that she's my pack and this damn restlessness prods me to push. Just like I have to with Lizzie.

My eyes widen at the realization that Veronica's pulling the same shit Lizzie does. I narrow my eyes right back at her and repeat the single word incredulously, "Mistaken?" She seems to be shocked at how brazen I am, but I'm not going to back down. This pull inside of my chest demands action.

My voice is tighter than I'd like when I ask, "Why were you crying?"

Veronica clicks her tongue while searching my eyes before she purses her lips. "Why does it matter to you?"

"I hurt for you. You're a member of my pack and I want to help you."

"I don't need help, little human." Her wicked grin returns and her hard mask resurfaces. "How could you possibly help me?"

"I can't answer that question until I know what the problem is." I stare straight back at Veronica, unaffected by her arrogant tone. She's not going to fool me any longer. We all have walls we build, brick by brick, to keep ourselves protected. Hers have tumbled down and I'll help her rebuild them if she needs, but only if that's the boundary she needs. My teeth sink into my bottom lip wondering if I should push her, and if so, how much harder.

Her shoulders relax and she leans back in her chair while tapping her bloodred nails on the desk. "I didn't like last night." Her cool expression and flat tone are at least a bit more genuine. I'll take the small opening she gave me.

"You didn't want him to claim you?"

She shakes her head gently. "It's not that. I'm honored to be his mate. I really am." She takes a deep breath and adds, "I didn't know fate would give me a mate at all."

"I don't understand. Don't you all have mates?"

Her response is to give me a soft smile that doesn't reach her dark brown eyes. "No, only werewolves, dear." She watches her fingers tap along the desk for a moment before continuing. "Other shifters too, I suppose." She breathes in heavily before meeting my questioning gaze. "Not vampires. We don't have mates."

"But you have Vince?"

"Only because Vince has me as a mate. Fate's a cruel bitch." She snorts a laugh although there's no humor in what she said.

"Why is it cruel?"

"Well, for starters, she gave Vince a bitch for a mate. And then for me ..." Her voice trails off and she straightens in her seat before staring into my eyes. "Fate decided to give me a mate. One person to love for my entirety. I will love him with everything I have, but I will live much longer than he will. I will watch him grow old, while I am ageless. I will hold his hand when he dies, yet I will live." Red tears brim around her eyes as she smirks.

"Like I said, fate's a bitch. I never planned this." She huffs that same humorless laugh. "I never wanted this. I never thought I'd have someone to love. And now that I have it, I'm not sure that I should. I wasn't made for this. It's not what I am." Her voice turns hard at the end and it makes my body stiffen with fear. She's a roller coaster of emotion ranging from disbelief to sadness and ending in anger. At first I'm taken aback by her honesty, but then I focus on what she said.

"You never thought you would love?" She can't truly mean that. "Do vampires not have the ability to love?"

She laughs, with real humor this time, and leans back in her seat while wiping away the blood rimming her eyes. I grimace inadvertently at the sight and unfortunately she sees my reaction.

"You don't know much about vampires, do you?"

"No. I'm sorry, I didn't—" She cuts me off before I can fully apologize.

"I've been a vampire for nearly two hundred years and I still despise some aspects of our species." She wipes her fingers on a tissue and places it on the desk as if she knows she'll need it again before trashing it; the bright red is vibrant against the stark white. "If I could change it, I would."

"You're two hundred years old?" Holy fuck. I don't have enough self-control to contain my shocked expression.

"Something like that." Her voice is flat. Then she tilts her head and a glint of happiness sparkles in her eyes. "Would you like to know how I came to be immortal? How I was changed?" Her smile widens, revealing her sharp white fangs. "I wasn't always like this." She shakes her head. "Vampires are a capricious species."

I clear my throat. From what I learned of vampires in school, that sounds about right. But then again, humans in general don't know much about them.

"Tell me." She quirks a brow and I suppress my smile. "Please." Her grin grows as we share a knowing look.

"I was a little older than twenty. I don't remember what day my birthday was because it's been so damn long. I was unmarried because I had been raised religious and thought I would become a nun. The day everything changed happened sometime around summer. I know that because there was a big thunderstorm that had just passed through our area, and where I lived the rainy season began in June." She rocks gently, glancing out the window as if watching her recollection playing out before her like she's watching a movie.

"I was in the rainforest foraging for my grandmother. She sent me out all the time to gather things. My mother and father had both passed away when I was a baby, leaving me alone with my grandmother to raise me by herself. She was in good health for her age and took care of me as any mother would." A sad smile pulls at her lips. "She always said I looked like my mother." That humorless huff of a laugh erupts from her throat. "I don't remember her at all. I used to be able to, but it was so long ago that I can't even picture her face anymore." Veronica falls silent as she tries and fails to recall her memory.

"I'm sorry." My voice brings her back to the present. Her dark eyes find mine and her grin returns.

"Don't be, dear. My first twenty years were good years. Even if I suffered loss, I was still grateful for my life." She visibly swallows. "At least until that day." I settle into my seat as I watch her pull her legs into her body. "I was gathering pandan leaves in the rainforest when I found some mangoes. They were delicious; I remember that well. They were nearly overripe but I'd cut one open to taste it. Fruit is best when it's almost too sweet, don't you think? It was a little treat for me. A reward for going out for my grandmother."

Her smile fades and her voice drops as she continues her tale. "I traveled to my usual area, where I knew I'd be able to find most of what she'd asked for. I was at the last pandan plant with only half of my basket full. I knew she'd need more leaves, so I went out a little farther. There was a large clearing and on the other side I spotted more bushes. The storm the previous night had left downed trees and broken branches in its wake, but somehow this clearing had been spared. It was so pretty. Undisturbed with dewdrops clinging to everything and sparkling in the light. So pure. I almost felt bad crossing through it to get to the other side." She gently shakes her head again and swallows. "But no one lived close to us and I didn't think I'd ruin it for anyone but myself. So I continued into the other side until my basket was full." Her lips pull down in a frown. "I knew my grandmother would be grateful. She would've been so happy to have a full basket."

Leaning forward in my seat, I clasp my hands. A hard pit forms in my stomach and my blood chills. I can tell I'm not going to like what I hear next. She clears her throat, but her dark eyes stay focused on her nails, tracing over the grain pattern in the walnut desk. She nods her head slowly. "I knew something bad was going to happen when I got back to the clearing. I could see so many large footprints in the dirt. They came from the left. I remember thinking there may have been four of them." The red tears brim in her eyes and spill over, trailing streaks of blood down her light brown skin. I part my lips, but before I can speak, she continues. "They were werewolves. I saw them shift in front of me. Well, two did. Two didn't." Her breath hitches.

"I don't have to tell you everything they did. But know that I didn't value my life afterward. I wished they'd just killed me. Instead, they left me mangled and damaged after they'd had their way with me. I was covered in bruises and bleeding out from the injuries they'd inflicted on me. Some of the plants I'd gathered had medicinal qualities; I used them to staunch my wounds. I still don't know how I made it back without dying. It was the longest journey of my life. Part of me wanted to stay and just succumb, but I was so scared they would come back."

"Where did you go?" I whisper the question, not sure I want to hear more but knowing I have to.

"Back to my grandmother's. Where else could I have gone? It was two hundred years ago. There were no phones to call for help. We lived in such a remote area, there were no hospitals nearby. The shamans in our area had all left due to religious persecution. There was no one but her." Her sad smile returns and she laughs before she tells me, "She scolded me. When she heard the door open, she yelled from the kitchen that I'd scared her and to never do that again. And then she came out and saw me.

"She looked so broken when she saw me. When she saw my bruised body and she realized what happened. I was barely clothed and covered in blood. My grandmother was a truly devout Catholic. She said the church would help us, that they would know what to do." She reaches across the desk for the crumpled tissue and regains some of her composure before continuing. "It took forever to reach the local priest, but he accused me of making everything up. That I must have imagined what I saw and experienced because werewolves would never do such a thing." She straightens and faces me. "They were supposed to protect us. We had a pact with them. Apparently they were allowed to do whatever they wanted so long as the vampires were kept at bay. What happened to me was nothing more than a small sacrifice in exchange for the security they provided." Her dark eyes harden as she spits out, "That's what the priest told me. 'It was a small sacrifice to pay!' That's the day I started to hate everyone. My grandmother was the only one who wanted justice. No one else dared to confront the wolves." She calms herself and wipes her eyes again. I can't even fathom her pain. To live through something so monstrous and survive, only to experience a horrible betrayal—my heart breaks for her with the injustice of it all.

"She died a few weeks later. I think the church's refusal to intervene was too hard on her. She was so angry at everyone else and felt like she had failed me, even though there was nothing she could have done differently. Her heart just couldn't take it. So I was left on my own, on the outskirts of the town. I lived in fear that the shifters would come back. One night I thought they did. I thought they'd come for me again." A wicked glint shines in her brown eyes. "But it wasn't the wolves." Her dark red, plump lips form an evil smirk. The look on her face is one of a scorned woman who's reaped her revenge. "No, it was three vampires. They'd come to kill everyone." She tilts her head and I hear her neck crack as she reclines in her seat and crosses her legs. Her characteristic collected facade replaces the emotional woman who I'd just been sitting with.

"They were going to kill me. Most of the town had already been slaughtered. They decided to punish everyone who'd sided with the wolves. Not that we had much of a choice in the matter of what the werewolves did. Obviously. When they saw me, they smiled. Like we were old friends. They'd heard what the wolves had done and offered me a choice: death or the chance to have vengeance. If I'd been smart, I would have chosen death. But then again, fate wouldn't have been able to curse my poor pup had I died all those years ago."

"You'd rather have died than become a vampire?"

She shakes her head and purses her lips. "Not now, no. But the things I did, all out of hate and to get revenge …" Her dark eyes narrow as she meets my stare. "There can be no forgiveness for all the innocent lives I've taken and all the times I sat back and watched as my coven ravaged villages for sport."

"Does your coven still …" I swallow hard, not able to get out the rest of the words.

"My old coven, I'm not sure. If they do, then they must be keeping quiet about it. The Authority has no use for those who make messes they have to clean up."

"So your old coven is the one who trained you. Natalia?"

"Natalia's a bitch." Her voice is hard and dripping with spite. "She was there when I was made a vampire. She taught me some things, although she's not as good as she thinks she is. Hate motivated me for decades, but when the years pass like days, you learn to let some things go in the name of self-interest. Natalia's still fueled by malice. I've no idea why, but I tired of her antics long before I'd even left that coven."

"What about your current coven?" Part of me is intrigued, wanting to meet more vampires and hear their stories; the other part is terrified.

"They're … vampires. There's not much to say beyond that truth." She stands up and heads to the door, opening it just before Vince enters. "You took your time, didn't you?"

He only huffs a humorless laugh, each hand holding a coffee. Vince's silver eyes find mine and he smiles, although it's subdued. "Hey, Grace," he says. Veronica may seem the same as she did before last night, but something has shifted in Vince. Something darker, something more careful.

Veronica asks Vince to give me my drink and holds the door open, telling me, "You can go now."

"I was really hoping to talk to you a bit more." Glancing between the two of them, I'm left feeling like an intruder.

"I'm happy you came to see me, sweet mate of my Alpha, but Vince will take care of me." Vince looks up from setting her coffee on the dresser and gives Veronica a semblance of a smile.

"I've got her, Grace." I feel the need to pry and protect Veronica, even if she doesn't think she needs it, but something in me settles and I know that I can leave them be. Something deep inside me is telling me that Vince will heal her. He is her mate. As I head back to the east wing of the estate, I expect the knot to form in my chest, objecting to my leaving. I rub my chest as I walk back to my room, waiting for the pull, but it never comes.

CHAPTER THREE

Devin

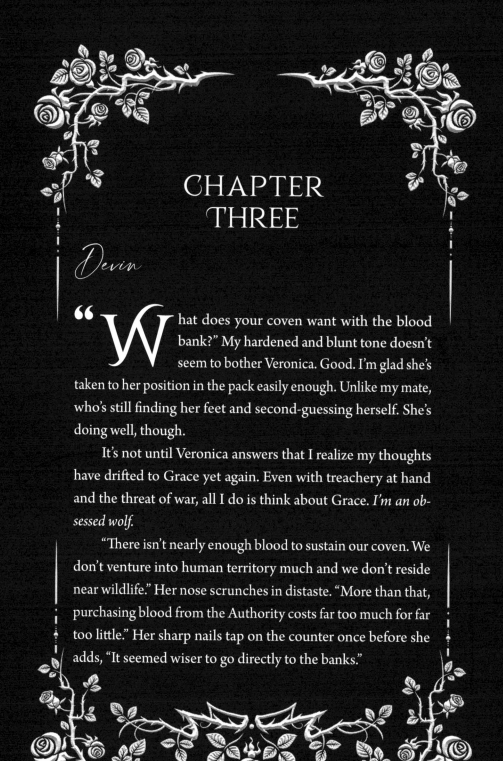

"What does your coven want with the blood bank?" My hardened and blunt tone doesn't seem to bother Veronica. Good. I'm glad she's taken to her position in the pack easily enough. Unlike my mate, who's still finding her feet and second-guessing herself. She's doing well, though.

It's not until Veronica answers that I realize my thoughts have drifted to Grace yet again. Even with treachery at hand and the threat of war, all I do is think about Grace. *I'm an obsessed wolf.*

"There isn't nearly enough blood to sustain our coven. We don't venture into human territory much and we don't reside near wildlife." Her nose scrunches in distaste. "More than that, purchasing blood from the Authority costs far too much for far too little." Her sharp nails tap on the counter once before she adds, "It seemed wiser to go directly to the banks."

"You have to order the blood for the coven?" It's difficult to keep my expression impassive. Much about vampires remains a mystery, even to other supernatural species. So long as laws aren't broken, they aren't required to divulge any information regarding any aspects of their way of life. There are plenty of whispers, though ...

"We don't *have* to order blood. But most of the humans won't sell theirs and like I said, our sources for acquiring it are limited."

"What about having a personal ..." I leave the remaining words unspoken.

"Drinking from humans? From their necks? It's been outlawed, as I'm sure you know."

"And your coven abides by the law?"

She swallows thickly, her gaze dropping for a fraction of a second before she nods.

"I see." When I see him, I'll be sure to ask Alec about the blood they sell to the covens. If they're drugging blood from the humans' blood banks, then I'm certain they'd be tainting the blood they sell to the covens as well. A tic in my jaw spasms. Thank fuck we don't drink that shit, but Veronica might.

"And do you plan on drinking the blood from the banks?" I don't miss that her body stills and tenses. "I *need* to know." Not only for her protection; I need to be sure she isn't a part of this scheme to poison other immortals. I'm fairly certain she has nothing to with it, but the way she glances at Vince and instinctively touches her neck where his claiming bite is, has my stomach knotting. As if she thinks being his mate will protect her if she's a part of anything as fucked as tainting blood.

Drawing herself to her full height, Veronica responds loud enough for Vince to hear, "If you'd rather I didn't drink from him—"

"Fuck that! What the fuck, Devin?" Vince's aggression takes me by surprise but as always, my face stays expressionless. My eyes narrow as they meet his and he backs down, no doubt feeling my anger.

"I want her to drink from me." His hands fist at his sides, but he relaxes them, reining in the initial indignation.

"He's your Alpha." Veronica's hushed words seem to relax him a bit.

As Vince comes closer, sidling up to the counter in the kitchen, Veronica's hand gentles on his arm. The touch is light but meaningful.

"This has nothing to do with her drinking from you." A look of relief flashes across Veronica's face. It appears she was only worried I'd make her stop drinking from Vince. Instantly her posture relaxes.

"Good. I want her to," Vince answers and then slides out a stool, the legs of it scraping against the floor as he does.

"So, you two are breaking the law?" I allow a little lightheartedness to enter my voice so Vince will calm the hell down.

Vince nods, letting a smirk grace his lips as he nods at me. "I'm a rulebreaker, Alpha," he jokes, but Veronica is less flippant.

"My entire coven is breaking the law. Most are pissed about the decree, but Natalia is essentially an inquisitor. She regularly visits our queen and the heads of the other covens. I was sent to observe members of the Authority after the queen's son was taken and punished for disobeying Natalia."

"He drank from a human?"

She nods. Vince's attention is focused on Veronica now, the reality sinking in hard that the Authority may step in. His anxiety and anger mix into a cocktail that's practically fucking palpable.

"Where did they take him?"

"To the Authority. To their dungeon. He was given a thousand lashes."

"A thousand?" The surprise is evident in Vince's voice. "A thousand silver lashes?"

She nods once and adds, "He was nearly dead when Natalia brought him back."

"For drinking from a vein?" How the hell is that reasonable?

"He did it in front of Natalia. The bitch had two enforcers take him in the middle of the night. Had they been seen, it would have been war. When she returned him, my queen nearly sent the entire coven to exact vengeance on the Authority. But she put her emotions in check, realizing it wouldn't have been wise. Not when we're so greatly outnumbered."

Vince's pulse still races. Not from fear of lashes, but from the danger his mate is in by staying at a coven clearly on the Authority's radar. His thoughts race but I silence them with a wave of my dominance as his Alpha.

"They allowed this?" I can't fathom that Alec would allow such violence. A thousand lashes just for drinking from a vein. Before she can reply, I ask, "The person offering the vein, they were willing?"

"She was willing. She's his partner. What's even more offensive is that Natalia violates the law herself. She only drinks from a vein, I know she does." I consider her words as she shakes her head.

"How do you know?"

"I've seen her do it for over a century now." Vince wraps his arm around Veronica's waist and pulls her closer to him. She leans into his touch, her hip nestled against him. A smile threatens at the sight of the two of them on agreeable terms after last night, but I hold back.

I don't know what happened between them, but she didn't run like I thought she might.

Perhaps she feels more for him than she lets on. Or perhaps her coven is truly in need.

Desperate times and desperate measures ...

"So that's why your queen sent you. Because her hand is being forced by the coven?" She nods once at my question. "And is it solely Natalia that's pushing the issue?"

"Mostly, but she has the backing of the other members. When they came to collect and imprison Stephan, she brought nearly a dozen other vampires with her."

"Was Alec there?" I hesitate to ask, but I have to make sure before I go to meet with him.

"No, only the vampires of the Authority." If I remember correctly, there are fourteen who are members of the Authority. That's more than most covens.

"Thank you, Veronica. Vince."

He immediately responds, "Yes, Alpha?" That's a much better tone, although he's tense. His emotions are unsteady and I consider him for a moment before speaking. I decide to let his anger from earlier go unchecked.

After all, I've heard having a vampire drink from you can be quite an experience. She's his mate and he's made his boundaries clear. I'll respect that.

"Are you sparring today?"

He nods and elaborates, "Dom and Caleb are going to go at it. I have to be around to see that." He glances at his mate and smiles. "And I thought it would be fun for them to see what Veronica can do."

I nod in agreement. Natalia taught Veronica, so I have no doubt she can handle herself just fine.

"I'll have to watch her at some point as well." First I'll speak with Alec. Too much right now is uncertain. Alec will tell me what I need to know, and then I'll be able to take action. I'm responsible for the pack and my mate needs safety above all else.

CHAPTER FOUR

Dom

Lizzie looks so fucking small on the sparring platform. My mate, my gorgeous mate. Last night was a damn dream come true. Holding her in my arms while I rutted into her tight pussy. I've waited all my life for her. She's mine now and she's eager to have me. A low, rumbling growl barrels through my chest at the memory of her soft whimpers and loud moans of pleasure. An asymmetric grin pulls at Caleb's chest when he hears the animalistic sound rip through me. She took us both just as she was made to.

"Fucking perfect." He mutters in my head so only I can hear him. *"You think this is going to work?"*

I shrug my shoulders.

"I have no idea, but it's worth a shot." We decided last night that teaching Lizzie to spar may help bring her wolf out again.

She's only felt her the one time since the offering and although I'm happy her wolf returned, it's fucking tearing up my sweet little mate.

She's been traumatized and her wolf abandoning her is a reminder of that. No matter how much she smiles and pretends it doesn't get to her, she wants her wolf to come back and stay. She wants to shift so badly; I know she does. I have no idea if she'll ever be able to, but I'll do everything I can to help her.

"Well, even if it doesn't coax her wolf out to play, she'll at least learn how to fight," Caleb comments and his thoughts turn darker. It's a side of Caleb I'm not comfortable with even if Lizzie is.

"You better not fucking bruise her." My statement, whispered aloud, carries a thinly veiled threat.

Caleb's reaction is dismissive. *"Have you seen our mate? I'm not the only one who's fucked up in our pairing, and if it's what she craves—"*

"We should've taken it easier on her."

"You didn't exactly think that last night," he rebuts.

The low growl is repressed as I tear my gaze from his. Shuffling my feet and kicking the floor, I avoid the sight of Lizzie's neck as guilt washes over me. Her hips are covered in bruises from where we gripped her, and her neck is covered in bites and bruises. Both of our marks are an angry red color.

I confess to him, *"I wish her wolf would come heal her. I hate seeing her so fucking wounded."*

"It might happen. It might not ... but she fucking loved it."

His comment doesn't help loosen the growing knot in my chest. He continues, *"Did you see her looking at herself this morning? She was delighted to see our marks."* His shoulder bumps into mine as he speaks. *"She'll heal up nice and the only thing that'll be left are two silver claiming marks on her neck. Proof she's ours."*

Imagining her beautiful slender neck with our scars on her makes my chest puff out in pride with a warmth spreading through me.

"Damn right she's ours." At my inner words, Lizzie glances over to us and smiles while walking toward the edge of the platform. Her leggings

are practically painted on and her sports bra leaves nothing to the imagination. I'm hard again just looking at her.

"So which one of you two is going to fight me?" Her tone is flirtatious and a blush creeps up her chest to her cheeks as her gaze slips from mine to Caleb's.

"Both of us." Caleb's answer doesn't lack an ounce of sex appeal and she bites into her bottom lip, rocking slightly on her feet.

The flirtation is ... well, it works her up. But he's out of his damn mind.

She can't handle both of us, I tell him.

He chuckles at my words as he climbs into the ring and it takes me a moment to register why. When I do, I let out a huff of a laugh.

"She won't be able to fight either of us off right now, but she'll learn." He answers me loud enough for her to hear.

"All right." I concede and follow Caleb onto the platform just as I see Veronica and Vince heading our way. A prick of unease flows through me. Vince has been ... off. He's bothered, and we can all feel it.

"Showtime isn't until later. We're training our baby girl first," Caleb calls out to them.

With the arrival of guests, Lizzie seems to second-guess our plans.

"Can I just watch?" Her tone makes it obvious she's a bit hesitant to get physical.

"Nope. You gotta learn a little something first." Caleb's answer is immediate and casual, but as I remind him, she's been through a lot. Anything could trigger a trauma response. I want to avoid that if possible.

"I'm scared," she barely whispers as Veronica and Vince come up to the platform.

"Nothing to be scared of, baby." He kisses her left cheek. It's only a peck, but it soothes her instantly. The bond between mates will do that and the anxiousness I feel also dissipates.

"Fine." She draws her shoulders back and raises her little fists while backing up to the edge of the platform. "But I want a kiss for every punch I get in."

I chuckle at the sight of her. Our sweet mate has a lot to learn.

"First of all, don't back yourself into a corner. Never," I say.

Caleb nods his head in agreement with me and adds, "It's even worse when you're outnumbered. Now get your ass back here."

She immediately walks back to join us at the center of the ring. He moves her easily, so that she's facing away from us. "So I should just stand here and wait?" she asks.

Caleb eyes her ass as he answers and then slips his hands around her hips before kissing her neck once again. "If you can't run, yes. Wait for your opponent to attack and watch carefully so you can block. Take your attacker off guard. If you can get in the first hit, make sure you make contact and really hurt them. Make it worth the energy."

"So if I can't run, hit first—" She's paying attention, even if Caleb appears to be preoccupied with other thoughts.

"Only hit if you can get a good hit in. If not, then you wait so you can block." Caleb interrupts her and I nod at his words although she can't see.

"How will I know if it'll be a good hit?"

"If you have easy access to the eyes, nose, throat or groin, then take the shot."

"Turn around and watch," I command her and she obeys instantly.

I put my hand up to Caleb's nose with my palm out and motion upward. "Like this, little one. That'll break the nose and push the bone into the brain."

Caleb turns sideways and elbows me in the gut. "Or shove your elbow right here. Clasp your hands and push with all your weight." The move knocks the wind out of me, but I only smile. "Cheap shot," I grunt.

"You want to try to land a hit instead of waiting for us to come from behind?"

She nods and says, "Yeah, let me try." Our little mate licks her lower lip, excitement running through her. It's a good sign.

"Any hint this has turned into anything ... alarming ... and I'm calling it off," I remind Caleb internally.

"Agreed," he answers back.

"All right," I offer to Lizzie, "I'm going to block it, but don't stop." She takes a deep breath and tries to palm strike my nose, but she's too damn slow and I'm able to snatch her wrist without much effort at all. "Faster, little one. Make it count."

She purses her lips when I release her hand, her eyes narrowing at the challenge. "But you know it's coming."

I nod my head at her deflated tone.

Caleb's arms are crossed over his chest as he tells her, "Your attackers may expect you to attack also. You have to be quick."

Appearing dejected, she rocks back and forth with her eyes on the ground. I part my lips and take a small step forward ready to comfort her, and that little hand of hers comes up from fucking nowhere and she actually lands the blow.

Square against my nose.

"Fuck!" My hands fly to my face. The stinging pain makes me wince and I think I'm bleeding.

Caleb's laughing his ass off and Vince is doing the same. I glance over to see Veronica full-on grinning, Vince's arm wrapped around her waist.

"Your girl got a hit on you, Dom. You a big softy now that you're mated?"

"Come on up here, Vince, and find out." That wipes the smile off his face; only for a second, though.

"Are you okay?" my mate questions softly. I don't miss the fact she's having second thoughts about this plan to coax out her wolf and her wide blue eyes are shining with vulnerability.

"Of course," I tell her and lean forward, giving her a peck on the right cheek, a twin kiss to match the one Caleb gave her earlier. Grinning down at her I add, "Now I know both you and Caleb take cheap shots."

That makes her genuinely smile and seeing her beautiful face light up fills my chest with warmth. The moment's interrupted, though … by her other mate.

"Good job, baby girl." Caleb gives her another small kiss on her cheek before raising his arms and getting into a boxing stance. "Now come get me, baby."

He looks ridiculous.

Lizzie just stands there shyly looking between the two of us. "You sure it's okay, Dom?" she says.

I chuckle at her concern and wipe my nose. The pain's already gone and I can feel it's mostly healed. "Yeah, little one. You did good. Now give me a kiss and don't ask again." She walks easily to me and brushes those soft, sweet lips of hers against mine. A rumble of satisfaction settles in my chest. I take a step back. "I wasn't expecting that one. You did well to take advantage of the situation and catch me off guard."

"Now we're ready, baby. Come on. It's not going to be easy." Caleb motions her forward and she practically lunges at him, aiming for his nose again. Caleb's quick to wrap his arms around her shoulders in a bear hug and tries to pull her into his chest to capture her, she quickly spins around so her back is to him. Shifting her hips, she drives an elbow into his side putting all her weight behind it. She moves fast. Faster than a human.

Caleb grunts and drops to the floor while I let out a bark of a laugh. I feel myself smile. Her eyes catch mine as I laugh and she stands confidently over Caleb's balled-up form.

Fuck, why does that turn me on like it does?

"You have such a beautiful smile," she tells me. Her kind words stoke the fire in me. I want nothing more than to pull her onto the ground and devour her body.

"Not now, jackass." Caleb's words resonate inside my head and snap me out of it. I walk forward to reward my little mate with a kiss.

"You're a natural," I say. She leans into my touch and then looks to Caleb for a kiss from him. The small act makes me chuckle.

"Okay, how do I hit the groin? You didn't show me."

Oh, fuck that.

"Vince, get up here," I yell out to the now pale fucker who only stops laughing once I call his name.

"Nah, I'm good, man." I look at Caleb and open my mouth, but he beats me to the punch.

"I got the last hit. You can take this one." He walks to our little mate and kisses her cheek. "Hit him hard, baby. If you can get a knee to his groin, you'll get him on the ground for sure."

Lizzie's hesitant to ask something but before I can tell her to say whatever's on her mind she asks, "Are you two letting me get these hits in?"

I shake my head adamantly, as does Caleb. "Not at all. I wasn't ready for that. You're much faster than I expected." His fingers brush the hair back away from her face while he leans forward and whispers to her, "You're as fast as a wolf. I didn't expect that." A blush creeps up her chest and into her cheeks.

"My turn," Veronica calls out from below. "You three obviously need a break before you start giving the two of us a different kind of show. Come, pup, I want to see what kind of damage you can do."

I take Lizzie's small hand in mine. "It will be good for you to watch." My eyes find Vince's. "And I'll enjoy watching Vince's mate beat the shit out of him." Caleb laughs on the other side of Lizzie before he pulls her hand to his mouth for another kiss.

She loves it when we kiss her. It keeps her smiling, keeps her happy. I imagine it keeps her thoughts from going elsewhere.

"Can we do it again after them?" Lizzie asks as we climb down.

"Of course. Especially now that we know you have some natural ability. Let's just take a moment, all right?"

"I'm happy she took that as well as she did." I speak to Caleb in my head.

"Yeah, that's our mate, though. She's such a wild spitfire."

"Sometimes, but other times she's so shy."

"Well, she did just meet us, Dom. She's gotta have some time to open up." He has a good point. *"And I think she's doing wonderfully."* I nod at his silent words.

He drops her hand to wrap his arm around her waist, pulling her into him and slightly away from me. Her hand squeezes mine and it gives me enough satisfaction to not be jealous of his possessive move.

"You did great, baby. Next time we'll be ready for you, though." She blushes as he whispers into her ear. Settling down on the ground next to Lizzie, I look up to see Veronica and Vince circling each other. "This should be a good show." I pull Lizzie closer to me and Caleb grins as he sits on her other side, knowing exactly what I'm doing. He can deal with me pulling cheap shots too.

He leans back resting on his forearms and concentrates on the two sparring. "Vampires are faster than us. Much faster, but we have far more strength than they do," I say. Lizzie nods, acknowledging my words.

I watch her pale blue eyes widen as Veronica lands a blow to Vince's chest before dropping to the ground to avoid Vince's attempt to grab her. She slides easily between his wide-legged stance and stands behind him, landing a kick to his back before he's even registered what's happened. He lands on all fours but quickly recovers, leaping and spinning in midair to snatch her wrist as she strikes. She's completely unaffected by his hold and lands a punch to his throat, right on his Adam's apple. The blow makes him loosen his grip on her enough for her to jump back to the other side of the ring as his hands fly to his throat. Vince growls his frustration and the two circle each other again.

The first round goes to Veronica. By a long shot.

"Holy shit, it's like a blur," Lizzie breathes out the words, clearly in awe.

"Yeah," I answer, equally impressed although I expected this. Still, it's something else to watch a vampire move and fight. The unease from earlier returns.

"Do you see how she kept fighting without hesitation? He had a grip on her, but she didn't let that stop her attack." I speak quietly into Lizzie's ear while she continues to watch. "You need to have that same tenacity. Never stop fighting." I notice movement from the corner of my eye and I glance at Caleb as he nods his head and smiles.

"Never stop fighting, baby."

She smiles at his words, but immediately winces as Veronica kicks

Vince hard in the chest. The telltale crunch of broken ribs resonates in the air.

Vince is knocked off-balance from the hit. Dropping to one knee, he's able to grab her ankle. She brings her other leg back and nearly lands another vicious kick to his face, but Vince tackles her to the platform with her beneath him. His crushing weight pins her in place. He releases her leg and reaches for her waist as she wriggles under him in an effort to get free. They wrestle for a moment and he pulls her hips toward his with a strong grip. Just as he smiles, thinking he's won, she throws her elbow back and it lands hard on his nose.

"Oh fuck," Caleb comments, his hand moving to his nose in empathy.

She's ruthless, and her skills are designed to take advantage of the natural instinct to protect the sensitive areas she targets.

"Oh!" Lizzie's hands flies to her nose too as she grimaces. Yeah, I know that fucking hurt. Vince doesn't release Veronica, though, which is obviously what she was counting on. Instead he drops all his weight onto her and his head lays against her back, caging her in. She struggles beneath him for a moment before realizing he's got her pinned. Despite her formidable fighting ability, she's physically outclassed in such a vulnerable position by his massive strength.

I barely hear Vince say "Gotcha" in a playful tone and then he kisses the crook of her neck. Veronica continues to struggle, though. Her breathing picks up until it's nearly panicked. Looking at Caleb, both confusion and concern are apparent on his face. Lizzie's shoulders hunch and she stirs uncomfortably between us.

"Get off of me!" Veronica shouts and pushes forcefully against Vince's massive frame. He props himself up on his knees, lifting his chest off of her back. In a blur of motion almost too quick to follow, she moves to stand on the other side of the ring.

Vince holds both his hands up while he stays still on his knees. "It's just me." Her shoulders rise and fall as her breathing slowly evens out. Slowly, he gets off the ground and walks calmly to her as if she's a cornered animal.

She swallows and shakes out her hair. "I know. I know." He takes her hand and leads her to the stairs.

"What the hell was that about?" I ask Vince in my head.

"Don't worry about it. I'll take care of her." I nod my head slightly as they walk past us. Lizzie looks to Veronica with concern in her eyes, but the vampire stares straight ahead, obviously still shaken and embarrassed by her reaction.

"She'll be all right, little one." I kiss her soft lips as Caleb rises.

"Come on, baby girl. We're going to show you how to block like Vince should've done." I snort at his words and help our little mate up, who's still watching Veronica leave.

CHAPTER FIVE

Vince

Veronica scowls when she sees the bed, her spine stiffening and she says, "You think you can chain me, pup?" There's humor in her voice and a little smirk on those beautiful full lips.

I love that nickname she's given me. *Pup.* The way the word spills from her lips makes my own lift in an asymmetric grin.

With every heavy step I take toward the pair of handcuffs dangling from the headboard, she follows behind me. I push aside the black velvet covering the cuffs so she can see the metal underneath. "They're silver. You won't be able to break out of these, babe." A thump in my chest makes me second-guess what I'm doing as she gasps and then goes still. It's hard to swallow with the flash of betrayal that lights across her eyes. Only for a moment, though. She needs this. She needs me to be a worthy mate. One who will heal her as much as she's already healed me.

With her gaze focused on the bright metal, she

noticeably swallows. Her dark eyes find mine while she shakes her head slightly.

My tone is soothing and I add a hint of playfulness although that thump in my chest happens again. "Don't you trust me, baby?"

She hesitates, merely staring at the cuffs in my hand. Eventually she settles on a muttered truth spoken just beneath her breath. "I don't want to do this."

I know she doesn't, but after seeing her triggered and scared again today, I'm not going to wait to show my mate she can trust me.

"How about if I promise to give you the key and do everything you command me to do?" I offer her. Her lips purse and she narrows her eyes. I need to sweeten the deal. "It's just me, baby. Just me and only for an hour." Her posture shifts slightly, but she keeps her arms crossed tight over her chest. "Just one hour," I say softly, taking a step closer to her. My hand rests on her shoulder, but only for a moment before she leaves me.

Her dark eyes find mine again before she clicks her tongue and walks over to trail her fingers along the velvet covering the silver cuffs.

"I tied it up here too, in case you want to grip it. There's no way it'll touch your skin, baby." Her fingers slip inside the cuff. They're quality, the best I could find, and nicely padded. They won't hurt her at all.

"Why?" she questions.

"You're afraid of giving up control ... even when it comes to your mate."

Swallowing thickly, she stares back at me, the truth of my words sinking deep into her.

"I only exist for you. I would die for you. And you don't trust me." It fucking kills me to say it out loud. "I have to do something, Veronica."

"Fine," she states with an elegance and finality only a woman like her can deliver. "Do it quickly before I change my mind."

I smirk at her response, even as I see her shoulders rise and fall with her deep intake of breath, the deep red silk shining in the dim light as she does. She doesn't wait for me to undress her as she sits at the foot of the bed and lies back with her wrists lifted above her head. The thin straps of her nightgown slide down her shoulders and she doesn't bother to pull them back into place.

She'll have plenty of slack until I get to her legs.

Any bit of heated excitement turns bitterly cold as I watch her hold her breath and close her eyes when the cuffs snap in place around her dainty wrists. With a heaviness I never imagined I'd feel when it came to my mate, I tug the handcuffs to ensure they're snug and secure before moving to the cuffs at the foot of the bed.

The room is quiet. So quiet, the click of the last shackle locking around her ankle sounds impossibly loud. A shudder runs through her body as I take her in.

A gorgeous vampire, laid out on my bed clad in only a thin whisper of silk that hides next to nothing from me. My hand gentles on her calf as I prepare to test her restraints, but she beats me to it, yanking against the restraints.

"Key." She says the single word with authority although a hint of panic lingers.

I give her a tight smile and prepare myself for her wrath with gritted teeth as I slip the key in between her lips. Instantly her eyes widen as she spits the key out. "Give me the key!" Heated anger I've never felt from her before radiates off her. So much so, my wolf retreats.

She yells again, the pain and desperation she's feeling coming through clearly as I pick the key up off the floor and move closer to place it back in her mouth.

Her gorgeous frame struggles against the chains, but her arms don't move far enough to reach me. Even if she had the key in her hands, she'd be unable to unlock the cuffs. She's utterly at my mercy and I can see the moment she realizes she needs me to free herself. Sadness and betrayal flash across her face; in that instant I nearly regret my decision.

"You fucking dog!"

"It's just for one hour." My voice is soft, but stern. She needs this. She hisses at my simple statement. "I'm still yours, Veronica. I'll do whatever you say."

"Untie me!"

"Anything but that." Her nostrils flare and her face reddens with rage. Her wrists pull against the restraints to no avail.

"If you come near me to do anything else … anything but untie me …" she trails off as I take a deep breath and lean close to kiss her cheek. Close enough for her to strike me with her fist across my jaw, which she does. I pull back, but I'm not far enough away to miss the second swing. The sharp, metallic tang of blood coats my mouth.

Fuck, my mate knows how to fight and make every blow count. The burning heat from her punches jolts me backward. I nearly fall off the bed, but I steady myself. "Babe, that hurt." I pinch my nose to stop the bleeding and straighten it before it heals crooked. Drops of blood fall to the comforter. As I feel my nose mending, I hear her sobs.

"Vince." She whimpers my name in between gasps. "Vince, I'm so sorry. Vincent."

Still hunched over, I wait until the pain of the blows has passed, until physically it no longer exists. It's only a memory.

I wipe my nose with the back of my hand and lean forward to kiss her on her tearstained cheek.

"Please forgive me. Forgive me, Vince, please. I'm so sorry. I—"

I cut her off, pressing her plump lips to mine and caress her face. "It's all right, baby. I knew you wouldn't like this. I knew …"

She shakes her head with her eyes shut tight and her lips pressed together, muting her panicked cries.

"It's not okay. It's not okay." Her words are rushed, a new panic taking over. "Vince, I'm sorry. I'm so sorry. I'm not okay."

I stroke her cheek until she opens her eyes and finds my silver gaze. "I forgive you, baby."

"I'm scared." She whispers the words before another tortured sobs erupts from her throat and she pulls against the chains again.

"It's all right, my love. I'm going to take care of you. I'm going to prove to you that you can trust me." Leaning in close, I kiss her again. Her mouth parts to grant me entry and I suckle her top lip before running my tongue along her sharp fangs.

"Please, Vince, I can't." She shakes her head and her deep brown eyes, rimmed in red, plead with me.

"I'm sorry, I can't. Not yet." Her head drops in defeat as she slowly nods and the sobs subside. "Give me a command, Veronica. I'm still yours."

Her dark eyes filled with red tears find mine and she says, "Hold me."

I lie down and settle my chest into her side before wrapping my powerful arms around her curves. I've never imagined her as this delicate before. I could easily crush her. She struggles against the shackles as another crying jag passes through her body; she trembles under my touch. A small part of me urges me to cave, not liking her reaction. My grip on her tightens. She needs this. She needs to learn to trust me. In time, I know she will.

"What do you want from me, Mistress?" I use her pet name, hoping that will calm her.

"I'm cold." Her softly uttered words contain a plea, not a command. Swallowing the lump in my throat, I pull the covers over our bodies and kiss the small dip in her throat.

"What else?" I need her to command me. I need her to find her strength.

"Just hold me." She sobs again and pulls against her chains as I lie back and gently place her head on my chest.

She cries silently. "I got you, babe. I promise." I barely speak the words, but my vow resonates through her, calming her. It hits me hard that she's not herself. She's not the strong, confident woman I know. She's so damn wounded. "I got you." I kiss her shiny black hair and let her cry.

Next time will be better. Next time I'll push her a little more. Until there is nothing between us but trust. Until she doesn't fear a damn thing in this world. Until she knows I will love her in her worst moments and through it all.

PART II

Blinded Obsession

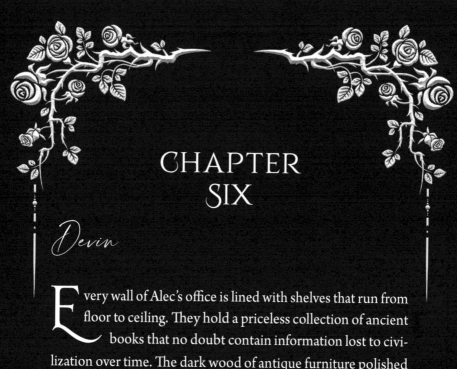

CHAPTER SIX

Devin

E very wall of Alec's office is lined with shelves that run from floor to ceiling. They hold a priceless collection of ancient books that no doubt contain information lost to civilization over time. The dark wood of antique furniture polished to a high shine, yet bearing the marks of history, adorns the office. In the very center of the three-story room sits a heavy desk with books stacked high upon its glossy surface. Two leather wingback chairs have been placed across from it. The pendant lamp above Alec's desk encompasses an open flame, matching the torches placed in sconces around the room.

If I wasn't aware that magic protects this space, I'd worry the texts would be in danger of being lost forever in a fire. It is common knowledge, though, that this room is heavily guarded by powerful wards.

I take a seat across from him and the old leather groans in protest. We're nearly matched in our attire: dark slacks and

simple button-down shirts. Although my clothes are custom tailored to fit my body perfectly. A pair of wire-rimmed glasses peek out from his shirt pocket and today he's opted for a navy blue tie.

It's not the first time I've come to visit him here, but this is the first time it's been to deliver bad news.

"I'd almost forgotten how comfortable these chairs are," I say as I sit back. Alec's emotions are easily read. He allows his aura to coat the air around him. He's peaceful and the comfort of his office makes it simple to follow his lead and adopt a relaxed nature. Vaguely I wonder if he already knows why I'm here.

With a grin that emphasizes the wrinkles around his eyes, he nods agreeably. "I prefer for my guests to feel at ease. Although, you don't seem as comfortable as I'd like."

"It would help if I was here for a different reason." His small smile slips a bit and the air turns cold, but only for a moment. He parts his lips, but a quiet knock at the door stops him from speaking.

A petite blond woman with an upturned nose pushes through the door using her backside as she carefully handles a silver tray loaded with teacups and a teapot. She turns and gracefully strides to the desk.

She sets the tray down gently, jostling the cups only the faintest bit. With a deep breath, she offers Alec a bright smile. Her dark brown eyes seek Alec's approval, shining with obvious affection. A humorous smirk plays at his lips and his light blue eyes find hers.

There's unmistakable romantic tension between them. So much so that I'm given the impression I'm intruding and I readjust in my seat.

"Thank you, dear."

Dear. My brow lifts, although I attempt to hide my reason.

Her gorgeous smile widens further as she leans across the desk to give him a peck on the cheek. I hurriedly avert my eyes as her blouse slips, revealing a bit more than I think she realized. All the sight of the two of them does, is remind me of my own mate. I already long for her.

It's not until I hear the click of the door closing that I'm brought back to the present.

Back to Alec and the matters at hand.

"She seems very nice." Alec grunts a response and lifts the teapot.

"Just sugar? Is my memory correct?" I nod and eye the old sorcerer in front of me. With a heavy sigh, he finally acknowledges the obvious. "She's quite nice. I enjoy her company."

"I think she enjoys yours as well." His eyes dart to the door with longing before he clears his throat and passes me a teacup with its accompanying saucer.

The porcelain clinks and it doesn't escape me that the dainty dishes look completely out of place in my callused hands.

"Your message was very vague. What is it that you need, old friend?"

His blunt response and dismissal of the conversation regarding the woman seems forced. I'm not sure why he seems so touchy about discussing her further. He's the leader of the Authority. The most powerful man I know, human or otherwise. Not because his magic is so much greater than that of the others, but because of his connections.

If he wants something, he's given it without question. I consider asking about the girl, but instead I move on to business. If he wanted to confide in me, he would. Besides, I hate to interfere. Still, the agreeable air seems dampened since she left and I don't care for the change.

"I wish you wouldn't call me that. I'm not nearly as old as you." He chuckles, knowing it's all in good humor. I almost smile at the sorcerer, but with the heavy situation weighing down on my shoulders, my body stays stiff. "Do you have somewhere more private we could speak?" He tilts his head and opens a drawer to pull out a notepad. A pen flies from the drawer and into his open hand before he scribbles something on a sheet of paper.

Away from meddling ears?

I nod my head once, maintaining eye contact while I set the teacup down on the desk.

"Of course. Let's head to the woods, shall we?" He snaps his fingers and the world blurs for only a moment before I'm sitting in the same comfortable chair, my hands still wrapped around the armrests, but in front of me is a babbling creek.

The morning light filters through the leaves onto the damp ground as a gentle wind passes. The shade of a large oak tree grants us privacy. It's a calm place that brings back memories.

I knew he'd bring us here. It's where we used to meet when I was younger. Back when I relied on him to get my footing as Alpha of my territory. Back when I struggled and worried I had made too many mistakes, and that I would fail my pack.

As I swallow down the recollections, a branch crunches under Alec's tread. "You didn't bring your chair," I comment. My head whirls for the span of a slow blink and then I feel settled once again. As if the world hadn't vanished and reappeared with the snap of his fingers.

"I have a feeling I'll be needing to stand." I get up from my seat to join him. We stand side by side watching the water flow over the small rocks. "Which one is it?"

"Which one?" I know what he's hinting at, but I'd rather he say it.

"Which one didn't you want to hear?" His hands are fisted and the balmy air around us stirs with irritation.

"Natalia." I answer honestly.

"Why is that?" His eyes darken, as does the sky. His anger isn't directed at me but I have to remind myself of that as I continue. I'm aware I'm one of a handful whom Alec shows this side to. The emotional, the part of him not ruled by logic. He doesn't need to hide in a cloud of comfort around me. He knows that. The sunless sky and chilled breeze are oddly comforting.

He echoes what stirs inside of me.

"What do you know about the blood you sell to the covens?" I'm relying on the last words of a dead man, but I have no doubt there's truth in what he said. And I trust Veronica's word.

"What blood?" Genuine confusion laces his question.

My fists clench at his ignorance. How the hell could they be conducting business right under his nose without him knowing? A tic in my jaw spasms with anger.

"The blood she's pushing on the covens." My hard words come out low, reflecting my disappointment with him. The clouds turn dark gray and thunder rumbles in the distance.

"She isn't—"

"She is," I say, cutting him off, and the seriousness of the accusation stretches between us.

He scowls and cracks his neck. The wind picks up and the water of the creek seems to heat, the steam rising.

"How did she get that by you?" I stare at him with disbelief. Alec is not a force to be taunted and that's exactly what Natalia's doing. It's not wise of her, yet she's getting away with it.

"Things have been distracting me lately." He slowly regains his composure as he closes his eyes and controls his breathing. His fingers flex, the clouds slowly parting to reveal the sun again and the simmering water cools.

"Things? What kind of *things*?" He glances at me before settling his eyes back upon the free-flowing water. Whatever is bothering him needs to be taken care of immediately. His position as head of the Authority is one that many covet, and they would all kill to have his place. He's all too aware of that fact, as many have tried before.

"Another time for that tale, old friend." He's never hesitated before to confide in me. I square my shoulders as I face him and wait for his eyes to meet mine. A different anxiousness settles through me as doubt creeps into my thoughts.

"We are friends, aren't we, Alec?"

"We are." He smiles warmly at me. It eases my discomfort. "Friends and allies."

"You have many friends."

"No, I have few friends and many allies. They're quite different. You are a friend who happens to be my ally. I have few allies who happen to be my friends."

"That doesn't sound reassuring." He grunts a laugh before sitting on the grass, fiddling with his tie as he stares across the creek. I follow suit.

"It's not. Allies will only stand by you while you have something for them. While you hunger for the same."

"Out with it, Alec. I don't speak in code."

He smiles at my impatience. "Another time. Now, back to Natalia. You're sure of this?"

"I am. She seems to have the backing of the vampires in the Authority."

He nods in understanding.

"I figured; they all work together. It's no matter. They'll face the same consequence." Absently, he plucks two blades of grass and twirls them between his forefinger and thumb. I watch as they lengthen in his grasp, their pale green hue turning more vibrant as they grow.

"They're tainting the blood. I'm thinking they're behind the abduction of the vampires who have gone missing recently. I'm sure they need test subjects."

His breathing stills and another round of thunder booms through the air. He crumples the grass in his fist and the stalks wither, turning brown, dying before my eyes. "Tainting it with what?"

"According to the shifter from Sarin's pack, Natalia made a deal with them. Drugs in exchange for control of Shadow Falls. She wants the blood bank so she can taint the blood she's forcing other vampires to drink. It's a new drug that voids their immortality."

Alec stares at me with disbelief evident in his expression. "I knew she was overstepping her boundaries with the vampires. But I had no idea she'd take it that far." His pale blue eyes search mine as he questions with a single breath, "Are you sure of this?"

"The shifter had nothing to gain and everything to lose by telling me this."

"We need to be certain, Devin. I can't get the backing of the rest of the Authority without irrefutable proof. This needs to be done quietly. No one can know. Not shifters, or vampires. And absolutely not the humans. There would be widespread panic." I already knew that would be his decision, but his sense of urgency regarding the matter is reassuring.

"I came prepared with a plan. Veronica's coven wants the blood bank, so we'll give it to them."

"And then?" His quizzical gaze meets mine.

"Then we'll have the ability to keep tabs on every move that is made."

Alec shakes his head. "This needs to happen quickly and quietly."

"I'll send her to her coven and gain permission for her to observe another town's bank. It'll be under the guise of seeing how things are done. A town where vampires have gone missing. Vince will go with her. Maybe he'll be able to tail them and sniff them out."

Alec nods once. "Do you need anything from me?"

"Not now, but when we're ready I'll need men to take them down."

"You won't have to worry about that. Keep me informed. When we have proof, you'll have the rest of the Authority on your side. It will be more than enough." His light blue eyes find mine and he smiles faintly before telling me, "She will pay greatly for this; I promise you that."

CHAPTER SEVEN

Veronica

The kitchen appears to be the meeting place for the dogs. It seems they prefer this room to the others.

I glance at Dom and Caleb before quickly averting my eyes. My chest thumps and I struggle to restrain my heart from beating faster.

Embarrassment floods through me still.

I know they saw evidence that I'm not well. If I could go back to yesterday and hide it, I would. Instead I'm trapped here, on an estate run by werewolves who are more than aware of my weakness.

Vince slips a hand down my arm, his thumb rubbing soothing circles as if he knows exactly what I'm thinking. I offer him my hand over his, all the while pretending to listen to whatever joke Caleb is making.

I laugh when appropriate and do everything I can to avoid

asking Vince what they're thinking. I already know; the sympathy is there every time Lizzie's eyes meet mine.

Focusing on keeping my breathing even, I slowly flex my hands under the table. My breath threatens to hitch and I start to slouch at the betrayal, but I keep my spine stiff and shoulders squared.

I wish he hadn't pinned me like that in front of them. I wish he wouldn't push me in private, let alone in front of them. I massage my wrists in my lap as anger consumes me. He fucking chained me.

The conversation continues without me. Devin needs to tell us what happened so I can get out of here. Back to the coven and back to safety.

Vince's large hand splays on my thigh; it's rough with calluses. My pup, my mate. My heart weakens at his touch.

The thought of leaving him behind has drifted to the forefront of my mind.

I know he only means to help me, but it's not working. It makes me feel weak and helpless to be anywhere near him. I refuse to be either.

I've worked too damn hard for nearly two centuries to be made so vulnerable. He hasn't lived my life and he'll never know what I've endured. There's no fix or cure.

His simple mind thinks love alone will fix this. I pull away from him, but he grips me harder and turns his head to face me. His silver stare bores into me, but I refuse to look back. My fingers tingle with the itch to touch him; my body wants me to crawl into his lap, but I won't. I shift in my seat so I'm sitting sideways. The move breaks the contact his hand had on my thigh and settles my back to him.

I look toward Devin, defying my mate and my own needs. His exhale is long and slightly shaken. My heart sinks knowing I've hurt him. I don't care, though. He knows what he did. He can deal with the consequences. He knows the immense pain he caused me. What happened in the room was too fucking much for me to give him my love right now. There's nothing but silence and damage between us now. I should have known this would happen.

The last of the wolves, Jude, filters in and the atmosphere changes instantly.

"I want to make this fast and simple." Devin takes a long breath, both of his hands resting on the edge of the counter. His shoulders flex and Caleb stops mid-conversation. "Save your questions until the end." He looks pointedly at his mate and she huffs, not quite in annoyance, but then gives a short nod. She's quite brazen for a little human. I rub my wrists again and look down remembering yesterday morning. Remembering how weak I was yet again for sharing something so personal, too personal, with her. I have no idea what made me want to talk to her. I wish I hadn't. They know too much and I don't like it.

The name *Natalia* catches my attention and my eyes fly to meet Devin's as he speaks. "It appears Natalia and several of the vampires from the Authority are on a mission to eliminate any vampires opposing them."

A chill flows through me. I've suspected that for decades. I've felt she wished to reign over our species, to become the one true holder of authority. To have it spoken by someone else sparks a slight fear that my dreaded thoughts could become reality.

"What's the endgame there?" Dom asks.

"From what we've been told, Natalia wants to destroy their immortality," Devin replies.

A crease forms between my brow. *Destroy their immortality?* How is that even possible?

As if answering my unspoken question, Devin continues. "They're poisoning the blood from the donation centers and most likely the blood being sold to the covens." A mixture of fear and shock widens my eyes as I stare back at Devin's serious expression. His mate glances up at him, looking very much out of place.

It takes great effort to keep my lips shut tight although I want to bombard him with questions of how these allegations came to be. My gaze falls to Grace's laced fingers she's struggling to keep still as Devin delivers exactly what I want to know.

Her heart races and it doesn't escape me that she may feel what I feel in this moment.

"The shifter that attempted to take our mates told us they made a deal with a vampire. That they were going to cede control of Shadow Falls in exchange for a steady drug supply. Sarin's pack will deal with the consequences of their actions. But for now, Alec has asked for our help in proving the dead shifter's allegations are true.

"Veronica's coven wanted to make a deal with us to have a blood bank built in Shadow Falls." Devin's gaze settles on me and everyone else follows suit. "You'll go to your queen and let her know that we're willing to grant that request. No one will mention anything about what we've learned."

My lips part to object. I can't allow my coven to continue drinking tainted blood. Devin speaks before I can, though.

"No one, Veronica. Not one fucking word."

Vince stiffens beside me, but Devin doesn't hesitate to add, "If Natalia or any of the other vampires who are in on this find out that we know what they're up to, we'll be in danger. They will come to kill us and attack the allies we have within the Authority, or they will run. This is the best chance we have at stopping them."

Pressing my lips tightly together, I nod. I don't fucking like it, but I understand and I will obey because without his help, I have no way of knowing what is true and who to trust. Most don't adhere to the law anyway. I cling to that knowledge.

"What about Sarin's pack? Days have passed since the offering and we haven't heard anything," Caleb says.

"You'd think they'd give a shit that we killed four of their members." Jude's response to Caleb earns a nod from Dom.

Lev huffs and snorts before saying, "Yeah, right. Like they care."

"How are we going deal with them?" Dom's voice comes out hard.

"I should've ended him rather than let him run," Devin says, his brows pinching together as he drums his fingers along the table.

"What do we know of their pack?" I ask as I realize I don't know a single thing about the rival pack.

"They fled to a stronghold they have in the mountains. Maybe ten men remain; a few women too, I think," Devin tells us.

"They're weak now. We could easily take them," Caleb says.

Devin's fist slams on the granite countertops, forcing his mate to take a step back. "I will not risk our pack." He calms, softening his voice to add, "We cannot take on too much at once. Understood?"

The pack answers in unison, all but his mate, who peers up at him with uncertainty. Not weeks ago, this human had nothing to fear beyond mortal concerns. And now she's found herself on the brink of war, her fate tied to a mate who will lead us to it. Without looking back at her, Devin's hand reaches out for her and she takes his hand with both of hers.

"Jude, you'll scout out his pack. We don't know enough to go on the offensive. I want to know everything. Come back with intel and a plan of attack. We won't give them any mercy this time."

Jude acknowledges the command with "Yes, Alpha," and the attention turns to us.

"Vince and Veronica will go to her coven. Tell them I want to know how the blood banks are run and go to Still Waters. Three vampires have been abducted. Find them. I want to know everything that's going on. You have four days. No more than that. I also want you to take your fucking cell phone this time, Vince."

"You got it, Alpha," my mate says.

"What drug could possibly make us mortals?" I'm still reeling over this revelation. With all my thoughts running wild, I simply can't imagine it. In centuries there's never even been a whisper of magic or otherwise that could reverse our immortality.

"We don't know. The drug in the shifter we captured is an amphetamine called Captagon. It's highly addictive, plus it keeps them awake and energized." Devin's gaze finds Jude's as he adds, "That could be a problem for you. I expect to hear back from both you and Vince, every hour on the hour. Call Lev. If Lev doesn't hear from you, we'll come immediately. Is that clear?"

They answer in unison, but my question is still left unanswered. "What about the blood, what's the poison?" I can't imagine this drug actually existing.

"We don't know, Veronica. Keep her safe, Vincent."

"That goes without saying," Vince responds, his arm wrapping around my waist protectively. Although there's a warmth to his words and touch, I can't help the irritation. As if I can't keep myself safe. I'm one of the elites of the immortals. Shaking off the disagreeable thoughts I ponder the idea of this rumored drug's existence.

Something I could take that would rid me of this immortality; the thought lights a need deep within me I didn't know I had.

I could be a mortal again. I could be mortal like my mate.

A chill stiffens my bones. I used to dream of what my life would have been like if that day in the rainforest almost two hundred years ago had played out differently. With the knowledge I have now, I'm certain it would've been fucking awful. Still, I've often found myself envious of humans. A small curl to my lips reveals a single fang and I graze the tip of my tongue across the sharp point. If I drank this tainted blood, would I still have my fangs? How long would I live? Long enough to grow old with my mate? A comforting warmth surges through my body at the thought.

I turn slowly in my seat in his direction. He immediately grabs my chair to pull me closer to him. My stomach churns at how cold I was to him just moments ago and so many times in the past few days. He doesn't deserve how harsh I am toward him. I'm certain of this truth, yet I can't help my reaction when he pushes me like he has. I know he means well, but I don't care for it. If I were mortal, though … everything could change. This weight and burden could drift away.

I would give anything to grow old with him. Could I bear children for him? There's no doubt in my mind that I would trade my immortality to have a child. I've lived long enough and experienced more than most would ever dream of. But the pull between Vince and me … this desire to carry a child, perhaps a wolf like him … I would give anything, drink anything. The temptation weighs heavy on my heart. I need to learn more of this drug. If it's true, if I could be mortal again, I would sacrifice everything to have it.

CHAPTER EIGHT

Grace

"How do you know you're pregnant? It's way too early to tell, isn't it?" I still can't wrap my head around the idea that Lizzie could be pregnant. That she even said it.

There's just no way to know that so quickly. It's not possible.

"Dom and Caleb are convinced. They said they can smell it."

"They can smell it?" My nose wrinkles slightly and I take in the sight of my best friend sitting at the end of the counter. In gray sweats and an oversized white T-shirt that I think is Caleb's, she's relaxed as can be as she drops this bombshell.

"They're sure?"

"It's too early for it to be certain, but that's what they said." Pulling the sleeves of my cream sweater over my hands, I keep my fingers tucked inside so I stop picking at the small tear in my jeans. Is she really pregnant? Everything has been too much too fast. I don't understand why she isn't freaking out right now.

"I don't feel any different. I'm just telling you what they said." She shrugs.

Lizzie pops a spoonful of yogurt into her mouth and closes her eyes before she tells me, "I fucking love strawberry yogurt. How come we never bought this before?"

I smile at her goofiness, although it's subdued. Seriously, it's just yogurt. "Didn't know you liked it." Shifting slightly on the barstool, I debate on getting into such a heavy topic, but it's too important not to. "Are you happy?"

Her bright eyes soften as she readjusts her stool and the legs drag on the floor. She puts her hand out on the table, palm up. I put my hand in hers and she squeezes in response. "Happier than I've ever been." Her reassuring words make my whole body relax.

"Are you really pregnant?" I can't fathom that in only days she knows she's pregnant. She shrugs her shoulders and goes back to scraping the plastic cup with her spoon, trying to get out as much as possible.

"They said between the two of them, there's no way they weren't going to knock me up during this last heat." She giggles into her cup, now licking the sides of it since the spoon isn't effective enough. I shake my head and hop off my perch to grab her another from the fridge.

"You're ready to be a mom?"

She smiles as she catches the new cup I toss at her. "I can't fucking wait, Grace. Can you just imagine it? A little baby, cooing at us, snuggling into my arms."

"They scream too, you know? And poop a lot." She laughs at my blunt statement and nods her head.

"Yeah, I know. They have their moments. But it's all worth it. All the late nights of them wanting to be held. When they're gone, I'll miss them. I may be irritated when they cry every time I put them down, but when they're older, I'll wish they'd let me hold them again."

I vaguely wonder if focusing on a baby is a way for her to cope with how different our lives are now. I wonder if it's all moving too fast. I worry for her, but I bite my tongue.

It's not my place and I'll stand with her through anything.

"It's not abnormal, Grace," Lizzie says softly, as if she knows exactly what I'm thinking. "When mates meet and the heat happens … this is what is expected."

She offers me a small smile as she pats my hand. "I've always wanted to be a mom, and I love my mates, truly. Both of them. Even if it's all too fast and there's so much to learn. When I was little, this was my happily ever after. Before … everything else. This was all I wanted."

Her doe eyes brim with tears and I wrap my arms around her in concern. "Fuck, I'm so damn hormonal, Grace." She lets out a sad laugh while tears slip down her cheeks. Wiping them away, she pulls back to tell me, "I don't just want a little baby; I want a family." She leans back farther, dropping her spoon and unopened yogurt into her lap. "I *have* a family."

"You do," I whisper, only just now realizing what she must be feeling. Reconciling her past and present, accepting love, and finally knowing she's safe. They'll protect her from everything.

"They love me so much and I love them too."

"Damn, girl," I joke to lighten the mood as she attempts to gather her composure, "you're definitely pregnant. All emotional." She laughs and pulls her legs into her chest, wiping her eyes.

"I hope I am." Her happiness makes me question my decision to wait. The way she's come round to them makes me wonder if I should do the same with Devin.

The thought of Lizzie holding a baby suddenly sends all sorts of emotions shooting through me, jealousy being the most prominent. It catches me off guard. I'm not a jealous person, and especially not of Lizzie. I want her to have happiness. It's quiet for a moment as I stand up, wanting to shake all of this off.

I shuffle to the fridge to find something to eat while I question my feelings. "What do you think it'll be like?"

"Having a baby?" Her eyes catch mine briefly before I look into the freezer.

"Yeah."

"Heaven. Well, sometimes heaven, sometimes hell. But it's all a phase and it will be worth the hard times."

"It's so much responsibility, so life changing." I snort at my own words. Everything has been so fucking life changing. It seems like every day there's something new, yet Devin is unaffected. Is this world of chaos and danger my normal now?

"It is, but I've always wanted a big family."

"Really?" Surprise coats the single word. "I never knew that."

She nods as I shut the fridge, a package of yogurt in my hand. She says, "I never really talked about it. It's not like I'd ever let a guy near me so ..." She breathes deep before tossing the cup at the trash can and missing. "Crap." Getting up, she walks over to clean up her mess.

"Is that why?" I question as I lean against the counter.

"Why what?"

"Why you never dated anyone?" I feel like a shit friend for not knowing any of this before. She's always been flirtatious but that's as far as things went. To be honest, none of the guys we would hang around with ever seemed like they were good enough for her, so I never questioned her not getting serious with anyone.

"I don't know. I just buried it all and tried not to think about it." She's pitching the cup in the trash; this time it makes it. "You know, I never thought I'd have kids. Since I'm latent, I didn't know if I could risk trying to have a family. What if I settled for some guy back in Shadow Falls? Obviously he would've been human. I peel back the lid slowly, taking my time and letting Lizzie say whatever's on her mind.

"If I settled down with some guy, I never could've told him about what I am. Heck ... I couldn't even tell you. And then if we had a baby, and that baby was a werewolf ..." She shakes her head as she trails off, the rose gold and moonstone earrings I gifted her gently chiming. Lizzie retakes her seat and spins on her stool. She bites her lip, obviously thinking about something. Finally she stops and looks at me as I take the seat next to her. "I always wanted to tell you, but I just couldn't. I didn't want to believe it was true. Some days I'd actually convince myself it was just a nightmare. It was so much easier living like that." She leans in and lays her head on my shoulder. "You're not mad at me, are you?"

Resting my head on top of hers, I answer honestly, "I could never be mad at you, babe. Besides, I knew you went through something and when you were ready, you'd tell me."

"I didn't think I would have ever been ready, though. I never wanted to deal with it, you know?" She leans back to look me in the eyes while I swirl the spoon in yogurt I don't even want to eat.

Setting it down on the counter with finality I nod slightly and tell her, "I know. I really do get it. You don't have to be worried about me. You know I still love you."

"I love you too." She kisses my cheek before going back to spinning on her seat.

All this heavy talk is making a lump form in my throat. My whole world is nothing like it was before. It's as if I'm living in a completely different reality and so much is out of my control.

I decide to change the subject to something I've been wondering about and something I'm certain Lizzie will want to hash out. "Are werewolf babies born human, or like …" I trail off as I think about getting pregnant with Devin's *pups*.

"Do you remember in biology when we talked about the difference between altricial and whatever the fuck the other word is?"

I just blink at her before stating flatly, "I fucking hated bio." My comment grants me a belly laugh from Lizzie that lights up her face and I'm forced to smile in return.

When she recovers, she starts one of her little tidbit tangents she's known for.

"Some babies are born and they're completely dependent on their mother, like humans and dogs, whereas other species give birth and the babies go on their merry way, fully independent, like"—she scrunches her nose in thought—"like sharks, I think."

"You're such a dork." My cheeks hurt from grinning at her. My best friend appears to be back to her usual happy-go-lucky self. For a moment, it all feels normal. For a moment, the smallest moment, I forget everything has changed.

"The first one is called altricial and that's what werewolves are."

"That doesn't really answer my question."

She stares blankly at me. How does she not get this?

"So your baby may be a werewolf, or definitely will be? And ... importantly, do they look like human when they're born or ..." I let the question hang between us, not wanting to imagine the alternative.

Her sarcastic smirk tells me she pities me for my complete lack of knowledge. "This form, as humans, is how they're delivered." I let out a deep breath at that statement. Her next, though, has me tensing right back up. "They'll be werewolf. So will yours, by the way." Lizzie raises her eyebrows at me before continuing. "I just don't know if they'll be latent like me or if they'll be normal."

Latent. My heart sinks as I watch her shoulders hunch. I don't fucking like her getting down on herself. "But you said you felt her, right? Your wolf?"

"Just the once since we've been here. I don't know why she left me." Her somber statement dampens her mood as she spins slowly on the stool.

"What brought her back?" Lizzie blushes at my question, which makes me really want to know what happened. Yes! This is a much better conversation to have. My cheeks burn and I lean in to whisper, "Was it the sex?"

She bites her lip again, looking shy. It's an odd look for her to give me when she tells me, "We didn't have sex, just did other stuff." She shakes her head and composes herself. "But we've had sex since then and she didn't come back. Unless—" Her eyes brighten and she takes a quick inhale.

"What? What was it that brought her back?" I love the hopeful light in her blue eyes.

"Caleb punished me with a belt—"

"What the fuck!" I jump out of my seat, causing it to fly backward and crash on the tile floor. *Punished?* My head spins as the word registers.

Every hair on my body stands on end as adrenaline has me seeing nearly red.

I practically scream as my body burns with anger. "I'll fucking kill him. Where the fuck is Dom?" My heart races as my hands ball into tight fists at my sides. *How the fuck could he hit her?*

"Knock it off, Grace!" Lizzie's quick to tug at my arm while scowling. "And shut your mouth about Dom." She hushes me with a tone I'm not used to and a hurt in her doe eyes that I don't understand. "He didn't do a damn thing to me." I step back, the wind taken out of my sails by her offended reaction.

"He hit you." Staring at her wide eyed with disbelief, I don't understand how she could possibly be defending him.

"First of all, Dom has never laid a finger on me." Her voice cracks as she speaks. "Dom loves me and so does Caleb. Caleb's the one who used a belt to get me to open up to him. And I fucking loved it." She points her finger at me and pushes out each choked-up word with a tone that brooks no disagreement. "You better not fucking judge me for it, Grace."

"I—" I don't know what to say. A numbness of regret runs through me. "I had no right to react that way. I'm sorry. I'm sorry, Lizzie." Putting my hands up in surrender, I walk toward her. My best friend is practically shaking with emotion. "I'm so sorry, babe, it was wrong of me to jump to conclusions." She leans into me for a hug.

"Please don't think badly of me. Don't hold it against him," she says softly. Lizzie pulls back with her hands on my shoulders and says, "Tell me you won't think badly of him. Please." My lips part, although I'm somehow able to hold my tongue. He hit her. He punished her.

"You liked it?" She nods her head and brushes the tears away with the back of her hand. "A belt?" She blushes again, bright red this time.

"I swear, Grace. It was … kinky and I loved it."

"Okay." I try to imagine it and then regret it. "If you're happy, then

I'm happy." Taking a deep breath, I look right into those baby blue eyes of hers when I tell her, "But if either of them hurts you, you know you can tell me, right?"

"It's a good hurt." Her cheeks flush beet red before she gives me a hug as if to end the conversation there. "I love them so damn much. I'm so fucking happy."

To each their own, I suppose. I don't know if I'll ever look at Caleb the same again. Between the pair of her mates there's no way I'd have guessed it was Caleb who'd be into that. An odd feeling comes over me as a weight seems to lift off my chest. I glance at my best friend, so happy and at peace with everything. I feel like I can let go, like for the first time in our lives, she doesn't need me. She has her mates now. Walking past her to pick up my fallen stool, Lizzie gasps and touches her chest.

"Lizzie?" The chair drops back to the floor at the sight of her shocked expression and her hand clutching her shirt.

"I feel my wolf, Grace. I feel her!" Staring at Lizzie, I'm frozen in place.

"What should I do?" I'd do anything for her, but I have no idea how to help her or what to do.

"I don't know. I don't know. I'm so scared she's going to leave me." Tears well in her eyes again. She rubs her chest before whispering, "Please don't leave me."

CHAPTER NINE

Vince

I've never been afraid of vampires. Never in my whole life have I even bothered with the thought of fearing bloodsuckers.

But holy fuck. Walking into the den of Veronica's coven, surrounded by vampires on all sides, I'd be lying if I said there wasn't a cold prick traveling down my spine and eliciting a hint of fear.

Veronica is the first vampire I've met who I've seen as more than an enemy. She's the first I've been able to interact with beyond strategizing about defense and offense. I've seen them before, of course, from the Authority, whenever Devin invited them into our estate, onto our territory. I've killed them when necessary. I've never had to question what would happen if they attacked. Our pack would have demolished them.

There is no pack with me now, though. On their turf and highly outnumbered, I'm not naive enough to think I stand a chance against them. If they decided I was their prey tonight, there isn't a thing I could do to win a fight against the coven.

Acutely aware of such facts, I wrap my arm casually around Veronica's waist. I may be humbled by the terrifying thought, but I'm sure as shit not going to let them know. In my periphery, I keep tabs on them watching me.

Swallowing thickly, I keep my pace even with Veronica's. The click of her heels is muted as she walks, the sound absorbed by the hardened earth.

Why the fuck do they live underground? They're wealthy beyond belief.

They've had hundreds of years to acquire riches and properties. It's known as fact among supernaturals that vampires are stacked with cash. They could afford to build mansions above ground where no sunlight would ever touch them. Yet they live in a fucking cave.

As I lick my lips, the salty air from the damp walls settles on the tip of my tongue. It's a refreshing taste. If I closed my eyes I could almost picture myself on a beach, but it's far too cold.

Again, I'm not a bitch, but why live like this when you could live anywhere? Fucking stupid, if you ask me. Of course, if they're going for intimidating, then they hit that nail on the fucking head. With only torches lining the pitch-black passageway, secured in sconces placed every few feet along the rock walls, it's dark for those whose sight is weak. Realizing I can see better than any of them puts a smirk on my lips.

A relatively large form passes in front of us down another dreary, fire-lit hall; he's a few inches shorter than me and only wearing a pair of white linen pants. His bare feet and chest reflect the light off his pale skin. I catch his scent and the sight of him clearly: human.

My forehead pinches in confusion for only a moment before I see the small scars along his neck. They form an interesting overlapping pattern, like the scales of a dragon. It must've taken hundreds of bites over a long period of time to make that kind of rough scar on the thin skin of his neck. They're only in a small patch on the right side. I lose sight of him as he walks farther through the passage and we continue straight ahead. With a glance down, I note that Veronica doesn't react.

The tunnel appears to end in front of us. No fire on the walls is present to light the path. It only takes a moment to spot the thick, dark red curtains pulled shut that are blocking our way. Veronica reaches forward, drawing one curtain aside. I take the other heavy panel and pull it back much farther than she can, then gesture for her to take the lead. She tries to hide it, but I see her small, satisfied smirk she immediately represses.

My chest constricts. I don't know whether we're okay or not. She's barely spoken to me since I let her off the bed. She's been glacial to me, icing me out. She hasn't tried to boss me around or even called me pup. Nothing. She's given me very little of her attention. She shies away from any physical contact between us. At least she's accepting my touch now that we're in her territory.

What worries me is that I don't know how I'll react if she continues to ignore me while we're here. Where I have no one but her. There's only so much I can hide and my wolf yearns for her touch and acceptance. Brushing off the unwanted feelings, I remind myself she's been more receptive since we left the estate. She's not giving me her full attention, but she's not ignoring me either.

At the thought, her hand briefly brushes against mine. As if she can perceive I need the reassurance. Veronica makes me weak. I would drop to my knees, begging for her to command me if that would ease the tension between us. If she told me to submit to her this very moment, I wouldn't hesitate.

She hasn't told me shit, though. Not a single word.

I'm not sure if she'll ever trust me. What little trust she had in me seems to have been diminished by me chaining her to the bed. It was only meant to help; to show her she didn't have any reason to fear me or my touch. That I would always be hers even if she had no physical control of me. It didn't work. I fucking failed her.

Again.

My chest constricts and my heart skips a beat momentarily. Nearly forgetting where we are, I remind myself to be more mindful of their hearing. Fuck.

After a minute, I shake it off. I *will* heal her. I will help my mate learn to trust me. It's going to take time and I need to accept that. Exhaling a long breath causes Veronica to take a peek at me. Her gorgeous dark eyes pierce through me, not hiding her concern.

Even if she hates herself for it, she cares for me. I know she does.

I smile down at her. Everything in me yearns to kiss her, but I hold myself back. I won't be able to contain myself if she rejects me. And we're in her territory, not mine. I repress the low growl from my wolf. He wants her. I haven't had her since the claiming and that didn't go well. I need to feel her body against mine. I need to give her pleasure and hear her moans of approval. Tightening my arm around her waist brings her closer to me. She stiffens slightly at first, which puts my wolf on high alert, but then she relaxes against me. He's still not happy. He paces restlessly inside me, knowing something's wrong, just not knowing what.

My focus leaves me as I sense a flood of warmth in front of me. Again the tunnel seems to end, but as I expect, thick curtains cut off the passage. I pull at the dark fabric to reveal a brightly lit room. Veronica doesn't hesitate to walk into the luxurious space and I follow her lead. She leaves my hold, but I'm quick to pull her ass back to me. She's mine. And all these fuckers are going to see that.

Apart from a raised brow, she doesn't object to my touch. *Good girl.*

The vast room is more of what I expected to see from her queen and ancient coven. The walls and ceiling are covered in ornate designs. Breathing in deep, I take in the scent of minerals. Gold. It's painted in gold. A closer look at the rough rock walls reveals luxury and decadence beyond belief. The masterful artistry on display must have taken decades to create. I have to squint to make out the hundreds of small fires blending together across the expansive space to make a literal wall of fire. The tone-on-tone metallic paint reflects the flames to the point where it nearly pains my eyes to stare straight ahead. Most of the furniture in the room appears ancient; the seats are intricately carved pieces lined with bloodred velvet fabric. It's completely at odds with the modern, clear acrylic table in the very center of the room.

The seat at the head of the table is taken by a tall, pale woman with smooth skin and black silky hair down to her small waist. Her sharp red nail pierces into her lip as her dark eyes find us. She rises in a blur of motion but then takes a small, slow step forward, making the black jewels adorning her dress clink together as she walks. She reeks of wealth and power. Her nearly black eyes have a youthful shine although I know better.

The other vampires in the room hardly take notice of our entry. But the humans, all wearing the same pants or halter dresses of white linen, take an obvious interest in our presence. All look to us but a single woman lying still on a plush white hide off to the right side of the room. For a moment I tense, thinking the human is dead. But the air carries no scent of decay. I watch her chest gently rise and fall. Fresh, open wounds on her neck indicate someone drank from her recently, but she's alone on the floor. My gut twists with the thought that the humans are here against their will, present only to satisfy the thirst of the vamps. The delight evident in the sets of eyes following our movement begs to differ with my assumption. I would quietly ask Veronica for confirmation, but vampires are known for their ability to hear at great distances.

My curiosity will have to wait.

The seductive voice of the black-eyed queen echoes gently off of the walls. "Veronica, my darling. You've brought a guest?"

A devious smile brightens Veronica's crimson lips. The firelight illuminates her tan skin. She's breathtaking in this lighting, glowing with a golden sheen. My pulse races and desire threatens to consume me. My gorgeous mate is in her element and she thrives here. I can feel her strength through our bond; I practically see her transform into the fierce warrior I met in the alley.

Before I claimed her.

Before I broke her. I shake off the thought. No, I'm *healing* her. She's hurting. Her ability to hide her pain is extraordinary. My eyes travel along her beautiful face, alight with mischief and seduction.

"A guest, or a snack?" a pale man with the same dark eyes says. In less time than it takes to blink, he makes his way across the room to stand in front of me. I swallow thickly, not letting their speed and number cause any more alarm than the initial shock. His clothes and the way his short blond hair is styled nearly make him look human. But his eyes give away his dependency on consuming blood.

"Braeden, you know I don't share." Veronica's voice is playful as she turns her back on her coven to pat the center of my chest. Her head tilts up at me and I don't waste a second to bend down and give her a small kiss on the lips. I keep my eyes closed longer than necessary, sending a clear sign to them that I don't fear their presence. They're no threat to me. At least that's what my actions suggest.

She waits until I open my eyes and I'm caught in her gaze for only a moment as she peers back up at me. There's something there, something between us, but it's quickly forgotten.

Veronica spins to face them, causing her leather skirt to flare around her. "I've found a mate, Adreana. I'll be staying with him for a while." A tic in my jaw spasms and my eyes harden on her back. *A while?* My stomach sinks as I realize the full weight of her words. My life span will be a blip in her existence.

"Of course, darling. Of course." The queen's eyes travel down my body with appreciation. I don't care for it. "So he's yours alone?"

Veronica nods her head slightly before walking past the table to a chaise longue in the corner of the room, extremely close to the wall of fire. "Funny that fate should give me a mate. Don't you think so, my queen?"

"It's odd. It's not completely unheard of, although I thought they were just rumors before."

Braeden appears by Veronica's side, but sits on the ground and stares at the fire with his knees pulled into his chest. He's so motionless he looks like he's made of stone. Veronica shifts her long legs onto the sofa in a very seductive move and pats the seat between her legs. I move deliberately with a casual pace and take my seat, a smirk begging to form on my lips. Her right calf rests on my thigh as her queen stalks toward us.

"What are the rumors, Adreana? I've no memory of a pairing like ours." My thumb rubs small circles on the inside of my mate's knee. She's relaxed and at peace, although it seems false. My eyes linger on her face, her expression one of disinterest; however, she's obviously curious. Her queen sits to my left and I lean back to give the two women an easy view of each other. I feel very much out of place in the quiet room, but I continue to follow Veronica's lead. I'd much rather have her queen's approval as quickly as possible to go to Still Waters and stake out the blood bank, but Veronica doesn't appear to be in any rush.

"I couldn't tell you, my dear. There was word that a vampire had mated with a wolf, and that was all to be said. I'm not sure he ever returned." Adreana's eyes focus on my fingers stroking the inside of Veronica's knee before traveling to her neck. "And you let him claim you, I see. Rather barbaric, wouldn't you agree." I don't let her words affect me in the least as I hold the queen's gaze. Veronica lets out a huff of a small laugh.

"It was quite primitive, but it suited my taste."

"If you say so. And what of the Alpha, is he willing to negotiate? I'm hoping this mating benefited us." Her voice rises toward the end.

"It did, my queen. Devin is willing to give us the bank and allow our control without any interference."

The queen laughs in obvious amusement, then says, "You toy with me, darling?"

Veronica's eyes spark with delight at her queen's approval. "I'd never. He of course desires a plan and would like my mate to receive information from a successful territory. He chose Still Waters. We're planning on taking our leave this evening, I believe."

"I see." The queen sighs and leans deep into the chaise, beckoning an onlooking human to come to her. The man smiles and rises slowly, kneeling in front of her, waiting for her next command. She gently runs her fingers through his thick brown hair.

We sit in silence for a moment. Braeden seems to grow bored and stands, walking to the young woman lying on the plush rug. He squats in front of her and runs his fingers down her chin. "Come, pet."

"I'm tired … You drank so much." She barely breathes the words as she leans into his touch. He chuckles deep and low.

"You need to sleep; would you prefer the floor to my bed?" His voice is full of humor.

"Your bed, please."

He lifts her in his arms as though she weighs nothing and saunters easily out of the room.

"And what do the Alpha and his pack think of the law? Are you expected to only drink from your mate?" The queen's alluring voice brings my eyes to hers, although she's not looking in our direction whatsoever. Her focus is on the man waiting patiently on his knees in front of her.

Veronica smiles easily and says, "He holds the same opinion as I." Her hand finds mine and she brings my fingers to her mouth to suck. My dick instantly hardens. With a quick inhale, I suppress my groan and the need to let my head fall back. The room's sweet smell and the heat of the fire add to the seductive quality of the unnaturally beautiful vampires. "My mate enjoys my touch and I continue to drink from him."

Although her voice is even, the queen's next statement holds a viciousness that's unexpected. "Do you think of me as a hypocritical bitch? Or a coward for bowing to Natalia's demand?"

Veronica sits up abruptly, her speed shocking me for a moment. She bows her head slightly with her lips grazing my knee. "Neither, my queen," she says and her softly spoken words tickle my knee.

"Up." Adreana rests her hand on Veronica's shoulder, and in turn my mate's dark eyes find her queen's. "I'm itching for a war, darling."

"We would stand at your side, if you so desired." My spine stiffens at the turn of the conversation.

This will all be taken care of shortly. The coven would only interfere. I keep my lips pressed tight and rest my hand lightly on Veronica's back, rubbing soothing circles. Her eyes close briefly at my touch, making my wolf pant with longing.

"For now, we'll build the bank. Her presence here will not be tolerated. Not after what she did to Stephan."

For the first time, I turn and look the queen in the eyes. "My Alpha was not pleased to hear what Natalia has done. He sends his sincere condolences."

Her dark eyes search mine for a long moment before she finally speaks. "Well thank you, my dearest wolf. Please send him my regards." Her hand stops in the human's hair and the lack of her touch has him seeking out her gaze. "Would you like me to drink from you, Jaret?"

"Please, my queen." His tone is deferential, but his green eyes practically beg her.

"Come." In a blur that leaves a gentle breeze in her wake, suddenly the queen is standing by the entrance. She passes through the heavy velvet curtains without a single glance over her shoulder as the human quickly follows her path. It's an abrupt end to the conversation to say the least.

"I need to pack, pup." The use of Veronica's pet name for me stirs my dick. My lips lift into a grin as she leans in for a kiss.

"Yes, Mistress." I feel her smile against my lips. Something deep inside me twists, knowing I'm playing into her hand. I'll give her this for now. A give-and-take of sorts. "When we get home, I want you chained again." My words turn the quiet room silent and I feel several pairs of dark eyes boring into me. My mate stiffens, but only for a moment. She leans back and stands.

"When we get back. Until then ..." Her words are left hanging in the air as she walks toward the exit. The blazing heat from the fire quickly fades, leaving me cold in its absence. I pull her frame into my chest and kiss the crook of her neck.

"I love you." Those eyes bore into me again as she turns in my embrace. Her hand rests on the center of my chest. Her lips part and close before her dark eyes find mine.

"I love you too, Vince," she says, barely speaking the words loud enough for me to hear. Her soft, plump lips press against mine in a chaste kiss. She hums her appreciation and turns, straightening her back and lifting her chin. Her strong voice returns. "Now come, pup; we're going to be late." My lips curl in a grin as I follow my mate down the dark, damp hall.

CHAPTER
TEN

Vince

I t's easy enough to catch the scent of the vampires among the humans. Special contacts disguise their eyes and they're dressed in the latest fashion trends unlike Veronica's coven, allowing them to blend into their surroundings. Even so, there are two I spot immediately. One near the entrance, appearing preoccupied at a desk as his fingers click along a keyboard. He pauses momentarily when we enter, but doesn't seem to care enough to fully stop his work. The other I scent is somewhere down the hall.

The building on the whole is small and sterile.

As we enter, I calculate every escape route available should we need one. In front of us are several couches and a small TV on the wall, playing some sort of animated comedy. There are three humans seated in the waiting room and I can smell blood being drawn from at least one more somewhere. I whisper softly to Veronica at the shell of her ear, "I thought the Authority only

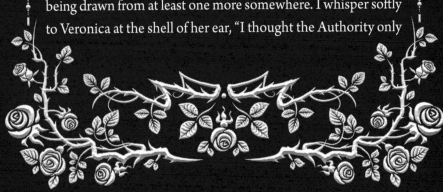

allowed humans to work the building and deliver the blood?" From what I know of their laws, there shouldn't be any vampires here at all.

"That was before vampires started going missing. They used to come alone once a day to pick up the blood and that was all. Now they have two in place at all times, although they aren't to present themselves as anything other than human." I grunt, taking in her words. A little warning would have been nice.

"Do you two have an appointment or are you walk-ins?" a peppy blond woman asks from the front desk. Her eyes drift down my body slowly as she licks her lower lip and clenches her thighs far too noticeably. Veronica surprises me by gripping my hand in a possessive response.

I must admit, her claiming me in such a subtle and human way is more than attractive. I squeeze her hand in return, reveling in the contact.

"Neither. We're here to take a look around, thanks." Her short dismissal nearly makes me laugh as she tugs me along.

"You're here for the tour?" The first vampire I made out rises and strides over, extending his hand for me to shake. Making eye contact, I grip him firmly. His gaze darts to Veronica's. Not that his coworker notices, but subtle clues indicate he's surprised; I'm guessing he didn't realize I was a werewolf. I grin at him before releasing his hand.

"Are you going to show us around or what?" I comment casually, still grinning.

He recovers quickly and says, "Right this way, miss ...?"

"Mrs." Veronica's response makes me snort a laugh. "Please call me by my first name, Veronica. I believe Melinda arranged the appointment." There's slight tension between the two but it's quickly eased.

He gives her a small smile while leading us through the hall. His demeanor turns professional as a short woman leaves the small room to our right with an adhesive bandage on her arm, obviously having just given blood. "Have a wonderful day," he tells her.

"You too," she replies. The woman leaves without even glancing in our direction.

The vampire's fangs aren't visible at all. He's obviously practiced a smile that hides them. I wonder how long he's hidden here among them and what he's heard. Humans have always left me curious. With my new mate, however, vampires may just become my new obsession.

"After you." He motions us into a small room, his button-down shirt shifting slightly as he does and the scent of vampire permeates the air. There's a simple desk with a computer that looks old as shit sitting in the corner. Behind it are a swivel chair and a cabinet housing a variety of equipment. A medical waste bin sits in one corner. Overall, everything looks very simple and not nearly as high tech as I was expecting.

"It's a bit outdated, isn't it?" I quirk a brow at the vampire and he smiles, revealing a bit of his fangs. With no humans around, he freely drops the act.

"Humans get suspicious of wealth."

I nod at his admission. "Makes sense."

Veronica takes the lead, asking him, "What changes have been made since the abductions? We want to know the ins and outs of operations. If you could also explain how vampires managed to disappear in human territory, I would appreciate that information as well."

Her nose wrinkles at the modest surroundings as she paces to the chair with her arms crossed listening to the vampire's response.

"Melinda said a member of Adreana's coven would be here. She didn't say anything about a wolf."

In a blur, she's beside me. "He's with me." With a smirk, she trails her nails along my arm. The move elicits a low growl of approval for the public display of affection.

"Is your Alpha open to relations with other covens?" His question is directed at me, although he noticeably swallows and doesn't make eye contact.

"No. We are willing to appease my mate's queen. That is all."

"I see. How … unusual." The vampire eyes Veronica's neck, lingering on my mark.

"I asked about the changes to protocol?" Veronica says coolly.

"As you can see, we have two of us on guard now. At all times. The three who were abducted were alone when it happened. Since then, we haven't allowed the rogue vampires a chance to take anyone else."

"Rogue vampires?" My hackles raise.

"It had to be other vampires." There's a pause and Veronica's gaze narrows. "There's no way it could've been anyone else. Humans wouldn't dare even if they had the ability to kidnap vampires. The wolves here in Still Waters respect our treaties. Our coven showed the security footage to the Authority. They haven't found anything yet."

"Who was it from the Authority that you spoke with?" My voice comes out hard and his gaze shifts from Veronica to me, back to her and then settles on me once again.

"I'm not sure. It was between them and my queen." He clasps his hands in front of him, not hiding his unease at my presence.

"It's no matter. Do you know why your queen is convinced it was vampires?"

He nods his head at Veronica's question, much more comfortable addressing her. It's probably better that way. Vampires naturally fear my kind and it should stay that way. "We could clearly see the vision of a running vampire. But only for a moment on the screen before Joshua left the property."

"So he was lured away by a vampire?"

"We have no doubt." With a curt nod, his voice is firm. "However, you have nothing to worry about. Although the Authority hasn't made any arrests, we haven't seen any strange activity since we've placed two of us on the property at all times. It is safe and operations have gone seamlessly since then."

"So you simply collect the blood and bring it back to your coven?"

"Yes. Nothing less and nothing more. I'm certain you won't encounter any problems." My eyes search the room for anything amiss. Devin's convinced they're poisoning the blood somehow. My eyes narrow as they zero in on the boxes behind the door.

"Where do you get your equipment?" I ask.

"The Authority sets you up with everything you need to start. It's cheaper than buying everything separately from the humans. And this way we avoid doing any more activity with them than we have to."

"Well, that's very convenient." Veronica voices my own thoughts. If I had to guess, I'd say the blood bags used to collect donations are what's poisoned; maybe they lace the plastic lining.

But what the hell do I know? We're going to have to test the materials after we place an order.

"Do you drink it?" I can't help but to ask if for no other reason than curiosity. A part of me feels complicit for knowing these vampires could be consuming drugs without knowing. It's obvious that Veronica's coven isn't adhering to the law, but how many other covens are as lenient as hers?

His eyes dart between the two of us before he replies, "Of course I do. It's law."

Veronica laughs a sweet, low seductive sound while trailing her fingers down my neck and resting them in the dip of my collarbone. "I prefer sweeter tastes."

"Wolves are sweeter?" His brows raise as he regards my wrists and neck curiously. The way his gaze lingers makes me think he must be hungry. Maybe they are only drinking what's been donated. When his eyes reach my hard stare, he flinches.

"I think we're good here," I state bluntly. I don't appreciate being looked at like I'm a fucking meal. Not by him anyway.

With a soft hum of agreement, Veronica laces her fingers between mine, peering up at me. The male vampire is quick to look away.

I lead Veronica out, loving that she holds on to my hand without hesitation.

Still, I can't help feeling a twisting knot deep in my gut. I just don't feel right. We haven't been intimate since the offering. My wolf isn't happy. My balls aren't either. Every few hours I'm rock hard for her and I'm going to need a release soon. Preferably before I lose my damn mind.

As we walk down the narrow hall, the scents mingle and that unsettled feeling turns into something else. "Let me do a lap and try to catch the scent."

Veronica pauses in the middle of the hall with me, the vampire to our backs. "Do you think you'll find anything?"

I shrug and tell her, "Possibly. A vampire's scent is much different from a human's."

"Oh," she says and purses her lips, "and what is it that we smell like?"

"More metallic and salty." That's the best response I can come up with. It's hard to describe their smell.

She huffs in distaste and says, "So you're saying I smell like a rock."

"No, you smell like honey and jasmine." I lean in close to her ear, backing her body against the handrail, then tell her, "You taste like them too." Heat dances between us instantly and she sucks in a breath, taken aback and very much weak for me. She lets her head fall back, which gives me a clear view of my mark on her. I bend down to kiss it, but she seems to realize my intention and pushes away from me. That twisting sickness in my stomach roils.

"Do a lap and see if you can smell anything." She maneuvers her way out of my hold and it takes everything in me not to react. Not to hold her still, press her against the wall and take her lips with mine. I watch her walk away from me, staying as still as I can.

Taking one deep breath and then another, my tense muscles relax. At least she's found her strength and is giving me orders again.

I follow her out of the blood bank walking a step or two behind. When she stops at the car and turns to face me, I step into her space. It fucking kills me when she stiffens as I cage her body in. Her eyes flash with fear, and then defiance as they narrow at me. She has no reason for either reaction.

I lean down and breathe in her sweet honey scent before kissing her neck. If I want to kiss my mark on her, I'm going to fucking kiss it. I leave an openmouthed kiss exactly where I want it and breathe into her neck, "My Mistress."

As I pull back, she doesn't react. There's a sadness in her eyes, followed by nothing. In a blink, nothing. It guts me.

How have we taken such a huge step back in our relationship? It was so fucking easy, so damn good before. My fists clench as I leave her and head for the back of the building, the thin skin over my knuckles going taut and turning white. My jog turns into a sprint. How the hell did I mess this up so fucking bad?

No. My fist pounds against the dumpster as I near the back exit, leaving a massive dent in the side. I look around and release the breath I was holding when I see that no one saw my outburst. I need to check my anger before it creates more trouble.

I didn't mess this up. I'm fixing it. I only have to think back to her lying on the ground in fear of me after claiming her. That's enough to solidify my decision to keep pushing her. She will learn to trust me again. The fucked-up part is that I think she's really pissed that now I know she can be shaken. Like it somehow makes her weak. That's a load of shit. My mate is anything but weak.

The building is small and it's easy enough to encircle it, drawing in air as I go.

I pause as I scent the air, detecting a number of vampires in the tall grass by the fence. It's easy to catch the trail. I move to follow it through the field but stop short, thinking I shouldn't leave my mate for too long. It's only a moment for me, only seconds until she's back in my sight. I can smell her and feel her even. The thought of leaving her alone, though, even if only for a moment? I don't fucking like it. That tightness in my chest eases as I see my mate's fingers on her neck, running along the little indents of the scar I gave her.

Knowing she very much feels me as I do her, I stride to the passenger side and open the door for her.

"I'll drive," she demands as she walks to the driver's side, ignoring my attempt to reconcile.

Just as she opens the door, I tell her, "It would be better if I drive. After all, I'll be trying to scent our way." She purses her lips and clicks her tongue against the roof of her mouth before striding toward me, her heels tapping out a staccato rhythm on the pavement. "Fine, pup."

Before she can slip into the seat, I wrap my hand around her waist, holding her there. Tension crackles between us as her chest rises and falls. My gaze is locked with hers.

"I want us to be okay," I admit to her in a whisper. Her fingers wrap around mine, releasing my grip as she swallows and says, "Me too."

That's all I get. But it's better than nothing.

It's silent in the car as I pick out the way to go. Veronica's still and quiet.

There's an out-of-sync energy that surrounds us and I despise it. The atmosphere is so different between us. It's as though we're at war, but neither of us wants to be fighting. It takes less than half an hour until I find a gravel road. It reeks of vampires. Far more than what I smelled back at the donation center. Braking, I stop the car. I squint down the road, but it's too difficult to make out what it leads to.

I look to my mate and tell her, "We should continue from here on foot." Watching her hand open the door, suddenly I'm not liking that she's with me. I'm slow. They could outrun me, but they could also grab her. They could take her and do to her whatever the hell they're doing to the other vampires. And what could I do? If they stay to fight, I'll win. My strength is unmatched. But their speed is superior. They could easily outrun me. They could take my mate captive and leave me nothing but a trail to follow.

"Wait." My voice is far too loud, considering vampires are close. She leans into the car with her hands braced on the doorframe.

"What the hell, Vince," she hisses. "You need to be quieter."

"Get in the car." Her eyes narrow at me, not liking my tone. "Baby, there are too many vamps. I don't trust it."

"We'll be fine, Vince."

"I won't be able to live with myself if something happens to you."

"I'll be fine; stop worrying. I can handle myself." She stresses the last part, shifting her stance and the gravel crunches beneath her heels.

"No, I can't live if something were to happen to you." Sadness flashes across her eyes and I don't understand it.

"You'll be just fine if I die. You'll have to learn to live with it." Her hard words seem out of place with the sorrow reflected in her dark eyes. It takes a moment for me to grasp what the hell's going on. My hand slams against the wheel in anger as it hits me. She's going to have to keep living after I die because she's a vampire, not a wolf. I'm such an insensitive asshole. She jolts at my harsh movement.

"I'm sorry. I wish things could be different." I barely get the words through my gritted teeth. I haven't really thought about the fact that my mate is immortal. What the hell is wrong with me? "Get in the car."

"I'll be fine, Vince."

"Get in the damn car right now, Veronica. I'm not going to risk losing you. I will *never* risk you." She fidgets outside the car, her feet gently moving the rocks beneath her again, and for a moment I think she's going to ignore me and walk down the path without me. Instead, she quietly gets in the car and shuts the door with a faint click, staring straight ahead while I gaze at her.

"You'll be fine if I die, Vince. You'll have to be fine and just keep living." Her head turns to face me and her cold dark eyes are devoid of emotion when she tells me, "You can't keep me by your side forever." Her words cut deep into me.

"I'll keep you safe for as long as I live, I promise you." I move to grasp her hand and she lets me. Even as the cords in her neck tighten with a swallow, she lets me hold her hand in mine. I brush my lips against her knuckles and turn her hand over to kiss her palm. "You're mine to keep by my side if I wish."

Her sigh is one that will stay with me. One of stubbornness, hardness, and a somber note of regret. It fucking kills me. She rests her hand in her lap while I start the car and leave the trail. I'll call Devin and tell him what we've discovered as soon as I swallow this lump climbing up my throat. There's no need for us to go down that path into God knows what by ourselves, most likely outnumbered. We're a pack for a reason.

"Do you want to talk about it?" I murmur the words while I drive us toward home. "We should make it there in a few hours. Plenty of time to talk." Before she can answer, my phone's timer goes off, indicating it's time to call Lev. I wait a moment and Veronica only shrugs, her gaze focused on the phone. Reluctantly, I put it on speaker and the other end rings once before Lev picks up.

"Yo, you good?"

Clearing my throat, I tell him, "Yeah, heading back now."

"No leads?" Lev's disappointment is obvious.

"We got something. We're going to need backup, though." I can practically feel his grin through the sounds of his howling laughter. My first thought is new to me: he doesn't have a mate to protect. There's not an ounce of worry for him. "We'll be back soon."

"Still, check in with me again in an hour. I don't need Devin up my ass."

"You got it." I end the conversation and glance at my mate. "Baby, talk to me."

"What do you want me to say?" she's quick to respond, but doesn't look back at me.

"Are we all right?" Her dark eyes find mine and I decide to pull over to have this conversation. There's a hint of worry laying heavy on my shoulders and I can't fucking stand it. Putting the car in park, I push the seat as far back as I can so I can pull my mate into my lap. She gasps as I lift her up and settle her right where I want her.

Both of her palms brace against my chest. Her eyes are wide and the vulnerability she tries to hide shines back at me. I'm gentle as I brush her hair back from her face with my knuckles. Her skin is smooth and that simple touch forces her to close her eyes.

"I need to know we're okay, baby. I know I pushed you. I was just trying to help and I'm worried I did the opposite of what I wanted."

"I know you were. It's fine." She shrugs off my concerns, the cords in her neck tensing as she swallows. My entire body bristles at how she tries to play it off. Her tone is glib, but her body language isn't.

"It's obviously not fine," I answer, my voice louder than I wish it was. She tenses but I don't stop, telling her, "You aren't the same. I'm sorry,

341

baby." Taking her chin in my hand, I force her to look at me. "I love you and I'm sorry."

"I know, and I love you too. I do." Her words act as a balm, easing the tension and numbing the burning concern that's had me twisted up all day long. Her hand rests on mine and she waits a moment before admitting, "I'm trying to be okay with being scared."

"You don't have anything to be scared of."

A soft smile that's far too sad pulls up her lips and she says, "I'm already scared of what I'm going to do when you're gone … and how that's going to feel."

"Baby," I breathe and my fingers spear through her hair. "Don't think about that."

All she does is huff and then her eyes drop to my lips. "I love you. You know that, don't you?"

My lips crash against hers instantly. Parting her lips with mine, I suckle her top lip. "I know," I groan. "I love you too." Her fangs gently graze my lips, making me moan into her mouth. She rocks her body against my hardening length.

"This. This is something I never dared to want or dream," she tells me as her back straightens and she spreads her legs wider.

My head is instantly cloudy with lust. Her lips drop to my neck and her fangs slip down my tender skin. I let my head fall back, giving her more room. "Don't tease me, baby. I need you so fucking bad."

"Aww, is my pup hurting?" A smile creeps onto my lips at her teasing. *That's my mate.*

"You know I am. I've been wanting inside you all damn day." She climbs off of me and my wolf growls at the loss of her touch, making my eyes instantly widen. I force my wolf to stay back, knowing she's not going to tease me. Not too much, at least.

She settles in her seat, making me think maybe she is just fucking with me. *Shit.* I can't take being teased like this. Not with this tension between us. Her hands slip up her skirt and she slides her lace panties down her slender, long legs. Over one heel and then the other until they're off. *Fuck yes.* My hands fly to my zipper so I can unleash my cock, precum already beading at my slit. I need to be inside of her as soon as fucking possible. I lift my ass up so I can pull down my jeans and stroke myself a few times, waiting for her to climb on top.

She gracefully straddles me more quickly than should be possible, and easily slides down my length before I can do anything to help her. *Fuck,* she's so damn wet and hot. And fucking tight. I moan as she pushes herself all the way onto my dick.

"Fuck, baby. You feel so fucking good." My hands rest on her hips and she stills for a moment. I close my eyes and hold my breath, hoping I haven't scared her off. I only dare to breathe again once she starts moving up and down, stroking my dick with her hot pussy. My hands remain on her hips and my fingertips dig into her flesh, but I don't dare take control. She'll give it to me when she's ready, but for now I'll be patient.

"You want me to let you go?" I offer and she only shakes her head, her eyes closed as she practically fucks herself on my cock.

I nip her neck. As I do, her dark nipples harden and I'm tempted to rip her clothes from her. To tear them off and take her how the beast in-side me wants to.

It's what the beast inside me wants, but there's not an ounce of me that would dare. That would risk frightening or triggering her in the least. I tilt my hips up so the angle lets me fill her deeper, lets me hit the back of her cunt and her bottom lip drops down with the faintest mewl of plea-sure. Giving her this is all I want.

"Tell me what to do, baby."

Her head falls forward to rest on my shoulder as her pace picks up and I have to let go of her to grab the wheel behind her. If my hands stay on her, I'm going to take control. I'm barely able to keep myself from buck-ing into her and pounding into that sweet heat of hers. The smell of her arousal and the little moans pouring from those dark red lips have me on edge. Sensing my growing need, Veronica stops and puts her hands on my shoulders.

"Take me, Vince." My eyes shoot to hers, finding her nothing but serious. "Take me again. I want you to claim me again."

I don't hesitate to take control. "Turn around." She quickly spins around and positions my cock at her hot entrance. Gripping her hips, I pound her wet hole as my heels dig into the floor of the car. I piston into her tight pussy and nip at her shoulder. She moans in pleasure at the feel of my teeth grazing her neck. I refuse to lose focus. I need to pay attention to her reaction and make sure I don't cross the line.

I concentrate on the sound of her soft whimpers as her pussy pulses around my dick with the need to come. My hand reaches around to her front and I rub ruthless circles against her clit. She writhes beautifully, the pleasure taking over. She throws her head back and it lands on my shoulder, exposing her neck to me and making it that much easier to put my teeth right where her claiming mark is. The time has passed to truly claim her, but I'll give her exactly what she wants. And at the next full moon, I'll sink my teeth into her neck and claim her as my mate once again.

It's not a normal thing, to claim a mate twice. But we both need this. And I'm sure as fuck not going to deny her. Her pussy spasms on my dick and nearly has me finding my release as I slam into her to the hilt, but my eyes are centered on her expression, making sure it's only pleasure that has her trembling in my arms.

"Vince," she says, moaning my name. I lick her neck and watch as her body jolts from my touch. It makes me smile. As aftershocks pulse through her body, I ease my still-hard dick out of her and push the head against her ass. Her eyes pop open at the foreign touch. "Vince." This time my name on her lips is a warning. I'm ready to push her a little. Now that she's sated and has more control than she did when she was chained, I think she'll give it to me.

Moving her arousal to her puckered hole, I press a finger in and then another, making sure there's enough to lubricate her.

"Grab the wheel, baby, and don't you dare let go." She hesitates to obey, but her delicate hands grip the wheel as I ease into her. Her sharp fangs sink into her bottom lip and the sight alone has me leaking more and more into her. I watch closely as inch by inch of my cock slowly disappears into her ass. *Fuck me.* I press in deeper and don't stop, burying myself to the hilt as she squirms on top of me.

"You are so fucking sexy, so damn strong and fierce," I tell her as I move in and out of her slowly. "And you know what I'm going to do with you? With my powerful mate?" I nip her earlobe as she moans in ecstasy. "I'm going to come in your ass."

Fuck, just saying the words almost has me losing it. Thrusting harder into her, I pick up my pace. Her arousal leaks out of her pussy, dripping between us and down my thighs. Veronica's moans match my groans and I kiss her neck frantically. My eyes don't leave her face, though.

I need to make sure she enjoys this. I'm going to push her and take from her, and make her fucking love it. I buck into her over and over again until I feel my balls tighten and lift, and that familiar tingle pricks at my spine. "I'm going to come in your tight ass and you better fucking come with me."

The rough pad of my thumb strokes her clit again and again, demanding another orgasm from her. My fangs dig into her neck; the move makes her body tremble as she screams out with another release. I dig my teeth further into her soft flesh as I pound into her ass four more times until I shoot wave after wave of cum into her. I don't let up on her clit or release her neck until I've drained every bit of her climax from her.

She lays limp in my arms as she comes down from the high. I smile in satisfaction, knowing I've taken her and she enjoyed me being in control. I lick away the bit of blood on her neck and kiss the new mark. A satisfied rumble barrels through my chest; my wolf is finally settling.

Nuzzling into the crook of her neck, I ask her, "Did you enjoy that, my mate?"

She softly murmurs, "I love you so much." Her heavy head drifts to the side as her lips find mine. Finally, I feel like everything is going to be all right. I nip her top lip, which makes her smile and my wolf howls with pride.

"Vince?"

"Yeah, baby?"

"I'm thirsty." Her dark eyes focus on my neck as she licks her lips. *Fuck, yeah.* My dick twitches, still inside her.

"Go ahead, baby," I tell her and arch my neck so she can dig in.

Her small laugh draws my attention back to her. "Can I take my hands off the wheel?" My smart-ass mate. I give her a kiss on her cheek.

"Yeah, baby, let go. I've got you."

PART III

Immortal Love

CHAPTER ELEVEN

Devin

"Come on, sweetheart, don't look at me like that." I don't even recognize my own voice as I plead with my mate to be reasonable. Yet again.

"Like what?"

"Like you're pissed at me and ready to fight." Steam is still drifting from the bathroom door I just walked out of and I can tell she's ready to lay into me again. I fucking love her fire, but damn, what the hell did I do now?

"I don't want to fight and I'm not mad." Grace crosses her legs in the center of the bed and lowers her head. I watch as she bunches the covers around her naked waist and pulls at the threads on the comforter.

"Then why are you pouting?" I don't understand my mate and her emotions. Humans should come with a fucking handbook.

"I don't want you to go. I'm nervous something bad is going

to happen." Her raw confession is laced with vulnerability as she looks up at me through her thick lashes. Her hazel eyes are brimming with unwarranted hope that I'll stay with her rather than head out to Still Waters.

Fuck.

Striding over to the bed, I run the towel over my face and hair once more before dropping it to the floor. The chill on my damp skin does nothing to calm my growing erection. Seeing her naked on a bed, how could I not be hard? Even if she is mad at me. Shit, her anger only fuels my fire. It only makes me want to tame her that much more.

"I won't be gone long." I pick her up easily and settle her ass in my lap where she fits just perfectly. She nestles her head into my chest and runs her fingers through that bit of hair above my belly button that trails down to something else I'd rather she play with. I shut down those thoughts and concentrate on my mate. I need to distract her and get her preoccupied with something before I go. "Have you decided what you want to do?" She surprises me when she nods into my chest. She lifts her chin and meets my eyes for the first time since I came into the room.

"I want to start a charity with Lizzie. For abused children."

"Humans?"

"Yes, of course." *Of course.* I resist the urge to tell her no. I can give this to her. It'll be a pain in the ass and she'll fight me with all the restrictions I'll have to put on her, but if she really wants it, I'll bend over backward to give it to her.

I'm not sure what part she doesn't understand, but that life and her are over. Or at least they're supposed to be. Those are the laws set forth. If a human is taken, they are dead to that world. If not, then the well-protected secrets of our lives can bleed into the human realm. We can't allow that to happen.

"It will have to be done under a false name. Also, you won't be able to make public appearances or be seen at all."

She readjusts in my lap before going back to picking at nothing on the blanket. "But I'll be able to see what they do, right? And set up events and monitor how they help the kids?"

A million questions filter through my mind in response. I shut them down one by one, reminding myself that she'll learn. She'll be happy here one day. I should count myself lucky, after all. She has no family to crave to return to. Lizzie is here with her and she's adjusted quickly given she didn't know a damn thing about us prior to being taken.

With that in mind, I concede.

"You can do it the same way I run the banks. Have cameras everywhere. Hire a dedicated go-between who acts on your behalf and relays everything. You can be involved as little or as much as you'd like. I prefer being a silent partner. If you'd rather be more involved, then you can. You have to set up a business plan and a budget while we're gone. When I get back I'll set up a meeting with my consultant to get a timeline established. He'll prepare everything you need to get started." It'll be easy enough and if it makes her happy, then I'm happy to give her whatever it'll cost.

Her smile presses against my chest. She tilts her head to nuzzle her nose across the base of my throat with her eyes closed. She's so damn beautiful when she's content. I wish I could make her this happy all the time.

"I thought of something for you to do while I'm away."

She sighs sleepily and stretches, apparently ready to start the day now that she's gotten the green light for her charity with Lizzie. "What's that, *Alpha*?" My dick twitches at her use of the word Alpha.

I groan and lean my head back. "Say it again."

She smirks knowingly and says, "What's that?"

"Don't toy with me, Grace," I scold her smart ass. I'm even more determined to hear it on her lips as I realize it's the first time she's called me Alpha.

Heat races through me as she rises on her knees and straddles my thighs, bringing her eyes level with my mouth. She lifts that defiant little chin up and I swear to God if she picks a fight, I'm going to flip her ass over and fuck her into the mattress. She lets her voice come out soft and seductive when she says, "Me?" Her hand trails over my shoulders, sending a shiver through my body. I resist the urge to shudder as her nails gently run down my back. She keeps my gaze as she bites her lower lip before saying, "I would never toy with you." She parts her lips and I can practically feel the word begging to come out of her mouth. I wait with bated breath as she whispers the word, "Alpha."

My palms grip that lush ass of hers and I pull her lips to mine, my fingers digging into her flesh. I moan into her mouth, ready to push her down and rut into her. I've been taking it easy on her since the claiming, but she's healing nicely and isn't sore. Besides, she'll have a few days to recover while I'm gone and I want her to feel me every time she moves for as long as I'm gone. I smile against her lips and flip her ass over. She gasps, taking in a sudden breath as she lands on her hands and I steady her hips until her knees find purchase on the bed.

I don't miss how she smiles and that her thighs clench. She knows what's coming.

"That's my good girl."

I run my fingers through her heat, finding her slick and ready for me. I groan in satisfaction and my wolf claws at me to fuck her. As I prod her with my fingers to test her readiness to take me, she pulls away, catching me off guard.

My first thought is that I hurt her, but she's not red or swollen. "You okay?"

She turns her head, looking away and giving a short, muffled response. My forehead pinches in confusion as I bring my hands up in defense. A tic in my jaw pulses at my eagerness to be inside my mate. I must've missed something. My dick protests my hesitation. I put both of my hands back on her hips and ask, "Sweetheart, what's wrong?"

"I don't know." I still behind my mate. I just want to fuck her, but I hold back, knowing there's something off.

Grace rolls onto her back; I withstand the need to keep her where I want her and fuck away whatever thought is bothering her. I keep my expression straight as she looks up at me while on her back. My hands instantly go to the curve of her waist, my eyes traveling to her breasts.

"What don't you know, sweetheart?" Goosebumps appear on her

body as I gently trail my fingers down her sensitive skin. She squirms under my touch.

"I don't know if I'm ready."

"Wait as long as you want to start it, my love. There's no rush and I'm sure Lizzie will understand."

"For a baby." I freeze at her confession. This is the one fight I've lost between us.

"I don't know if I'm ready." She picks at the blanket again and the loss of her eyes on me makes me want to rip the damn thing off the bed and rip it to fucking shreds. "Did you know Lizzie's pregnant?"

I grunt at the thought and tell her, "It's way too early to tell." Licking my lips, I bend down to take her nipple in my mouth. She doesn't protest. In fact, she runs her fingers through the back of my hair. Her nails gently scratch my scalp, urging me to do as I'd like. I pull away releasing my tight hold on her with a *pop*. Grace slaps my arm as I admire the bright pink mark on her breast.

"Dom and Caleb are convinced," she says. A low growl vibrates up my chest and out of my throat. I'm happy for them, if she really is pregnant, but I don't really give a shit about that right now. I'm far more concerned with the fact that my own mate is taking active steps to avoid getting pregnant. And she's currently avoiding getting fucked. Another low growl leaves me.

"I'm sure they both think the baby is theirs too." My head shakes of its own accord at their arrogance. "They can't know yet. It's too early to scent it."

Grace's face falls. "Oh. If she's not, she's going to be really upset."

"Don't worry about her, sweetheart. Her heat will come again and then Dom and Caleb will be fighting each other to be inside her." The more I think about it, the more I'm worried about her delivering pups. I don't think either of them will be truly content if they don't father the first pup. I keep my mouth shut, though. Grace tends to worry and intervene, and none of that is something she should be concerning herself with.

Running a hand down my face, I wish we were talking about us rather than them.

"She's so ready to be a mother. We've never talked about it, but she's sure she's ready." Her head falls to the side and she sighs while her eyes meet my gaze. "How can you know for sure that you're ready?"

I don't understand her question, either because I've always known I'd have pups or because all the blood in my body is currently pounding in my throbbing dick. "What do you need to be ready?" If she'll just tell me, I'll fucking give it to her.

"To feel ready. Once we have a baby, we can't go back and we've just met each other."

"What the fuck does just meeting each other have to do with anything?" A hint of my anger comes out in my words and Grace narrows her eyes at me.

"We haven't had time with just the two of us. If I start popping out babies, then we really won't get any time for just the two of us."

"We'll have plenty of time while you're pregnant. Once the pups come, we'll hire help if you'd like time alone. That's an easy fix."

"I just don't *know* that I'm ready." I resist the urge to sigh in exasperation. She's fucking killing me here.

"It'll drive me crazy every heat, to know you're actively working against getting pregnant. Everything in me wants to breed you." My wolf howls in agreement. "Do you think you'll ever know that you're ready?" I pinch her chin between my forefinger and thumb, then ask her, "What are you afraid of?" Her hazel eyes widen at my question and she whips her head out of my grasp in anger.

"I'm not afraid! I just don't know." Her anger catches me off guard. We already covered this. I fucking caved already. I gave her what she wanted, but she's still fucking fighting with me.

"You told me that you weren't ready, so we're waiting. There's no reason to fight. Why are you yelling at me?"

"I'm not yelling!" She practically screams the words and I just stare back at her unreasonable ass.

After a moment, a heavy sigh leaves me and I climb off the bed. My hard dick protests the movement, bobbing up and down with every movement. I rake my fingers through my hair.

"Where are you going?" she asks and I respond by grabbing her angry ass by the ankles, then dragging her to the edge of the bed.

"Nowhere, sweetheart." I flip her over and prop her ass up for me.

"Devin!" She scolds me but with my hand against her shoulders, her back bows perfectly. I half expect her to protest, to do anything other than close her eyes and moan.

"You worry too much," I tell her and then give her cunt a languid lick. "Right now I need you to do anything but that."

She writhes slightly, a sight to behold. The second I slip two of my fingers into her greedy pussy, she melts against my touch. Her back arches and she rests her head on the bed as I curve my fingers and stroke her sweet spot. I push my thumb against her clit without any mercy.

"You've got to come, sweetheart. You're too wound up." She moans something incoherent into the mattress and I smirk at the sight of my gorgeous mate letting her arousal get the best of her. She's not in heat anymore. This is just her, loving my touch and letting it soothe her.

I kiss the small of her back as her skin heats and she pulls slightly away from the sensation. Her pussy tightens on my fingers as a bit of her honey drips down my hand. Picking up my pace, I fuck her ruthlessly with my fingers. All her small whimpers fuel me and I can't help but think this is perfect. Pregnancy or not, we have time. So long as she's mine, it doesn't matter.

I lean my chest against her back and lick my mark before growling the command, "Give it to me," at the shell of her ear, letting the heat of my breath tickle her neck. She obeys like the perfect fucking mate she is and comes on my fingers. "Good girl."

Her body is still shaking with aftershocks as I thrust my dick in to the hilt. *Fucking perfect.* Her pulsing heat feels so damn good, trying to milk my cock. Her pussy knows exactly what she wants; at least I can satisfy part of her. Rocking into her slowly at first, I take my time enjoying the feel of her warmth. But I know my mate likes it rough.

I pull her closer to the edge and piston into her without any warning. She screams into the mattress as her little hands fist the blanket and her hips buck against mine. Her small body thrashes against my hold, but I don't let up. Instead I reach around her hips and start circling her throbbing clit.

"Fuck!" She lifts her head to scream and I know everyone in this damn estate is going to hear my mate come. And I fucking love it. Let them hear how I please her. How she submits to me. I slam into her wanting more of her cries of pleasure. My hips rock against hers as I pound into her tight sheath. My dick hits her cervix and I fucking love the feel of it.

She moans out my name as I push myself inside her deeper and hold it there. She claws at the sheets to get away from the pain of me stretching her and pushing her to her limit, but I know she fucking loves every second of it. "I want a baby." She barely says the words through her panted breaths.

My eyes widen at the admission. *Fuck!* Now that her heat's gone, now she wants a baby. I slam into her, punishing that sweet pussy as I lose myself in her. I'll fill her with my cum and do my damnedest to knock her up even though the odds are not at all in our favor.

As my cock pulses inside of her, I lean down and groan in the crook of her neck, "You want my cum? Your greedy pussy wants my cum, doesn't it?" I smack her ass so hard my palm stings and watch a red mark form on her flesh. I spank her ass again and again until she finally answers.

"Yes!" She moans out as another wave of arousal makes fucking her that much easier. Gripping her hips, I angle her to take the punishing fuck as deep as possible. I slam into her over and over again. Even as I feel her pulse around my dick and coat it with her cum, I don't stop.

I push deep into her as she thrashes on the bed beneath me. The sight and feel of her like this has my balls drawing up and a cold sweat breaks out over my skin. It takes four long, deep strokes to have her screaming in ecstasy. Her pussy tries to milk my cock and when I feel the tight walls squeeze and flutter around me, it's enough to set me off. I come hard and I stay deep inside her even when I know I'm spent. I pick her ass up and leave her like that.

"Don't move." I slip out of her only to get a cloth from the bathroom. My dick is at half-mast but when I come back to the room it springs to life at the sight of my mate, head down and ass up. Her hazel eyes watch me closely as I stride back to her. I smirk at my feisty mate, subdued from her orgasm. Her chest and cheeks are flushed, and her breathing is still ragged. "I prefer you much more when you're sated."

"Mmm." She murmurs a sound of agreement although I imagine she'll give me hell for it when she's more coherent. "I prefer you fucking me to telling me no," she manages. Her voice is coated in sarcasm but her smile is genuine. A deep, low chuckle rolls through me at her barely spoken words.

CHAPTER TWELVE

Dom

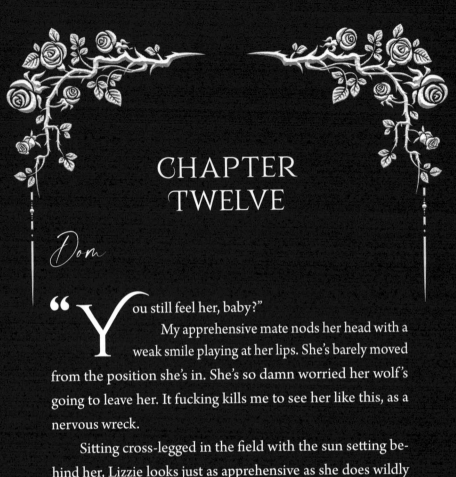

"Y̶ou still feel her, baby?"

My apprehensive mate nods her head with a weak smile playing at her lips. She's barely moved from the position she's in. She's so damn worried her wolf's going to leave her. It fucking kills me to see her like this, as a nervous wreck.

Sitting cross-legged in the field with the sun setting behind her, Lizzie looks just as apprehensive as she does wildly beautiful.

"Smile, baby. It's a good thing that she hasn't left." Lizzie's hand rubs against her chest like she's petting her wolf. Like the kids at my old pack used to do. I chuckle at her. If it wasn't heartbreaking, she'd be adorable right now.

"Do you think she'll stay this time?" Her question is whispered, like she'll scare her wolf off if she speaks any louder. The half smirk on my lips vanishes when she peers up at me with tears brimming. My poor mate.

I shrug, trying to make light of the situation. I've noticed she mirrors what I'm feeling. If I'm serious, so is she; if I'm not, she's not either. "Sometimes my wolf goes on hiatus. It happens to all of us, and it's okay when it does."

"That's right, baby girl," Caleb says from behind me as he pulls his shirt over his head. He strips in the field, getting ready to shift. "My wolf loves going for a run, though." He smiles at our mate, eating up the distance between the two of them to help her up. It works. She stands easily enough although her hand stays on her chest. "He's especially excited that you're going to ride him, baby."

She smacks his arm and takes two small steps away from him before she says in a sultry voice, "Don't make it sound so dirty." He grabs her small hips and pulls her body into him to kiss his mark on her neck.

"You know you want to ride me." She blushes at his teasing words and I can't help loving that warmth of happiness that flows through me. I kick off my boots and watch the two of them. The sight of her smile makes me radiate with pride. We've come such a long way. I know she's always going to want her wolf to show herself. Being latent will only make it worse, but I'll do everything in my power to help her and her wolf.

"You want to get naked too, little one?" My dick hardens at the thought of our mate exposed and bared to us. "Your wolf may want to come out more if she feels the wind on your skin." I have no fucking clue if that's really true, but I don't mind telling a little fib so I can feel her bare pussy on my back. Caleb glances at me for a second like I'm a fucking liar and I don't give a shit. Then he smiles at my deviousness and plays along.

"Strip, baby girl." He gives her neck a hard open-mouthed kiss before releasing her. She bites her lip, but nods her head and starts undressing. I stroke my dick at the sight of her curves. Her full breasts bounce as she pulls the little dress over her head. There's a bit of a chill in the air, but the temperature's nice enough. She should enjoy the feel of the sun kissing her skin. She bends over to put her clothes in a neat pile and I groan at the sight of her. My wolf wants me to push her down and take her. Caleb's palming his dick and I can see he wants the same thing. A low, possessive growl rips through me. The sound makes Lizzie jump a bit.

In the blink of an eye, Caleb shifts easily.

His black wolf trots to our mate and lowers his head. She's so small next to his beast. He licks her cheek, making her grin and she pushes his snout away letting out a peal of feminine laughter as she does. He whuffs and I shift as she spears her fingers through his thick fur.

The familiar crack of my bones is comforting and feels natural as I change form. My vision is heightened and my control waning but present. My wolf trots to her with ease and pride. He's a bit smug that he's larger than Caleb's wolf.

I shuffle back as Caleb lowers himself flat to the ground and she straddles him. My wolf whimpers with desire to see her wolf. He can smell her and he wants her more than anything. I huff at his impatience and rein him in. He may never get to see his mate, but at least he can smell her now.

Caleb takes off without warning, making Lizzie cry out and then laugh as she clings to his fur. He heads straight to the forest and I know he must want to take her to the clearing where we claimed her. I round the bend and sprint, pushing my limbs and straining my muscles to get there first. I hurl my body over the boulders in my path and duck under a fallen tree. The wind rustles through my fur as my wolf strains and I push him to run faster. I hope she sees me. The bark of passing trees barely grazes my fur as I spring forward. I don't stop running even as my breathing quickens and my muscles tighten; I want her to see my wolf at his best. He huffs in agreement and leaps through the trees.

I slow my sprint as I round the bend and come to the clearing. Panting but proud. I trot toward the entrance and wait for them to come through the path. My wolf starts pacing and I give him control. He doesn't like that we let her out of our sight; he doesn't want to share our mate right now. I shake my body, ridding myself of the leaves and debris that cling to me from my run. I calm my breath and wait impatiently. After a moment I close my eyes and try to hear where they could be. I hear a laugh to my left and my wolf snorts at me, wasting no time to head to the stream. Damn, I thought he'd take her here.

"You fucker." I hear Caleb laugh in my head at my words as I sprint to get to the stream. I'm faster in my wolf form so it doesn't take long to catch sight of them. My wolf growls low at the sight of Caleb pounding into Lizzie from behind. His fingers dig into her hips and each thrust makes her breasts bounce.

"I couldn't help it," he groans out in my head as I shift and make my way toward them.

"Selfish prick." He laughs at my admonishment.

"Admit it, you would've done the same thing." I nod at his words as he continues thrusting into her. Lizzie moans in pleasure as her knees scrape against the ground and her palms dig into the dirt. Her long blond hair flows over her shoulder as she takes every one of Caleb's thrusts. Her head arches back with her eyes closed and her full lips parted while she whimpers for more.

Walking confidently up to my mate, I put my hand on her throat and drag it up to her chin. Her soft blue eyes slowly open and stare right into mine. She peeks at my erection and then looks back up to meet my gaze. Her mouth is agape with pleasure while Caleb continues thrusting into her. I stroke my dick a few times, watching how her body jolts with each of his powerful strokes. The remnant of a faint bruise on her neck can be made out and part of me wishes Caleb would go easy on her, knowing her pussy must be aching still too. But her loud moans and her body pushing back against his hips, keep my mouth shut.

I slip the tip of my cock between her lips and she shifts forward to take more of me into her mouth. My head falls back and I let out a groan as her warm mouth sucks down my dick. Her tongue massages the underside and makes me leak down her throat. She moans as I pulse in her mouth and the vibrations make my legs tremble with the heated anticipation and need to release. I gather her long hair in my hands and wrap it around my wrist. Gripping the hair at the nape of her head, I push myself into her mouth until I feel her throat give and constrict around my length. Fuck, she feels so fucking good. I pull out and give her a moment to catch her breath before sliding my dick to the back of her throat again.

Out of fucking nowhere, Caleb's fist comes down on my arm, making me drop my hand from her hair. She whimpers from the slight pain and I shoot fucking daggers at Caleb. My wolf rears back and snarls at him.

"I can't fucking see when you do that." He doesn't slow his rhythm as he voices his concern in my head. It takes me a moment to register his words as Lizzie diligently takes my dick back into her mouth, oblivious to the fact that I'm two seconds away from ripping her other mate's head off.

"What?" My wolf snarls again, not liking that my attention is being pulled away from our mate's touch.

He shoves himself deep into Lizzie and holds her there, making her moan around my dick and try to push away from the intensity of his shallow movement.

"Don't fucking think of coming in her. I'm up next." I pull my dick out of Lizzie's mouth and push it back in slowly as he withdraws and strokes himself, aiming his dick at the small of her back. With his right hand wrapped tightly around his dick, his left moves between her legs making her writhe beneath him.

"Hold still, baby girl." He watches as I fuck her mouth, just waiting for the chance to get into her pussy.

"Switch with me." I hear his voice in my head, but I don't register his meaning until he's pushing me out of his way to shove his dick into her mouth. My anger is barely contained. *"You better come in her pussy. If not, I'm going again."* I'm tired of him being in my head when all I want to do is give and take pleasure from our mate.

I grunt at him as I push my length into her heat. "Fuck, you feel so good." I start out nice and slow and within seconds she pushes against me, wanting more. I can't deny my mate. I rut into her with a primal need. I don't even realize Caleb's found his release until he commands her, "Swallow every drop."

I glance up from where my dick's ruthlessly pounding into her pussy to see her lick her lips and shudder with her impending orgasm. Caleb reaches down and pinches her nipples while biting her throat. She arches her neck and the sight of my mark on her has me coming in waves in her pussy. I reach around and pinch her clit to make sure she gets off and she does. *Holy fuck.* Waves of heat crash through me and make me dig my heels into the dirt. Pushing myself deeper into her, I wait for the aftershocks we're both feeling to subside before pulling out.

When I finally catch my breath and open my eyes, I see Caleb squatting in front of our mate, kissing her and nibbling her lip. She's still panting and struggling to stay up on all fours. Her skin's flushed and her legs are still quivering from the intensity of her release. I take her small body in my arms and roll us to the ground, cradling her with her back to my chest. I lift her body on top of mine and run my hands over her trembling limbs, comforting her as best as I can.

"Don't be selfish." I ignore Caleb's scolding. I just want to fucking hold my mate.

"You had her first and I didn't give you shit about it, did I?"

"I didn't get to come in her. I count that as you giving me shit."

"Stop it!" Lizzie shouts and lifts her head from my chest to glare at the two of us. I blink at her pissed-off expression.

"How the fuck did she hear us?"

"Lizzie, can you hear us, little one?" I question her telepathically and wait for her response. I get nothing, not a damn thing.

"I'm sorry, baby girl." The fuckface decides he's going to scoop her off my chest to cuddle her and I grit my teeth to keep Lizzie from sensing how pissed I am. I don't want her getting upset again.

"Knock it the fuck off, asshole." I fucking hate that he's taking her from me. I only just lay down with her.

"You knock it off! You can keep petting her, but I get to hold her now."

"I told you two to stop it!" Lizzie pushes off of Caleb and makes to stand with her back toward us.

"You can hear us?" I'm overwhelmed with happiness, but as I search for her wolf, I can't feel her or hear her.

"*Talk to us.*" Caleb pleads with her in my head, but she doesn't respond. Instead her shoulders start shaking and that gets both of us up on our feet.

"Don't cry, little one. We won't fight. I promise." I still don't know how the fuck she knew we were fighting. Rubbing her shoulders I try to console her, but she only sobs harder.

"You can't hear me!"

Caleb looks to me before answering her, "We heard you, baby. We'll stop fighting. Dom's just a little moody today."

"No, you can't hear me! I keep talking to you. I can hear you, but you can't hear me." Her voice cracks and the realization breaks my fucking heart.

"Your wolf can hear us?" My wolf paces inside of me at the mention of his mate.

Lizzie nods and buries her head into Caleb's chest while reaching for my hand. I take her little hand in mine and squeeze it while gently rubbing her back.

"Try again." My softly spoken words are meant to offer her comfort, but her head rears back and she practically spits at me.

"I am! I'm screaming in my head and you can't hear me!" Tears spill down her reddened cheeks as she shudders from the chill of the air.

"Let's go home," Caleb speaks into Lizzie's hair, but he glances at me with a pained look. I'm sure I share his expression. We don't know how to help our mate. I don't like feeling helpless but that's exactly the situation I'm in right now.

"It's all right, little one. She isn't ready for us to hear her, that's all."

"We'll keep on loving you and one day she'll learn to trust us and let us in."

"You can't know that," Lizzie says. Her words are hard, but then she softens her tone to add, "What if she never does?" She sobs into Caleb's chest. My poor mate.

Caleb pulls away so she has to look at him when he answers, "Then she never does and life will go on. Everything will still be perfect. It might even be a good thing. When we have pups, you'll be able to listen in and they won't hear you."

I chuckle at Caleb's reasoning and add, "Our pups won't be able to get away with shit." Lizzie looks between the two of us as a small smile plays at her lips.

"You two won't be able to get away with anything either." She wipes under her eyes and rubs her hands against her thighs, pulling herself together. "I really don't like it when you fight."

"I'm sorry, baby, I was just fucking with Dom. I'll stop." Fucking Caleb, why's he gotta be the hero?

"I'll stop too. I don't want you to get upset." She cuddles into my chest and I kiss her hair. Her warmth and touch are everything. I can't imagine hearing but not being heard. My poor mate.

"I love you two," she whispers and molds her body to mine. Caleb and I both murmur our love for her and as unfortunate as it is, there's a bond that's unbreakable. It's stronger with every small step. Forward or backward.

"Time to go home, baby. They'll be heading out soon and I'm sure Grace is going to be lonely with Devin leaving her behind. You want to ride one of us, or do you just want to walk?" Caleb runs his hand up and down her back while he talks and I can tell she's losing her energy.

"My feet are going to hurt if we walk."

"Piggyback ride?" he suggests. A grin covers his face and I snort a laugh at his words.

Her head turns to face Caleb and she smiles as she says, "You're going to make such a good father." She leans away from him and gives me a kiss on the lips before looking into my eyes. "You too, Dom. You're going to make a great dad too." My chest fills with a sense of pride that spreads warmth through my entire body. "I got to ride you up here, so

I'll ride Dom back." She pats Caleb's chest and gives him a quick kiss on the lips.

"*We're going to be just fine, little one.*" I say the words in my head and she meets my eyes, acknowledging that she heard me. I reward her with a quick kiss.

"We love you, baby." Caleb kisses his mark before he shifts. I follow his lead and shift in front of our mate. She runs her hands through my hair before settling on top of me and gripping onto my fur.

"I love you too. Both of you."

CHAPTER THIRTEEN

Devin

With my car parked behind Vince and Veronica, I kill the ignition. The rumble fades as he does the same and all that's left is the quiet, dark night.

Neither of us gets out just yet ... there's a third party we're waiting on. I check the clock and he should be here soon. It only took a few hours to get here, but I'm already missing my mate. Lev was pissed he had to stay behind, but I wanted him and the Betas to keep our human mates safe.

Vince is attached to the coven and I'm Alpha; this task falls squarely on our shoulders.

I glance in the rearview to see Alec park behind me. There's a man seated on the passenger side I don't recognize. I've never met him before and I'm not sure I like the fact that he's here. A heads-up would have been nice. It takes me a second to register that he's a vampire and there's another vamp in the back

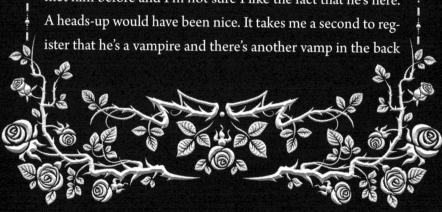

of Alec's car. I'm not sure why Alec thinks he can trust them and I'm real fucking reluctant to let my guard down.

This surprise isn't something I would ever expect from Alec. Bristling and already irritated, I message Vince that it's time.

I shut the door as quietly as I can and wait for him to walk with me to the edge of the gravel path. It'd be far too noisy to drive up the path. It would give our arrival away as well. They'd have plenty of time to bolt, so we'll be taking it by foot.

Veronica leans against their car, eyeing the fuck out of the two vampires Alec brought. She isn't subtle and I'm guessing she's not too keen on the fact they're here either.

"How many do you think?" I question Vince.

"No clue." He takes a whiff of the air and adds, "It's stronger than yesterday."

"Just the three of you?" Alec's steps are so quiet I didn't notice he'd come up behind me. I don't give that shit away, though. I continue looking down the gravel road and nod before turning to face him.

"I didn't want our mates to be left alone."

Alec nods and says, "Makes sense." He takes a deep breath and motions the two vampires to come over to us.

"I want to introduce you to my allies, Devin." He stares hard at me while he speaks. *Allies?* My spine stiffens and my wolf raises his hackles. I suppress his growl. These are not friends. Alec's lip rises in an asymmetrical grin as my stern response registers with him that I've understood his meaning.

"They're enemies, Vince." I speak the words calmly to Vince so he can pick up what Alec has insinuated. The fact that Alec confirmed my gut feeling heightens the anticipation for a fight. Vince makes no outward sign that he's heard me, but I can feel his anger and readiness to rip them apart. He calls Veronica over and wraps a possessive arm around her before murmuring something in her ear. I can't hear what it is, but the two vampires huff humorously with thinly veiled judgement at Vince's display of affection.

My eyes stay on Veronica, watching her as she takes in the knowledge Vince is giving her. She narrows her eyes at Vince and takes in a heavy inhale before nodding in understanding. He responds with a kiss in her hair.

"Nice to meet you two," I begin and wait for Alec to give me any more clues or signals. The plan was easy enough before, but this adds a speed bump I wasn't expecting and now I second-guess if the plans we had are realistic at all. Has our cover been blown and this is nothing more than a setup? We could be walking into a giant trap for all I know.

"This is Marcus and Theo," Alec says, pointing to his left and then right. The vampires nod respectively. "Meet Devin, the Alpha of the Shadows Fall pack. This is Vince, and his mate."

"So you're the vampire who aligned with the werewolves?" Vampire Prick Number One speaks over Alec to Veronica. "I didn't realize wolves even mated vampires."

Vince appears calm and easygoing on the outside, like he always does, but I know inwardly he's fuming. He looks to his mate with a smirk and rubs her back. She leans into his embrace before engaging with the vampire who spoke. "It's rare. I got lucky, I guess," she tells him. One of the two snorts at her response and her calm smile turns to ice.

"She's going to fuck them up. I can feel it." Vince smiles at his mate like everything's fine while his irate voice echoes in my head.

"Did you tell her what's going on?"

"Can't. They would hear. But she'll pick it up fast."

"Devin, your guns are in the trunk. Marcus and Theo, I brought guns for you too." Alec pops his trunk with a click of his key fob and the vampires and I head to the car trailing behind him. I have no fucking clue what guns he's talking about, but I'm happy to accept whatever gifts he's decided to lend me. Adrenaline courses through me, every muscle tense as I round the car on high alert. I grin at the sight, not at all disappointed.

There are three semiautomatic pistols and an assault rifle.

"Fuck yeah." Vince's voice booms with excitement. "The rifle's mine, right, Alpha?"

I see Alec nod from the corner of my eye as he hands two of the pistols to Marcus and Theo, then stuffs the third into a holster at his hip.

"I don't think so, Vince." I pull the strap over my body and secure the weapon.

"Careful. It's all silver," Alec says.

"Silver?" Theo looks to Alec for confirmation while examining the bullets.

"I took the liberty of preloading everything." He meets the vampires' curious expressions and adds, "Aim to wound, but if you have to, killing is acceptable." The vampires exchange a glance, then nod and mutter that they understand, seemingly content with the orders.

"What's the plan?" I speak aloud, waiting for more direction and any information Alec can give me.

"Friends will be on the left," he says and turns to face the vampires. "That's where the exit is, correct?"

"No, the exit is on the right side. They're coming through there," one of them replies although neither look at him. The vampires are still examining the bullets rather than giving us their full attention. *Friends on the left.*

"Ah, got it." He looks me in the eyes and there's a beat that's serious and prolonged before he tells me, The Authority will get them from the right."

"Vince, you got that?" I start a silent dialogue with him.

"Yeah, stay to the left. Is it just the vamps we're ambushing?"

"No idea. You sure you want to bring Veronica in on this?"

"They fucked with her coven. There's no way she's not getting in on the action."

"You have to keep her safe." I know he already knows, but I can't help giving the command regardless. My mate is human, but even if Grace wasn't as vulnerable as she is, even if she was a vampire like Veronica, I still wouldn't want her here.

"I told her to stay with me. She'll listen." I hope Vince's right.

"You expect them to be waiting for us?" Marcus asks Alec.

"Absolutely." He doesn't hesitate to answer. "If they're still monitoring the blood banks, they know we're onto them. If they planted a spy in the system, they know. I think it's fair to assume they know we're coming for them. They may already know we're here now."

"So we're walking into an ambush?" I question as though I have no idea what Alec is really orchestrating.

"We're going to ambush the ambush." His silver eyes flicker with anger, but he keeps it contained and flashes a wide smile, radiating a false sense of trust and calm.

My blood heats as I draw in a single deep breath. There won't be time for hesitation. Masses have been slaughtered in seconds. We'll be in and it will be over in minutes at most.

Gripping the handle of the gun, I nod. "After you," I say and motion for Alec to lead the way, the two vampires following close behind him.

I'm locked and loaded and ready to get this shit over and done with so I can get back to Grace. My pulse races as we stalk down the grass that surrounds the gravel road. Each step quiet and in line with that of the others. I'd be quieter in wolf form, nearly silent as the vampires are now, but that would render my gun useless. And surely Alec gave it to me for a specific purpose.

Veronica hisses to reprimand her mate as Vince steps on a twig, breaking it and disrupting the quiet trail to our target. I doubt the vampires can hear us this far out, but it's best to keep perfect form until we're there.

I'm not sure if this is going to be a bloodbath, or if Alec has a plan to capture the vampires and force them to face a trial. With every silent step, my heart races faster, prepared for what may come. It's slow and steady, and every second tense and wound tight. We're only about halfway there when a loud bang shocks the quiet night. It came from the warehouse a mile or two in front of us.

The vampires take off almost too fast to register, forming a blur in front of us. I push my limbs as fast as they can go, but it doesn't even come close in comparison. Veronica's form rushes past me and the gust of wind from her speed comes a second later.

"Stop." Vince forces the word out as he gains momentum and nearly passes me. Veronica halts just outside the stairs to the warehouse. She's fuming with rage and her chest is frantically heaving in air as her fists shake at her sides. Her dark eyes follow us as we get closer to her.

"Stay behind me." Veronica doesn't respond aloud to Vince's command, but she doesn't go in without him either.

The tension between those two is thick. It's an unwanted distraction at this moment. If they can't do this, if my attention is spent on the two of them being safe, this could all go to shit.

"I've got her," he reassures me and I keep moving, passing her, following Alec as he sprints toward the double doors. All I can do is trust that he's right, that she'll catch on and that she'll listen to him.

As I rush to come up behind Alec, keeping to his left, he lifts his hands and gestures in the air. The doors are torn off their hinges and crash hard on the cement as he nears them. It's eerily quiet. Not at all what I expected. There's a noticeable lack of gunshots or screaming. *Nothing.* I don't trust it. My heart hammers in my chest. I slow my pace, planting one foot in front of the other and stand to the right of the opening as Vince and Veronica come up from behind me.

"I'll go in first, follow behind. Don't get blocked in, Vince. If I go down, run. Don't look back."

"Fuck off, Dev. That shit's not happening." I growl at his response, but quietly make my way through the doors. I sweep the room, aiming my gun to the right and left, quickly taking in my surroundings.

There are too many people in this space for me to feel anything close to comfortable. On the left half of the room are two witches, both female and both with pissed-off expressions and clearly irritated. I don't recognize either of them, but their green eyes and wild red hair suggest they're related.

In the center of the room are three humans bound and gagged, tied to chairs with silver rope. The acrid smell of their urine makes me cringe as they audibly struggle, their eyes wide with fear.

I walk in a slow line across the room, keeping my left shoulder pointed at the witches and my gun trained on the center of the room. Alec stands

372

before the humans, but his eyes are on the eleven vampires off to the right. Behind them are two more sorcerers and a shifter, that fucker, Remy. Carol is also among them. If my math's right, that makes eleven vampires and one shifter against three sorcerers, three witches, and the three of us. The numbers aren't in our favor. But with our strength and the magic on our side, we should come out the victors, with little to no casualties. If they're smart, they'll surrender. But then again, if they were smart, they wouldn't have crossed Alec.

Natalia stands in front of Alec, waiting for him to speak. She appears confident and strong before him, but the miasma of fear surrounds her. "We got here just before you. Luckily they were easy to round up."

"Humans?" His question is laced with disbelief.

"We found two dead vampires in a silver cage in the back." She gestures at them, then faces Alec and stares into his eyes as she faintly laughs. "These humans tried to outrun us."

Heat engulfs me as the tension swells.

"Humans!" The room shakes with his anger as he roars the word. The witches to my left spread their arms wide as thunder explodes above us; the doors and windows of the warehouse suddenly close in on themselves, crumpling the steel and brick in an unnatural way, caging all of us in and cutting out all light save for the three large dome lights above us.

Fuck. My pulse hammers and I stay steady, prepared but on edge. Waiting and praying I don't react too slowly.

Natalia shudders at the witches' display of power. The vampires behind her shift slightly on their feet. Marcus and Theo slip their pointer fingers onto the trigger of the guns Alec gave them. They may be fast, but with nowhere to run, their speed will be irrelevant. Adrenaline spikes through me. A sweat breaks out along my skin and I welcome it. I crave to let my beast out, but I wait. Alec will give me a sign when it's time. My body begs to shift, I remember the gun and fight the need to shift even harder.

"Stay behind me." I hear Vince's command come from my right, but my eyes stay forward, focused on the scene in front of me.

"You thought I'd fall for this?" Alec sneers at Natalia.

"Fall for what? You think I'd betray you?" Her eyes flash with anxiety, but her voice is level.

"I know you would." Alec speaks his words slowly as Natalia's anger gets the best of her. Waves of fear drift from the line of vampires. I watch Remy as he slowly retreats from the crowd. He has no escape now that the witches have closed everything off.

Natalia's shoulders rise and fall as she slowly backs away from Alec. Her gaze stays glued to him as she nears the line of vampires behind her. She's a caged animal with wild, desperate eyes. The realization that she's trapped and Alec knows what she's done hits both her and the rogue vampires in unison.

I steady my breathing and concentrate on the location of each vampire. Remy is the only other enemy to watch for. But he'll be slow enough to see coming. Just as I clench my fist, all hell breaks loose. The quiet is shattered with shrieks of pain and growls of rage.

I'm not sure who to take down first, but as I block a vicious attack from one vampire, I witness Theo and Marcus aim their guns at Alec and pull the trigger. In a split second, everything seems to slow. A shock of white shoots through both Theo and Marcus, forcing them to the ground as their bodies shake uncontrollably. Their limbs continue to twitch, rendering them useless.

Gritting my teeth, I keep an internal count. Two down, ten to go. Alec was smart enough to level the playing field immediately by sabotaging their weapons. I growl in triumph that we were the first to take the numbers down.

The vampires spread out in a blur behind them and attack in pairs. The two sorcerers and Carol are instantly surrounded. A beam of blue sends two vampires flying in the air and slamming against the wall behind me; it won't kill them, but at least it gives us time to get to the other side.

With every muscle wound tight, I run forward trying to reach Carol as two vampires attack her in unison. One behind her and one in front. Both of them bite into her neck and pin her to the ground. Witches have power, but their strength and speed are poor. She's knocked down to the ground as they drain her of her blood, weakening her. As soon as I reach her petite body, I jerk the nearest vampire off of her. His fangs rip her flesh, spraying blood in front of me as I grab his chin in my right hand and hold his body still with my left arm. He frantically pulls against me, trying to gain freedom, but I strain my muscles against his struggle and twist his neck, shattering his spine. His bones crack and I drop his limp body, knowing that's another one gone.

I lunge for the other vampire, prepared to fight him off of Carol, but he's convulsing on the ground with blood that's nearly black spewing from his mouth. My eyes find Carol on the ground, barely moving. Her wounds are seeping and I bend to cover them with my hand and stop the flow until she can heal herself. She coughs blood from her cherry lips and smiles at me.

"Silver doesn't hurt us, even in our blood." Her eyes twinkle with trickery as she pushes my hands away. They're soaked with her blood and I realize she knew about Alec's plan. Who else knew?

Adopting a protective stance over her weak body, I take in what remains of the chaos as she hums and slowly heals her wounds. It's taking far too long, but I can't leave her alone and vulnerable. I stand guard and scan the room, searching out Vince and Veronica. Veronica's going head to head with Natalia, and Vince is fighting off Remy. He's not fully committed to this battle, his gaze darting to his mate with distress far too often. A snarl rips up my throat from my chest. Alec is fighting off two vampires at once, and the other two sorcerers and two witches are facing off with a vampire each. We're on the verge of losing this battle. My blood heats and pumps through me, urging me to fight.

A roar leaves me as I allow the anger to take over. The pure rage and animosity. The need to return to my mate and end this battle just as quickly as it began.

Carol slowly rises to her feet. She's still weak and in no condition to be left alone, though. If a vampire attacks her, she won't make it. Even so, I can't just stand back and watch them die; Alec is being slashed repeatedly as the vampires break through his defense and get in small hits each time. Blood sprays from his wounds as knives slit his flesh.

"Go." Her weakly spoken word is all I need to run to Alec. I push my back against his, giving him support as I wait for the inevitable blows. With our backs protected, the vampires can only attack us head-on, giving us a better chance at defending ourselves. In a blink, a gash is slashed across my face. Another blur and a gush of wind whip in front of my face. My arm reaches in front of me, but I catch nothing. The fucker is too fast. My wolf roars in anger.

Thump, thump, my blood pounds.

"Your gun!" Alec reminds me of the weapon strapped to my body. My fingers reach for the trigger at the same time that the vampire attacking me tears it from my body. The instant the trigger is pulled, there's a loud bang and a blinding flash of white. Instinctively I reach up to shield my eyes from the bright light. As I drop my hand and open my eyes, I gaze in wonder. Everything has slowed before me. The once loud surroundings are now a haze of white noise.

The gun is slowly being turned to face me as the pale vampire points it in my direction. I'm able to easily snatch the gun from the vampire's grasp and smash it across his face as his body seemingly continues to defy time and gravity.

Cold drifts around me as I move, seamlessly and easily while others are trapped for only a moment in this warped field.

I watch in awe as time speeds once again and the sound of screams ring in my ears, seeming louder than before. The vampire crashes on the ground and time returns to normal. My finger pulls the trigger and I welcome the flash of white as I barrel toward the still vampire and rip his throat out with my fangs. The magic relents quicker than before and time ceases to still for me as I watch Alec take the strike of a blade across his throat. I pull the trigger a third time and don't wait for the flash of light. I ram my body into the vampire, whose fangs are bared, prepared to feast on Alec's weakened body. I smash his head into the cement floor over and over without mercy. Even as time resumes, I continue bashing him into the hard, unforgiving ground until his skull breaks and his struggle becomes nothing.

Alec's body falls to the ground and he reaches for his throat. I crawl on the floor to reach him, but his eyes find mine before darting behind me in warning. I turn prepared for an attack, adrenaline spiking through my veins, but instead I see both Veronica and Vince losing their respective battles. Fear crushes down on me. Natalia and Veronica are each armed with blades, and they both have several pierced into their bodies. Veronica is much worse off, though, with a glaring gash down the front of her chest. Her body heaves, but her eyes are focused on vengeance.

Vince is struggling beneath Remy, both with their fangs out and snarling as they attempt to reach each other's throats. I quickly pull the trigger waiting for time to stop, for the moment to easily rip Remy into two, but time no longer obeys. I pull the trigger over and over as I run toward the two werewolves, wrapped around each other in a fight to the death. I toss the gun aside in a fit of anger as the magic no longer grants me an advantage and barrel into Remy's body, forcing him off of Vince. The second I have him pinned under me, Vince rises and quickly wraps his hands around Remy's throat, pulling with all his weight. I push my body on top of Remy's and wrench against Vince's strength. Remy screams in terror and pain as his neck snaps from the strain and his body goes limp.

I rise quickly, preparing for more, only to find myself surrounded by bloodshed. Carol hovers over Alec. Two sorcerers are surrounding the witches with white light. The vampires all lay dead, scattered in pieces across the large room.

The only noise is a violent hiss as Natalia and Veronica circle each other in the center of the room. Their dark, distorted dance of death has them weaving in and out among the humans who are still tied to the chairs, which have toppled over. Vince races to the center of the room, ready to help his mate.

"Behind me!" The bellowed command and the blur of Veronica's vision comes to form, her back to his. Natalia's body whips in front of Veronica's as Vince bends forward and Veronica leans her back against his as she wraps her legs around Natalia's neck, forcing the vampire to claw and slash at her legs. Vince moves as fast as he can, pushing the two vampires to the ground before grabbing Natalia's arms and pinning them behind her back. Veronica's legs bear several wounds. A deep gash in her upper thigh seeps blood as she squeezes her thighs around Natalia's neck, cutting off her oxygen.

Natalia struggles violently as she's forcefully contained between the two members of my pack. Veronica reaches forward and grips both sides of Natalia's mouth as she screams; she pulls with all her force against the vampire's jaws until they finally snap and separate. A shattered scream ricochets against the hard walls as Natalia's life is ended.

Vince releases the dead vampire, but Veronica's dark eyes are fixated on Natalia's tormented face. Her body is covered in blood and still badly wounded, but she disregards Vince as he tries to take her in his arms. Her fingers wrap around one of Natalia's fangs and she rips out the pair in turn before smiling in triumph at her dreadful victory. Vince raises his brows in question at his mate when she finally looks at him.

"For my queen." Her softly spoken words offer an explanation that Vince accepts as she heaves in a steadying breath. He opens his arms to her and she immediately goes to him, finally resting in his embrace.

They're safe. My pack is safe. Even that knowledge doesn't grant me reprieve, though. I need my mate. With my shoulders heaving as I attempt to calm, all I know is that I need my mate.

"I'm glad they used the guns I gave them." Alec's voice resonates in the quiet warehouse as he walks slowly to where Theo's and Marcus's bodies lay, still trembling in shock. "They'll talk if they want to live. All we need is one to tell us what we want to know."

"Is it over?" I question, eager to leave and return to Grace.

Alec glances around the room before settling his kind eyes on me. His large hand raises and slaps against my shoulder.

"It's never over, my dear friend. But this battle has come to an end." He gives me a weak smile before walking to join Carol. No one has escaped unscathed, but we'll all heal. Except for the vampires who dared to betray the Authority. Two will live to give answers, but they won't live long after.

I will get back to my mate. I will love her and she will love me.

Heaving in a breath, I know that's all that matters. With death surrounding us and corruption in every corner of our world, our pack is safe and that's all that matters.

Grace

Devin hasn't taken his hands off of me. A warmth swept over me the second he stepped foot on the estate, and it hasn't left. With every soft hum that vibrates up his strong chest, it only intensifies. It's not the heat, it's something else that sparks between us. With his back braced against the threshold to the kitchen, he holds me close to him, his hand running soothing strokes up and down my back. His chin rests on the top of my head and every so often, he kisses my crown.

Each time he does, a smile is pulled to my lips.

Even if he was broken and bruised when he arrived, the shower seems to have cleansed all of that away. For each of them, every member of my pack.

The night has set and the sun will no doubt be rising soon, but the adrenaline hasn't left the room.

I shift against Devin to peek at Veronica and Vince in the corner nook of the room. Something's changed between them, something possessive and raw. Something that's dropped her guard and that's not the only noticeable change between them but it's so hard to place what's changed.

"Did something happen?" I whisper the question to Devin, peeking up at him through my thick lashes, exhaustion beginning to weigh my eyes down.

"Nothing that didn't have to happen. It all happened as it should." He kisses my temple and the warmth spreads throughout me once again as I close my eyes, feeling a familiar comfort I associate solely with my mate wash over me. "Fate conspired in our favor."

I can't help but whisper back, "Something's changed," and when I open my eyes, Veronica's sharp gaze meets mine. There's only a knowing look that she gives me before Vince cups her chin in his large hand and kisses her. He takes her lips with his and the gentleness between them is genuine and it shouldn't surprise me so, but it does. It's not unlike Caleb, Dom and Lizzie.

"A lot has changed very quickly, sweetheart," Devin murmurs into my hair and I shake my head, refusing to let the shift go.

"Something ... something in the air is different," I say and the moment the thought leaves me, a chill runs down my shoulders. Devin's hand soothes the goosebumps that appear on my arm, running down my arm in the chill's wake.

In only his shirt and a baggy pair of gray sweats, I know I don't look glamourous, but I wanted to smell him. I wanted to feel him here when he was away. It helped, but not much. The lonesomeness that came over me ... Lizzie felt it too. As if she heard her name in my thoughts, she glances over to me with a gentle simper. But my friend doesn't give me too much attention for too long. How could she, with both beasts on either side of her? Just as Devin hasn't stopped touching me, they haven't stopped touching Lizzie. The atmosphere is far more joyous between them, and I do feel the same relief, the same contentedness. I can't deny I feel whole in his arms.

I thought it would go away, though, this uncanny sensation, when Devin and the pack came back an hour ago, but it didn't. I repeat, more sternly, "Something's changed."

"The new moon is coming," Devin responds as if it's an obvious answer.

"What does that mean?"

"It just brings a different energy, different powers."

"Powers?" I question and he only smiles down at me, his dark and hungry gaze flashing with desire. Sucking in a breath, I try to steady my racing heart as he tucks a lock of hair behind my ear.

"You have so much to learn, Grace."

That I can't deny.

I can't help but feel like this is only the end of a chapter for a story that hasn't finished yet. It's an eerie feeling that washes over me, and one that's only dimmed when Devin kisses me.

"I love you," Devin whispers at the shell of my ear and the warmth of his breath against the crook of my neck does more to me than any other feeling could. When he holds me like this and kisses me, it's as if the entire world can wait. It could stop, it could vanish, and I wouldn't even notice.

"I love you too," I whisper, my eyes closed as he takes my lips with his and deepens it.

CHAPTER FOURTEEN

Vince

Three days later

I know something's off as I walk to our room. A metallic tinge of blood coats the air. It smells god awful and reminds me of death. It's been quiet for days since we've been back and there's no reason to fear an attack, but that fucking smell makes my skin crawl and my body shake with anxiousness. The scent gets stronger and I find myself picking up my pace as a sick churning stirs in my stomach. *My mate.*

I grip the doorknob so tightly it nearly breaks off in my grasp as the door bashes violently against the wall. Veronica's form is a blur as she spins to face me. Seeing she's safe calms the beast clawing inside me. My frantic breathing eases as I walk to her. The sense of peace is fleeting as I study her face.

With wide eyes so black they match the silk negligee she wears, my mate looks as though she's been caught with her hand in the cookie jar. I grin and look past her to the large walnut desk. My smile falls instantly. My mate swallows and opens her mouth, but I silence her with a glare.

At least a dozen blood bags line its polished surface. They've been opened and drained, and it looks like she's been scraping the insides of the bag with a razor. There's a small pile of white powder in the center of the desk. The poison. She's collecting the poison designed to corrupt her immortality.

Unable to breathe, I stare into her eyes and search for an answer.

This isn't real. It can't be true. Disbelief comes in waves. What the hell is she doing with this shit? My blood runs cold as all manner of possibilities race through me.

"Did you drink the blood?" That's the first concern on my mind. I don't think my mate would hurt herself by drinking this shit. She can't. She wouldn't. She drinks from me daily. I can give her everything she needs.

"No." Her voice is small and her eyes are brimming with bloodied tears.

I nod my head and back away from the desk, walking to the bed with my back to her. If she's collecting this drug, it can't be for anything good. I think of any enemy she could have that's vampire, but I come up with nothing. I haven't the faintest clue why she would be harvesting this weapon. And it's one fucked-up weapon. They found four vampires at the warehouse; their fangs were barely visible and their immortality gone. Two were already dead and the other two were no stronger than humans. They needed a complete blood transfusion and to be bitten and turned again. They're still weak, though, nowhere near the vampires they used to be. There's no reason Veronica should have this shit here.

What the fuck is she doing? Did her queen give her orders without me knowing?

"Explain." The single word falls hard between us. I hope she can sense my disappointment and the agony at being kept in the dark. She's up to something, something of grave proportions. If she's hurting and planning revenge, she should've told me. Why wouldn't my own mate confide in me?

"I don't want this anymore." Her chest rises and falls with the admission, pain laced in her tone.

What the fuck? My heart sinks at her words. A spiked lump forms in my throat. She doesn't want me anymore? If she thinks she can run from me, she's dead fucking wrong. I'll always find her and bring her back to me.

"What have I done that makes you want to leave me?" Her head tilts and confusion is easily read on her face.

A beat passes and a hard lump grows in my throat.

"Why would I want to leave you?" Her softly spoken question instantly eases my body and I struggle to hide the fact that I'm fucking crumbling on the inside.

"You said you don't want this anymore?" I need her to clarify her words, and I fucking hope it's something I can handle. Because this shit is fucked beyond recognition and I'm failing to see what the hell is going on.

"I—" Her eyes look around the room as if searching for an answer I'll find acceptable.

I move into her space and growl out the words, "Answer me."

She stares straight into my eyes as she speaks, "I don't want to be immortal. I can't live when you die. I don't want to. I don't want this. A life without you isn't one worth living."

I stare into her dark eyes as my heart clenches in agony. My poor mate. Taking her head in my hands, I kiss her plump lips and lick across the seam for her to part for me. My tongue rubs along her bottom lip and caresses hers, while I allow the pain to subside and find the words to give her peace.

What do I know of immortality and how she's feeling? I know I would want to die if she was taken from me. I wouldn't want to go on without her. But my mate is strong and is destined to live once I've been buried in the dirt. I would never wish her to be in pain, but to want her to give up her immortality? Never.

I part from her and miss the warmth immediately. "What about our children? You're blessed to be able to care for them and watch them grow once I'm gone. You'll have peace loving them when I can't."

Tears fall from her eyes. "I don't know that I can ever give you pups,

Vince." She sniffs and turns her back to me to take a tissue from the package on the desk. How did I not know this? How have I let myself be so blind to the cost of her immortality.

"You think this poison will give you that ability?"

"I don't know, but it's worth it to try if it can."

My head spins. How could she be so reckless? "But we haven't even tried without resorting to something like this. Something that could destroy you!"

She lifts her chin and defiantly tells me, "I will give it all up to be the mate you deserve!"

"You are the mate I deserve, Veronica. You're more than that." I push her against the wall and cage her in with my body. She moves easily, not resisting in the least. "Tell me you haven't taken the drug. Please tell me you haven't."

Her shoulders shake with her sobs and then she says, "Only a little." I feel my heart fall and the crushing weight of guilt push through my limbs.

"Veronica." I place a hand on her neck and kiss my mark on the other side. "Don't. Don't do this. I love you just the way you are. I don't want this. I just want you."

"But I want to give you more. I want to be more for you." My head shakes at her words.

"How can you think so little of yourself? You're perfect in every way." I kiss her forehead as tears slip down my cheeks. "I've failed you as a mate." Her hands shove against my chest.

"Don't you dare say that; you've shown me glimpses of the kind of life that is possible without the burden of immortality. You've given me hope and desire for more. How could you think you've failed me?"

"You're drugging yourself to be something you're not!" She cowers from my words and the sinking feeling of defeat races through me. "Promise me you won't take any more." She refuses to look at me and sobs harder. "Promise me, Veronica." She slowly shakes her head, but I'm not going to accept that. There has to be another way.

"Just wait for me, then." Her eyes finally find mine at my desperate words. "We can try without it. We can wait until the Authority is done with their testing." I pull her into my arms and let her head rest against my shoulder. I stroke her back and settle some as her breathing relaxes. "We can try without it." I kiss her hair, inhaling the sweet floral scent of jasmine and add, "We have time to wait."

"I'll wait." She whispers the words.

"Promise me. Promise me you'll tell me if you think about it again."

"I will, I promise."

I kiss her hair again. "We can try without it. I will give you everything you need. I promise you, my love." She sniffles and kisses the crook of my neck. The feel of her soft lips against my skin brings a warmth to my chilled blood. "I love you, Veronica."

"I will love you forever, Vince."

ABOUT THE AUTHOR

Thank you so much for reading my romances. I'm just a stay at home mom and avid reader turned author and I couldn't be happier.

I hope you love my books as much as I do!

More by Willow Winters
WWW.WILLOWWINTERSWRITES.COM/BOOKS